Sparks Fly at Midnight

Sparks Fly at Midnight

CHRISTIN HEPNER

Copyright © 2021 Christin Hepner

All rights reserved. No part of this publication may be reproduced, distributed, or transmitted in any form or by any means, including photocopying, recording, or other electronic or mechanical methods, without the prior written permission of the publisher, except in the case of brief quotations embodied in critical reviews and certain other noncommercial uses permitted by copyright law. For permission requests, write to the publisher, addressed "Attention: Book Rights and Permission," at the address below.

Published in the United States of America

ISBN 978-1-955243-29-2 (SC)
ISBN 978-1-955243-30-8 (HC)
ISBN 978-1-955243-28-5 (Ebook)

Christin Hepner
222 West 6th Street
Suite 400, San Pedro, CA, 90731
www.stellarliterary.com
Order Information and Rights Permission:

Quantity sales. Special discounts might be available on quantity purchases by corporations, associations, and others. For details, contact the publisher at the address above.

For Book Rights Adaptation and other Rights Permission. Call us at toll-free 1-888-945-8513 or send us an email at admin@stellarliterary.com.

In memory of Leonard Bishop and Grant Hepner

To my mentors: Pastors Gary and Carolyn Ward, Cathy Hedge, Mark Rogers, Det. Ryan Runyan, Reyne Lehman,

My family and encouragers: my husband, Terry Hepner; Tim and Michelle Hepner; Tracy and Shanon Woodward; and Grant Hepner

Thank you, friends and family members, for your steadfast loyalty.

Contents

Chapter 1	8
Chapter 2	14
Chapter 3	22
Chapter 4	32
Chapter 5	37
Chapter 6	41
Chapter 7	52
Chapter 8	67
Chapter 9	71
Chapter 10	83
Chapter 11	87
Chapter 12	92
Chapter 13	98
Chapter 14	115
Chapter 15	121
Chapter 16	124
Chapter 17	131

Chapter 18	145
Chapter 19	151
Chapter 20	163
Chapter 21	179
Chapter 22	184
Chapter 23	188
Chapter 24	198
Chapter 25	205
Chapter 26	213
Chapter 27	217
Chapter 28	234
Chapter 29	238
Chapter 30	242
Chapter 31	258
Chapter 32	265
Chapter 33	269
Chapter 34	284
Chapter 35	288
Chapter 36	292
Chapter 37	297
Chapter 38	308
Chapter 39	314
Chapter 40	322

Chapter 41	337
Chapter 42	348
Chapter 43	351
Chapter 44	356
Chapter 45	361
Chapter 46	376
Chapter 47	409
Chapter 48	416
Chapter 49	418
Chapter 50	425
Chapter 51	430
Chapter 52	446
Chapter 53	449
Chapter 54	454
Chapter 55	463
Chapter 56	479
Chapter 57	484
Chapter 58	489
Chapter 59	499

Chapter 1

Manhattan, Kansas

March 22, 2016

The ringing of the phone caused Brooke to bolt upright in bed, her heart thumping wildly against her chest. Squinting, she looked at the clock on the nightstand and inhaled deeply. Raking her fingers through her hair, she exhaled and sank back down into the soft pillow moaning, "Not another accident." She rolled over to her side, reaching for the receiver. Clearing her throat, she answered, "This is Dr. Kaufmann."

Dr. Brooke Kaufmann, an orthopedic doctor, was on call for the next twenty-four hours. The voice on the other end spoke in a hoarse whisper.

"Cliff, is that you?" Brooke asked.

"Yes, it's me. I'm at the ranch."

She turned to look at the clock on the nightstand. "What are you doing at the ranch at this hour?"

"It's your parents." A short silence slipped by. "There is no easy way to say this. Their home is on fire. You need to be here."

"What do you mean *on fire*?" Brooke could hear the wail of the sirens in the background.

"Brooke, I really can't talk now. Please come."

"Cliff, Mom and Daddy ... are they all right?" Her voice quavered.

"I don't know. I just got here myself."

"I'll be there in twenty minutes." Hanging up the receiver, she swung her legs over the side of the bed. "Fire," she said. "Oh, Mother, Daddy always said that one day you'd burn down the house with your smoking!"

Reaching for her clothes, she slipped on her jeans, fumbling with the buttons to her top. With mismatched socks and a half-buttoned blouse, she flew through the open bedroom door, tripping over the heels that she had kicked off before stepping into the shower. Upon entering the kitchen, she flipped on the light switch, turning on the overhead fluorescent light. The dark room suddenly came to life. She made a mental note of the things she needed to do.

First, call Hank and see if he will take my calls. She hit the speed dial button and then set the phone on her shoulder, cradling the receiver to free her hands. Hurriedly, she tucked her blouse into her pants. Her eyes scanned the countertop for her keys and her cell phone.

"Come on, Hank. Pick up the phone!" she said in an agitated voice.

A voice thick with sleep answered, "This is Dr. Colbert."

"Hank, this is Brooke. Can you take my calls for me?"

"What's up?" He yawned.

"An emergency in the family."

"An emergency? What kind of emergency?"

"Cliff just called. My parents' home is on fire."

"I am so very sorry to hear that, Brooke. I hope that they're all right, and don't you worry, I'll take your calls."

"Thanks, Hank. I owe you one. Don't forget to call the answering service."

"Don't worry about a thing. I'll take care of it. Drive safe, and call me later!" Hank ordered.

Hanging up the phone, she pulled open a drawer and then slammed it shut. "Where did I put them? Why is it always the keys that you can't find when you're in a hurry?"

Once again agitated, she raked her fingers through her hair and looked around the room frantically. *Check your coat pocket*, she thought. Pivoting on her toes, she went to the mudroom, snatched her coat off the hook, and stuck her hand into the pocket. Her fingers touched the cold keys, and she pulled them out, clutching them close to her chest. "Next time," she scolded herself, "put them where they belong." Brooke rushed out the back door, letting it slam behind her.

With a closed fist, she struck the button to the garage door opener harder than normal and then shook her hand in pain. "Ouch!" she wailed. The light blinked on, and the grinding of the chain slowly raised the door, allowing the wind to scatter the leaves. The moment she climbed into the gray SUV, she leaned forward, nervously fumbling with the keys, and clumsily inserted the key into the ignition. The engine sparked to life, and she threw the car into reverse, pressed firmly on the gas pedal, screeched the tires as she backed out of the garage, and sped down the driveway. *Don't forget to close the garage door*, she thought. Striking the button, she sent the garage door into the down position.

"Everything is going to be okay. Mom and Dad will be outside waving as you drive in. Mom will be upset at the loss of her beautiful Victorian home, and Dad, well, he'll say, 'Thank God we're alive! All of this can be replaced.'" Brooke smiled and whispered, "That's my dad. He's always looking on the positive side of things."

Upon turning the corner onto Kimball Avenue, she sped down the lamp-lit street. A storm had recently passed through the town. Tree limbs littered the lawns, but Brooke paid no attention to the mess. The homes that lined the street showed no evidence of life behind the dark windows. Brooke came to a stop sign and quickly glanced to her left. As she saw no cars coming in her direction, her foot came down heavily on the gas. Her tires screamed, blackening the asphalt as she turned onto Highway 177, which led out of the city.

The headlights of a car coming toward her brimmed over the hill. Her headlights bounced off the approaching car, and she saw the unlit lights on the roof of the black-and-white patrol car as it zipped past her. Brooke flew past the patrol car doing ninety miles per hour.

"My luck! It would have to be a cop! Well, you're going to have to follow me in. I'm not pulling over!" Brooke said angrily.

Chapter 2

Officer Dan Phillips, calling it a night, was headed for the station when he clocked Dr. Brooke Kaufmann doing ninety in a fifty zone. He slammed on his brakes; the tires screeched, and smoke and dust hurled high into the night air, drifting into the open fields. Black tread marks burned deep into the pavement. Switching on the lights and siren, he then picked up the two-way radio, calling in to the station. "This is 41 Riley."

"Go ahead, 41 Riley," the dispatcher answered.

"Requesting 10-28 on Riley, RAC 248, Kansas. I've clocked this dumb broad doing ninety. She's driving like her place is on fire!"

Officer Phillips could hear the clicking of the keyboard. "Forty-One Riley, that license plate number belongs to the chief's wife, Dr. Brooke Kaufmann, and that dumb broad is, in fact, going to a fire. The chief radioed in at twelve thirty this morning saying that Dr. Kaufmann's parents' home was in flames. It does not sound good. You might want to escort Dr. Kaufmann in—the address is 1540 East Fifty-Seventh Avenue—and see that she makes it in safe. Do you copy? 10-4."

"Copy, 10-4." *Ah shit, how was I to know that she was the chief's wife!* he thought. The sirens continued to wail loudly.

fff

Clenching her teeth, Brooke looked into the rearview mirror and saw the flashing red, white, and blue lights against the dark, velvety night. She shouted obscenities as she watched the lights close in on her. Her body fought to contain the rage she felt at that moment.

fff

"She is not going to slow down, is she?" Officer Phillips said to himself and accelerated to catch up with the speeding SUV. He pulled alongside of her and spoke into his handheld speaker. "Dr. Kaufmann, I've been instructed to escort you to your parents' home. Please follow me in!" Speeding up, Officer Phillips eased the patrol car in front of the gray SUV and then gradually slowed down to slow Brooke down.

fff

Brooke's foot came down hard on the brakes to avoid rear-ending the officer's car. Her fist came down onto the steering wheel, and angry words spewed past her lips. With no other recourse, Brooke unwillingly followed behind the patrol car.

Turning onto East Fifty-Seventh Avenue, to Brooke's horror, she could see the night sky lit up in an orange hue. The closer she got to the fire, the more evident the magnitude became. Brooke could see the flames licking the trees that stood close to the house. As she rounded the curve in the road, the bright red and white lights of the fire trucks caught her eye. The firefighters frantically sprayed water on the house gutted by the flames. Glass from the windows popped and crashed to the ground. Flames leaped from the glassless windows. A section of the roof fell in. Sparks, like fireflies, were cast high into the cool night air.

Brooke slowed her car to a stop and sat in horror as she watched the flames destroy her childhood home.

fff

Off in the distance, a ghostly figure stood in the dark shadows of the barn. Deep sadness overcame her at the death of her only friend, whom she thought might one day be able to help her. Now, Sharon was gone.

fff

Cliff ran over to the car and opened the door for Brooke as she, in shock, mechanically turned off the engine. Her eyes moved swiftly, searching for her parents. She looked up at Cliff with quizzical eyes, searching his face for a sign of hope. "Where's Mom and Dad?"

Cliff reached for Brooke's hand, and she timidly took hold of his, swinging her legs out of the Suburban. Looking around her, she asked again, "Where's Mom and Dad, Cliff? I don't see them!" Brooke searched his soot-covered face for an answer.

"It doesn't look like they made it out, Brooke."

"What do you mean they didn't make it out?" Brooke's eyes widened with fear.

"I'm sorry, Brooke. When I got here, the house was already engulfed in flames. I haven't seen them."

Brooke shook her head with a stagnant, appalled look on her face. "No!" she screamed as she tore her arm away from Cliff's grip and ran toward the house. "Where are you, Daddy, Mom? Please answer me!" Brooke called out.

Cliff ran after her to restrain her, "What are you doing, Brooke? Come away from there! There's nothing you can do."

Tears streamed down Brooke's cheeks, as she frantically attempted in vain to free herself from her husband's grip. She pleaded, "I've got to find them, Cliff. They just might be out there." She pointed to the fields. "Daddy would have gotten himself and Mom out. I just know he would have. He must have taken Mom down to the stream, away from the fire. I need a flashlight!" Brooke screamed hysterically.

Officer Phillips, seeing her anguish, ran to his patrol car. Throwing open the trunk, he reached in and returned with the flashlight she had asked for.

"I'll take that." Cliff snatched the flashlight from his hand.

"Please, Cliff, we've got to find them!" she pleaded.

With a gentle touch, Cliff placed his arm around his distraught wife's shoulder and assured her that they would find them. *Dead or alive, we will find them*, Cliff thought. "Come with us, Officer." Cliff ordered. The officer obeyed, and they followed the narrow dirt path down to the little creek that Doc, Brooke's dad, took daily to check on the cattle.

The beam of light moved from side to side. They searched for a footprint, a house shoe, anything that might have been left along the path. Brooke called out repeatedly, "Daddy, where are you? Please answer me!" Her desperate calls resonated through the night air. "Please, Daddy, Mom, where are you?" she screamed. A sob caught in her throat.

Cliff pulled her into his arms, where she collapsed in uncontrollable sobs.

"I'm so sorry. They're not out here, Brooke. Please come back with me." Cliff gently helped her up from her position on her knees and led her back to the SUV. "There isn't anything that we can do until first light," he stated with defeat in his voice.

Brooke, whose face was smudged with black ash from her tears, looked up into Cliff's brown eyes. She reached up and, with her thumb, tried to wipe off a dark streak of soot that marked his face. "How did the fire start?"

"I honestly wish I could answer that question for you. We won't know until the ashes cool. It might have been that storm that blew through earlier tonight. Lightning may have struck the house. I don't have the answers for you, Brooke."

Brooke fell against Cliff's chest and sobbed helplessly. "What happened here?" she asked.

Officer Phillips had disappeared to the back of the house and returned to the chief's side. Nervously he cleared his throat and then said, "Excuse me, sir. I have something to show you."

"Okay, I'll be right with you."

Cliff glanced at his beautiful wife, whose world had just fallen apart; not wanting to leave her but knowing the parameters of his duty, he placed his index finger below her chin and lifted it ever so gently, raising her focus to his face. "Babe, I need you to sit right here." His heart broke for her as he opened the door to the SUV and gently hoisted her in.

With the glow of the fire as their light, Cliff and Officer Phillips walked back to the side of the house.

"Look." Officer Phillips directed the flashlight beam to an antique silver candlestick lying in the tall grass. Puzzled, Cliff kneeled to get a better look and then raised his gaze toward the flames within the house, an agonized look in his eyes. With his training and experience, Cliff knew immediately what they were up against. "Mark the area off; this is a crime scene. Let's get this into evidence. I don't want anything tampered with, stolen, or destroyed." *Shit!* Clifford thought to himself. *The storm has probably washed most of the evidence away.*

"There is something else that you need to see, Chief." Officer Phillips led the way to a rock at the back of the house next to the gravel road. "Here, sir." He pointed to the wet brown manila envelope.

Cliff tilted his head to read the typed name and address. *Attn: Parole Board.* Cliff's eyes glowed with rage. "Get me an evidence envelope," he demanded as he removed a white handkerchief from his inner coat pocket, bending over to retrieve the evidence off the waterlogged rock.

Chapter 3

At two in the morning, a cloud of thick black smoke spiraled upward like fingers grasping for the crescent moon. A sudden gust of wind blew, scattering the black fumes, and Brooke watched as the smoke dissipated into the blackness of the night.

The firefighters' faces were blackened with soot with white crease lines streaked across their foreheads. Their shoulders drooped in fatigue. It had been a long night. With their work completed, they loaded the hose back into the fire truck. Slowly, they dragged their weary bodies back to the truck and collapsed in their seats. Their gaze drifted to the burned-out structure, shaking their heads in sadness for not being able to save the occupants. The diesel engine groaned and knocked, as it began its slow climb up the hill to the highway and back to the station.

The fire chief, Bob Hall, stood next to Brooke and watched the fire trucks round the bend and fade into the early dawn. The early morning air was chilly, and yet sweat beads had formed on Bob's forehead. He removed his hard hat and wiped the sweat from his brow with his jacket sleeve. Lowering his head, he ran his fingers along the rim of his hat and placed it back on his head, contemplating what he would say. Bob felt a deep sadness for Brooke as he observed her red and swollen eyes.

Bob finally spoke. "I'm so sorry, Brooke. You know how I felt about your parents. I would have done anything for them. They were very good people." Shoving his cold hands into his coat pockets, he studied Brooke's face and then said, "If there is anything that I can do, please don't hesitate to call."

"Thank you, Bob. Thank you for all your efforts." Brooke's voice quivered. She walked over to Bob, wrapped her arms around his neck, dug her face into his shoulder, and sobbed. His heart raced. Long-lost feelings for the woman he had once loved suddenly and unexpectedly rose to the surface, leaving him bewildered and confused.

When she let him go, he stepped back and away from her, and reality set in. He shrugged, lowered his head, and stuffed his hands into his pant pockets. "I've got to get back to the station now. Again, I'm truly sorry for your loss." He grabbed the back of his neck as a sign of discomfort, turned, and walked toward his car. Once there, he removed his hard hat, tossed it onto the seat, and slid into the cab. He looked over at Brooke and sighed—*A love that was never meant to be*—and then drove off into the first appearance of dawn.

fff

As the first glow of light became visible over the horizon, a rooster crowed off in the distance. The headlights of a car came around the curve in the road headed toward the house. Detective Pete Paulino pulled alongside the chief's car.

"Hey," he said. "Isn't this the home of your in-laws, Chief?"

"Yes, Paulino, it is."

The detective inhaled deeply. "I gather that they didn't make it out?"

"No, they didn't. There's good evidence that it was a break-in. Doc may have surprised the intruder."

"That's really too bad. What did you find?"

"A silver candlestick lying in the grass at the side of the house."

Paulino shook his head in disgust. "I'll get on it right away. It will be daylight before you know it. Soon, people will be coming out to see what happened. Don't want inquisitive people disturbing the evidence or walking off with it either." He heaved his heavy body out of the car and then went to the trunk to retrieve his camera and kit.

Cliff looked over at Officer Phillips, fatigue etched deep on his face. "When was your shift over?

"Midnight, sir."

"Get out of here. Go home, and get some sleep. I'll get someone else to seal off the rest of the area. We've got enough men around to do the work."

"What about Dr. Kaufmann? Do you want me to run her home, sir? She must be exhausted."

"No, you go on. I won't be here much longer. She seems to be asleep in the Suburban. Thanks for your offer though."

fff

Officer Dan Phillips turned and walked toward his patrol car, passing by the SUV. He looked in on Brooke. Her eyes were closed.

Officer Phillips lowered his head; sadness engulfed him over her tragic loss.

fff

Paulino walked over to the chief and observed as Officer Phillips slowly shuffled to his patrol car. "See you later, Phillips."

Phillips raised his arm and waved without turning.

"How's she holding up?" the detective asked as he looked over at Dr. Kaufmann.

"Well, it's hard to say right now."

"Why don't you take her home, Chief? She shouldn't be out here."

"I can't get her to go home without me."

"Then go home!" Paulino said.

"I will shortly. Are you ready to get started?"

The detective shook his head sadly and held up the camera. "As ready as I'll ever be. Let's get to work."

"I'll show you where the car was hidden. Paw prints overlay human footprints," Cliff added.

The grass, wet from the night's rain, glittered in the first glow of dawn, and the rain had collected in pools in the deep recesses in the ground. Along a slope, Cliff pointed out a number of good shoe prints. Dog paw indents were deep in the mud alongside the tire treads and with human footprints.

"Yep, there are a lot of paw prints, and it looks like it is a very big dog. They overlap the human's prints," Paulino said. "It will be hard to find good prints and separate them. But, on a positive note," he added, "it can and will be done."

Cliff sighed. "Poor Max, I had to put him in his pen when he scared one of the firefighters when he jumped on the door of the fire truck." Cliff chuckled. "The driver claims that Max nearly gave him a heart attack. Max is a big Newfoundland dog, and they don't make the greatest watchdogs. They are known to be real teddy bears. But Max is a very protective of Doc and his grandchildren. He never leaves Sharon's side when he sees her outside. These prints indicate he knew the intruder."

"Well, from what I can see, I believe you're correct on that point. Max did know the intruders. See where the paw prints are overlapping human ones? No sign of a struggle or a dog attacking a person. It appears to me the dog was walking with the intruder." Paulino continued taking pictures as he focused on the shoe prints. "I'll go get the plaster for casting those prints," he added.

"I'll go with you. I need to check on my wife," the chief said.

Paulino followed behind the chief and noted the mud that had caked on Cliff's shoes and the cuffs of his pant legs. "The missus may have to throw those pants away. She'll never get them clean."

An officer who had left the worksite to investigate the surrounding area called out, "Chief, you got to see what we found here in the barn."

"What is it?"

"There's an open safe in here."

Cliff moved at a fast pace and entered the barn. "Well, well, what have we here?" Excitement coursed through Cliff's body. *Absolutely perfect!*

fff

The smile on Cliff's face sent anger that raged through the gentle spirit of the shadowy form of Marianne, and she paced in fury.

fff

Everything is beginning to fall into place, Cliff thought. *The safe has been found and, of all places, in the barn. We assume that Max knew the intruder, or he would have barked, waking Doc and Sharon.* Cliff chuckled under his breath and smiled.

The emotional strain of the night suddenly overpowered him, and fatigue settled in. A chill from the cool morning mist ran up his spine.

"Hey, Chief, help is coming. Why don't you take the Doc home? You look like you're ready to drop."

"Yeah, it's been a long night. I am tired. You've got everything under control. I'll see you later this afternoon."

Cliff heard a car door slam shut, and he went to the barn door to see who had driven in. Brooke was standing outside of the SUV and directing two detectives his way.

"Paulino is in there, guys." Cliff pointed as they walked past.

"Sorry about this, Chief," Detective Powell said as he walked past, laying his hand on Cliff's shoulder.

"It's a terrible tragedy. My sincere condolences to you and the missus," Detective Ramos added.

"Oh, by the way, Ramos, at the back of the house, there is a manila envelope lying on a rock. Take it into evidence."

"I'll get on it right away, Chief."

Cliff turned and walked toward the SUV.

fff

Brooke took note of his clothing as he walked toward her. His jacket and pants were covered with soot and mud. He rubbed his coarse chin and ran his hand through his hair in fatigue, his shoulders slouched. A chill seemed to run up his spine, and he quivered, stuffing his hands down deep into his coat pockets.

A stick lay along the path, and he looked down at his shoes. Removing his hands from his pockets, he picked up the stick to scrape off the mud from the sole of his shoes. A shiver tingled down Brooke's neck and coursed through her body. Unable to stop shaking, she got into the SUV and slid over for Cliff, who got into the driver's seat.

"Let's go home, babe." Cliff looked over at Brooke; the early morning sunlight struck her face, bringing his attention to the tear imprints that had etched their presence on her face. Her auburn hair glowed in the rising sun as her teeth chattered from the cool morning chill enveloping her.

Cliff reached over and took hold of her hands. "Your hands are like ice!"

"I'm fine," Brooke answered. "Just a little cold, that's all." She placed her hands between her knees in a feeble attempt to control the shivers that surged through her body. She snuggled close to Cliff as he turned the key in the ignition. The motor rolled over and came to life. He reached over, turned the heat on, and then slumped back in his seat.

"Exhausted?" Brooke inquired, momentarily forgetting the reality at hand.

"I'm fine, Babe." Cliff shrugged off his exhaustion, caring only for the well-being of Brooke. He hesitated to look up, fearing he'd see more tears, which would devastate him further. Diverting his attention from her, he glanced over at the destroyed house that once was his wife's childhood home.

Brooke followed his gaze, and they both sat for a long moment, staring at the once massive Victorian-style home now reduced to rubble.

Tears began to flow down Brooke's tearstained cheeks once again. She laid her head on Cliff's shoulder in a vain attempt to hide her sorrow. She held her breath, hoping her husband wouldn't notice. Of course, Cliff's sixth sense kicked in, and his heart dropped with each sniffle he heard.

In a light-hearted attempt to alter the mood in the car, Brooke wiped her nose on Cliff's shirt, with a giggle and a grunt. Cliff looked at her and cringed. He handed her his hankie, and she blew her nose. "Look." She raised her head from Cliff's shoulder and pointed toward the northwest. "Dark storm clouds are coming in again. Looks like we're in for another bad one."

"Yes, we are," Cliff exhaled. "I'll be right back, Brooke. I need to make sure Paulino and the others are aware of the next round of storms coming in. They're going to have to work fast before the rain washes any more of the evidence away."

Chapter 4

Lightning zigzagged across the early morning sky. Thunderous booms sent ripples across the sky, as if to alert the living of the majestic powers held by only One. The passionate displeasure of an evil deed angered the heavens. The storm gathered in intensity, and an angry bolt of lightning struck a tree, severing a large limb and setting it on fire, burning as if it were being cauterized of its unproductive branches.

The velocity of the oncoming storm paralyzed Brooke with fear. Her thoughts of Wednesday night's service flashed through her mind. Pastor Ward quoted the Bible and said, "The branch in me that does not bear fruit, He takes away: and every branch that bears fruit, he prunes it, that it may bring forth more fruit." Pastor put it into words that they could understand. "The trunk of a tree is like the human body. The branches supply the needed nourishment for survival. Without the branches, the tree dies. God's Word is the heart that nourishes our soul," Pastor Ward had said. "We are commissioned to take that Word (God's word) and feed the world with His Good News. For those with hard hearts who choose to go their own way, God will sever you from the trunk, and it shall be tossed into the pit of fire." To Brooke, this was a terrifying thought, and she quivered.

A hair-raiser, the pit of fire ... hell. Brooke squirmed with anxiety as she waited for Cliff to return.

****

The electrical discharge of energy a few hundred feet from Cliff caused the hair on his head and arms to stand at attention with the static in the air. In fright, he bolted for the Suburban, jumped in, and slammed the door shut. "Wow, that was a close one! I could feel the electricity bounce off my body. I really thought I was a goner."

"I saw that. Are you all right?" Brooke looked at Cliff with concern.

"I'm all right. Just a little shaken." He held out his trembling hands. "I'm just glad that it was that tree that Mother Nature decided to take her fury out on and not me!"

"I am in total agreement with that. Will Detective Paulino and the others get everything before the rain hits?" Brooke asked.

"They're almost done. I bet with that bolt of lightning; they are as eager as we are to get out of here." Cliff stared at the angry clouds. "But we can't afford to lose evidence, and Paulino knows that," he added.

"The first storm moved out too quickly. Now this one is way too late coming in. Where was this rain when Daddy and Mom needed it the most?" Brooke's voice trembled with emotion as her volume rose, and sudden anger hit. "Just a few hours earlier and they could have been spared. I know that the thunder would have woken Dad." Her voice trailed off, and anger returned to sorrow. Her thoughts reverted to yesterday's conversation with her father. Abruptly, Brooke stated, "I saw him only yesterday."

fff

Cliff's thoughts were on the problem at hand. *Everything is already falling into place: the rain, the footprints, the tire tracks in the mud … and that safe placed in the right place by Dallas, no less. Beautiful! If it weren't for the rain, we would not have gathered the evidence we have now. Any sooner and it would have all been washed away. We're gonna get 'em!* A slight grin creased his face.

"Are you listening to me?" Brooke asked.

"What did you say, babe?" he answered in a surprised tone.

"I asked you if I had mentioned anything to you about seeing Daddy yesterday at the hospital."

"No, I'm sorry. I don't remember you telling me. What was he doing at the hospital?"

"Wilma Bethel fell and broke her hip, and he went in to see her."

"Wilma is in the hospital? That's too bad. How'd she fall?"

"She slipped and fell at work. We talked for a while, and he said that after the hospital, he was going to head over to Mattie's house. He had read in the paper that her ex-husband would be going before the parole board soon; rumor had it that Cooper planned on moving back into town, and Daddy was worried about Mattie. So, he had gathered letters from the community to make sure he stays put. Well, when Daddy heard that Cooper had been released, he couldn't understand why the parole board had completely disregarded the petitions to keep him in prison. So, Daddy was worried, and he said he was going to check in on Mattie to make sure that she was all right."

"Hmmm, well, there was a manila envelope found out back lying on a rock. It was soaked from the rain. I'll have to take a look at it later today. And if Myke Cooper has any smarts, he'll stay away from Mattie, the kids, and this town." Cliff's voice rose, and his right eyebrow arched as it did when he was in deep thought. "I'll make his life miserable if he returns."

Brooke's hand went to her quivering lips. "I can't believe that Daddy and Mom didn't make it out. What am I going to tell Mattie, Jenner, and Morgan? I can't do it, Cliff!" A sob broke loose.

Cliff patted Brooke's knee. "Don't you worry about a thing. I'll call your brother and sisters this morning. I'll take care of it for you."

The sky lit up and rumbled. The loud boom resonated in the distance and crackled as lightning flashed across the early dawn's sky, once again with a promise of more rain to follow.

Chapter 5

Dr. Kent Brookfield, a retired family physician, rolled over in bed. His eyes fluttered open, and he could hear the March wind whistling through the trees. He looked over at his sleeping wife; the momentum of her breathing was steady and peaceful. A strand of gray hair lay across her closed hazel eyes. The years of smoking had wrinkled her face, aging her appearance by ten years. He could smell the cigarettes on her breath from the night before.

Kent, or Doc, as he was known by everyone in town, moved himself out of bed slowly, slipping on his house shoes, not wanting to disturb her. He then made his way down the hall, stopping in front of the decorative mirror. He stared at his reflection and then ran the palm of his hand over his platinum-white hair. Doc's smoky-blue eyes stared back at him. They had lost their glow from the many years of caring for an ill wife. *You could use a cup of coffee in each of those baby blues this morning*, he thought. *That should put back the shine and zest.*

Turning, he slowly shuffled into the kitchen. As he reached over the sink, Doc pulled back the window curtains and groaned softly. "Oh, a bleak morning! I had hoped for the sun to be out." Instead, he was staring out at a thick haze of gray fog that cast a heavy curtain that hung over the earth, blocking out the early morning rays. After turning the coffeemaker on, he stepped out onto the back porch and inhaled deeply as he gazed out into the fog. *Very soon, the wildlife and the open fields will be gone, lost to progress. Lord, I pray that I am doing the right thing.* He turned, went back into the house, and poured himself a cup of coffee. *Oh!* He set his cup down. *I nearly forgot! I can't leave until I call Mary Beth.*

Doc picked up the phone and dialed her number. A cheerful voice answered, "Hello, this is Mary Beth speaking."

"Mary Beth, I'm so very glad that I caught you at home! This is Dr. Brookfield."

"Oh, Doc," Mary Beth answered. "I was just about to walk out the door when I heard the phone ring. Has something come up this morning?"

"Oh, no, I'm not calling to cancel on you, Mary Beth. Just calling to let you know that I have an appointment in town this morning and Sharon is asleep. You go right ahead and get your cleaning done. Don't worry about her. A truck could hit the house, and she'd sleep right through it. The door won't be locked."

Mary Beth chuckled. She knew Sharon was a heavy sleeper and that she normally slept until noon. "You have a safe drive into town, and don't you worry about a thing. I'll look after Mrs. Brookfield when she wakes."

"Thanks, Mary Beth."

Doc took another sip of his coffee and stepped out the door, looking out at the fog. He grinned fondly. He could remember the days when Sharon enjoyed a brisk early morning walk out in the field. How she loved to watch the wildlife from the screened-in porch. Oh, and the excitement that lit her eyes when the deer came to feed from the pan of pellets, she had put out for them. That was before, when she was still in better health. Spring was her favorite season of the year. It was when the calves, colts, and fawns were born.

One spring, Sharon found a young fawn that had lost her mother. She brought the fawn home and fed her with a bottle until the fawn could survive on her own. Sharon named her Little Miss. Little Miss had free rein of the place, and the dogs treated her like one of their own. As Little

Miss grew, she began wandering farther away from home. Little Miss was not afraid of people, and it worried Sharon. She feared that a hunter would shoot her, so she went out, bought a wide red collar, and called the newspaper to tell Little Miss's story. For many years after that, Route 154 became a busy road. People would drive by to get a glimpse of the friendly deer with the red collar.

Each spring, Little Miss would come by to show off her fawns. One year, she showed up at the house with twins. Doc smiled; the way Sharon behaved; one might have thought they were her grandchildren. Then one day, the fawns showed up without their mother. *A sad day in our lives*, Doc remembered with a frown. They went out and searched for Little Miss every morning and evening for a week. Sharon was devastated that she would not be seeing Little Miss again. She now contented herself with watching Little Miss's offspring from the screened-in porch.

Chapter 6

A strong burst of cold wind came up from behind, astounding Doc. Heavy goose bumps raised the hair on his arms and sent chills down his back. He glanced down at his watch; it was 7:30 a.m. *Must get moving, or I'll be late for my appointment with Alexis.*

He went back into the house to peek in on Sharon. She was sound asleep. Satisfied that she would be all right until Mary Beth got there, he dressed. At the hall closet, he slipped on his black leather jacket. The sound of coughing drifted down the hallway. He stood for a long moment listening for her to call out. Satisfied that Sharon had drifted back to sleep, he went out and headed to town.

Doc's plans were to stop off in town for breakfast before his scheduled appointment with Alexis Shoemaker. He drove his champagne-colored Chevy Blazer into the parking stall in front of Rick's Café. The curtains in the café had been pulled back to allow what little sun there was to flood the room. As he stepped from the Blazer, the crisp Kansas air nipped at his ears. Zipping up his jacket, he pulled the collar up around his neck to cover his ears, shielding them from the cold. He hurriedly walked up to the door and pushed it open. The smell of bacon permeated the air, causing his stomach to grumble. Doc removed his gloves and stuffed them into his pocket. His ears were red from the cold, and his platinum hair was untidy from the wind. He ran his fingers through his hair, flattening it.

Rick's Café had a quaint atmosphere with collages littering the walls. Old photographs and paraphernalia of the 1800s were scattered throughout the restaurant. A picture of Rick's great-great-grandparents standing by their dugout home hung on the wall behind the register. Another old snapshot of them standing by their buckboard loaded with supplies hung next to it. The serious faces of the grownups in all the photos had deep ridges from the many hard years out on the open Kansas plain, where the wind had little mercy. Kent paused at a picture of adults and children bent over a stream panning for gold. They were Wilma's great-great-grandparents. They had panned enough gold in Colorado to open up this restaurant, and it had been passed down through generations of family members. The miners' gold pans were nailed next to the pictures belonging to Wilma's great-great-grandmother, and the pans contained many dings and scratches from the years of use out in the Colorado streams.

Then there was that old wagon wheel leaned against the wall next to the fireplace that had belonged to Rick's great-great-grandpa and had made the trek to and from the Colorado gold fields. The fire danced and glowed an iridescent yellow and orange, welcoming him into the restaurant.

The morning *Daily News* lay neatly stacked next to the register. Doc picked up the paper and read the headlines. He then heard the louver doors squeak open. A waitress he had never seen before stepped out from behind the swinging doors. She took the apron tied around her heavy waist into both hands and wiped them dry. Smiling at him, she said cheerfully, "Good morning! Take a seat anywhere. I'll be with you in just a minute."

As she turned and went back into the kitchen, he took a mental note, *Oh, I'd say, fifties*. She was short in stature with curly light-brown hair. Doc grinned at her size. Her broad hips jiggled as if stuffed with Jell-O.

Doc tucked the morning paper under his arm and strolled over to a table close to the fireplace. He held his hands out to the heat that radiated from it. The waitress returned and handed him a menu. "I don't need a menu." Doc smiled up at her, and she blushed. "I know what I want. I'll have the biscuits and gravy with two sausage patties and a cup of coffee. Thank you."

She wrote the order down on the bill and returned to the kitchen.

Doc reread the headlines: "Explosion; Fire Destroys Building, 21 Left Homeless."

Wow, he thought. *Thank God, no one was killed.* The picture in the paper showed the charred remains of a once three-story building. Firefighters stood with hoses fixed on the fire, with other people standing in the background.

He read on: "City in Financial Trouble."

I'm going to have to write the city commissioners again in protest, Doc thought. *They've approved another pay raise for themselves and the county workers. Where do they plan to get the money when there is a shortfall in the treasury? There goes our property tax and sales taxes up again for the third consecutive year.*

He shook his head in annoyance. Sharon had been talking about retiring to Florida. *I just might check into it.* His eyes drifted over to the obituaries. *Oh my, Floyd Crow passed away on Monday. Sharon will grieve over his passing.* Doc sniffed. *That old goat was once sweet on my wife! God rest his soul.*

He turned the page and continued to read. A small article on page 2 caught his attention: "Local man up for parole: Myke Cooper will go before the parole board on March 26, 2006." *I wonder why the prison authority didn't notify me about this. Did they contact Mattie? Well, it's a good thing that Cliff called yesterday to warn me. I'll cover my bases and get a petition circulated around town today. They are not going to let that wife abuser out of prison. I'll do everything in my power to keep him behind bars. He's a no-good drunken bum!*

Doc sniffed again in contempt. *I wonder if Mattie has seen this article yet. They should have locked him up and thrown the key away. If that drunken bum knows what's good for him, he won't show his face in this town, or I'll make his life miserable*, Doc thought angrily.

Just as quickly as those thoughts had entered his mind, Doc's conscience was pricked at the ugliness of his anger. Quickly, he repented. *Oh, Lord, forgive me for those thoughts! Cooper could have changed his ways. I pray for Mattie and the children's sake that he has. God's Word says, "Judge not lease yea be judged," so I should not judge Myke. God is the one and only true judge.*

The waitress came from the kitchen and set Doc's breakfast in front of him. He smiled up at her and said, "Thank you, miss."

"Just call me Joan, Dr. Brookfield."

Doc set the paper down and stared at the waitress. He had never seen this woman in town before. *Should I know this woman?* he thought. "Thank you, Joan. Have you worked here long?"

"Oh, no, I'm new in town. I started this job two days ago when—"

"Hey, Doc," a male voice rang out. "How are you? I haven't seen you out and about in a long time!" Rick lifted his once-white apron and wiped his hands, allowing the louver doors to swing closed behind him. Rick, a heavyset man with thinning white hair, slid himself into the chair in front of Doc.

"It has been a long time, Rick. How's the wife?" Doc asked.

"You go right ahead and eat. Don't let me keep you from your food, Doc."

The four biscuits cut in half had been loaded down with thick white gravy. Two sausage patties lay to the side. Doc's mouth watered. He could almost taste it. He laughed. "Don't worry, Rick. Nothing is going to keep me from slopping down this good stuff. You go right ahead and talk while I eat."

"It's good to see you enjoying the food, Doc. Well, Wilma is in the hospital. She took a bad fall three days ago and broke her hip."

"That's too bad. I wondered where she was. I was looking forward to one of her jolly hugs. How'd she fall?"

"Oh, Doc, I feel terrible about that." He dropped his head and stared at his hands. "It's my fault. I spilled some cooking oil on the floor, and she slipped on the mess. I feel so bad. I knew I should have cleaned it up right away …" His voice trailed off. Lowering his head once again, he twisted his fingers together and sighed deeply. "I get after the workers for being sloppy and look at what I did. I've asked myself, what if it was one of the workers? I would have been getting sued right now."

"Accidents happen, Rick. It's just one of those things. You can't go around beating yourself up. She'll heal and be good as new in no time. And a good lesson learned. I'll stop by to see her at the hospital before returning home."

"Oh, she'd like that, Doc. Wilma was sure glad that your daughter did the surgery on her. I remember when Brooke walked through them doors looking for her first job. How time flies! She just loved watching all your children grow up. We think highly of them all, Doc."

"Well, I'm happy to hear that. By the way, how is your son Shanon?"

"He's up in Kansas City working road construction. Shanon's the big man there. He loves to bark out orders, including sometimes to the bosses." Rick chuckled.

"Shanon and his wife, Tracy, they have three kids. We haven't seen the baby yet with Wilma in the hospital."

"So Shanon's got a newborn."

"Yeah, a little girl, Christina Maria. They call her Chrissie. She was born on the day Wilma had her surgery. Not to change the subject, Doc, but did you read that they might be letting Myke Cooper out of jail?"

"Yeah, I sure did. He's trouble!"

"Didn't he threaten to kill you and Mattie at the trial for putting him behind bars?"

"That he did! He's one mean-spirited person when intoxicated. If Mattie hadn't pressed charges, she might not be alive today."

"Well, we don't need the likes of him around here!" Rick shook his head. "Putting her and them kids through hell like that. If I see him around here, I oughta—"

"Rick, that's exactly why I stopped by … well, that and the biscuits and gravy." He chuckled. "I need your help. Will you have your customers sign a protest petition to keep Cooper in prison?"

"Heck, yeah. For that little lady, I'll do that. When do you need it?"

"Yesterday!" Doc laughed. "Nah, as soon as I can get the petition drawn up. After I leave here, I'm going over to the lawyer's office. Here's a rough draft I put together." Doc handed him the sheet.

"I'll be the first to sign. I feel special." Rick smiled.

"Okay, sure, Rick." Doc smirked playfully. "I'm going to make the rounds this morning to some of the businesses on Poyntz. I'm going to gather enough signatures and possibly get it in the afternoon mail."

"You're on a tight schedule, Doc."

"Yep!" Doc wiped his mouth with the napkin from his lap. They heard the door open and close, allowing a gust of the north breeze to enter the restaurant.

"Well, I hate to rush off, but I've got to get going, Doc. Don't ya worry about a thing. Gotcha ya covered." Waving the paper in the air, Rick scooted back to the kitchen. "I've got another customer to feed. Don't let that bum ruin your day, Doc! I'll get this petition signed for ya."

It's always easier to tell people not to let others spoil your day, especially when they're not directly involved, Doc thought. *But Rick means well and I understand.*

In a flashback, Doc could still see the fear in Mattie's brown eyes. It would be forever engraved deeply in his mind. Mattie's right eye was red and swollen shut, and wild panic flashed in her one good eye. Her shirt was torn and bloody. She was carrying a screaming toddler when she dashed out in front of Doc's car. He slammed on his brakes as he sucked in his breath and gritted his teeth. "Oh, Lord, stop this car!" He prayed out loud.

With her one free hand, Mattie reached out and touched the hood of the car as if to stop it. Doc came inches from hitting her and the child she held in her arm. He remembered throwing open the car door and running to her side, asking her if she was all right. She handed him the frightened and screaming child and then she crumpled to the ground. A blond-haired little boy ran from behind a tree and out into the street, screaming, "Mommy, Mommy!"

A crazed man stood in the doorway waving a gun and yelling obscenities. "Mattie, get back here!" Then a shot rang out, breaking the silence of the early afternoon. Birds nesting in a tree squawked and took flight.

Doc remembered placing the screaming toddler into the car and gathering the woman into his arms. The little boy clung to her bloody shirt, refusing to let go, and screamed for his mother to get up. To this day, Doc could not remember how he managed to get them into the backseat of the car. He drove past that house with the crazed man spewing profanities and wondered if he would shoot at the car as he drove past.

That afternoon, the police found Myke Cooper passed out on the couch with a revolver lying across his chest.

fff

Doc stared out the window of Rick's Café toward the courthouse. A sequence of words spoken by Myke Cooper after his sentencing replayed in Kent's mind: "You're going to pay dearly for what you did to me, Doc! You and Mattie will pay! I'll kill you both," Myke had snarled angrily. Hate penetrated through his eyes as he was led away.

Mattie lay in a comatose state for three weeks. Nine months later, she filed for divorce. Then the threatening letters from Myke Cooper began arriving. He would send detailed descriptions of how he would kill Mattie and take the children away from her. Then he went into descriptive details about how he would deal with Doc and Sharon.

The prison warden assured Doc that the letters would stop. Myke claimed that he had no intention of carrying out his threats and that he was just trying to scare them. Doc wasn't so sure.

Now, he might be free to terrorize Doc, Sharon, Mattie, and her children. *This man is a deranged lunatic when he's drunk.* Did he get the help he needed in prison? *Probably not*, Doc thought.

Chapter 7

The sign on the door of Mattie's Therapeutic Massage Studio read "Closed." Doc smiled as he walked past the door. *Mattie has done well at putting her life back together*, he thought, and he continued down the hall to the office of Alexis Shoemaker.

Doc walked up to the door and paused. His hand came to rest on the doorknob; he read the calligraphy writing on the door: Alexis Shoemaker, attorney-at-law. He pushed open the door and walked in. A young woman was leaned over the coffee table straightening the magazines. She looked up and smiled. "Can I help you?"

Closing the door behind him, Doc turned and answered, "I have a nine o'clock appointment with Ms. Shoemaker."

Doc watched the young woman saunter over to her desk. The gentle sway of her hips was so different from that of Joan's at the café. Doc grinned.

"Oh, yes, Dr. Kent Brookfield. Have a seat, and I'll tell Ms. Shoemaker that you're here." She picked up the phone and spoke into the receiver. "Dr. Brookfield is here, Ms. Shoemaker."

All right, thank you," Ms. Shoemaker answered.

fff

Nicole turned to Doc, and in her most professional voice, she said, "Ms. Shoemaker will be with you in a minute."

Doc looked at his watch. "I'm early and in no rush." He then asked, "Are you new in town?"

"Yes, I am," she answered.

"Where are you from?"

"I'm from North Platte, Nebraska."

"That is not a very big town. I'd guess it's about the size of Manhattan or a little smaller in population," Doc said, making small talk. "Would you, by chance, know a woman by the name of Loretta Martin?"

A look of complete surprise flashed across Nicole's face. She stopped what she was doing and stared at Doc for a long moment. "Did you say Loretta Martin? Do you know her? Loretta Martin is … was my mother. How do you know her?" An astounded look wrinkled her forehead as she tipped her head quizzically. "Have you been to North Platte?" she asked.

"No, I haven't. Do you mind my asking your name?"

A stern, defiant, and puzzled look flashed across her face. "How do you know my mother?" she asked again.

Doc stiffened, looking intently into her eyes. He could see by her expression that she was not going to answer his question until he answered hers.

"To answer your question, your mother worked for me approximately twenty years ago here in Manhattan. She was my nurse for five years before she returned home to North Platte. And your name?" he asked.

A woebegone look crinkled her face, and she stammered, "Nicole Martin."

Doc's head tilted back, and he inhaled deeply. "How is your mother these days?"

The poor child seemed to fall into a daze. Her eyes were fixed, and her voice was in a low whisper. "Mama died a year ago in a hit-and-run car accident."

Her voice amplified in his head. *Dead ...* "When?" he asked.

"Last April."

The desk intercom cut in. "Nicole, send Dr. Brookfield in please."

"Yes, ma'am. You can go in now, Dr. Brookfield."

His legs felt like jelly. Doc pivoted away from her desk and walked toward the closed door. Pausing, he turned with a heavy heart to look back at Nicole. *What a beautiful young woman she turned out to be. Such a shame. Tragic shame! All those lost years without any contact with my own daughter.* He then opened the door and disappeared into Alexis's office, the door closing behind him.

Doc looked across the room at Alexis. Her long black hair was pulled back into a tight bun, which emphasized her heart-shaped face.

Alexis looked up from her work. "Kent, I'll be with you in just a minute. Have a seat." She squinted and tipped her head to the side. Something was not right with Doc.

"Are you all right?" she asked.

"Oh, yes. I'm fine."

"All right then. Just give me a moment. I have one last notation I need to jot down." Alexis returned to the paperwork in front of her.

Doc sank down into the brown leather chair that Alexis had directed him to sit in. He then took in a deep breath and exhaled loudly. Alexis looked up at him again. "Are you sure you're all right?"

"Go ahead and finish what you are doing and we'll talk when you're done. I'm in no hurry." He sat back and watched her work. His thoughts drifted back to the conversation that he had had with Nicole. For the past year, he had wondered what had happened to Loretta. Well, now he knew. It was agonizing for him to know that Loretta was deceased. He had loved her, and yet it was a love not to be.

Loretta was such a compassionate person, and the patients just loved her. *Now what am I going to do about our daughter, Loretta?* He let out another deep sigh.

Doc smiled. *I cannot get over how much Nicole looks so much like Brooke. The same skin tone, the auburn hair, and those green eyes. My fervent prayer has been answered. But, Lord, I never expected it to be like this, here in this place! It truly is an answered prayer. I will finally get to know my one lost child before I die. All children need to know their identities. What Loretta did was wrong. So wrong! But I knew that one day our daughter would come looking for me.*

How and when do I tell her who I am? Doc smiled sadly. Looking over at Alexis, he thought. *Now my other problem—how do I get Jesse and Alexis together?* Doc chuckled to himself. *Those two kids just could not get along growing up. It almost seemed like a love-hate situation. Well, the next time he is in town, I have to get them together. They would make a fine couple. They have the same things in common; they are both lawyers and workaholics. She'll have him spinning on his heels in no time.*

Doc remembered the day he delivered Alexis. It was a hard birth for her mother. Alexis wanted to come feet first into this world. Doc smiled at the memory. Alexis was like a cat, always landing on her feet. Children had a way of growing up before you knew it. She went off to college and made her folks proud. She graduated in the upper 5 percent of her class and went off to law school. The year she graduated from law school, her father became ill, and she returned home to help her mother in caring for him. Doc remembered her telling him it was just for a year or two. She had a job offer at a prestigious law firm in Chicago. They would hold the position open for her, and when she was ready, the job was hers. Her ailing father passed of cancer eight months later. The strain of his illness had taken its toll on her mother, and six months later, she too passed. Alexis was burying another loved one.

Doc could never figure out why she didn't leave after the death of her mother. She had that job in Chicago waiting for her, and many other offers from large law firms in the big city had come through. She turned them all down.

Doc sat admiring Alexis's beauty and then asked, "Working on a serious case?"

Alexis laid her pen down and smiled, avoiding his question. Pushing back her chair, she stood and walked around the desk. Her serious emerald-green eyes were almost as green as the carpet she was walking on. She extended her slender hand in greeting. "What important business brought you to town this morning, Kent? I hope everything is all right with you and Sharon."

"I'm in good health, thanks to the good Lord. But … Sharon, well, she's not doing well after two strokes. She's having a hard time getting around and refuses to take her medication, as she should. I don't want to do it, but if she continues to neglect her health, I may be forced to temporarily institutionalize her to get her back on track."

"I'm really sorry to hear that, Kent. What can I do to help?"

"We could have handled this over the phone, but I didn't want Sharon to overhear our conversation and get all upset. Edward's Resort and Amusement Park has made me an offer I can't refuse. They want to buy my three thousand acres, and they're willing to pay five million for it."

Alexis whistled and sat at the edge of her desk. "That's a lot of money, Kent. What do they plan on doing with all that land?"

"A theme park centered on Dorothy, Toto, and her red shoes. It will bring in a lot of revenue and jobs to this small college town."

"All right." Alexis crossed her legs. Her right arm wrapped around her waist, while her left hand cupped her chin and nose. She stared off in deep thought. "It hardly makes any sense. Why this town? We're nowhere close to a metropolitan city. This is a small college town with small goals. People in small towns value their privacy. A theme park will rattle their cage. I wonder how the town's people will take the news of a theme park in their backyard."

"I've given this town my life," Doc said. "It's now time for me to think of my wife and living out our lives, not looking over our shoulder. Did you read in last night's paper that Myke Cooper is going before the parole board? He threatened our lives. I don't want to have to worry about that bum. Besides, growth never hurt any town, Alexis. It would be a boost to the economy. The government has pulled out The Big Red One from Fort Riley and moved it to Germany. That hurt our economy. The amusement park would help to compensate for the lost revenue the county has suffered. Five million dollars is a pebble tossed into a very large pond. Think of the ripple effect a small rock could make in this community's pond!"

Alexis shrugged. "Well, Doc, it's your land and you can do whatever you want with it, but when word gets out … well, I'd hate to think of the repercussions that'll follow." Then she added, "Not to change the subject, but are you going to get a petition circulated around town to try and stop Cooper's release?"

"I most certainly have." Doc pulled a piece of paper from his breast pocket. "I didn't read about Myke appearing before the parole board until this morning. I quickly put this rough draft together at Rick's Café this morning. Here, add your name to the petition. We need every name that we can get our hands on."

"You bet I'll sign! By the way, have you checked into the zoning regulations on the land?" Alexis scribbled her name on the petition and passed the paper back to Doc.

"Edwards Resort and Amusement Park will take care of that. In fact, I believe that it has already been approved from farming to commercial."

"So, tell me. What do you want me to do?"

"My will. I want to make sure Sharon is taken care of in case I should depart from this world before she does. I don't want the children to feel the burden of caring for their ailing mother. When the land is signed over next week, I am taking Sharon to look at a retirement community in Florida. I'll use the excuse that we need a vacation. Sharon will make the final decision as to whether she wants to retire in Florida or remain here in Kansas. The selling of the land will be hard enough on her. I want her to be happy. I know she'll be upset with me for a while, but in the end, she'll see that I'm right. My primary concern is that Sharon will be taken care of. Then, when we're both gone, there will be enough money to pay the inheritance taxes and other taxes, and then the money is to be divided among the five children."

"Wait a minute. Last time I counted, you had four children. You said five?"

"Yes, I did say five—Brooke, the eldest; Jesse; Jenner; Morgan; and Nicole Martin. Nicole is the youngest of my children."

Alexis shot a look of surprise at Doc and waited for an explanation. When none came forth, she asked, "Can I assume that you're talking about my receptionist, Nicole Martin, in the other room? She is your daughter?"

"Yes, and if at all possible, I'd like to shield her from the ugly gossip. Nicole is never to know where the money came from. Only under extreme circumstances is she to be told; otherwise, it must remain anonymous."

Alexis squinted at Doc. "Are you sure you want to handle it in this way? Don't you think she has the right to know that you're her father?"

"It was quite a shock for me to find my long-lost daughter here in your office. I haven't sorted any of this out myself. How will she? Yes, and you may well be right. But how do I tell her that I am her father? She may rather not know who I am. She may hate me!"

"I don't believe she hates you. Do you mind my asking how this all came about?"

Doc drew a long breath in. "The last time I saw Nicole, she was only a week old. Her mother left town in a huff, barring me from ever seeing our daughter. I was a fool to agree to her terms. Loretta left town and took the baby back to North Platte, Nebraska."

"Did Sharon know about this?"

"She may have had her suspicions. I couldn't leave Sharon. We had three small children, and Sharon was pregnant with Morgan. Morgan and Nicole are only a month apart. It was a foolish affair that I have regretted. Sharon had a very hard pregnancy with Morgan and came close to losing her twice. Make one mistake and a person pays for a lifetime with regret. Loretta paid dearly, and so did Nicole. How has this affected her life, and how can I make it right by her? If only I could turn the clock back and make things right; however, that can never happen." Doc slouched in the chair and folded his hands in his lap. "I'm not a deadbeat father. I've sent Loretta monthly checks to support our daughter." He paused, searching his thoughts.

Then he asked, "Do you know anything about her? I lost track of Nicole last year. Not that Loretta gave me any information concerning her. Loretta's box had been closed and checks were returned. 'Address Unknown.' I ... I thought that Loretta had moved away or gotten married. It was quite a shock to see Nicole in your office and to hear that her mother was killed in a hit-and-run auto accident."

Alexis sighed. "Nicole's mother told her that she had friends who went to K-State, and they spoke very highly of the university. Nicole wants to be a veterinarian, and K-State has a strong program. She is a good kid and religious. She has tried to get me to go to church with her. I have told her maybe one day. That day hasn't come yet. I like her, Kent." A wisp of sadness could be seen in Alexis's eyes. "Oh, Doc, before I forget, I figured you would want to add this to the signatures." Walking back around her desk, Alexis shuffled through some papers. "Yes, here it is. I had Nicole type this up this morning. It's my letter to the parole board. I was going to put this in the mail, but since you're here, I'll let you send it with your petition."

Doc chuckled. "I'm really glad to have this. Thanks. I'll certainly add it to my mail."

"I want him kept in prison as much as you and Mattie," Alexis added.

ƒ ƒ ƒ

Unable to work, Nicole sat staring out the window. Dr. Brookfield's revelation of knowing her mother twenty years ago startled her. How could that be? Her mother had told her that she was born in North Platte and that she had never ventured south over the Nebraska line. *It can't be. Dr. Brookfield must be mistaken. Mom and I had an open relationship. She would never lie to me about something like this.* A questionable doubt began to gnaw at her. *Why would you lie to me, Mom?*

Doc stepped out of Alexis's office, closing the door behind him. "It is really nice to see a pretty face sitting behind that desk," he said. He pulled a handkerchief from his pocket and did not notice the crumpled paper that fell from his jacket pocket. "You have a nice day, young lady."

"You have a good one too, sir," Nicole answered and watched the door close behind him. She then heard him blow his nose in the hallway.

The office intercom startled Nicole. "Nicole, could you please bring me a cup of coffee and a cinnamon roll?"

"Right away, Ms. Shoemaker."

Nicole got up and went to the small kitchen. The short counter, sink, and cupboards ran along one wall. The room contained a small refrigerator, microwave, and a coffeepot that held freshly brewed coffee. Ms. Shoemaker had stopped at the bakery before coming to the office, and doughnuts sat on the counter. Nicole opened the cupboard door, removed a paper plate, and placed the cinnamon roll on it. She then poured the coffee into the purple mug with the emblem of the K-State mascot, the power cat, and poured herself a cup. She'd return for hers later.

On the way to Alexis's office, Nicole noticed the crumpled paper on the floor and stepped over it as she opened the door to her boss's office. She walked gingerly up to her desk and set the coffee and cinnamon roll down. "Can I get you anything else?" she asked.

Alexis looked up from what she was doing and smiled. Nicole thought she detected sadness in her eyes.

"Can I get you anything else?" Nicole repeated.

"No, that will be all for now." Alexis added, "Is something troubling you?"

Nicole looked at her quizzically and then answered, "Well, Dr. Brookfield said something very odd."

"What did he say?"

"He said he knew my mother." When Nicole was by the door, she turned. "How could he have known her?"

"What do you mean he knew your mother?"

"I'm not really sure. Mom said she had never been south of the Nebraska line, but Dr. Brookfield said she worked for him twenty years ago. He must be mistaken." She then walked out and closed the door behind her. She walked over to the crumpled note on the floor, picked it up, and unfolded it. "Pick up Sharon's medication at Rex's Pharmacy, a box of her favorite dark chocolate, and note paper," it read.

"Huh." She turned the note over in her hand and stared at the handwriting. She then went back into the kitchen and tossed the note into the trash. Looking down at the rolls, she could not decide which one she wanted—jellyroll or cinnamon roll? They both looked good. She picked up her cup and took a sip. Her eyes returned to the trash can. Something about that note bothered her. She walked over to the can and retrieved the crumpled paper. Staring down at the note, she shrugged her shoulders and placed the note into her blazer pocket. *It will come to me later*, she thought.

Chapter 8

Summer 2001

The dark-blue 1944 Datsun rattled noisily down the main street of the popular college hangout in Aggieville in Manhattan, Kansas. Heads turned to watch the steam billow out from under the hood of the car. Myke Cooper eased the car to the curb. He got out and then slammed the door, cursing. In agitation, he tossed back his long blond hair and hissed in anger. His fist came down on the hood of the car in a fit of rage, adding another dent. He then walked over to the tire, giving it a swift kick before popping up the hood.

Two college students walked past, laughing under their breath.

"Need some help?" one asked.

"Nah!" Myke answered in a harsh tone. "I've got a leak in the damn radiator. Just need water." He went to the trunk and popped it open; his clothing lay heaped in a pile among his household items. Shuffling through the clothing, he seemed to be looking for something, and then he cursed out loud, choosing some choice words. Then he said, "Found it!" He pulled out an empty gallon milk container.

"Know where I can get some water around here?" Myke asked.

"Try Buddies," a tall Asian man answered. He pointed across the street to a brown one-story wooden building with a four-foot wall that enclosed the courtyard.

"Just got into town?" a short, slender man asked with his hands jammed down his jean pockets, watching with interest.

"Yeah, sure did, and this stupid car does this to me," Myke said, kicking the tire.

The Asian fellow then added, "You're lucky it didn't happen on I-70!"

"Yeah, yeah!" Myke answered, slamming his fist down onto the hood. "Pile of junk!"

"You've got quite a temper there, guy," the young man added. He pulled his hand from his pocket and held it out to Myke. "Gordon Harris is my name, but everyone calls me Gordo. This here is Pang Woo. Got a place to stay?"

"As a matter of fact, I don't. Do you know of any place I can hang at for a while?"

"Got money?" Pang asked.

"Yep." Myke dug into his pocket and came up with a wad of crumpled bills. "Yeah, I got money. You got a place for me to stay?"

"Yeah, we have a room. It will cost you 125 bucks, and we share the monthly bills. You want a phone; you pay for it. We've been stuck with too many long-distance phone bills when our so-called friend skipped town. He left us with an outrageous bill that we have to pay. The phone company don't care who made the calls; they just want their money. Still want the room?"

"Yeah, I'll need a place to lay up for a while. Ah, heck … there goes the money to repair the radiator. Can you lower the rent a little? I'll need some money to live off of until I can find me a job."

Pang and Gordo looked at each other. They needed the money to make the rent payment due at the end of the month.

Myke counted the money in his hand and showed it to them. "See, this is all I got, 125 dollars." He neglected to tell them of the fifty dollars he had stashed away in his sock.

Gordo and Pang looked at the wad of bills and then grinned at each other.

"Okay, how about a hundred dollars? You can live off twenty-five dollars, can't you?"

"I've lived off less." Myke recounted the money and handed it to Gordo. "I have no choice. I'm just glad you guys came by."

"Come on. Let's get you that water you need for your radiator. Then you can take us home." Pang smiled.

Chapter 9

The first time Mattie Holland set eyes on Myke Cooper was the day she saw him slam his fist into the hood of his car. Mattie, a tall brunette, stood at the window of the sporting goods store in Aggieville, watching the scene. When she saw Myke look up at her, she became embarrassed and quickly turned to the wall lined with sneakers. She looked over her shoulder and saw him watching her, and she blushed.

"Know her?" Myke pointed to Mattie.

Gordo looked at the young girl. "Nah, see her sweatshirt? She's in high school."

"Too bad," Myke answered.

"There are lots of hot chicks at K-State. No need to be looking at the high school girls," Gordo said.

Myke thought to himself, *I'm really not that much older than she is.* He just looked older because he'd been on his own since he was fourteen years old. He had had a rough life, and that made a person grow up much too fast. He sighed.

Two days later, Myke found work at a pizza place delivering pizza around town. He hadn't worked there very long when he found himself in front of a white ranch house in the upper-class neighborhood. Myke went up to the door and rang the doorbell. A young woman came to the door, and it was the young high school girl from the sporting goods store.

"Hey, I've seen you before!" she said. "You're the guy with the broken radiator. Did you get it fixed?"

"Not yet," Myke answered. "Did you order a large sausage with extra cheese and a large supreme special?"

"Yeah, sure did. Come in." She hollered, "Dad, the pizza's here!" Then she smiled up at him. "I'm Mattie Holland." Mattie's dad came to the door and handed him the money. "Keep the change, son."

Myke's eyes grew large. "Thanks!" He smiled. It was the biggest tip he'd gotten all day. Myke looked up at Mattie and said, "See you around, gorgeous."

Mattie blushed as she watched him walk down the path to his car. She didn't ask him where he went to school or, for that matter, if he was in high school or college. *Oh well,* she thought. *I'll look for him tomorrow in the hallway. If he's not there, I'll go to the Pizza Palace for a Coke.*

After cheerleading practice, Mattie talked some of her girlfriends on the squad into going down to the Pizza Palace for a Coke. The girls on the team made comments in front of her about this college boy she was chasing after. What Mattie didn't know was that Myke had never graduated high school. He was a runaway, a kid who lived off the streets in various states of his choosing, never staying in one place for long. If it weren't for his car trouble, he would have driven on to Topeka and then on to Kansas City. Now, he was stuck in the small town of Manhattan, which they called Wildcat Country, until he could raise the money to get his car fixed.

Mattie soon fell head over heels for Myke Cooper and spent her days after school hanging around the Pizza Palace. He had promised her a real date when he received his first paycheck. When that day arrived, he brushed his first paycheck across her nose. "Smell that money? Wanna go out for pizza?" He grinned.

"Pizza!" She wrinkled her nose. "How about Mexican?"

"I was just joking about the pizza!" He smiled. "I've eaten enough burnt ones here!"

El Matador Cantina was her pick. They shared their dreams and goals for the future over a plate of enchiladas and cheese dip. Mattie had wanted to go to law school and had applied to Harvard University. She glowed with excitement at the thought of leaving Manhattan—to her parents' displeasure.

Myke lowered his head. "I dropped out of high school. I once had a dream of joining the navy. I wanted to be a pilot flying off an aircraft carrier." He closed his eyes and held out his arms as if he were soaring above puffy white clouds. He opened his eyes. "That will never happen. Dreams are for fools."

"What are you talking about? You can always return to high school. Come in tomorrow and talk to the school counselor. They can help you, Myke. I'll help you."

"I'll think about it."

"I'll tell you what, I'll go talk to Miss Shaw tomorrow. She can help you."

Wide-eyed, Myke exclaimed, "No, don't do that! If she finds out … the school will turn me in to the authorities. I'm a runaway, and I've been running for three years. Please, Mattie, don't talk to the counselor," Myke pleaded.

Mattie agreed. That was the beginning of a relationship that she would regret.

fff

Mattie had been the envy of every female in her school. She had been voted most likely to succeed in her senior year, lettered for four years of cheerleading, and was looking forward to college in the fall of that year. She fell hard for Myke that winter, and by summer, she was pregnant. Her parents were devastated when they learned of her pregnancy. Mattie had been offered a full scholarship to the prestigious Harvard University; a dream come true. Her parents offered their support on the condition that she place the baby up for adoption and leave Myke. She refused, ran off to Vegas with false identification, and married him.

Myke worked at fast-food places. He was trying to support a young wife and a newborn and found it difficult. He turned to gambling and drinking at the casinos, trying to make a fast buck. Mattie was forced to find work, so she took a job at the local grocery store and depended on friends to help with the baby. Then the beatings began. Fearful for her and baby Jakie's life, she made a desperate call to her parents. They wired her money for a bus ticket home. Hating the thought that her parents were right about Myke, she swallowed her pride and boarded the bus headed for home with an infant in tow.

Mattie later got word that Myke was sentenced to five years in prison for theft and possession of a stolen firearm. He served only three years of his five-year prison term and then returned to Manhattan with the stipulation that he would check in with the parole board once a month. Mattie took Myke back against her parents' angry protests, and she found herself pregnant again with their second child.

fff

It was Thursday, March 9, and a late snow had blanketed the ground. Buttoning up her son's coat, Mattie looked lovingly into the blue eyes of her seven-year-old and gently raked her fingers through his blond hair. *He is so much like his daddy,* she thought, *so sweet and gentle with a big heart but a bad temper with a short fuse. I pray that he never hits the bottle like his daddy.*

"Remember what we talked about last night?" she asked her son.

"No."

"Remember the call I got from the school yesterday?"

"Oh yeah, I remember now. It was about me and Billy fighting in school."

"If Billy bothers you again, you're to go and tell Mrs. Bailey, right?"

"What if he says bad things about my daddy again?"

"The best thing to do is to ignore him and walk away."

"I'll try, but if Billy calls me a sissy pants again, I'm going to punch him in the mouth."

"No, you won't! You're to tell Mrs. Bailey, or you're going to be in trouble again, and you will be grounded when you get home. Do you understand me, young man?"

Lowering his head, Jakie answered, "Yes, um."

She kissed him on the tip of his nose and tousled his hair, sending him out the door where the other children were waiting for him. "Have a good day, children!" she hollered out the door after them.

Oh, Lord, she prayed, *be with Jakie in school this morning, and please help him to be an obedient child.* She went into the kitchen and loaded the dirty breakfast dishes into the dishwasher. Her first appointment at the massage parlor was at one thirty. She was in no great hurry to get dressed or get Dana ready for day care.

Mattie picked up the unread daily newspaper and sat down in her easy chair. Dana, her nearly four-year-old daughter, sat in front of the television with her doll by her side. She was watching her favorite morning shows, *Zoo Babies* and *Purple Dinosaur*. Her long light-brown hair was uncombed, and she sat with her thumb in her mouth and her blanket tucked under her nose.

She'll be contented for the next half hour, Mattie thought, picking up the paper to read. "City Budget Approved," the headline read.

Taxes going up again! How can we continue to live in a town that has the highest taxes in the state? We don't need two more schools and a new swimming pool in this community. What's wrong with the pool we've got? It's plenty big for a town this size. In addition, pay raises for the county commissioners and employees when the county is in financial trouble! Who do they think they're fooling?

She rustled the paper in agitation and turned the page. "Local Man Up for Parole." *Huh, who could that be?* She read on. "Myke Cooper."

"Oh, no!" She gasped and continued to read. "Cooper will be going before the …"

Dana turned to stare at her mother. "What's the matter, Mommy?" she asked with her thumb resting on her lip.

"Nothing, baby. What's Purple Dinosaur doing?" Dana's attention diverted back to the television and the singing purple dinosaur. "I'm gonna catch you and love you with all of my might …"

Mattie's heart beat wildly in her chest. *They can't let him out! They just can't!* Mattie heard a soft tapping on the decorative stained-glass door. She looked up to see a shadow standing there. Lowering the recliner's footrest, she quickly went to open the door. Doc was standing there. "I just got through reading the news. They can't let Myke out of prison! What are we going to do, Doc?"

"That's why I'm here, Mattie." He held up the paper. "Cliff got word that he was going before the parole board and called me yesterday. I read it this morning in the newspaper."

"Come in, Doc." She ushered him into the kitchen. Again, she asked, "What are we going to do?" Deep concern filtered through her voice.

He pulled out a chair and sat, watching her pace across the kitchen floor with her hand to her temple. Her fingers traced the scar line on her cheek that Myke had there put when he had knocked her off her feet and she struck her head on the tub. She remembered waking up in the hospital with Myke standing over her. "You're awake!" The look in his eyes had frightened her. "You're to tell the doctor that you slipped on the wet floor in the bathroom and hit your head on the tub. That's what you're to say. Understand? It was all an accident." It was one of the many vivid memories of the many lies she told to cover up the beatings inflicted on her by her husband.

Dana heard the voices and went to see who her mommy was talking to in the kitchen. She peeked around the corner, and with wide eyes, she flew across the room into the arms of Dr. Brookfield. "Did you come to see me?" she exclaimed.

"What a delightful child." He chuckled. "You're one of my favorite girls, Dana!"

"Yes'r, I am!" she exclaimed. "Did you bring me a p'esent?"

"Well, now, let me see." He reached into his shirt pocket, pulled out a stick of sugar-free gum, and handed it to her.

"I like gum!" she exclaimed. "Can I have it, Mommy?"

"Sure, you can, baby. What do you say?"

"Thank you, Doc."

Mattie let her daughter visit while she made a fresh pot of coffee. She reached for a cup in the cupboard and accidentally let it slip through her fingers. It went crashing to the floor, shattering into small pieces.

"Uh-oh." Dana looked up at Doc.

"Stay where you are, Dana. Accidents happen." With shaking hands, Mattie went to the closet to get the broom to clean up the mess. "Let's try this again." She took another cup off the shelf and filled it with coffee. The cup rattled on the saucer.

"Here, let me get that," Doc said. "We don't want another accident, do we, Dana?"

"No," Dana exclaimed in a gruff voice.

Mattie leaned over and whispered in Dana's ear. "Go on, Dana. Doc and I need to talk."

"I don't wanna go! I wanna stay here with Doc."

"Dana, Mommy's not going to tell you again. You can visit after the grown-up talk."

Dana's lip drooped to her chin and she slowly slid off Doc's lap and left the room.

"She loves you, Doc. Talks about you all the time." A worried look creased Mattie's brow as she sighed deeply. "He said he'd kill us for putting him in jail."

"I know," Doc said. "First thing: I got a petition started this morning protesting his release. Ms. Shoemaker has written a very strong letter on our behalf to keep Myke in prison where he belongs."

"I'm so scared, Doc." She held out her shaking hands. "I won't be able to sleep for fear that he'll try to break in and kill me and take the kids. I'm afraid he'll hurt them."

"Stay calm, Mattie. He's not out yet. Besides, you have my number and the number to the police station. I will talk to my son-in-law Cliff, and he'll have his officers cruise by your house throughout the day to make sure he doesn't bother you. Talk to the neighbors and tell them to call the police if they see anyone loitering around the place. Check your windows and doors every night to make sure they are locked, and I'll have the locksmith come in and put a deadbolt on today. Let's hope he's smart enough to stay away!"

"He said he would never let his kids go. What if he tries to kidnap them?"

"Don't you worry; he wouldn't dare touch the kids. Call Jakie's school and tell them no one is to remove him from the school premises," Doc hissed.

Dana came around the corner and asked, "Are you grown-ups done talkin' yet?"

Mattie smiled down at her daughter and nodded her head.

Dana flew across the room and hopped back onto Doc's lap.

Chapter 10

It was getting close to one in the afternoon when Doc pulled into the circular driveway of his white Victorian home with burgundy shutters. He had planned to have the house painted that summer, but the selling of the land changed all that. It would be foolish, he thought, to put money into a house only to have it torn down later.

Sharon heard the car drive up and hurried to the door. She stood in the doorway, resting her weight on her cane. Her left hand was resting on her hip. Great displeasure showed in her face.

I'm in trouble, he thought. He could see it written all over her face. It was a good thing he had stopped off at the candy store.

"Where have you been?" she demanded.

Doc walked up the steps with a look of dismay on his face. His hands were behind his back, and he answered, "Went to town to see Alexis and to buy you this." He pulled the box of chocolates out from behind his back and handed it to her.

"Oh, Kent, you always know how to wiggle yourself out of trouble. Have you had lunch?" she asked. "And why did you go in to see Alexis?" She walked into the house as she tore into the box of dark chocolates.

"To answer your first question, no, I haven't had lunch, and secondly, I needed a petition drawn up to keep Myke Cooper in jail." *Half of the true story*, he thought. "Then I had to walk the petition around to get the signatures of the people in the community. And I need yours and Mary Beth's."

"Oh, you mean that awful man that once worked for us that you fired due to his drinking on the job and him beating up his lovely wife, nearly killing her?"

"That's the one."

"Let me sign it. I know that Mary Beth will also sign it." Sharon took the petition to Mary Beth and returned it to

Doc signed. She set the petition on his desk and then added her name to the list of people.

"Good!" Doc took the petition, folded it, and placed it into a manila envelope.

"Mary Beth has lunch ready."

"Tell Mary Beth I'll be right back. I'm going to run this petition to the mailbox before the letter carrier comes this afternoon."

"Oh, let me take it!" Sharon said with excitement in her voice. "I so need the exercise after all those chocolates. Plus, I really want to do something to help."

"All right," Doc answered, handing her the large manila envelope. "Take your cane with you. I don't want you falling and hurting yourself again!"

"Don't worry. I'll take it slow, and I'll be careful," she said, happily heading for the front door.

Doc hollered after her, "Don't forget your jacket!"

"I've got it!" She rolled her eyes.

The fog had cleared by midmorning, and the sun was a welcome blessing. Sharon walked up the lane headed for the mailbox and stopped to watch a couple of squirrels chase each other around a tree. Sharon slowly made her way to a rock and sat, laying the manila envelope at her side. A deer appeared, and her heart raced with excitement. *Darn*, she thought. *I should have brought a carrot or celery stick with me.* Sitting very still, she watched the deer nibble at the early spring grass. The buck cautiously lifted his head, made eye contact with Sharon, and then quickly sprinted away. Sadly, Sharon got up and walked back toward the house. She stopped suddenly. Standing by the barn door, she saw that sad woman looking in her direction. Sharon wondered why she was so sad. She seemed to be beckoning Sharon to follow her. She wanted to help her, but every time Sharon got too close to her, she would disappear. Sharon tried to tell Doc about the sad woman, but he and the others could never see her. *They think I'm crazy*, Sharon thought. Saddened, Sharon waved at the strange woman as she slowly vaporized.

Chapter 11

Mayor Phil Stokes hung up the phone and loosened his tie in agitation. Gritting his teeth, he brought his fist down onto the mahogany desk with great force. His full cup of hot coffee rattled, spilling the contents over the side.

"You've really made me mad, Kent!" He hit the intercom button and bellowed, "Sophie, bring me in some paper towels, will you!" Picking up the papers on his desk, he shook the coffee off into the trash.

Sophie entered with the paper towels. "Had an accident here, I see."

"Yes, a little accident." Phil spoke in an irritated voice.

"Here, let me clean up this mess for you … There, anything else?" She smiled, although she could see the anger on his face.

"Is there anything wrong?" Sophie asked.

"Yeah, plenty. Stay close. I may need you later." Phil snatched up the phone and dialed Doc's home number. He drummed his fingers impatiently on the desk while he waited for Doc to answer. The receiver was picked up, and a familiar voice answered, "Hello, Brookfield's home."

"Doc, this is Phil."

"How are you doing, Phil?"

"I've got a question for you, and I'm hoping there is no truth to this rumor."

"Uh-huh, go on. What's your question, Phil?"

"I've just gotten word that you're selling the Lazy-B Ranch to an amusement park. Of all things, an amusement park!"

"You heard right, Phil. They've made me an offer I simply couldn't turn down."

"Doc, you can't sell prime farmland to an amusement park! You've got one of the best spreads in this county—rich soil for hay and wheat, not to mention the best grazing land for cattle. You will ruin the quality of life in this community. The zoning board will never approve of it, Doc! You can't do this to this town!"

"Well, Phil, if you or the townspeople want to make me an offer, I'd be glad to sell the land to you."

"You know that we don't have that kind of money laying round. Besides, that land isn't worth five million," Phil said angrily.

"Well, that's what they're willing to pay, and anyone in their right mind wouldn't turn it down. I know you wouldn't, Phil."

"That's beside the point, Doc. I'll do everything in my power, as mayor and your banker, to stop it from going through!"

"Well, do what you feel like you have to do, but it is a done deal, Phil. You can't stop it."

"We'll see about that!" Phil slammed the receiver down. Reaching over, he pressed the intercom button and, in an angry voice, called out, "Sophie, call the city commissioners for an emergency meeting tonight at seven o'clock sharp at my home. Tell them that I will not accept any excuses."

"Yes, sir. Do you want me to give them a reason for the meeting?" Sophie asked timidly.

"No! Just tell them to show up, and no excuses!"

Five minutes later, the phone rang, and Phil hit the intercom.

"What is it, Sophie?"

Sophie cleared her throat. "I'm sorry to bother you, Mr. Stokes, but Mr. Forrester is on line one, and he is saying that it's urgent that he speaks to you."

"Thank you, Sophie. I'll take the call." Phil picked up the line and answered, "Yes, Ed, what can I do for you?"

"What's going on, Phil?"

"I need all of the city commissioners to show up at the house for a closed-door meeting. I'll explain tonight."

"You're calling for an illegal meeting, Phil. Something big going down?"

"Yeah, you can say that."

"Can't you tell me over the phone what it is? I promised Marge that I would take her out to dinner tonight. It's our anniversary."

"Send her flowers, buy her a bracelet—or better yet, buy her a box of chocolates to add to her waistline. Do what you have to, but I need everyone at this meeting tonight."

"That comment about my wife's waistline was uncalled for, Phil," Ed said in a defensive tone.

"Just be at my house no later than seven o'clock tonight, Ed."

Chapter 12

Alexis was on her way to a dinner engagement when she heard angry voices and profanity spewing from Smokie's Bar and Grill. Glass shattered loudly. Alexis peered in through the smoke-filled window to see a chair flying through the air. Obscene language followed, and someone hollered, "Call the cops!"

More glass shattered as a chair came flying through the bar window, followed by a woman's scream. To Alexis's shock, a body slammed through the closed door and landed at her feet; the impact had broken the door from its hinges. The young man, who was in shock, lay there moaning at her feet. The jagged cut on his face was spewing blood.

Myke Cooper stormed out the door and stood over the young man—a broken beer bottle with blood on the jagged edge in his hand. Myke snarled. "I'll kill you for that."

The man on the ground pleaded for his life. "I'm sorry, man. I'm sorry. I was just joking."

"Jokes like that one is not appreciated, especially when it concerns my woman," Myke snarled. "You insult her, you insult me! Get up and fight like a man!"

Alexis stood immobilized, staring into the drunken face of Myke Cooper.

"Like I said, get up! It's time for you to die!"

The young man rolled over and grabbed hold of Alexis's ankle in a desperate attempt to raise himself, startling her. She yanked her foot away and looked down into his eyes. Fear and pain emitted from his eyes.

Evil permeated through Myke's. He reached down to grab the defenseless young man, the jagged beer bottle still in his hand. Myke then raised his hand, ready to plunge it into the young man's body once more.

"Stop!" Alexis screamed. "Don't hurt him anymore."

They heard the sound of screaming sirens coming down street, and the large crowd dispersed, allowing the ambulance and police vehicles to pass through.

Coming up behind Myke, a stranger threw his arm around Myke's neck and put him in a headlock. Myke fell back against his attacker, and a violent struggle to free himself took place. The attacker released his hold on Myke and fell back in pain. Myke had violently plunged the broken bottle into the man's leg, leaving a broken piece behind that protruded out of his leg.

Myke screamed, "Come on! I'll take y'all on, one by one!" Myke curled his upper lip under his nose and snarled like a dog.

fff

Troy Frederick, prosecuting attorney, Alexis's dinner date, had been watching her walk down the street when the young man came slamming out of the door. Troy bolted from his seat and rushed out the door of the restaurant, using his hands to part the crowd to get to Alexis's side. He took hold of her arm, startling her. She pivoted quickly to see Troy standing behind her.

"Come on, Alexis. Let the police handle this," he said to her.

The rotating lights could be seen over the heads of the crowd. A sudden piercing scream blocked out the sounds of the approaching ambulance. Myke had a woman by her hair; he was dragging her toward the alley, the broken bottle poised against her throat, threatening to kill her if anyone came near. The victim's hands held on to her hair as she struggled to free herself. Pain and fear crossed her face. She cried out. "Let me go! Someone, please help me!"

Two police officers went in pursuit of the woman in need of help while the others pushed the crowd to the side, allowing the paramedic to get to the injured men. One injured young man sat at the curb, blood running from between his fingers. The paramedic rushed to his side tending to the gash on his cheek, which was bleeding profusely. Another paramedic rushed over to the young man bleeding from the gash in his leg, glass sticking out of the wound. The paramedic dropped to his knees, looking at the woman pressing against the wound, and said, "I'll take over. You've done a great job at stopping the bleeding." The young woman who was applying pressure to stop the bleeding identified herself as a nurse and began barking orders to the paramedic.

They could hear a woman's desperate screams for help. "Help me! Someone please help me!"

"Over there!" Someone pointed.

The officers' hands went immediately to their holsters. "Let her go!" one officer yelled out.

The officers slowly moved in on Myke. "You don't want to do this, son. Let her go, and come with us," the officer said.

Reality set in, and Myke realized he was finished. "Here,

you want her? Take her!" He shoved the woman toward the officers. She stumbled and fell forward into the arms of one of the officers sobbing. She held tightly to the officer who had caught her. When they looked up, Myke had vanished down the alley.

Aggieville was sealed off, and patrol cars with flashing lights cruised up and down the streets, spotlights scanning both sides of the alley. Someone from a second-floor window hollered, "He's in the dumpster."

Two police officers pulled up to the dumpster. One lifted the lid as the other unbuckled his revolver. "Come outta there with your hands raised!"

Myke slowly stood, his hands above his head. "Don't shoot."

The took him to the station and booked him on aggravated assault and battery with a deadly weapon, attempted murder, making terroristic threats, and attempted kidnapping charges. His sentence should have been ten years; however, because of an error (an incorrect entry in the presentence investigation report at sentencing), he was released on bond after serving only three years.

Mattie knew deep down that she should have filed for divorce then. Her parents offered her their support, but she loved him. A week later, he beat her in a drunken rage, nearly killing her.

fff

Alexis pondered the letter she had written to the parole board. Did she make her case against Mr. Cooper strong enough to keep him behind bars? *He's a drunken lunatic and desperately in need of help before he kills someone. He certainly won't get the help he needs in prison. I've dealt with that board many times. Letters don't carry much weight. The parolee's attitude and how he answers the questions weigh heavily on whether he remains in prison or is let out on parole. Myke may be uneducated, but he's no dummy.*

Chapter 13

January 14, 2016

Leavenworth, Kansas

They walked side by side—two strangers housed in separate sections of the prison. They were dressed in blue jeans. One had on a red Chiefs football T-shirt, while the other was wearing a K-State Wildcat shirt. Myke Cooper and Pico Sanchez stood in front of the security door, waiting for the buzzer to sound. No words passed their lips. They both seemed anxious to get far away from that place of cold steel and concrete. They finally heard a buzzing sound, and the gate clanged opening slowly, allowing them to step out into freedom. Myke looked over his shoulder, fearing that a guard would call out that they had made a mistake and he was to return to his cell.

His heart raced wildly as he hurriedly stepped out into the sunlight. He then heard the door closing behind him and felt relief flood his soul. Myke inhaled deeply, taking in a delicious breath of freedom's air—the first in three years.

"Do you smell that?" he asked the young man walking next to him.

"Smell what?" Pico asked.

"That sweet smell of freedom, fool." Myke held his face up to the sun. The warm rays felt so good. *Freedom*, he thought. Pausing, he realized no one had shouted out for him to stop. So, he slowly turned to look back at the high, cold limestone walls and the high gate that no longer imprisoned him. "I hate that place!" Myke hissed. "I'll kill myself or anyone who tries to put me back in that stinking hole again."

"There's always a bright side to everything," the Chiefs football fan walking next to Myke answered. "We could have been in a worse place than this one. In Mexico, they starve and beat their prisoners. By the end of the first year, many make it out in a box, *amigo*. That was a luxury hotel as far as I'm concerned. Good food and smelly roommates.

The drawback, no women, but still better than Mexico. My name is Pico Sanchez. What's yours, *amigo*?"

"Myke Cooper." He held out his hand to shake Pico's.

A white-and-blue bus pulled alongside the curb, and the two men got on. "Going to Kansas City?" the driver asked.

"For now," Myke answered. He handed the driver the voucher.

The driver looked from Myke to Pico and asked, "Just got out, huh?" He punched a hole in the voucher and handed it back to Myke. The driver had a smug look on his face.

Myke snorted and moved toward the rear of the bus.

Pico handed the driver his voucher. "Don't harass me, my friend! Your business is to collect the fare only."

Myke grinned at his newfound friend and watched him walking past the seats with passengers who stared at him as he walked past, saying to one man, "What you looking at?"

Pico, a muscular Hispanic, had gained quite a reputation at Leavenworth Prison. It was rumored that he had killed a guy with one punch, shoving his nose into his skull. Myke later found out it was a false rumor. He had made up the story to survive in prison.

Pico's hair was curly and black; a large scar ran from the edge of his nose to his jawline. His front teeth were spaced far apart, causing a slight lisp, which Myke found annoying. But he was humorous, and Myke couldn't help but like the guy. His life story was very interesting. He was not ashamed to tell of his brushes with the law. He claimed that he had been sent up for breaking and entering, theft, and arson.

"How did you get that scar?" Myke asked.

"Oh, this," He ran his finger across his cheek. "Me and my friend Angelo, we were always getting into trouble. One day, me and Angelo rode our bikes to the edge of town where this beautiful white church stood. It was so beautiful with stained-glass windows. One window showed Jesus holding a lamb. The next window, the Holy Book lay open on a pedestal. Angelo, my friend picked up a rock and threw it at the window. He missed, hitting the window frame. I laughed, and Angelo got really mad. Like a dummy, I threw the next rock, and that beautiful stained-glass window shattered and it showered down on us. A large piece of the glass struck me in the face, cutting me badly. It was almost as if God's hand was punishing me for my bad deed. The surgeon who stitched up my face said I was very lucky that it didn't take out my left eye. To add to my pain, my father told me that scar would be a constant reminder of the evil deed I had done."

It was just like Pico to say what he did next. He said that he didn't feel badly for what he had done until Angelo told his sister. With her big mouth, she screamed, "I'm telling Papa." He took off after her and threatened her by the inch of her life when Papa came around the corner.

He said, "What are you going to tell me, Anna?"

"I was dead meat," Pico said. "My papa turned every color in the rainbow. He took me by the collar and marched me and Angelo back to the church to face Father Dominic. In the confessional, our penance was to say one Hail Mary and Our Father. After some thought, Father Dominic added five acts of contrition."

Angelo and Pico's restitution for their sins that day was to clean up the broken glass and pay for the window. Pico found the jagged piece of glass with the hand of Jesus smeared with his blood. He said it sent shivers down his spine. He then added that his father was right; God did it to teach him a lesson.

The stories he told of his life made Myke look like a saint. Pico also told Myke of his breaking into a house early one morning, thinking nobody was home. Pico was out to make his old lady happy. She was always complaining about something. A baby was on the way, and she felt that she deserved something better than shoddy paper plates. She wanted good china dishes and silverware to set on her table. When he told her that they didn't have the money for stuff like that, she got mad. With hormones blaring, she said that she had made a big mistake marrying him. She should have married his best friend, Enrico, the plumber. "He could buy me the fine china and silverware." She had sneered at him.

Enraged, Pico stormed out the door. He was determined to prove that he could provide for his wife and unborn child. He had overheard his wife talk about a neighbor who was going to be out of town over the weekend. *That's it!* Pico thought to himself. *I am fed up with having nothing and being unable to provide for my family. I'll show her that I can provide for her and the baby even if it kills me.*

Pico said he wasn't very quiet when he broke the glass to the back door. After unlocking the door, glass crunching under his feet, he walked into the kitchen, turning on his flashlight. He went about his business looking for valuables and said he wasn't very quiet about it, thinking nobody was home. But soon, he realized his big mistake. First off, the people were poorer than he was. They had no china or fine silverware. They ate from plastic dishes and had no microwave to steal. The silverware was cheap dime store stuff too.

He then felt the cold steel of a rifle pressed to the back of his head and nearly dropped a brick in his pants.

A very low, gruff voice behind him spoke. "Put. It. Back!"

Pico turned in surprise. Somehow, pure adrenaline kicked in, and he was able to throw a quick thrust, knocking the rifle away from his head, catching the gunman by surprise and knocking the owner off his feet. Pico went flying to the kitchen door. Glass crunched under his shoes, and he ran as fast as he could out the back door. Out of breath, he had to stop. *Man, I gotta quit smoking!* He gagged.

The old man went flying out the kitchen door behind Pico, glass crunching under his house shoes. Pico turned and saw this old large man thundering after him in his underwear, and Pico ran like a scared rabbit. "This old guy, mind you," Pico said, "was older than my dad and bigger. He come running after me, tackled me to the ground, and he sat on my chest, screaming, 'Stop what you're doing! Stealing goes against God's Ten Commandments! Thou shall not steal! Repent of your wicked ways!'" Pico said. He recounted how he almost vomited from the weight on his chest and this dude's bad breath.

"The old man was loco! I told him, I even begged him, 'I didn't take your cheap stuff. I didn't want it anyway.' But this guy, he wanted to fight me." As always, Pico was laughing.

Someone called the cops, and he heard the sirens coming down the street. "Get off me, you crazy old goat." Pico said he struck the man with a hard blow, and he rolled off of him. He then got up and took off, headed down the alley. Police cars with searchlights came down the alley with their sirens blaring, lights flashing, and brakes screeching to a halt. The door to the police car flew open, and a neighbor hollered through an open window, "He's hiding behind that bush!" Pivoting around in Pico's direction, the police pointed their guns and flashlights at him, yelling, "Drop to the ground!"

Soon thereafter, a search warrant had been issued to search Pico's home, where they found stolen stereo units, televisions, and jewelry, along with some of the items from a house that had burned to the ground earlier that year. Pico was then slapped with arson and theft.

"Did you do it? Burn down that house?" Myke asked him.

"I don't remember. They said I did it." Pico scratched his head. "Alcohol and drugs don't mix, *amigo*. I don't remember a thing about that one, other than a helluva of a hangover and being behind bars." Then he asked Myke, "So what'd you do to get put in the slammer?"

"A misunderstanding with my old lady."

"Must've been one helluva misunderstanding to get you sent up to the big house."

"Like you, I was drunk and did drugs. My memories of that day are hazy," Myke said. "I was charged with attempted murder."

"You gotta be kidding me! Your own wife?"

"No, I'm not kidding. My ex. Well, she was my wife then. She divorced me when they put me in the slammer. The cops claimed that I smashed her face."

"Damn, *amigo*. That's bad." The look on Pico's face made Myke mad.

"What do you mean bad? Like you not remembering burning down that house? I don't remember hitting her. The cops found me out cold on the couch, a revolver lying across my chest. They say that I had fired that gun at my wife. Would I have killed her and my kids? Hell, no! Well, I don't think so. Not my kids, anyway. People say I'm real mean when I'm drunk. Mattie has accused me of being ugly sober or drunk. Maybe she's right. Yeah, I have hit her before, smacked her across the face for talking back and tossed her across the room like a sack of potatoes. Real men don't take that from their women. Women are supposed to look pretty, not have a sassy mouth. That's what my uncle Joe taught me, while making his own wife, Mable, as an example."

As a child, Myke had felt sorry for his aunt Mable; she always cried. Myke would spend summers with them to help his uncle Joe in his hardware store, and Uncle Joe would tutor him. "A woman respects her man and does as he says. No questions asked," he'd say.

"My dad never hit my mom. He only cheated around on her." Myke sneered.

"Hey, *amigo*, you and me, we think alike!" Pico retorted. "The only way to get a woman's respect is to demand it."

On parting, Pico handed Myke his phone number. "Call me, *amigo*, when you get settled in. We'll go out and have a beer, or should I say, a Coke together. We gotta stay away from the hard stuff." Pico laughed.

A car pulled up alongside the curb. "That's my woman. Gonna have to listen to her nag all the way home. *Buenos Dias, amigo.*" A look of regret was on Pico's face.

At first, Myke thought of getting on another bus to Manhattan but then decided against it. He had a restraining order against him in Manhattan. It prevented him from having any contact with his ex-wife, and he needed a court order to see his children. *Maybe*, he thought, *I'd be better off finding me a job in the big city for a while.*

Myke pulled out the list of apartments that he had stuffed into his pocket earlier: "King's Motel on Fourth and Main: studio and one-bedroom apartments." *I'll try this one first. It doesn't sound too bad*, Myke thought.

It was not a very far walk, and he was glad. The air was chilly, and without a hat, his ears were cold. He finally reached King's Motel, a red-brick building that was five stories high. *Could be worse, but the inside will tell the story*, he thought.

After pushing the door open, he walked up to the front counter. The manager of the motel sat behind a desk, smoking a pipe. He was bent over working on a crossword puzzle. He looked to be in his mid-sixties, and Myke stood there looking at him. *Why, that old geezer*. Finally, he cleared his throat to get his attention.

Looking up from the magazine, the old geezer said, "Need a room, son?"

"Yeah," Myke answered. "Your sign says weekly rates. How much do you charge for a week?"

"You've come to the right place." He smiled broadly, got up, and walked around the desk. "I have the cleanest rooms this side of town. You want a studio or one-bedroom?"

"Just me. A studio will do."

He reached over and pulled a key off a nail. "Follow me, young man. By the way, my name is Gus. Some call me Gramps. But for now, you can call me Gus."

Gus walked with a limp and dragged his left foot up the three flights of stairs.

"Hurt your leg?" Myke asked.

"Sure did! That ice storm dumped an inch of ice on us the other day. I stepped out the back door unaware of the ice and slid down three steps on my backside," he said as he rubbed his buttocks. "It's a good thing I didn't break my hip when I fell. I just bruised it, nothing broken. The doctor told me to take it easy for a couple of weeks." Gus opened the door to the room. "We haven't gotten to this room yet. I know it needs painting, and I had hoped to get this room done by next weekend. I'll give you a special rate, and I'll take off twenty-five dollars."

Myke looked around the room. The room was small and dreary. A brown sofa bed was placed against the north wall. Both armrests were worn through with cotton fiber poking through the holes.

"We're going to replace that sofa bed and chairs. It's on order and hasn't come in yet," Gus added.

Myke nodded his head, letting him know that he understood. A nineteen-inch television sat on the coffee table next to the window. "Colored?" Myke asked.

"Nope, black-and-white only. Just outta prison?" Gus asked.

Taken aback by Gus's question, he snapped in agitation. "What? What kind of question is that?"

"They all come here to stay right off the bus. I've got the best rates in town."

Myke felt the anger well up inside of him. He owed Gus no explanations. "Well, I'm just passing through. How much do you want for the room with the twenty-five dollars off?"

"It will be a hundred a week in advance. I usually charge $125. But since this room has not been painted and the sofa bed and chairs are on order, I'm giving you a good price. But once they are replaced, the rate goes up to $125."

Yeah, right, Myke thought. *I bet you tell that to everyone. A rip-off for a cockroach-infested dump.* "I'll take it for a week." He handed Gus a one-hundred-dollar bill.

A greedy grin creased Gus's wrinkled face. A gaping hole revealed several missing teeth. The rest were stained brown from years of smoking.

Gus handed Myke the key to the apartment and closed the door behind him.

Myke went to the bathroom to wash his hands and looked down into a sink of black mold and rust stains. The tub was no different. He cringed at the filth. *Prison was a lot cleaner than this dump.* He then walked over to the kitchen cabinets and pulled open the doors. A couple of roaches scurried in panic as their tranquil darkness was disrupted by the light of day. Myke wondered if Gus was charging them a hundred dollars a week too. A disgusted smirk formed on Myke's lips.

Well, he thought, *let's check the refrigerator and see if there are any little tenants there too.*

Swinging the door open, he leaned against it. There were no roaches, and it was empty. *Well, what did you expect?* he asked himself. *A T-bone steak and a six-pack of beer welcoming you back to the real world?*

He would have to get groceries to get him through the week. He went over to the couch and pulled out his wallet. He began counting what money he had left. One hundred twenty-five dollars. He cursed. He picked up the apartment key and his coat and then went down the three flights of stairs to look for a pay phone.

Gus, in a brown plaid shirt, sat hunched over at his desk, again deeply engrossed in his crossword puzzle. From the corner of his lips, his pipe dangled, and smoke loomed heavily above his head.

"Have you got a phone I can use?" Myke asked.

"Local or long distance?"

"Local."

"You can use the phone on the counter. It will cost ya fifty cents. Long distance calls, you'll have to use the pay phone at Gappie's grocery store on Fifth and Pine."

After digging deep into his pocket for the fifty cents, Myke slammed it down on the counter. "It only costs thirty-five cents at the pay phone!"

Gus handed him the phone book and answered, "You can go to Gappie's grocery store and pay the thirty-five cents. Your choice."

Glaring at the old man, Myke shoved the phone book back at Gus. "I don't need this. Is there a charge for me to look at the phone book too?" he asked sarcastically as he reached into his pocket and pulled out the slip of paper that Pico had scribbled his phone number on. He dialed the number.

A woman answered the phone.

"Is Pico home?" Myke asked.

"Yeah, just a minute." He could hear her yell, "Hey, Pico, telephone!"

Myke heard Pico yell back. "Who is it?"

"How should I know? I'm not your secretary."

"Give me that phone … Yeah, this is Pico."

"Hey, Pico, this is Myke. You don't sound so good on your end."

"Hey, back at you, *amigo*. I could be doing better. Sometimes, I think I was better off in prison. She's already telling me I gotta get a job or get out. Can you believe that? I just got out of prison, and she's already nagging me!"

"Man, I'm sorry to hear that."

"Where you staying, amigo?"

In the background, Myke could hear a child crying. A sinking feeling of remorse stirred in Myke's gut. He wanted to go home and ask Mattie to forgive him. He wanted Mattie and his kids back. Sighing, Myke answered, "At the King's Motel on Fourth and Main. Do you know where it is?"

"Yeah, I know where it is. It's a cockroach-infested dump!" Pico snickered.

Myke laughed and looked up at Gus, who was staring at him, listening to the one-way conversation. "Yeah, I've got roommates, all right," Myke answered. "You know of any good place nearby that I can go for a good burger?"

"Amigo, I know of a good joint that has the best burger, and it's only a couple of blocks from where you're staying. Benny's Place, best burgers and fries in town. It's two blocks east from you on Fifth and General. You want me to meet you there?"

"What about your wife and kid?"

"What about 'em? I'll see you at seven o'clock."

"Yeah, sure. I gotta go to the grocery store first, and I'll see you at seven, sharp."

Chapter 14

Jim Anderson, a tall, lean man with salt-and-pepper-colored hair, stepped out of his car as Vinnie Cynova pulled up behind him. Jim waited at the curb for Vinnie. He stuck his hands into his pockets and watched Vinnie gather up some materials from the backseat. He finally looked up, stepping around the black Lincoln. "How's it going, Jim?"

"Not too bad, Vinnie." They exchanged handshakes. "Do you know what this meeting is all about?" Jim asked.

Vinnie, an Italian lawyer in private practice, was a man who turned heads. His light-brown eyes had a way of sending messages to women. A different woman hung from his arm weekly. Vinnie tossed his cigarette to the pavement and crushed it under his shoe. "It's gotta be important for him to call an illegal meet. If the press gets ahold of this, we're chopped liver, and we'll get nailed to the wall for not posting a twenty-four-hour notice."

The two men walked up to the door, and Vinnie rang the doorbell. The door opened, and Phil Stokes greeted them. "Thanks for coming. Take a seat in my study. I'll be with you shortly."

Vinnie and Jim entered a small, quaint, nicely decorated room. An electric fireplace sat in the corner and glowed brightly. Brown leather furniture as well as a mahogany desk placed close to the fireplace added to the masculine atmosphere with family portraits covering the walls. A Boston fern sat on a stand in front of the window with chairs set up in the room to accommodate the board members who would be in attendance.

Ed Forrester was the last member to enter the room. He glared at Phil. "I am in hot water over this meeting! Marge is accusing me of having an affair. The box of chocolates and flowers you suggested did not appease her anger."

The men in the room sat quietly, avoiding Ed's angry stare. Ed dropped himself into a chair next to the fern.

Vinnie spoke in a low voice. "Phil, this is an illegal meeting. Do you know what the press will do to us when they hear of this?"

"Yes, I know!" Phil glared at Vinnie.

Vinnie was, as usual, immaculately dressed in his blue suit, his nails filed and manicured. His shoes were spit-shined every morning, and not a hair on his head stood out of place.

Mr. Do-it-right Vinnie Cynova, Phil thought in irritation. "The only way the press will get ahold of this is if someone leaks it!" he said, glaring directly at Vinnie.

Phil's glare then moved to Ed Forrester, a hardware store owner with greasy gray hair that needed washing, not to mention a haircut. His shirttail hung out of his pants, and his brown shoes were scuffed and worn with age. He shook his head. *And his wife's accusing him of having an affair. Get a life, Marge!*

Colin Ward, the senior member and pastor, sat next to Ed. His blue eyes stared intently at Phil, waiting to hear the explanation of this emergency meeting.

"Judge me not, Pastor," Phil said in a low voice, so none could hear.

Then there was Sid Meek, a short man whose large

belly hung over his belt. Sid was a gourmet cook and the owner of one of the finest restaurants in town. He not only enjoyed cooking; he loved to eat, and his waistline told his story.

Phil looked around the room, and his eyes settled on Ed Forrester's angry face once again. Phil then decided not to prolong the meeting any longer than necessary, saying, "Since this is an informal meeting, I'm going to dispense with the formalities and get straight to the point. I've been told today that Dr. Kent Brookfield is selling his land to an amusement park. I spoke with Doc this morning, and he said that once the zoning board passes the rezoning from farmland to commercial, it is a signed and done deal. I've made an appointment with the zoning commissioner to get this rezoning stopped, and I need all of your support and input before I meet with the zoning board."

"Phil," Sid Meek said, "I've just talked with Mark Reed. He was in the restaurant for lunch today, and it was the first time that I heard about the selling of Doc's land. Mark said that the zoning board had already passed the rezoning. It's too late to stop it."

"What do you mean it has been passed? I've just gotten wind of the selling of the land today, and now you're telling me the rezoning has been approved?"

"It happened late last night from what Mark said. It's

also rumored that money may have been slipped under the table to get the rezoning done as quickly and as quietly as possible before the news broke. It sounds to me like someone got very greedy and didn't worry about the consequences of his actions," Sid added.

"So, are you saying that Mark took bribe money, Sid?" Phil's eyes narrowed.

"No, that is not what I'm saying. It may have been others on the zoning board," Sid added in defense of Mark Reed.

"So, Doc already knew that it had passed. No wonder he sounded so smug over the phone. Well, my bank holds the mortgage to a small parcel of land south of the ranch, and it hasn't been paid for yet."

Phil rubbed his forehead in agitation. The zoning board may have approved it, but I'll find some way to stop it. I won't allow an amusement park in my town. Never"

"Now, Phil, what harm would an amusement park do to this community? It would bring in revenue that this town most certainly could use. It would lower taxes and boost the economy," Sid Meek added. "Besides, it would be great business for my restaurant."

"I'll tell you what it would do," Phil snapped. "The crime rate will triple, meaning, more police protection for the community, thus raising our taxes. This small town will be no different from the big cities like Kansas City, New York, or Chicago with their traffic pollution, and who knows what will follow!" Phil said angrily. "And besides, prime farmland will be lost!"

"I'll check into this tomorrow, Phil, and I'll get right back with you," Vinnie Cynova said sympathetically.

Reverend Ward, who had sat through the meeting quietly, finally spoke. "Deeds done in darkness can only end in disaster. Be careful as to what you say of others. Make sure before you point a finger at someone and claim money went under the table that this is a fact! Evil, in the end, is always exposed."

Phil paced the carpet, listening to the reverend. Strong displeasure showed on his face. *I don't need to be preached at today, not today!* His thoughts exploded.

"Phil, I don't think there is anything more we can do tonight until Vinnie gets back to you on this issue," Ed Forrester added.

"Go home, Ed. All of you, go home. This meeting is adjourned."

Chapter 15

Nicole slid open the louver doors to her closet, hung up her sweater, and kicked off her shoes. Stepping back, she looked up at the suitcase that she had brought with her from Nebraska. She could never bring herself to open it and wondered why she just didn't toss it into the trash.

The old worn brown suitcase that Nicole had found hidden under her mother's bed now lay on the shelf in her closet. The leather-wrapped handle had cracked with age, and the hinge was rusted and tarnished. Lowering it off the shelf, Nicole gently placed it on the bed and ran her hand across the dry brown leather. Sadness engulfed her, and her heart began palpitating in her chest. It brought sadness into her mother's life, and Nicole was afraid of what was inside of it. *Why, didn't I just throw it out after her death? Well,* she thought, *you've hung on to it for a reason …*

She tugged at the clasp that refused to snap open and then hit it with her fist in frustration. It popped open to her surprise, startling her. With both hands, she lifted the lid gingerly. Inside of the suitcase were stacks of letters neatly tied together with a red bow. *Mother's favorite color.* Nicole smiled sadly. Were these the letters she had seen her mother reading?

That was such a long time ago, she thought. She remembered those sad days when she came home from school to find her mother in tears. Her mother always managed to explain the tears away. Her answers were always the same. She explained it away as a sad movie or a letter from Aunt Sadie reporting on her grandma's health, which was failing. Great-Grandma Becky eventually was placed in a nursing home because of Alzheimer's disease, and she no longer recognized anyone. It saddened Nicole's mother deeply to hear of her deteriorating condition and not be able to visit her in Virginia.

Nicole's mother would tell her to think back on the good times with Great-Grandma Becky and how she made her feel so special.

Yes, G. G. Becky—as Nicole called her—made her feel very special. Nicole could still remember the smell of her hands as she cupped her face in her warm hands—the smell of jasmine. She once told Nicole that she was one of God's most precious children, that God had chosen her to be in this family who dearly loved her. Nicole was a blessing from God.

Fond memories, she thought as she smiled to herself. Returning to the old suitcase, Nicole untied one of the bundles' red bows and removed a letter. She read the stationary heading: "St. Mary's Hospital; Manhattan, Kansas." The letter was short, and Nicole read it quickly. The writer asked how her mother was doing and asked about Nicole. It was signed, Kent.

Nicole tore open each letter, and they all read the same, ending with an apology. What startled her was the money that fell out of each letter that her mother had not opened.

Chapter 16

In the wee hours of the morning, ice pellets, followed by large snowflakes, had pelted the earth. The ice had covered the streets in a sheet, and then the snow blanketed the ice. Myke stood in the doorway of the motel surveying the packed snow. A chill ran up his spine, and he zipped his coat and pulled his collar over his ears. The snowplows had packed the snow along the street curb and stained it a dirty brown. He then jammed his hands into his pockets, lowered his head, and cast his eyes to the ground.

He heard the jingle of a doorbell, and he looked up to see a man in a tattered brown tweed jacket walk out of the hardware store. He paused to pull down the brown bowler hat to keep the wind from carrying it away. He tucked a bag under his arm as he walked past Scottie's Liquor Store.

Myke licked his lips; it had been three years since his last drink. Closing his eyes, Myke could almost taste the brown liquid sliding down his throat. Shaking his head, he forced himself to walk away as remorse filled his gut. Flashbacks of the past rushed through his mind. He had turned out just like his mother. Everything that he despised, he had become, and to add to it, he was a wife beater, which cost him his marriage. It took willpower that Myke had not realized he possessed to turn from alcohol. He surprised himself.

Thank you, God! Myke smiled. *If it wasn't for You, Lord, I would have run back to the bottle.*

Myke had returned to God in prison before his release. A fellow inmate had finally convinced him to attend one of the meetings held once a week at the prison. Myke held deep resentment and hatred for the church after what had happened behind closed doors. A priest he had respected, trusted, and loved did bad things to him, and he wanted nothing more to do with the church or with God. His friend in prison told Myke that he needed to forgive all the wrong that was done to him. "Hate eats away at a man's soul," his cellmate told him. Myke's heart was hard with anger. He didn't want to forgive, and he didn't want God in his life. What had God done to help him?

Well, Myke finally gave in and went to one of the meetings just to shut his cellmate up. The sermon turned out to be on forgiveness and letting go of the past. "Turn and never look back," the preacher had said. "Ask God to come into your life and take control. Let Him do the driving. Just say these simple words, 'Lord God, I need help and I can't do this alone.'"

Myke repeated after the pastor, and—*wham!*—the Holy Spirit came and touched his heart. Myke felt the hate of the past lift from his shoulders, and he felt like a new man.

fff

At seven o'clock in the evening, Myke walked through the doors of Benny's Place. He could smell the hamburgers and ribs, which awakened his senses, telling him he was famished. The concrete floor was littered with empty peanut shells, and the jukebox played an oldie by Johnny Cash, "Waiting for a Train." Myke's foot began to tap with the beat as he looked around for a place to sit. The words bellowed from the jukebox, "My pocketbook is empty. My heart is full of pain. I'm a thousand miles away from home, waiting for a train." A pang of homesickness hit Myke like a slow-moving train, and his heart ached for his children. He wanted to go home.

Myke thought of joining a handful of people who sat close to the potbelly stove, warming their hands. He could feel the warmth coming from it. Then a hand came down on Myke's shoulder, causing him to jump. Turning around, he saw Pico standing there with that gap-toothed smile. "What's up, man?"

"Pico, you scared me," Myke said and cursed.

Laughing, Pico pointed to a table in the corner. "Let's sit over there."

The waitress came over to their table and asked, "What can I get ya?"

"Two beers," Pico answered. "Nah, make that one beer and a Coke. Add two juicy cheeseburgers with fries, and make that separate checks."

Scribbling the order on a pad, the waitress then asked, "Anything else?"

Myke looked over at Pico. "Who's the Coke for?"

"What's with you, man? You know you can't drink anymore!"

"Who made you my mother?"

"You know you'll pay if you're caught drinking!" Pico hissed in Myke's ear. "Besides, you gave up drinking since you found God, remember?"

"Man, I hate it when you're right," Myke added.

A look of disgust came over Pico's face, and he told the waitress, "Cancel the beer and make that two Cokes. I can't let my friend here sit and watch me drink a beer. That would be heartless of me. Sorry, man, I wasn't thinking."

Alcohol had always been Myke's weakness. Myke was glad that Pico was there to remind him. He then looked up. *Sorry, Lord, I am new at this.* Then he turned to his friend. "Hey, Pico, thanks for caring. I don't want to be sent back up again for something as stupid as a beer. Man, that's rough, no beer. So, Pico, how's your old lady treating you today? Is she being good to you?" Myke winked.

"No, I wish. Nag, nag, nag. That's all she does is nag. It's getting old man, and I've been out of the pen for only a few hours! She's constantly yelling, 'Pay attention to your son when he's talking to you, Pico. Pico do this. Pico do that.' Today she yelled at me to go out and look for a job. 'You're not living off me!' she hollered, and then she called me a lazy bum!"

Here was Myke's opening. "You know what I've decided to do?"

"What?" Pico asked.

"I'm going back home. I hate big city life. Maybe my old lady will take me back."

"And what if she doesn't? You almost killed her, remember."

"I haven't thought that far ahead. I'll think of something."

"Yeah, like rob a bank."

"Shut up, Pico! You wanna get into trouble with that kind of talk? Somebody could be listening. That kind of talk can get us both thrown back into prison."

Pico's hands flew up. "Oh, forgive me, man!"

The waitress brought their Cokes and cheeseburgers.

Between bites, Pico asked, "Are you going to pay a visit to that rich doctor friend that put you in the slammer?"

"He's no friend! And what do you mean pay him a visit?"

"You know, all that money, furs, and jewelry his old ladies got."

"Keep your voice down, Pico! What're you talking about—stealing?"

"Well, yeah, he stole three years of your life, man. It's time to get even. I can show you the ropes."

Myke looked around the room to see if anyone was within earshot. "Then what, Pico?" he whispered.

"We'll take off for Mexico and live a life of ease."

"Man, you're crazy, Pico, real crazy. And what does one of God's Ten Commandments say? 'Thou shall not steal.'"

"Aw, there you go, getting holier-than-thou on me. I hate that." Pico drew in a breath. "Okay, when are you going to leave for Manhattan?"

"I'm leaving on Thursday, on the two-o'clock-bus."

"If you see me on Thursday, I'll be going with you. It all depends on the old lady. If she doesn't get off my case, I'm history."

Chapter 17

Nicole's stomach grumbled. Looking up at the library clock, she saw it was 6:10 p.m. She closed her history book, shoved it into her backpack, and zipped it closed. She then headed out the door toward her car. A stranger walked past her saying, "It's snowing outside. Watch your step. It's slick."

"Thanks for the warning." She smiled.

Passing through the swinging doors, she saw, to her delight, large snowflakes slowly drifting and dancing toward earth. It was wet snow, and the children across the street were having a snowball fight. She could hear the screams and loud laughter. *Oh, to be young again*, she thought.

Nicole's gray Mazda was blanketed with snow. She scooped up a handful of snow and then packed it into a ball. With a sheepish grin, she looked around for a victim.

A tall, good-looking young man with light hair walked out of the library door, a backpack slung over his shoulder. His hands were tucked in his pockets, and his head was lowered. He was looking down at the ground. *The perfect target!* The purple power cat on the back of his backpack was calling to her, beckoning her as if it had a purple bull's-eye right in the center. She couldn't resist the urge. The snowball went flying, missing the purple bull's-eye and striking that gorgeous blond stranger in the back of the head. *Oh no!* she thought.

He shook his head and ran his hand along his collar, knocking the snow from it.

"Oops!" Nicole lowered her head and cringed. She busied herself at the task, brushing the snow from the windshield.

"Hey," he hollered. "Who threw that?" He looked in Nicole's direction. She was the only one out in the parking lot.

"Hey, you!"

Oh no, it's Reid Starr! And he's looking straight at me! "Me?" She asked, pointing at herself and pivoting around to see if anyone was behind her, she could blame.

"Yes, you! Did you throw that snowball?"

Raising her hands in defense, Nicole answered, "Me, throw a snowball at you ... what snowball?"

Reid bent over, picked up a handful of snow, and began packing it lightly in his bare hands.

"No, wait!" Before Nicole could complete her sentence, a stinging cold struck her in the face, paralyzing her for a second. Startled, she gasped at the freezing cold. In anger, she screamed, "How dare you!"

"How dare me! You struck first." Reid came over, laughing. "Sorry about that. I figured it was you who threw that snowball. I saw you packing that snowball from the library door and wondered who your intended victim was. Here, use my shirttail to dry off your face."

Cringing, Nicole forced a weak smile. She bent down and took hold of his shirt. "I don't know what came over me," she said. "It was all in fun. I'm sorry. Will you accept my apology?"

"Only if you have dinner with me," he replied. "My name is Reid Starr. What's yours?"

"Hi!" she answered. *Boy, Nicole, you really know how to pick 'em.* "I'm not sure I want to tell you who I am, considering what I did to you."

He laughed. "You never know, I might have done the same to you. It was all in fun, and I do forgive you. But see that it doesn't happen again, okay?" He smiled.

Extending her hand, she said, "First off, my name is Nicole Martin." She fought to conceal her giddiness, and she could feel the freezing sting on her face quickly heat up to a warm blush.

He took her hand in his. "Glad to finally meet you, Nicole."

"You're in my writing class on Monday and Wednesday, aren't you?"

"Oh, you mean Professor Bishop's class. Isn't he the most enlightening teacher you've ever had? I have learned so much from his class," she said.

"Yeah, he challenges me, and sometimes he makes me mad. He told me once that I'm capable of doing better writing and that I'm letting basketball interfere with my creativity." After a pause, Reid added, "Well?"

"Well what?"

"Dinner, you, me, dinner?"

"What about Amber?"

"What about her?" He shrugged his shoulders.

"Well, aren't you two going together?"

"No, we broke up a month or so ago." He stared at Nicole intently, waiting for an answer.

"Well?" he asked again.

"Oh, yeah, sure! Where do you want to meet?"

"Do you know where the Belly-Bop Bar and Deli is on Bluemont?"

"I sure do. It's my favorite place to eat."

"Good. I'll see you there in ten minutes?"

"It's a date," Nicole said enthusiastically and then cringed with embarrassment. *Did I just say it's a date? I can be such a dork sometimes.*

Reid walked back to his car. Nicole watched him bend over and scoop up a handful of snow. Underhandedly, he tossed it at her. She screamed as snow hit her coat. "I never make promises I can't keep. See you at Belly-Bop?"

"Okay," she said with a laugh. What a way to get a date with the most popular guy on campus.

I can't believe that I hit Reid Starr in the head with a snowball, and he asked me out! Me! I've been told that he's one of the most arrogant, conceited basketball players on the court. Reid won the MVP award and became front-page news. Everyone wanted to be associated with Reid Starr, especially the women. Amber had her hands full trying to protect her property, her man.

ƒƒƒ

Reid was standing at the door of the Belly-Bop watching for Nicole. When he saw her, his heart flip-flopped, a feeling he had never experienced before. *This girl is different*, Reid thought to himself. He held the door open for her. A cold draft blew in from the open door, causing the patrons to snarl and shiver.

One of the customers yelled, "Close that door!"

Nicole ran in, and he quickly shut the door behind her. "I was beginning to wonder if you were going to come," he said jokingly, smiling down at her.

"I had to circle twice before I found a parking spot. Aggieville is always such a busy place at night."

"Aggieville is always such a busy place all the time." Reid chuckled.

The room was the size of a large, oversized walk-in closet. It was packed with students and faculty members, and there was no place to turn around, let alone sit. Two workers stood behind the bar. One was making a drink, and the other was taking orders and ringing up a sale. Eight people sat at the bar talking or watching a football game. Four booths that held four people, sometimes six if they squeezed in together, ran along one wall. Facing the street were three small round tables with two high-backed stools.

A couple got up and gathered their belongings and then headed for the door. The table was quickly cleaned off, and Reid and Nicole sat down.

The waitress came over. "What can I get you to drink?" she asked.

"Just water for me, thanks," Nicole answered.

"Make that two," Reid added. "We're the heavy drinkers here." He smiled at Nicole.

"So is Manhattan your home?" he asked.

"No, I'm from Nebraska."

"Yo, Starr!" a voice called out.

"Hey, man, what's up, Joe?"

"Who's your new girlfriend?" Joe asked.

Nicole recognized the girl standing next to Joe as one of Amber's friends, Annette. She glared at Nicole, sizing her up, causing Nicole to feel very uneasy.

Reid placed his arm around Nicole's shoulder. "This is Nicole Martin."

"I've seen you around campus," Annette said with an icy glare. "You're in Professor Bishop's creative writing class, aren't you?"

"Yes, I am," Nicole answered politely.

Reid picked up on the tension between Nicole and Annette.

"Talk to you later, Joe," he said dismissively.

The waitress stood behind, Joe balancing their drinks in both hands. Joe stepped aside. "Yeah, later, Reid. Nice to meet you, Nicole. Oh, by the way, are you going to Smitty's party tonight?"

"Yeah, Reid, why don't you and your new friend join us there?" Annette snapped sarcastically, glaring at Nicole.

"No, I can't. Not tonight," Reid answered.

"Yeah, sure, man, I understand." Joe winked.

"She's not that kind of girl." Reid looked at Joe in annoyance as Joe and Annette walked out the door. "He can be such a jerk," he offered apologetically.

"Yeah, I'll bet he didn't mean anything by it," Nicole said. "Thanks for defending me."

"A remark like that really shows no moral character in a person. That Joe can be a real jerk. Don't let him bother you."

"I won't. A jerk is born every second." Nicole smiled over at Reid with admiration. Even though she had told him that the remark and wink hadn't bothered her, it secretly did. No male had ever defended her in that way.

After dinner, Reid walked Nicole to her car; his head lowered, and he seemed to be in deep thought.

"Why so quiet?" Nicole asked.

"I would really like to see you again. Would you consider going out on another date with me?"

"I'd really like that."

"Great, I'll see you in class tomorrow. Oh, one more thing, I really want to apologize for Joe. He's not like some of the guys on my team, and I ... Okay ... well, some of the guys on my team are Christians like me, and we have taken an oath of abstinence. One day, Joe attended our campus meeting to see what it was all about, and the topic was abstinence. Joe thought it was hilarious. He had never in his life heard of guys our age abstaining from sex. He laughed his way out the door, clutching his sides from the laughing cramps. Once you take a stand for something you truly believe in, you're labeled," he explained.

Reid had been labeled a goodie-two-shoes, but he didn't mind it. In fact, he took pride in it. "People don't understand the truth in God's Word. We would not have unwanted pregnancies, abortions, AIDS, and all the sexually transmitted diseases if it weren't for promiscuous sex. I believe that Amber put Joe up to coming to our meeting. Amber and me, we weren't on the same page when it came to that topic, and Joe is the same way."

"He was mocking you then, wasn't he?"

"Yep, I guess in his warped way, he simply doesn't get it. Joe's feelings are if a girl is available and willing, he's not going to turn a good thing down."

"That's pretty sad for him. He'll pay the price, if he hasn't already."

"Yeah … he's like a little kid who thinks it won't happen to me. He's even said he does not use precautions," Reid continued. "I told him the story of a kid I grew up with who contracted AIDS while in high school. His dreams of playing college football came to an abrupt end. He lost his scholarship soon after being diagnosed."

"Oh, Reid, how tragic. How is he?"

"He passed away three months go."

"I'm truly sorry."

"Well, he's gone and no longer in pain. He stopped taking his medication when he fell into major depression. He wanted to die. He had lost all his friends who were afraid to get near him. Nobody would call or talk to him except for me. When he walked down the street, people would cross to the other side of the street and whisper to each other about him. They treated him as if he were a leper. He couldn't take it anymore, so he tried to kill himself and nearly succeeded once.

"The doctors tried to give him hope by telling him that scientists were close to a cure. But that was a lie, and he told me that he knew it was. I try to call him at least once a month and visit whenever I could. My mother and Rob's mother are good friends, so Mom kept me informed until his death. The sad thing is that young people today have this foolish idea that they're invincible." Reid sighed and shook his head in sorrow. "He was a good friend."

"I am truly sorry. How awful!" She shook her head in disbelief over the cruelty of people.

"I gathered you must be a Christian too," he said.

"Yes, I am. It's much easier to understand a person when you share the same beliefs in God."

"I'm glad that we are of one mind, Nicole. You're so different from Amber. I wish I had …" Reid paused. "It doesn't matter anymore. It's over and done with, and I've gotta admit I'm glad. She's not what God wanted for me."

fff

Reid and Nicole's conversation continued in Nicole's car. They talked into the early morning hours about God, beliefs, and dreams for the future. When it became clear that Nicole was getting tired, he offered to take her home in his car. She agreed, they switched cars, and Reid drove her home. At her apartment, he walked her to her door, kissed her forehead, and said he would see her in class that afternoon.

He made it early to Professor Bishop's class that afternoon and saved a seat for her. When he saw her walk in, he stood and waved her over. *She made it to class.* He was beginning to wonder if he had kept her out too late.

"Hi," she said. "Thanks for saving me a seat."

Professor Bishop walked into the classroom and placed the graded papers on his desk. His eyes quickly scanned the room as he announced in his gruff, authoritative tone, "Good job to some of you on the essay. As for the rest, better luck on the next test. More effort needed." He began handing out the graded test papers and talked about the next assignment. Professor Bishop did not waste any time; he was a nonstop talker, and when discussion was opened to the group, he wanted to see hands raised.

After class, Reid said to Nicole, "I've got my jeep. Let me take you home. Or did you drive?"

She had walked to class that morning, and it was bitterly cold. Therefore, she eagerly accepted the ride to her car. They had left her car in the parking lot early, and she needed to get it before it was towed away.

Reid had followed her to her apartment in his car. She had left her billfold on the seat of his car. Reid caught up to her at her door.

"You forgot this again." He handed the billfold to her. "Here, let me help you. He took the key from her hand, unlocked the door for her, and pushed it open. "At your service, madam."

"I have got to be more careful of my wallet," she said. "One of my bad habits ... Would you like to come in and have a cup of hot chocolate?"

"I sure would." Reid entered the apartment. *Nice and neat*, he thought, and then he sat down. Cuddles, Nicole's cat, jumped up onto his lap and purred.

"I hope you're not allergic to cats." She handed him the hot chocolate.

"That, I don't know. I haven't been around cats much."

"Cuddles likes you. She doesn't usually jump up on people's laps."

They had a nice afternoon visiting and getting acquainted. It was getting late, and Reid still had basketball practice. "Well," he said, "I've gotta go. Got practice in half an hour." He bent over and kissed Nicole's forehead.

Her heart skipped a beat, and she could feel the heat entering her cheeks. She lowered her head. The heat she felt always turned her cheeks beet red. Reid smiled at her and slowly backed away. Then he turned, walked toward the door, and closed it behind him.

"I think I've fallen in love, Cuddles."

Cuddles sat on the window ledge and watched Reid's jeep drive down the street. She then jumped from the window ledge where she had been perched and came over to Nicole, purring loudly and rubbing herself against Nicole's leg. Nicole reached down, picked her up, and stroked her long white angora fur. "Sorry, Cuddles, I forgot to feed you this morning. I bet you're hungry!" She set Cuddles back on the floor.

Chapter 18

Man, I'm going to be so glad to be rid of this big town! I hate this place, Myke thought as he cursed under his breath. *Once I'm on that bus, I'm never coming back here.*

The bus terminal he entered was ancient and dingy. Its walls were a drab dirty white, and a musty odor hung heavily in the air. Large posters of New York City, Chicago, Los Angeles, and Dallas hung on the walls.

His footsteps echoed down the hall as his boots hit the brown cobblestone floor. A gray-haired woman peered over her tortoise-framed glasses and watched the stranger approach the wire cage window.

"Can I help you?" she asked.

"Yeah, I called a couple of days ago to reserve a seat to Manhattan."

"Your name?"

"Myke Cooper."

"That will be $157 for a one-way ticket to New York, New York. That's as close to Manhattan as I can get you."

"Wait a minute. I don't want to go to New York! I wanna go to Manhattan, Kansas. The Little Apple, not the Big Apple."

"Oh, I'm sorry. I misunderstood. Let me check." She turned to her computer and clicked away at the keys. "Here we are. Manhattan, Kansas. That will be twenty-six dollars. A big difference from $157, isn't it?" An embarrassed giggle escaped from her throat.

Myke counted out twenty-six dollars and passed it through the small opening in the window. "The change in cities, how will it affect the time the bus will leave for Manhattan?" Myke asked.

"Not by much, just thirty minutes. Will you be traveling alone this trip?"

"Yes, I am."

"No, you're not!" a voice behind Myke answered. "I'm traveling with him."

Myke sharply turned around. "Hey, Pico, glad to see you, man! So you decided you weren't putting up with your old lady's nagging?" Myke chuckled.

"Yeah, you could say that." Removing his wallet from his back pocket, Pico asked, "How much to where he's going?"

"That will be twenty-six dollars."

He handed her thirty dollars, and in exchange, she returned his four dollars with his ticket.

"What made you change your mind?" Myke asked.

"My old lady and her boyfriend kicked me out," Pico said angrily, rubbing his knuckles.

"She has a boyfriend? That's bad news, man."

"Apparently so," Pico answered.

"Oh, man! What happened? Tell me about it."

"That whore was sleeping with another guy while I was locked up. Now I understand how you felt when you punched out your old lady. Rage can make you do things you never believed you were capable of doing." Pico cursed and spit on the ground.

"So, tell me what happened."

"Val, my soon-to-be ex-wife, and her boyfriend ..." Pico stopped talking as the expression on his face turned to anger.

"Yeah, Ted had been keeping my wife company at night. That son of a b … he came over last night, and my three-year-old son, Jose, ran up to this guy and called him daddy." Pico's voice cracked with emotion. "My kid calling another man daddy!" He swore in anger. He turned his back to Myke and hit the wall with a thunderous blow. He shook his hand in pain, and then he walked over to the large plate-glass window and folded his arms across his chest. Myke could see the reflection of his face, tears streaming down his cheeks. His shoulders slouched forward, quivering. Throwing back his head, Pico took in a gulp of air and wiped away the tears.

"Then that turkey asked Val, 'Didn't you tell him?'" Pico continued. "The whore cowered like a scared rat and began to whimper. She told her lover that she tried to tell me many times but was afraid. Then Val, with her lover at her side, asked me for a divorce." He quivered with emotion. "I went to jail because of her! Everything I did was for her." Pico attempted to hide how distraught he was, tapping one fist into his other palm, squeezing and pursing his lips together. "Amigo, I went crazy with anger. I couldn't control myself. Before I knew it, I was going after her. Everything seemed like it was in slow motion. It was as if I was watching myself from across the room, and I couldn't stop myself. I ran after her and tried to hit her. I would have busted her face in. Lucky for her, that gringo stepped in front of her, and I hit his chest instead. Then I found myself airborne and then hitting the floor." Pico swore, rubbing his backside. "I don't remember the punch he inflicted on my face. That gringo planted his heavy foot on my chest, snarling like a mad dog. See where he hit me?" Pico turned his head to show Myke the bruise on his cheek. "And my kid ... my kid was hanging on to Val's legs, screaming and crying. My kid is the only reason I didn't fight back anymore. He was scared." Pico moaned with utter sorrow in his voice. "Then that gringo grabbed me by the collar and lifted me off the floor, his face in mine, and he told me if I ever came back, he'll kill me."

Pico turned from the window. "My kid calling that gringo daddy. You know how that hurts. I'll never get over that. Val might as well have taken a knife and stabbed me in the heart and ended it right there." He walked over to the bench and sat next to Myke, his hands folded between his legs. His head drooped low. "Man, if I had a gun on me, I would have shot Teddy right where he stood."

Myke was silent. He searched through his own emotions and experiences for the right words for Pico. Finding none, all he was able to say was, "Man, I'm sorry about what happened, *amigo*." A sorrowful silence filled the room. Myke then inquired, "Where'd you sleep last night?"

"Here at the bus station over on that bench." Pico pointed to a bench across the room, far away from any doors that might open and bring in a cold draft. "And this place gets pretty cold at night."

"Why didn't you come to my place?"

"I don't know. I guess I just wanted to be alone to think."

Myke decided to change the subject. "Where'd you get all that money?"

Pico chuckled. "I emptied Val's ATM account. Boy, will she be surprised when she tries to withdraw money or write a check and it bounces. It will serve her right for what she did to me."

Chapter 19

Cuddles came into Nicole's life six months before her mother was killed by a drunken driver. She had always wanted a cat, but her granddad was allergic to them. On the day she left for college, her mother handed her a large basket with a pink bow tied to the handle. In the basket was a little ball of long white fur, her blue eyes peeking out from the pink tissue paper that made up her bed. A little pink bow was clipped to the top of the kitten's head. In surprise, Nicole asked, "Is she mine to keep?" Now, looking back, she smiled painfully. That was the last time she saw her mother alive.

Nicole closed her eyes, and she could see her mother's hand brushing away her auburn hair from her eyes. Her mother's blue eyes were smiling back at her. "Yes," she had told her. "You'll need someone to keep you company while you're away at college." Painful memories. Six months later, her mother was killed by a drunken driver going down the wrong side of the street. Her mother made it to work in an ambulance and died before Nicole could get to her bedside. Nicole blinked back the tears forming along the rim of her eyelids. *Oh, Mother,* Nicole thought sorrowfully, *why did you have to leave me? I miss you so!*

Nicole stared at her mother's picture on the entertainment center, tears rolling down her cheeks. She quickly brushed them away. *You would have liked Reid, Mom. He is everything you said you wanted to see in a man for me. He is kind, gentle, treats me with respect, and most of all, he is a Christian.*

Sighing deeply, Nicole bent over and picked Cuddles up, running her hand through her long white angora fur. "Cuddles, that man you just saw at the door, he's Reid Starr. He asked me out to dinner tonight, me! And one day, I'm going to marry him!"

When she set Cuddles down on the floor, the cat followed her into the kitchen and sat next to her dish. She was not the least bit interested in what Nicole had to say about Reid; she just wanted to be fed. Nicole laid her backpack on the table and rattled on.

"Reid is so handsome and tall. And he asked if he could call me again!" She giggled like a high school girl. "Are you listening, Cuddles?"

Cuddles meowed back at her, twitching her tail in agitation. Crouching low, she positioned herself and sprang up to Nicole's leg, sinking her claws into her jeans and into her thigh.

"Ouch!" Nicole hollered, grabbing hold of Cuddles by the nape of her neck. Nicole scolded, "Bad kitty!"

Setting Cuddles on the floor next to her dish, she rubbed the spot where her claws had caught deep into her thigh. All thoughts of Reid had vanished with the pain.

ƒƒƒ

Dr. Brookfield's appearance at the office had disrupted her week. His comment about knowing her mother and her working for him had greatly upset Nicole. She had been unable to pay attention in class for the past week. She realized her mother had lived a very secretive life.

Walking into the bedroom, Nicole went to the closet and kicked off her shoes. Her mother's brown suitcase caught her eye once again. Nicole reached up, removed it from the shelf, and set it on the bed. The old leather suitcase held mysteries of her mother's past life, a life that suggested that her mother knew of someone here in Manhattan, Kansas.

Who is this Kent? Well, I'm going to find out who this person is.

Nicole opened the suitcase for what seemed like the umpteenth time. She stared down at the neatly tied stack of letters, contemplating at length the meaning behind them. The letter at the top was postmarked November 11, 1982. Nicole would have been nearly a year old then.

Stroking Cuddles' fur, Nicole took in a long breath. "What do you think, Cuddles?" The cat suddenly sprang from her arms, her front paws grabbing hold of the luggage lid and her back claws digging deep into the fabric, tearing it away. She then pushed off and sprang away from the suitcase as the lid fell closed.

"Oh, Cuddles, what am I going to do with you?" Cuddles' bright-blue eyes stared back at Nicole for just a moment, and then she playfully ran off into the kitchen.

Nicole raised the lid, and to her surprise, letters tumbled out from the tear in the lining. She picked them up, and her eyes grew large with surprise. She then turned them over in her hand. They were unopened letters. She counted them and there were thirteen in all. *Mother, why would you hide these letters? And why did you sew them behind the lining?*

She fanned the letters through her fingers, and one with bold letters written on it stood out among the rest.

Her name was written in bold black letters: NICOLE. *Oh my*, Nicole thought as she tore open the letter.

My Dearest Nicole,

With your curiosity, I knew you would find these letters after my death. These letters may answer your questions and take you to Manhattan, Kansas. There is an excellent college there. I do know you'll go looking for answers in Manhattan. All I can say is that it is too painful for me to talk about it. I am deeply sorry that I have kept you in the dark concerning your father.

On another note, I am sure you could use this money. My heart's wish is that you stay strong in the Lord and lean on Him for all of your needs, and I pray that you can forgive me. I truly love you very much.

Love,

Mom

Nicole sat on the bed next to the letters and opened the first one. Five crisp hundred-dollar bills were wrapped in tissue paper, but no note was enclosed in it like the others she had read. She tore into the other twelve letters, and they all contained five crisp hundred-dollar bills. She fanned the bills through her fingers, confused. *Money? Mother, what's going on? Why all this money, and why did you hide it? You hoped that these letters would answer my questions concerning my father. What ... is there a secret code that I am missing? I'm more confused than I have ever been. Forgive you ... for what?*

Thirteen envelopes and with five hundred dollars in each. She looked up at the ceiling, calculating the total amount. *Why, that makes the total amount come to $6,500. Not including the money I've put in the drawer.* Her hands fell to her lap. She sat dumbfounded at what she had found. *Oh, Mother, I don't know what to make of this ... What's with all this cash? And who would be sending money to you anyway? Why were you hiding it? What were you doing at nights, Mom? Were you at the hospital working ...? No, no, I won't allow my thoughts to take that path. You would never ...* she thought. *What am I to do with all this money? There is no denying that I could use this fun money. I could buy the blue jeans and sweater that I saw at the mall. And, oh, that purple ski jacket too.*

Her thoughts ran wild. *Now, Nicole, control yourself,* Nicole scolded herself. Fanning the bills through her fingers, she then slapped them across her palm. *Thank you, Mom. I'll worry about it later. I'll put this money in the bank tomorrow when the door opens.*

Nicole got up and went to the dresser, a smile creasing her lips. She pulled open the drawer and placed the bills under a pair of jeans. She closed the suitcase and got up, and then she walked to the kitchen to get her books that lay on the table. She went into the living room, plopped herself down on the couch, and curled her feet under her. Unable to concentrate on her assignment, she slammed the book closed, scaring Cuddles. *Why hide the money, Mom?*

Nicole was, by no means, a destitute person. Her full scholarship was paying for her four years at the university, and her mother and grandparents had put money aside to help her with living expenses.

This is awful, she thought. *I'm unable to stay focused in class, and for some reason, I am so glad to be in the safety of my apartment. And yet, I still can't focus on the class assignment.* In frustration, she slammed her book down on the coffee table. *A shower,* she thought, *just might do the trick in settling the tension of this stressful day. Then I'll just turn in early. Tomorrow is Saturday. I've got all day tomorrow to work on this chemistry assignment.*

She took the contents from her blazer pocket and laid them on the dresser. The crumpled note fell to the floor, and she bent over to retrieve it. Smoothing out the creases, she looked at the note and then smiled at the handwriting of a doctor. It read, *"Pick up Sharon's medication at Rex's Pharmacy, a box of her favorite dark chocolates, and note paper."*

Her thoughts returned to that day Dr. Brookfield walked into Ms. Shoemaker's office. His face had turned ash white when she told him that Loretta Martin was her mother. Then, when she told him that her mother had been killed by a drunken driver, she thought he was going to fall over. How oddly that day had gone.

She went into the bathroom and stripped off her clothing. Cuddles pushed open the door and ran over to her, rubbing herself against Nicole's bare leg. Leaning into the shower, Nicole turned on the water and adjusted the temperature. She then stepped in and held her head under the showerhead, allowing the warm water to run down her back.

Nicole's thoughts went back to the note. *I've seen that handwriting.* She stepped out from the tub and hurriedly dried herself down, slipping on her robe and wrapping her hair in the towel.

Cuddles lay on the brown leather suitcase watching Nicole come in from the bathroom. Her tail swished back and forth gently. Nicole's heart seemed to skip a beat as she retrieved the note from the dresser. *It couldn't be.* She picked Cuddles up, set her on the bed, and snapped open the suitcase. She then picked up one of the letters, removed it from the envelope, and held the note up against the letter.

"Oh, my!" Her hand came to rest on the dresser to steady herself. She glanced up at the picture of her mother. The picture had been taken at the park, and her mother was pushing her on the swing. *Are these letters his letters, Mother? What was he to you? Was he your lover?* She compared the uniform strokes of the S's, R's, and the crossing of the T's. They were identical.

Her thoughts reverted. *All these years, I've wondered who my father was and what caused him to stay away. Didn't he love me?* Nicole had wanted answers long ago, but her mother refused to provide them. She would always say the same thing. "You don't need a dad. You have me, Grandma, and Granddad."

Nicole could feel the anger rise to the surface. Why the lies? She was confused, and she felt a deep emptiness and a longing to talk to her mother. Nicole wanted the truth, and now it was too late to get answers. The truth went to the grave with her mother—forever lost and remaining her secret.

The doorbell rang, startling Nicole back to reality. She raised her hand to her head, touching the towel that twirled around it. *Who could that be at this hour?* There was a soft knock and a voice called out, "Nicole, it's Reid. I know you're in there. Please answer the door."

"What are you doing here?" she asked, cracking the door open.

"You asked me to hold this for you." Reid held up her pocketbook. "I thought you might need it tomorrow."

"Oh yeah, you're right. I would have missed it later this morning. Come in, Reid, and thanks for running it by."

"Are you all right?" he asked.

"Well, no." Her eyes began to tear, and she placed her head on his shoulder.

"What's wrong, Nicole?" Reid wrapped his arms around her, nearly knocking the towel off her head.

She placed the towel back in place and smiled between her tears. "Come into the kitchen. Can I offer you a cup of hot chocolate?" She turned the stove on and then filled the kettle with water.

"Yeah, I'd like that," Reid answered.

"I'll be right back. Cuddles will keep you company."

"It's nice to see you again Cuddles." Reid bended over to pet her.

"I hope you like cats and that you're not allergic to them," she called from the bedroom. "Oh, I believe I asked you that question once before."

"Yes, you did ask that question. And no, I haven't been around cats much, so I really don't know," Reid answered. "Are you okay?" he asked.

Nicole walked back into the kitchen with her mother's suitcase in tow. She came around the corner and emptied the contents of the suitcase on the table. She inhaled deeply and then said, "I believe I've found my father." There was a troubled looked in her eyes as she said it.

"Your father?" Reid eyed Nicole quizzically.

"Yes, my father. I believe that Dr. Brookfield is my dad. I found these letters under my mother's bed when I was cleaning out her room after her death. Tell me, what do you think?" She held up the note and one of the letters for him to look at. "Let me get dressed and put a comb through my hair first. I'll be right back."

fff

As soon as Nicole left, Reid studied the letter and the note. *I believe she's right. I'm no handwriting expert, but they look like they are written by the same person.*

Chapter 20

The Red Line Express pulled into the bus station on Seventeenth Street in Manhattan, Kansas. Engraved in the white granite stone above the door was the name "Murphy's Building" and the year it was built—1945. It was a two-story red-brick building with benches along one wall. From the bus, Myke watched the wind pick up the leaves and swirl them around, blowing them across the walkway under a bench.

The driver announced, "We're in Manhattan, for those of you who will be disembarking. Our next stop will be Junction City."

Gathering up their small duffel bags, Myke and Pico made their way to the front of the bus. Once outside, Pico asked, "Where are we gonna sleep tonight? I hope it's not on some park bench. It is not the time of year we'd want to sleep outdoors."

"I have this friend that owes me a favor. I'll call him. Don't worry."

The driver stepped from the bus and lit a cigarette. Lifting his head, he puffed a white circle of smoke into the air and looked at Myke and Pico.

"Is there a phone around here?" Myke asked the driver.

The bus driver pointed. "Around that corner."

"Thanks. Watch the bags, Pico." Myke went around the corner where the phone was and deposited the coins into the slot. After dialing the number, he leaned against the wall and waited for someone to answer.

"Hey, Ozzie, this is Myke Cooper. How are you doing, man?"

"Hey, Myke, where are you?"

"I'm here in Manhattan. We just got off the bus from Kansas City."

"They let you out of the slammer already? I thought you had another eight years."

"A loophole in the system and they had to let me out early. I've got a question for you. Do you have room for me and my friend for a couple of days? Oh … yeah, I hear ya. I understand. Talk to you later."

Pico came up behind Myke with both bags in tow. "Don't sound too good," he said.

"Ozzie can't help, not this time. He got married last week, but he recommended this motel along Fort Riley Boulevard."

Myke dug deep into his pocket for the needed coins to make the call. He dialed the number, and the person on the other end spoke with a heavy accent. Myke asked, "What are your rates? … Okay, can you hold for just a minute while I ask my friend?" Placing his hand on the mouthpiece, he turned to Pico and said, "The owner claims it's clean with cable, HBO, a kitchenette, daily, weekly, and monthly rates. Only thing is the weekly rate is $145. How much money have you got on you, Pico? I've got $125 after buying groceries in Kansas City."

Pico removed his wallet from his pocket and counted his money. "I've got $474 of Val's money." He smiled. "What's the split?"

Myke looked up at the clouds, calculating the cost for each of them. "That comes out to $72.50 for each of us."

"That's okay with me," Pico answered.

Myke then returned to the phone. "We'll take it. Hold a room for me. My name is Myke Cooper, and I'll be there in twenty minutes." Myke deposited money into the pay phone to call for a cab. "The cabdriver should be here in ten minutes."

It was a short drive to the motel. The cabdriver pulled up in front of the door. "That'll be $4.50," the driver said.

"Pay him, Pico."

"Pay him! Half of that cab fare is your responsibility. Remember, everything divided in half."

"That leaves me with only $50.25. I can't live on that!" In agitation, Myke pulled out $2.25 and slapped the money into Pico's hand. "I paid for the phone calls, remember."

The cabdriver looked over his sunglasses at them. Pico handed the driver a five-dollar bill and then stood with his hand out, waiting for his change.

"What, no tip? You want your fifty cents?" the driver said.

Pico stood unmoved with his hand out.

"Tightwad!" the cabbie snarled and went to the change dispenser. He clicked out the fifty cents, slapped it into Pico's hand, and said, "I got kids to feed too, you know!"

"Fifty cents ain't gonna feed your kids. I just got out of prison! Don't tell me your hard-luck story! You made them kids, not me."

In anger, the cabbie hit the gas, burning rubber behind him.

"Ozzie said this place was decent. I wonder if he ever stayed here," Myke said.

The outside of the motel was in desperate need of a paint job.

He turned to Pico. "Hey, Pico, maybe we can offer to paint this place for free room and board. Whaddya think?"

"Uh-huh, not a bad idea." Then he added, "But it will be a lot of work. There's only one problem."

"What's that?"

"This motel has a section where there are two floors. I don't do heights."

"What else are you afraid of? I thought you were a tough guy."

"I am tough. Just don't like heights, that's all."

The motel owner, a Middle Eastern-looking man, sat with his feet on a table. Two young children sat on stools beside him, watching cartoons. Upon seeing them enter, he swung his legs off the table and hurried over to the counter. "How can I help you?" He smiled broadly.

"I called earlier, and you said that you had a vacancy."

"I do, I do! For the two of you?" He looked at Pico.

"Yeah. You quoted me $145 for both of us for a week, right?"

"I guess if I said that, then it is so. But I usually charge an extra ten dollars for additional people."

"In that case, we'll go someplace else."

"Oh, no, no, no! No, $145 for the two of you will be fine."

"Now, if we choose to stay longer, the price will be the same, right?" Myke asked.

"Longer, oh, sure! It will be the same."

"It's a deal. Show us our room. By the way, I didn't catch your name."

"Just call me Sher Shan." Sher Shan turned and went to get the key in another room.

Myke then turned to Pico and winked. "He didn't ask for the money up front."

"Maybe if we're lucky, he'll forget." Pico smiled.

Sher Shan came around the counter. "Follow me, please. I'll take you to your room. My wife, she does a good job of keeping it clean. You won't be disappointed. The room I'm taking you to has one bedroom with twin beds. I believe you'll find it comfortable."

When they got to the room, Sher Shan inserted the key into the door of room 3 and pushed it open. "Go ahead and look around. I'll be back to collect the rent money when you find everything in order. If you need anything, call the front desk. The phone number is in the little handbook, okay?"

Sher Shan closed the door behind him.

"Well, heck," Pico said. "I was hoping that he'd forget about collecting the money for the rent."

"You're unbelievable, Pico."

The room was small with a couch and a chair, a television against one wall, a small kitchenette with a table, and two chairs placed under the windowsill.

Pico went over and turned on the TV set. "Well, look at that. It's color, and it even has a remote control!" He sat down and began to channel surf, while Myke went into the bedroom.

The bedspreads were old and faded but clean. Myke

went over and pushed on the mattress. The springs squeaked. *Could be worse*, he thought. The bathroom was his next stop. The mirror in the bathroom had a crack and had turned gray behind the glass. A torn and molded white shower curtain closed off the shower.

Pico went to answer a knock on the door. "Sher Shan is back!"

"You take room?" Sher Shan asked.

"Yeah, we'll take it." Pico handed him his $72.50, and Myke fished in his pocket, pulling out the amount needed to make it $145.

Sher Shan smiled with great satisfaction, counting the money as he walked away. Then, he turned and said, "My wife asked me to ask you how you like the room. Very clean, is it not?"

"Yeah, it's okay. It could be cleaner."

"Not clean!" Sher Shan looked at Myke with a startled look. "My wife, she will be very disappointed to hear it's not clean!"

"It's the shower curtain. It's torn and molded!" Myke answered him.

"I'll take care of the shower curtain right away!" Sher Shan turned and rushed off.

"Well, heck! I had hoped he would knock some money off the rent."

Pico looked at Myke, flashing him a disappointed look. "Oh, well, it was a nice try anyway, amigo."

The door was left ajar when Sher Shan returned. "Your new shower curtain. So sorry that it was not changed. Anything else?" he asked.

"No, everything is just fine."

A broad grin creased Sher Shan's dark face, and his dark eyes flashed with delight. "Very good, very good. I will get your receipt right away, okay?" He disappeared from the doorway once again.

"Hey, isn't he going to hang that damn thing up?" Pico asked.

"I guess not. Here." Myke tossed the shower curtain to Pico. "You do it."

"Thanks a lot!" Pico gave Myke a nasty look and went to the bathroom to hang up the curtain.

I've got more important things to do now that I am back home. It isn't gonna kill you to hang up that blanketly-blank shower curtain, Pico, Myke thought. He went over to the table where the phone hung, looking for the phone book. Pulling open the cabinet drawer, he found what he was looking for. Lifting the phone book from the drawer, he let the pages slip through his fingers until he came to the C section. "You know, Pico, I haven't seen my kids in three years. I wonder how tall Jakie has gotten and if Dana would even remember me." Myke plopped himself down on the chair next to the phone and began thumbing through the pages looking for his wife's name. "She's not listed! Now, what'll I do, Pico?"

"Well, where did you live before you were sent up?" Pico asked. "It's still daylight. Let's go find something to eat. Then maybe we can walk over to the house if it's not too far."

"No, it's not. Maybe five blocks up."

After a quick hamburger, which was what seemed to be their daily diet, they walked to the old street where he and Mattie had lived before, he was arrested and convicted for attempted murder. Myke wondered if she still lived in the gray house that stood before them.

"Not bad," Pico said. "Are we going to stand out here and just stare at the house, amigo?"

"She's not doing a very good job of keeping up the place."

"Yeah, you're right. The hedges should have been trimmed away from the house last summer," Pico said, looking around the neighborhood. The trees had budded out, and the grass had begun to turn green, coming out of its dormant winter stage. "Nice neighborhood. Not bad at all," he added.

Myke walked up to the door and knocked. The door slowly opened, and Myke saw an eye peeking through the small crack in the door that was held on a short chain. "What do you want?"

"Is Mattie Cooper home?"

"Nobody by that name lives here." The door slammed shut in his face.

"Hey, lady!" Myke pounded on the door. "Do you know where Mattie Cooper moved to?"

"Nope! Never heard of her," the woman said through the closed door.

"Too bad your old lady moved. How you gonna find her now?" Pico asked.

"I've got friends in this town."

When they returned to the motel, Myke made a couple of phone calls and was finally able to get Mattie's new address from an old friend. Lance told Myke that Dr. Brookfield had moved Mattie and the kids to one of his rentals in the older section of town.

"Do me a favor," Lance had said. "Don't tell Mattie it was me who told you where to find her."

"No problem. I won't say a word, promise. By the way, for old times' sake, you wanna meet me and my friend at the Diamond Bar and Grill for a couple of drinks tonight?"

"Nah, I can't. The kids are sick, and so is the wife. Somebody's got to take care of them."

"Since when did sick kids keep you from partying, Lance?"

"My wife, she's got the flu and can't get out of bed. Somebody's got to be here for the kids. Sorry, another time."

"Yeah, sure, I'll see you around."

The next morning, Pico and Myke went looking for the house on Sunset Circle. It was in a quiet neighborhood close to the school. *Nice*, he thought. *She didn't do too badly. Wonder if she sleeping with the Doc? She must be to live in a place like that!* Myke sneered.

The small two-story limestone house at the end of a cul-de-sac had a blue bike leaning up against the house and a tricycle parked beside it. It surprised Myke that Mattie would allow the children to leave their bikes outdoors. "I don't know how many times I've had to tell her not to leave stuff lying around. Someone could come along and steal the kids' bikes! How many times did I warn her about stuff like that?" he said angrily.

"Well, you're right," Pico said. "But aren't you going to ring the doorbell?"

"I am!" Myke snapped, unable to take his eyes off the door. "I can't believe she painted the front door dark green. Why in the hell did she paint it that color anyway? She knows I hate that color."

"Maybe she painted it that color because she knew you hated it." Pico laughed.

"Shut up, Pico!" Myke hissed as he pressed the doorbell. They could hear the chimes ringing inside and a little girl's voice saying, "Mommy, someone's at the door."

"Could that be my little Dana?" A feeling of excitement came over Myke. Then he heard footsteps on bare floor.

"Who is it?" Mattie asked.

"It's her, Pico. That's her voice." Myke smiled at Pico nervously. "Mattie, it's me, Myke."

After a long pause, she answered, a quiver in her voice, "When did you get out?"

"A week ago. I've been in Kansas City. Just arrived in Manhattan late yesterday."

"How did you find me, Myke?"

"I can't tell you my source. Mattie, I really want to see you and the kids. Please open the door."

"You're in violation of your probation, aren't you? You've got a restraining order placed against you, and you can't come near me or the children, Myke."

"Come on, Mattie. Give me another chance, please! I promise you I will never hit you again! Promise to God."

"You've made promises before, and the last time you nearly killed me," she said. "Besides, you don't even know God. You're in bed with the devil, Myke! Go away. Leave the kids and me alone! Please don't make me call the police."

"I've changed, Mattie."

Pico mumbled repeatedly, "*Ay mama mia*, merciful God, *ay mama mia!*" He quickly touched his forehead with his finger, making the sign of the cross.

"What are you doing, you idiot?" Myke demanded, slapping at his hands. "Are you loco?"

"Oh, Lord, what have I gotten myself into? She said you're sleeping with the devil, *amigo*! Are you?"

"Me, sleep with the devil? You and I slept in the same room," Myke hissed at Pico. "Did you see the devil in bed with me?"

"Well, no, *amigo*." Pico stared at him.

"Gee whiz, Pico!" Myke shot him a dirty look. "Mattie, please let me see my kids!" he begged.

He then heard a little voice on the other end say, "Who's that man, Mommy?"

"Open that damn door, Mattie!"

fff

Dana heard the angry voice on the other side of the door. "Who's that, Mommy?"

"Nobody, Dana. Why don't you go to the kitchen and color in your coloring book? I'll be with you in just a minute." Mattie watched Dana walk back into the kitchen.

When Dana was out of earshot, Mattie said, "Go away, Myke. You don't have custody or privileges with the kids. You wanna see the kids, go talk to your lawyer."

"Open this damn door," he shouted. "Or I'll kick it in!"

"I've called the police, Myke, and they are on their way. Please, Myke, don't come back." Her voice was trembling in fear.

fff

"We need to get out of here. Right now, amigo! You heard her. She said she called the cops. You'll get arrested and sent back to prison for breaking your probation, and then where will I be?" Pico pulled hard at his arm.

"Let go, Pico!" Myke cursed at him. "Let go of me!" Jerking his arm away from Pico's tight grip, Myke tilted his head and heard the sirens wailing down the street.

"Forget you, man! I'm out of here." Pico took off in the opposite direction, running toward the cemetery. He then collapsed behind a tombstone. Myke, heaving for breath, fell next to him.

Myke growled. "I can't believe that she called the cops on me and wouldn't let me see my own kids!"

Panting, Pico answered, "There's nothing you can do about it, unless you take her to court. And your chances of winning don't look so good, amigo."

"She's really made me mad now. I'll get even with her and Dr. Brookfield for making my life a living hell. That's a promise, you hear me, Pico? And I'll get my kids back too!"

"What has happened to you, amigo? You're talking crazy. What happened to God and turning your life around?" Pico stared at Myke in disbelief.

Chapter 21

Phil Stokes stared stonily at his bourbon, watching the ice cubes swirl around in his glass. He felt that the only way to soothe his anger and frustrations was with a drink. Lifting the glass to his lips, he let the liquid rush down his throat. He puckered his lips in satisfaction and held the glass out, staring at the yellowish-brown liquid. The hour-long meeting with Mark Adams, the zoning commissioner, had left him highly agitated and frustrated.

Mark, you are messing with the wrong person! I could have you destroyed in this community. Who do you think I am? A nobody or an idiot? Well, I'll show you, Phil thought angrily.

Mark Adams had been at his oak desk putting a binder together when Phil peeked into his office earlier that day. "Busy?" Phil asked.

"Not too busy. Come in, Phil. Find yourself a place to sit, and I'll be with you in a moment."

Looking around the familiar office, Phil noted that nothing had changed. In one corner of the room, an array of pictures of Phil, his wife, and their three children on a skiing trip to Colorado and pictures of a fishing trip to Alaska were on display. Since then, they had had an addition to their family, but no new photos disturbed the familiar pattern.

Mark's blond hair had begun to thin and recede since the last time Phil had seen him.

"How's the family, Mark?" Phil asked him.

"Oh, April had a bout with the flu last week. That has made its round in our home, and she is finally beginning to feel like her old self again. I don't know how she does it. Our four kids drove me haggard. Jimmy, the nine-month-old, had me going full speed until nap time and again until bedtime."

They both laughed.

"I know what you're saying, and I wouldn't trade places

with you for anything. Our youngest is now five years old, and I promise you, it does get easier as they get older."

Mark leaned back in his chair and rested his elbows on the armrest with his fingers intertwined in front of him. "How can I help you, Phil?"

"I'll get right to the point, Mark. I have talked with Dr. Brookfield, and he has told me that he is selling his farmland to Edwards Resort and Amusement Park. What are the chances of stopping that farmland from being zoned commercial?"

Mark moved uneasily in his chair, and he cast his eyes down at his hands. "Why do you want to see it stopped, Phil?"

"The loss of prime agricultural farmland, for one thing, and your primary concern should be the community's welfare. Personal property taxes have risen for four consecutive years now, and the townspeople are complaining bitterly. I know what you are going to say, that it will help the community by bringing in revenue. Well, it won't. Crime rates will be on the upswing, adding an additional burden to the police department—meaning, added officers, more patrol vehicles, and a larger prison. There'll be higher taxes in the long run."

"Now, Phil, you're getting upset over nothing. I don't see how it could hurt this community. That farmland has not been a working farm for over two years. Besides, Kent wants to move to a retirement village. It's his land, and he can do whatever he wants with it."

"Now, come on, Mark, let's get real. An amusement park in our backyard? Why here in Manhattan? Why not in a larger community, say, Topeka or Wichita?"

"It was Edwards Resort and Amusement Park's choice. They chose Manhattan. It is a good town, a growing town. Look around you, Phil. Can't you see how this would help the growth of this town? Think of all that money entering this community. You know how the merchants are struggling to keep their doors open. You of all people should know how many of the merchants have had to close their doors this year due to poor sales! You're the banker in this community, Phil, and you're the only one who has been in my office about this."

In anger, Phil retorted, "There was no public announcement made about this, Mark. I heard money has been passed under the table—large amounts of money—to get this passed quickly. Did the money fall into your pocket, Mark, or the other commissioners'?"

He pointed at the pictures on the wall. "Is that the way you fund all those expensive vacations your family takes?"

"Now, Phil, you have no right to accuse me of taking bribe money! Where did you hear this rumor from?" Mark replied in anger.

"Privileged information, Mark! You could be in a lot of trouble. Watch your back. Heads will roll, and your head just might be one of them." Phil got up smugly and walked to the door, breathing in heavily. His hand came to rest on the doorknob. "This isn't over yet, Mark!" He turned and then slammed the door behind him.

Mark's secretary jumped at the slamming of the door. "Is everything all right, Phil?" she asked.

"Everything is just fine, Fran. You have a good day!"

Chapter 22

Myke's words were slurred when he said, "Come on, Pico, just one more drink."

"No, amigo. You were not supposed to be drinking. I know what you are going through, so I let it slide, but you've had enough to drink! Let's get back to the motel."

"Just one more for the road, Pico. It helps to dent the pain in my heart. I want my family back." Myke cradled his head on his arm.

"Well, your problems will still be there tomorrow. You can't drink your problems away, amigo. Get up. Let's go!" Pico said, taking Myke's arm firmly.

"Let go of me! I'm going to kill that jackass." Myke pushed Pico's hand away.

"Shhh, keep it down, Myke. You're talking crazy. Let's get out of here. You're drunk, amigo."

"Leave me alone, Pico!"

Pico stood, looking down at Myke. He was torn between anger and pity. He told himself to leave the drunken bum right where he sat. *His wife is right. He is ugly when drunk*, Pico thought. *If I leave him and he is arrested, he's back in the slammer. Say goodbye to getting even with the Brookfield's and all that money!*

Pico moaned in annoyance and looked around him. At the other end of the bar in a dark corner, a man sat partially hidden. Pico had not noticed him before, but the stranger seemed to be watching them. *What did he hear?* Pico thought. Leaning over, he whispered into Myke's ear, "There's a man at the other end of the bar watching us."

Myke raised his head and, with bleary eyes, stared down the long bar. "I don't see anybody!" Myke slurred.

"See him now?" Pico asked as a figure stepped into the light. "Yeah, I see him. He might be a cop."

"He just might be. We'll find out soon enough. He's coming our way. Let's get up and walk in the other direction," Pico said, but then he added, "Too late."

A well-dressed man in a navy suit strolled over to where Myke sat with Pico standing over him. The man set his drink down. "Mind if I join you two?"

They stared at the stranger, and Pico answered, "Help yourself. We're leaving."

"Don't rush off. You're Myke Cooper, aren't you?" The stranger stared at Myke.

"Maybe I am, and maybe I'm not. Why?" Myke answered.

"Well, if you're Myke Cooper, I followed your trial, and I thought you got a real bad deal—ten years for smacking your wife when she asked for it? A real bad deal."

fff

Phil lifted his glass and emptied it. He signaled for the bartender. "Bartender, another round for me and my friends." He looked over at Myke. "What are you two drinking?"

"He's not. He's had enough for one night," Pico answered.

"Well, what are you drinking?" Phil smiled at Pico. "I'm buying."

"I'm not drinking. I'm the designated driver," he answered sarcastically. Pico had a thing with well-dressed men, especially ones wearing suits. They intimidated him. The air they carried about them had a superior, high, and mighty attitude, and he felt put down by it.

"Come on, Pico. You heard what he said. He's our friend!" Myke slurred.

"Let me introduce myself. My name is Phil Stokes, and I'm the president of Prairie Bank and Trust Company." Phil extended his hand. *Two dumb ducks in a pond. How lucky can a guy get?* Phil thought.

fff

Meanwhile, Pico had a thought of his own. *Oh, get out of our faces. Why does he want to be our friend? We're nobodies, dirt under his shoe, little cockroaches, and he wants to be our friend? Give me a break!*

Chapter 23

The radio in Officer Dan Phillips patrol car cracked with static, and the dispatcher's voice cut in. "Riley 41, can you respond to a disturbance call at 809 Sunset Circle?"

Officer Phillips picked up the small handheld receiver and answered, "Dispatcher, this is Riley 41. Can you repeat that address? Over."

"It's 809 Sunset Circle, Riley 41."

"I'm two blocks away. Will take the call. Over and out." Officer Phillips drove by the cemetery surrounded by the limestone walls. The iron gates were usually left open to allow visitors.

fff

Pico peered around the tombstone that he was hiding behind and saw the flashing lights. The siren had been turned off. He watched the patrol car pass the gates and turn down the street lined with stately homes, maple trees, and neatly manicured lawns.

A water tower he had not noticed before stood impressively tall, overlooking the neighborhood. The face of a purple cat was painted on the water tower, and he stared at it for a long moment. To his south, a school bell rang. School was in session, and kids were flying out of the school door, headed for the mobile school classrooms.

fff

"Riley 41, reporting in. I'm at 809 Sunset Circle, over."

"Pursue with caution, Riley 41, over." Officer Phillips got out of the patrol car, his eyes alert to any suspicious person or persons loitering in the area.

He stared up at the impressive white colonial home with burgundy shutters. He jumped out of the patrol car, closed the door, and locked it. A silver bike and a red tricycle stood against the front porch. Officer Phillips's hand immediately went to his holster and rested on the wooden grip of his gun, a habit he had developed from his police academy training. Walking to the back of the house, he saw toys scattered about the yard. A swing set sat idle, and a yellow bucket lay on its side in the sandbox. Nothing seemed to be disturbed, and the back door had not been tampered with. He returned to the front of the house and rang the doorbell.

A child's voice called out, "Mommy, someone's at the door! Can I open it this time?"

"No, Dana. I'll get it."

Officer Phillips heard footsteps approaching the door, and it slowly opened. A blue eye peered through the small opening in the crack of the doorway.

"Ma'am, I'm Officer Phillips responding to a disturbance call from this address."

ƒƒƒ

Officer Phillips removed his sunglasses, and Mattie immediately recognized the tall dark-haired figure. He wore a navy jacket with a silver star identifying him as an officer of the police department.

Mattie quickly undid the chain and swung open the door. "Dan, I'm so glad it's you!" She drew in a deep, shaky breath, and her eyes filled with tears.

ƒƒƒ

Officer Phillips took a step back, his mouth gaped in surprise. He had not seen Mattie since high school. Dan and Mattie had been high school sweethearts until Myke came along. Soon after, Mattie broke it off with him, and his world had crumbled around him. They had planned on going to the same university and one day getting married. After the breakup, he began drinking and partying to escape his painful world. His parents were concerned for him and thought that it would be in his best interest to send him off to his uncle, who was a police officer in Chicago. There he finished off his senior year. Dan attended college in Chicago for two years and then returned to Manhattan to join the police force. He had heard that Mattie had returned to town with a baby five years ago but had not seen her until now.

Dan cleared his throat. "What's going on, Mattie? A disturbance call came in from this address. Are you all right?"

"Yes, I am now. Myke … my ex-husband, is out of prison, and he was just here." Mattie dropped her head. "He's the biggest mistake of my life, Dan. Myke has a restraining order to stay away from me and the kids." She paused, taking in a deep, nervous breath, and tears began to roll down her cheeks. "Myke heard Dana's voice and demanded to see her. I wouldn't open the door, and he became angry. I then told him that I was going to call the police." Reaching into her pocket, she pulled out a tissue and blew her nose.

"Do you know where he might have gone or where he is staying?" Dan asked.

"No, I don't know where he went, and he didn't say where he was staying. Someone was with him, and he sounded Hispanic." "Do you want to press charges against him for breaking his restraining order?"

"No, I don't want to anger him. I just want to send him a reminder and a warning that he needs to get a court order before I'll let him see the children." The phone began to ring in the kitchen. "Please come in, Dan. I need to get the phone." Mattie hurried around the corner to answer it.

Dan heard her say, "Oh, Doc, Myke's back in town. What am I going to do?" She sobbed.

Dan walked into the kitchen and looked around him. The dishwasher door had been left open, and the box of dishwasher soap sat on the door ready to be poured into the dispenser. The refrigerator was covered with drawings and children's photos. A little girl stuck her head out from under the table. "Are you a policeman?" she asked.

"Yes, I am," Dan answered. "What are you doing under the table?"

"There was a man at the door, and he scared Mommy and me. Are you going to put that bad man in jail?"

"Yes, I'll take him in for questioning when I catch up to him. What's your name?"

"I'm Dana. What's yours?"

"I'm Officer Phillips, and your mommy and I went to school together a long time ago. We are friends, and you can call me Dan if you like. You want to come out from under the table? It's safe now."

Mattie hung up the phone and saw something move under the table. "Oh, Dana, honey! I'm sorry, I didn't see you there."

Dana grabbed hold of Mattie's legs. "Is that bad man gone now, Mommy?"

"Yes, he's gone. You can go back into the other room and watch the television while Mommy talks to the officer, okay?"

"You mean Dan!" Dana corrected her mother.

"Yes," she said and smiled. "Dan and I need to talk, okay?"

Dana slowly walked to the doorway and then suddenly turned. "Are you in trouble, Mommy?"

"No, I'm not. Now go on."

"Is that bad man in trouble?"

"Why do you think that, Dana? Do you think he should be in trouble for scaring us?" Mattie asked her.

"He should be in trouble. He's a bad man!" Dana said with a frown.

"Officer Phillips and I need to talk now. Scoot!"

Dana disappeared through the archway into the other room.

"She's full of questions, isn't she?"

Mattie smiled proudly. "That was Dr. Brookfield on the phone. He will be here shortly. Dr. Brookfield is very good friend of my family and has been a big help to me and the children."

"You did the right thing in calling the police, Mattie."

"I pray that I did." A foreboding look eclipsed her eyes.

The doorbell rang, and a voice hollered in, "Mattie, it's me."

Mattie hurried out of the kitchen to greet Doc at the door. A look of concern emitted from his blue eyes as he asked, "Are you and Dana all right?"

A mute cry of relief escaped, and she hiccupped, saying, "I'm pretty shaken. I didn't expect Myke to show up at my front door this morning. But I'm okay now, Doc, uh ... Officer Phillips here is an old friend."

Dan removed his hat, placed it under his arm, and then extended his right hand. "We know each other," he said. "It's good to see you again, Dr. Brookfield."

"I've known Officer Phillips's family for years," Doc said to Mattie with a smile. "His mother was my nurse for fifteen years before I retired." He then turned to Dan. "Good to see you, son. And how are your folks?"

"They were in Arizona for the winter and will be home shortly." Dan smiled.

Doc's attention was drawn back to Mattie. "Did Myke hurt you or Dana?"

"No," she answered. "I wouldn't let him in. He threatened to kick the door in if I didn't open the door and let him see Dana." Her shaking fingers went to her lips, and she choked back a sob. Tears brimmed on her eyelids. "I simply can't go through this again. I can't, and I won't!" She choked back a sob, and the tears began to roll down her cheeks.

Dan ached to take her in his arms, to comfort her and wipe away her tears, but he restrained himself. He was surprised to feel the love he once had for her grab hold of his heart once again. They had both lost a great deal in life. She gave up a full scholarship to Harvard University to marry that loser, and he had simply lost his drive for life.

Dan cleared his throat. "Ah, excuse me, sir. Shall I put in a formal complaint against her ex-husband?"

Doc looked over at Mattie and asked, "Did he threaten you or the children?"

"Well, no, he didn't. He never had the chance. I told him that I had called the police. When he heard the siren, he and that other man ran off."

"He had someone with him?" Doc asked.

"Yes, he did, and from the peephole, he looked Hispanic," Mattie answered.

"You did the right thing," Doc said, and then he looked over at Dan. "Right now, I believe a warning is all that is needed. Now, if he comes here again, yes, have him arrested." Looking back at Mattie, Doc then added, "That was good advice you gave Myke, Mattie. He does need to go through the legal system to see his children."

Dan looked at both Mattie and Doc. "Are you sure that's the course you want to take?"

"For right now, we don't want to anger Myke. We're not sure what he's capable of doing now that he's out of prison. A warning will be all that is needed for the moment."

"I hope you're doing the right thing. I'll turn my report over to my supervisor. Mattie, my advice to you is that you keep your doors locked and know where your children are at all times. Do you have a cell phone?" Dan asked.

"No," she answered.

"Get one. Phone lines can be cut, and you won't be able to get a hold of us if that should happen."

"I'll get her one today," Doc volunteered.

Dan placed his hat back on his head and touched the tip of the brim. "I'll check on you later, if that's okay with you, Mattie?"

"I'd really appreciate that, Dan. Thank you."

"If you like, I can give you my cell number, and you can call me anytime you need me."

"I would really like that, Dan, and thank you."

Dan scribbled his number on a note pad and handed it to her. "Be safe."

Chapter 24

The hinges to the gymnasium door squeaked eerily as Nicole pushed it slightly open, peering through the slit in the door. Darkness loomed before her, and a menacing feeling of danger swept over her. Frightened, she quickly backed away, allowing the door to swing closed. The dark and distant past awakened her consciousness, and her heart raced wildly, sending spasms of chills through her body. Nicole stood frozen as the inner warning in her screamed out for her to run. A childhood fear was looming before her.

A menacing man in a black cape sprang out at her. His red collar stood high behind his head and accented his white face. Thick black lines were drawn above and below his eyes, making him look sinister. His lips stretched into a grin, revealing fangs with blood caked between. His eyes were a bloodshot red. She stared up at him, frozen in fear. She wanted to run, but her legs wouldn't move. Nicole clung tightly to the hand of her babysitter, Mollie. Then without warning, a deep-throated laughter suddenly splintered from his wide-open mouth. His claw like hands sprang to her shoulders.

Nicole swallowed hard at the memory. *You were only a child of five at the time, nothing to be afraid of now*, she told herself. *That was a long time ago. A Halloween party, just to scare little kids. Well, you're not that little kid anymore, and Dracula is only fiction.*

In the gymnasium, she willed her legs to move, but they refused to comply; her knees were locked tight. *Reid's waiting for you. Go on! You can do it*, she told herself. *All it takes is one step in front of another. God is with you, go!*

Hesitantly, she pushed open the door and stepped in, and the door closed behind her. A window somewhere in the building must have been left open. She could feel a sudden rush of a breeze and heard what sounded like paper scraping across the floor, or maybe someone shuffling down the dark hall. Her heart pounded wildly against her chest and cold sweat beads formed on her forehead. She fell back against the door as she stared into the blackness.

Fear turned into terror, and her mind screamed, *Run from this place!* She couldn't move. Her feet were cemented to the floor. He eyes darted wildly, searching in the blackness.

Calm down, she told herself. You're hyperventilating. Your imagination is going to take you over the edge. Remember when you were a little girl and you were afraid? Mom would snuggle you close and tell you God is always with you. So, call on Him. He is your safe place, and you have nothing to fear.

Nicole could remember answering her mother, "But God doesn't have skin that I can snuggle up to, and you do." *Well, God, I'm scared, and I could sure use some skin. How about a hand?*

Nicole then heard muffled voices far off and a screeching sound as something scraped against the floor. Light filtered through the crack in the double doors that led to the basketball court. Her heart delivered heavy blows to her chest. Every ounce of courage that she was able to muster up caused her to spring forward and rush toward the doors. She pushed open the door, and light from the gymnasium temporarily blinded her. She fell back against the door frame. Her hand went to her forehead to shield her eyes from the bright light. Quivering, she drew in a long, deep breath. The coach yelled and waved the players off the court. Then she saw him.

Reid waved at her to get her attention, beckoning her down. Nicole waved back weakly and, on shaky legs, made her descent down the steep stairs to the first row of seats. Her pounding heart slowly returned to its normal rhythm.

The huddle broke, and the players returned to the court. Reid took a slight detour and hurried over to her. "It will be another half hour of practice. Glad you made it! I'll talk to you later." He backed away slowly, staring at her.

What ... that stare? she thought. *Did I forget something?*

The coach called out to Reid, "What do you think you're doing, Starr? Didn't you hear the whistle blow? Practice isn't over yet. Get back on the court where you belong!"

Nicole heard Reid apologize as he hurried back to join the team.

She found the momentum of the practice enthralling, and her fears were quickly forgotten. A final whistle blew, and the exhausted players came to a screeching halt. Reid threw a towel around his neck and used one end to wipe the sweat from his forehead as he walked toward her.

"Well, what did you think of the practice?" he asked.

"I must say, it was exciting!" she answered.

He took hold of her hand and helped her to her feet. "Come with me," he said. "You can wait in the coach's office while I shower and dress. Have you had dinner yet?" He smiled at her.

"No, I haven't."

"That's good. Neither have I."

Reid took Nicole to the coach's sitting room and then disappeared down the hall to the locker room.

The coach's waiting room consisted of a dark-brown leather sofa placed against one wall. A coffee table sat in front of the sofa, which was cluttered with sports magazines. Nicole walked over to a wall where photographs of previous coaches dated back to the early 1920s. Then she felt the presence of someone standing behind her.

"Ready?" Reid smiled down at her.

Turning her head, she looked up at him and smiled back. "Yes, I'm ready, and I'm starved."

"How does Mexican sound to you?" he asked.

The hour was late, and the restaurant was nearly empty. Mexican sombreros and guitars decorated the walls. A shelf close to the ceiling held beautiful vases of various sizes, painted and inlayed with colored glass birds, cougars, and temples.

The waiter took their order and later brought them drinks with a bowl of chips and salsa.

Dipping his chip, Reid asked, "You looked frightened at the gym this evening. Did something scare you?"

Nicole hadn't realized that fear had shown on her face. How was she going to explain to him her fear of dark places and that horrible night when she was only five years old and her babysitter and neighbor, Mollie, asked her grandparents if she could take Nicole trick-or-treating. What she didn't tell Nicole's grandparents was that she was going to hook up with friends and that they were going to a haunted house where their other friends were working. It was Nicole's very first time, and she was excited, but she had no idea what a haunted house was all about. She was soon to find out.

They went to an old two-story house decorated for haunting. They walked through the front door and immediately saw an ugly witch with a large black wart on her crooked nose. She stood over a kettle chanting, "Bubble, bubble, toil, and trouble, hee-hee-hee!" Steam rose to the ceiling, and the witch asked, "Wanna taste my brew?" Seeing the fear in Nicole's eyes, the witch grinned broadly, tossing her head back as a wicked laugh escaped her throat and pierced the cool night air. Horrified, Nicole clung to Mollie's hand. This was not what she had expected, and she was terrified.

Then, someone screamed, "It's Dracula!" Unspeakable fear grabbed hold of Nicole as Dracula sprang out and grabbed hold of her shoulder. She felt something warm run down her legs, and it formed a puddle at her feet. Dracula pointed at the floor and began laughing hysterically, holding his stomach.

Mollie exclaimed, "Oh, Paul, look what you did! You scared the kid."

"You brought her. What did you expect?"

Nicole stood there, looking up at Dracula, unable to move. Then there was a sudden yank on her arm, and she was being dragged toward the door. Mollie's friends followed behind, laughing.

For years after, Nicole suffered from night terrors. That dark, foreboding hallway in the auditorium with the sound of the wind and movement brought back those horrible memories. It was the most frightening and humiliating experience for a child her age to endure. How was she to tell him of her fears? Would he understand or would he make fun of her like Mollie's friends did?

Well, not tonight. Maybe one day I'll tell him when the moment is right.

Chapter 25

Man, it didn't take me long to screw up, Myke thought. *How stupid can you get?* He lay his head on his arm. *All you've got to show for your night out is this terrible hangover.* He groaned in misery.

"Here, try this." Pico handed him a cup of black coffee. "It's not a cure for your hangover, but it'll give you a jump start this morning. And you need to call your friend Phil, the banker."

"Phil, Why?"

"You don't remember him telling you that he has a friend at the warehouse who owes him a favor?"

"I can't remember much of anything. Tell me what he said."

"Man, you were really wasted last night! You really don't remember what he said?"

"No, Pico, I don't." Myke pressed his head into his hands. "What did we talk about?"

"Well, he said for you to call him around ten this morning. He's going to check with his friend about a job for us at the warehouse. It's now five after ten. He gave you his business card. Check your pockets."

Rummaging through his jacket pockets, Myke pulled out Phil's card. His unsteady hand shook and he was unable to focus his eyes on the numbers. He handed the card to Pico. "Read the phone number to me."

Oh God, forgive me for my weak moment. I really messed up, didn't I? But it was all Mattie's fault.

Pico read the numbers, and Myke dialed. "Can you get me a glass of water? My mouth feels like cotton."

Pico went into the kitchen and returned, handing him the glass of iced water.

A woman on the other end picked up the phone and spoke. "Mayor Phil Stokes's office. May I help you?"

"I'd like to speak to Mr. Stokes."

"Mr. Stokes's line is busy at this moment. Can I take a message?" the voice on the other end of the line said.

"Yeah, tell him that Myke Cooper called, and he can call me at—"

"Mr. Cooper, Mr. Stokes's line is open now. Let me transfer you to him."

"Okay, thank you."

After a pause, he heard, "Well, Cooper, how are you feeling this morning?"

"I've had better days."

"I bet you've got a nasty hangover this morning."

"Yeah, something like that. I've had worse though …"

"Do you remember our conversation last night?"

"Yeah, I remember last night," Myke lied. "I wasn't that drunk. Did you call your friend at Big Harry's?"

"I did, and he said he'd have an opening in about one week or so and for you and your friend to go in and put your applications in. Will that work?"

"Yeah, that'll work."

"Good, go down and put in your application. I'll keep in touch with you and see how things are going with you and your friend Pico, if that's okay with you."

"No problem. You do that, and, hey, thanks." Myke hung up the phone.

"Man, why didn't you hit him up for some cash? He's not only the mayor, but the big boss of a bank!" Pico yelled.

Cringing, Myke's hands went to his ears. "Don't yell! My head hurts!" Pushing back the chair and slowly getting up, he announced, "I'm going to shower, and hopefully it will make me feel better. We've gotta go and get our applications in at Big Harry's if we wanna work." He slowly made his way to the bathroom and then added, "And we gotta make plans." He stopped at the bathroom door and placed his hand on the doorknob to steady himself. Turning slowly, he looked back at Pico.

Pico's eyes narrowed. "What's your plan?"

"We're going to the bank, if you know what I mean."

A toothy grin flashed across Pico's face. "Doc's place!"

"Yeah."

Dressed in new blue jeans and a Western-style button-down shirt, Myke felt confident. "How do I look, Pico? And, hey, thanks for the loan."

"Real good, amigo! If he doesn't hire you, I will." Pico laughed. "How do I look?" He pranced around the room holding up his pant leg to show off his new boots. "Pretty nice, huh?"

"Real sharp, Pico. We'd better get going. It's going to be a long walk to Big Harry's Warehouse. No bus service in this small town."

"How about calling a cab?" Pico asked.

"No, cabs cost too much, and we need the money. They always take the long way to get anywhere, clicking up the bucks real fast. We could try to hitchhike, but in this town, people are too cautious. They'll never pick up two men, especially when they're strangers in their town."

Later that afternoon, they reached the warehouse. They figured it was a good two miles and were thankful that it was cool out. Lifting his arm, Myke smelled his armpit, and Pico followed suit. He didn't want to offend anyone with body odor, and they didn't have the extra funds for deodorant.

"I hope I don't smell too bad. Whatta you think, Pico?"

"From here, I can't smell anything. How about me?" He lifted his arm again and took a deep whiff.

"Nah, you're good." Myke gave him the thumbs-up.

The writing on the door in large black bold letters read "Personnel." A young dark-haired woman sat behind the desk. She looked up. "Can I help you?"

"Yes, my friend and me, we're here to apply for a job," Myke answered.

"And your names?" she asked.

"My name is Myke Cooper."

"And, my name is Pico Sanchez."

"Oh, yes, Mr. Cummings is expecting you." She smiled, handed them the applications, and directed them to sit in an area with a sofa, two chairs, and a coffee table with magazines neatly stacked upon it. They did as she directed.

Leaning over, Myke whispered in Pico's ear, "How do you like that, Pico? We must be pretty important."

"Yeah, I think we've got the jobs, thanks to Mr. Stokes. I'm beginning to really like this town and Mr. Stokes." A satisfied look flashed across Pico's face.

The interviews went well, and Mr. Cummings said he'd be in touch in a week or two. Back at the motel, they stopped off at the front desk to ask for a paper and a pencil. Sher Shan seemed delighted to see them.

"You find job?" he asked, handing Myke a pen with the motel logo on it.

"We should be hearing in a week or two about the job at the warehouse," Myke answered.

"Very good, very good!" Sher Shan exclaimed at their news, giving them the thumbs-up.

Myke and Pico returned to their room after their job interview with Mr. Cummings.

Myke sat down at the coffee table, setting the note pad down, and he drew up a rough draft of the basement floor from memory. "This is what I remember of the basement. Dallas, Doc's ranch foreman, he would have me stack firewood in the furnace room to feed that monster furnace. The safe was hidden in a corner of the room when I saw it. And, the only reason I saw it was that there was a golf ball in that room and I kicked it. It rolled and hit the safe." Myke put an X mark on the table. "That's where I saw the safe." Pointing to the X on the paper.

"The monster!" was all that Pico heard. "Docs got a monster in the basement. Forget you, you can go by yourself." he said.

"No, Pico, that is what Doc called the furnace, because it burns up so much firewood to keep that big house warm."

"Sheesh! You like to scare me, don't you? I'm glad to hear that there is no monster in that basement."

"Man, you're unreal, Pico. Your own shadow would scare you."

"Give me a break," he retorted. "How do you know that there is anything important in that safe?"

"Because I asked Dallas about the safe, and he told me that Doc kept his important papers and Sharon's jewelry in it. He didn't know what else, but he could imagine all the money in there. Doc liked to pay for things in cash."

Chapter 26

Myke had met Dallas Wilcox five years earlier at the Brick House Grill and Patio. His friend John had pointed Dallas out and said that he was looking for help at the ranch where he worked. If Myke was interested, he'd introduce him. Myke told John he was very interested and in need of a job. John took Myke over to meet Dallas, and he was hired on the spot and told to report to work on Monday.

He showed up early Monday morning and was in for a rude awakening! Myke, a streetwise kid from Washington, DC, knew nothing about cattle, and here he was being thrown in with them. He had no idea what he was getting himself into. Rounding up cattle was something he thought was only done in the 1800s and in the movies. He had to help separate the cows from the calves and move the cows into a fenced-in area. Once they had them separated, the calves were chased into a chute and out into another pen where they were roped and pulled to the ground. The cowboys would then swoop down on the calves. One would use a dehorn clip and clip off the horns, while another sprinkled power onto the wound to stop the bleeding. Another cowboy would vaccinate and brand the calves. Myke nearly lost his stomach when a cowboy whipped out his knife, sliced open a male calf's sack, and popped out the testicles. Never in his life had he witnessed such a horrible thing being done to an animal.

Myke went home with flashbacks of the poor calf being sliced open and smelling like the smelly cattle. The odor clung to his clothing, hair, and skin.

When he got home that night, Mattie had a fit as he walked through the door. She shooed him out to the back porch, telling him to leave his shoes out on the porch and undress there too. Mattie said he filled up the house with the smell of all the cow dung he'd dragged in on his shoes and clothing. He was tired, hungry, and disgusted, and her remarks made him mad. But he had made a vow never to hit her again and he planned on keeping his word, so he did as she asked and undressed on the enclosed porch. Talk about humiliation. Then on top of that, she rushed him into the shower before feeding him! Myke was growling mad. But the shower did manage to soothe his anger, and he felt much better after it. He hated to admit it, but Mattie was right.

Myke told himself that he would stick it out for a week. He desperately needed this second job. His first job couldn't pay for the mounting bills that threatened to drown them in debt. Mattie seemed a lot happier that summer, and her complaining lessened. She did what she could to help. She babysat people's children and ironed clothes to put food on the table and to buy the needed formula and diapers.

When fall rolled around, Mattie's friends went off to college, and she fell into depression. She began to complain about money again. She wanted to go to college and felt that life had passed her by. She blamed Myke and the baby for holding her back, and Myke began drinking again. Nothing he did seemed to satisfy her. Then one day, he came home drunk, and she lit in on him. That was a big mistake on her part. Myke hit her, knocking her to the floor. The next morning, he saw the black eye he had given her. He could not remember hitting her. She said he did and that he had broken his promise. Feeling badly, Myke began staying out late at the ranch working long hours, and that didn't help the situation.

At the end of fall, Dallas presented Myke with a Stetson cowboy hat and said he was now a full-fledged cowboy. Myke was so very proud of that hat and all that he had accomplished that summer.

He worked for Doc under Dallas for three years. By the third year, he was drinking heavily and showing up for work either drunk or with a hangover. At first, Dallas pretended not to notice, until it became a steady pattern. He could no longer ignore the problem, and in a real somber mood, Dallas warned Myke that if he came to work again drunk, he'd fire him. "When working with animals," he told Myke, "you need to be alert. You can't turn your back on them!"

Well, that day, Daisy, the horse, threw Myke off her back, and he separated his shoulder. When Doc saw the condition Myke was in when Dallas brought him into the hospital, Doc asked Dallas, "What happened?"

Dallas pulled Doc over to the side, and they talked. Dallas didn't have to fire Mike; Doc fired him that day in the ER.

Chapter 27

The full moon in its full glory stared down on earth. It was not a good omen. The stillness of the night gave Myke an eerie feeling he could not shake. He searched the night sky for the promise of rain that had been forecasted earlier that evening. To the east, the stars sparkled brightly in the night sky, as they did to the south and north. Myke turned to the west; billowing clouds were forming. He smiled to himself and thought, *Think positive. Tonight's the night!*

"Look, Pico," Myke said, pointing to the storm clouds. "Yeah, it will be a good night."

"Ah, amigo, a good omen for a successful night."

"Yeah, a very good omen." Myke smiled. "Better get moving; we've got things to do."

"That we do. As the song goes, 'Let it rain! Let it rain!'" Pico grinned and playfully wagged his eyebrows up and down as he sang.

"'Let it snow,' not rain. 'Let it snow, let it snow.' We don't need snow, not tonight."

"Ah, amigo, you are so right. But, look, it's gonna rain. You gringos got no sense of humor."

Changing the subject, Myke said, "I got a friend who will let me borrow his car. Come on. Let's get moving."

ƒƒƒ

A faint light glowed from a bedroom window in the row of duplexes. "This is the appointed night for vengeance, Chuck Walker."

Pico felt a drop of rain hit his cheek and looked up, wiping the wetness from his face. "Amigo ..." Before he could complete his sentence, the heavy clouds let loose the droplets of moisture, and they heard the crash of thunder, which was followed by a flash of lightning. "Just what we asked for. Rain."

"Yeah, sleep soundly, Chuck."

Chuck was once Myke's closest friend, and he had turned against him. It gave Myke great pleasure at getting one over on him. When Mattie had filed for divorce, Chuck testified on her behalf. His testimony helped put Myke in jail.

Myke grinned with delight. The heavy clouds hid the moon, darkening the night. "It couldn't be more perfect, Pico! The rain will wash away the tracks and whatever we leave behind."

"*Si*, amigo, a most perfect night. And look, we are getting wet. The rain has come."

Off in the distance, a dog barked. *We must move quickly*, Myke thought. The Shelby Cobra was parked in the driveway. He glowed with eagerness and rubbed his cold hands together in anticipation. *She's still a beauty. Chuck, you made it easy for me. A car like the Shelby should have been parked in a garage, not in the driveway.*

"Come on, Pico, I found the car; we're good to go," Myke whispered.

Pico walked behind Myke, asking, "What kind of car is this?" as he ran his hand across the red paint finish.

"It's a Shelby Cobra with a 302 V-8 engine. A muscle Mustang! Isn't she beautiful? It'll be great to be behind the driver's wheel again." Myke spoke in a low voice.

The car was locked, and Myke went to the front of the car, reached under the hood, popped the lid open, and quietly and slowly raised it.

Good boy, Chuck, he thought as he pulled the little black box away from the frame of the car where Chuck kept the emergency key. With care, he slowly lowered the hood and heard it latch. He then went around to the door, unlocked it, and got in. Reaching over, he unlocked the door for Pico.

"Isn't she sweet, Pico?"

"Yeah, amigo, she's a real sweet car!"

"I offered to buy this baby from Chuck when he was on hard times, and he wouldn't part with her. I really can't blame him." Myke ran his hands over the dashboard and smiled. "Don't forget to check the radio before starting up the Shelby," he reminded himself aloud.

"What did you say?" Pico asked.

Smiling, Myke answered, "Chuck and me, we spent hours installing an insane speaker box with twelve-inch subwoofers to shake the fillings out of our teeth and drive the neighbors crazy. If that radio is on, we'll wake the whole neighborhood up." Reaching over, he turned the knob to the off position. "Chuck is so predictable. The radio was on and turned up high. I don't know how his wife puts up with him."

"By the way, how'd you know that the key would be under the hood?" Pico asked.

"Chuck's old lady has a real bad habit of locking her keys in the car." Myke laughed, looking up at the window. "Amber, that's his wife, once locked the door with the baby still in his car seat. She called Chuck at work, screaming hysterically, and, man, he went ballistic."

Turning the key to the ignition, Myke froze as the engine ignited. His palm gripped the steering wheel tightly.

Pico saw the look on Myke's face. "What's the matter?" Myke's head fell to the steering wheel, his heart thumping hard against his chest and his knuckles white from the tight grip on the wheel. "I forgot about the glass pack muffler that I helped Chuck replace before I was sent up."

"Well, it's a good thing he replaced it, or we'd be knee-deep in trouble. She's purring like a kitten." Pico laughed. "Scared you, didn't it?"

Myke added some choice words and said, "You better believe it did! We would have woken the neighborhood up, not to mention Chuck and his family, and here I was worried about the radio! This place would have been swarming with cops like bees out of a hive."

The rain was coming down hard, banging loudly on the roof. Easing the car away from the curb, Myke's heart still pumped hard and his hands shook. "I need a smoke really bad, and here I was trying to quit. There's a Fast Eddie's up the street. Run in and get me a pack of cigarettes, will ya, and a bottle of Coke?" Myke handed Pico a ten-dollar bill. "And while you're at it, get yourself something to drink. It's on me."

"I was gonna ask. Thanks, big spender." Pico grinned.

The rain subsided as quickly as it had begun, and the moon peeked out from behind a cluster of clouds as they moved past.

Myke turned off the engine and the headlights as they approached the driveway of the Brookfield's home, allowing the car to slowly coast down the hill toward the house. As Myke rolled the windows down, cold wind blew against his face. "It doesn't look like it rained as hard here as it did in the city."

"Yeah, it doesn't. I've been watching the clouds. I hope the rain holds off until we're done; then it can let loose and soak the ground," Pico answered.

Reaching into his pocket, Myke's fingers hooked onto the short chain attached to a long, thin metal whistle. Removing it from his pocket, he placed it against his lips and hung his head out the window. With a steady flow of air, Myke blew the tune "Take Me Out to the Ballgame" into the whistle.

"What are you doing, amigo? Are you going to let them know we are coming to rob their place with that whistle?" Pico looked at Myke, thinking that Myke had lost his mind.

Chuckling, Myke held the whistle away from his lips and waved it back and forth. "My friend, this is a dog whistle. Only a dog can hear this pitch. You see, they have this big black dog that knows my call. Watch. You'll see."

Pico's hands went to his chest. "Amigo, you gave me quite a scare there for a moment."

Coasting the car off the gravel road, he hid it between a cluster of cedar trees and tall weeds. He held the whistle out the window once again and blew the same tune; his eyes swiftly scanned the area. "I don't see him, Pico." Myke got out of the car and raised the whistle to his lips.

Pico hissed. "Are you sure that no one can hear that whistle but that dog?"

"Yeah, I'm sure. Can you hear it?"

"Well, no."

Myke squinted to see beyond the dark night. A feeling of uneasiness crept in, and he wondered if something could have happened to Max. As a young pup, Max would pounce on cars that came down the lane. His nails would leave scratch marks on the paint finish. He hoped that Doc hadn't gotten rid of him. With a deep sigh, Myke said, "Well, if Max won't answer, maybe the ghost will." A feeling of sadness nudged at his heart. "I really liked that dog, Pico. He was a gentle and handsome dog."

"*What ghost?*" Pico cried.

Smiling, Myke knew that he had gotten to Pico once again. "Mrs. Brookfield once told me that she saw a woman in a long light-green dress dating back to the pioneer days. The woman, Mrs. Brookfield claimed, would stand at the barn looking toward the house. Why, Mrs. Brookfield could never figure out why she stood there with a forlorn look on her face. She wore a white bonnet on her head with black curls flowing down her shoulders. Then she'd disappear in a cloud of vapor. Doc never believed her story because he never saw the ghost himself. He claimed there was no such thing as a ghost."

"Where'd she see the ghost?" Pico asked, looking around frantically, his eyes wide with fright.

"I never saw that ghost myself, so don't spaz out, Pico."

"Ghosts aren't something you kid about, *amigo!*"

"Why would I lie to you? And where is that dog?" Myke was beginning to worry, and he blew into the whistle again.

"What if the dog is in the house? He'll start barking because he hears you calling him, and he'll wake them up."

"They don't keep him in the house. He's too big."

Myke saw the brush move and then heard something moving through the tall weeds. Then, out pounced Max. In his excitement, Max jumped up on Myke, placing his large muddy paws on his shoulders. Max's large eyes stared into Myke's, and he was panting. His large tongue swiped across Myke's face and he whimpered, his tail swinging back and forth in excitement. Saliva hung from the corners of his mouth.

At seeing Max, Pico leaped onto the hood of the car. "Wow, that's one big black dog! Look at the size of that animal, and you call that thing a dog? It looks more like a black bear! What kind of dog is that anyway?"

"He's a Newfoundland. They're great with kids—aren't you, Max? You're a great big pussy cat!" Myke said, tousling Max's ears.

"Will that pussycat bite?" Pico asked.

"I've never known him to, but there's always a first time." A malicious grin creased Myke's lips as he looked over at Pico.

Max's tail swished back and forth, striking the car with

a thump. Myke ran his hand over Max's head and told him, "Yeah, I'm glad to see you too, old boy. But I've got work to do. Go home!" Max slid his big paws off Myke's shoulders, leaving a streak of mud down the front of his shirt, and pranced away, back to his doghouse.

Myke turned to Pico. "You're okay now. You can get off the hood of the car," he told him, laughing. He then brushed his shirt, only to make the mud smear even worse. "We'll be able to move around freely now."

"Look at your shirt. You're a mess," Pico said in disgust.

The semi-soggy leaves crackled under their shoes, and Myke could see Pico cringe with every step.

"Won't they hear us coming?" Pico whispered.

"No," Myke answered. "The bedrooms are on the other side of the house."

Removing the latex gloves from his pocket, Myke slipped them on, and Pico did the same. He reached for the doorknob to the French door and found it unlocked. *Sharon, you're as dependable as Max.*

A night light glowed down the hallway. "Stay close to the wall and don't walk into anything," Myke whispered over his shoulder. Creeping across the room, they walked past the pool table. *A couch should be a foot away to the left,* Myke thought, and he extended his hand out. He felt the thick padding of the armrest. *Good, nothing has changed.* He stepped over a golf ball on the floor. "Watch out for the golf ball." Myke whispered.

Too late. Pico's foot found the golf ball that glowed in the dark, and it went across the floor, hitting the wall with a thump and rolling back toward him. "What was that?" Pico whispered.

"Sheesh, Pico! I told you to watch out for that golf ball," Myke whispered back. Myke's body then stiffened. He thought he heard the creaking of the floorboards upstairs. "Do you hear anything?" Myke held his hand up and placed his finger across his lips. He pointed at the floor. Light that filtered from under the door quickly flickered off.

Pico whispered in his ear, "Why'd you stop?"

"Didn't you see that light under that door go off?"

"I saw nothing. It's dark down here. Maybe it's another night light that just burnt out," Pico whispered back.

Myke hadn't thought of that, and he shook off that uneasy feeling again. But then again, Myke's dad used to tell him when he was a little boy—that was before he decided to dump Myke and his mom—to always go with your gut feeling. It had saved his dad's life many times when he was on a case.

"I don't know, Pico. I don't have good feelings about this job tonight."

"Ah, come on! You are getting spooked!" Pico whispered. "Maybe it's that ghost …" He snickered.

"Smart-ass," Myke hissed back as he opened the door to the furnace room. The room was warm from the heat that the furnace was generating. Eager to see the safe, Pico stepped around Myke to get a better look at the room. "Hey, close that door behind you and turn on the light," Myke snapped.

"Oh, yeah. The only light we're getting is from that monster furnace. Some light would help." Pico went back and flipped the light switch. "Now, we can see. Hey, where's the safe you said was in here?"

The light that had flickered off was not a bulb burning out. The one light bulb in the room was just turned on by Pico. The hair on Myke's arms stood. "That, I don't know. It's not here. Something heavy has been moved, and it looks like it might have been a safe." Wheel trails left in the dust led to the door.

"Somebody got to the safe before us." Pico swore.

Myke had an eerie feeling that someone had been in the room with them. Myke thought he saw a shadow move back into the dark recesses of the room where a door to the bathroom was placed, in an obscure part of the house. That person may have exited that door into the bathroom. Someone who might have been in that room knew the floor plan of where the door was placed.

"Now, what are we gonna do?" Pico asked.

"I don't know!" Myke swore. "If you wanna know what I think, I think we need to get out of here. Like, right now."

"Wait. Let's make a quick trip upstairs. Maybe we can find some cash or something."

Myke stood pondering that question, and against his better judgment, he gave in. "I know where the missus keeps her purse. I'm short on cash and in desperate need of money."

The house was old, and the floorboards creaked as they made their way up the stairs, setting Myke's nerves on edge. A shadow cast on the wall made him jump. It was Pico's shadow. Pico's heavy breathing seemed to amplify in Myke's ear.

fff

The full moon filtered into the room through the large windows. Pico rubbed his hands greedily and headed for the dining room. He saw two silver candlestick holders sitting on the formal dining room table. *So, the Doc's wife has a fondness for silver.* Pico's eyes glowed with excitement. He picked up one of the candlesticks and held it up to the light. *I'd take these to Val. Maybe she'll take me back after she sees what I brought her and drop that gringo.* He then went to the china cabinet and pulled open a drawer. He saw real silverware, and in a dish was a diamond earring that Mrs. Brookfield must have hidden. Pico put the earrings in his pocket. *Val will go crazy for this! Ah, shucks, can't take that beautiful china. Maybe I'll come back later.* Pico grinned.

Myke went to the pantry where he knew Mrs. Brookfield hung her purse. He removed it from the hook and took the wallet out of the purse, stuffing the bills into his pocket. Pico came up from behind and leaned over Myke's shoulder, scaring him.

"Pass me that credit card, will you!" Pico whispered in his ear.

"Don't scare me like that!" Myke jeered, handing him the wallet. "Help yourself, and let's get out of here before we wake them."

Pico patted the linen tablecloth he carried like a sack. "Maybe my Val will take me back after she sees what I have for her." Pico winked.

"Yeah, yeah, and what if she doesn't? What are you going to do then? She's got a boyfriend, remember?"

"Then I'll go to Mexico. I have family there. I haven't seen my grandparents in a long time. My grandmother would appreciate these gifts." Pico slid the tablecloth onto his shoulder, smiling with great satisfaction. He then stiffened and raised his head, smelling the air. "Do you smell smoke?" He sniffed the air again and looked around him. "Something burning?"

"Yeah, I do smell smoke. We'd better get out of here!" Myke took the wallet from Pico and tossed it into the laundry basket. "We don't want to get caught with this on us."

"Look!" Pico pointed. Smoke billowed from a room down the hall.

A flicker of yellow-orange flames spat out of the doorway. Shadows danced on the dark walls, lighting the hallway leading to the master bedroom. Flames burst out of the room, igniting a small table in the hallway, and crawled along the ceiling rapidly.

There's no way Doc and the missus can make it out of the bedroom now other than a window. I hope they make it out! Myke thought. *Maybe I should just yell fire. Wake up, Doc. The window, use the window to get out!* But fear stopped Myke from calling out. Doc would recognize his voice.

Pico stood transfixed, staring at the flames. "Move, Pico!" Myke grabbed Pico's arm and pulled him toward the door. "We've gotta get out of this house! The fire is coming our way fast! Move, Pico!"

The flames licked the walls and ceiling. Myke could feel the heat on his face, and he drew back for a moment. Pico pushed Myke out the door, and the flames leaped out at them like fingers trying to draw them back into the house. Once out on the lawn, Myke turned and looked back at the house. He saw the curtains burst out in a blaze in the mudroom. From the corner of his eye, Myke saw movement near the barn door. The shadow moved quickly into the safety of darkness. A fleeting thought crossed his mind: *Sharon's ghost!*

Pico grabbed hold of Myke and tugged at his arm. "Come on, amigo. We got to get out of here before the fire trucks and police get here."

Myke's face was drained of color. His only thought was to get out of there as fast as possible. Once in the car, he turned the ignition key, shifted into reverse, and gunned the engine. The car jerked, leaping backward and skidding in the gravel. Mud clods were tossed into the air from the mud trapped in the threads of the tires. In the distance, he could hear Max barking.

The bulky clouds released small droplets of rain that hit the windshield. With the tense moment behind them, Myke asked Pico, "Did you see somebody standing by the barn?"

"No, amigo." Pico's eyes widened. "Why? Did you see that ghost?"

"I don't know. I've never believed in ghosts before, but tonight … I don' know what to believe."

"Well, if there was a ghost out there, I'm glad it was you who saw it. I'd have a hard time dealing with a ghost." Pico stared out the window, looking at the fire. The look on his face sent a chill down Myke's spine.

"Look at that fire!" Excitement flashed across Pico's face as he watched the fire lick the trees.

The shrill sound of fire trucks reached them before they saw the flashing lights coming toward them, passing them by.

"Man, I'd like to watch them put out that fire. I bet the house burns to the ground first," Pico said with a hint of remorse only for not being there to witness it.

Chapter 28

The banging at the door startled Nicole awake. Her hand went to her eyes, and she squinted at the light penetrating her bedroom. She lay motionless, listening to the quiet in her room until the pounding started up again. *Who could that be at this hour of the morning*? she thought. Cuddles stared at her; her ears drawn back.

A voice called out, "Nicole, it's Reid."

Nicole swung her legs over the side of the bed, grabbed hold of her robe, and slipped it over her shoulders. Hurrying past the dresser, she snatched the hairbrush off the top and sent the brush through her long auburn hair. Her heart palpitated against her chest. She leaned against the door and said, "What are you doing here at this hour of the morning, Reid?"

"Open the door. I've got something to show you."

Nicole slid the safety chain from its holding place and cracked the door open to peer out. "What is it?" she asked.

"Have you read this morning's news yet?"

"No, why? You startled me out of bed."

"Read the headline." Reid held the paper up for her to see. Wrapping her bathrobe tightly across her chest, she opened the door wide, allowing Reid to enter. He handed her the newspaper, and she took it from him and walked toward the sofa reading: "Prominent Manhattan physician killed in house fire." Reid walked in and closed the door behind him. Nicole went to the sofa and sat down. He followed behind her and sat next to her.

"No, it can't be ..." she whispered. "I didn't get a chance to talk to him!"

Reid put his arm around her shoulder. "I know, Nicole, and I'm truly sorry."

She laid her head on his shoulder, choking back a sob. "I have so many unanswered questions."

Reid patted her hand in sympathy. "An untimely death. What a tragic shame. Let me put on a pot of coffee, or would you rather have hot chocolate?"

"This morning, I would rather have coffee."

He turned and walked into the kitchen, where he opened the cupboard doors, looking for the coffee and filters. Cuddles rubbed up against his leg and meowed. He leaned over and stroked her head.

Nicole called out, "The coffee and filters are in the cupboard above the coffeepot, and could you feed Cuddles for me? Her food is under the sink. She's hungry."

"Have you finished reading the article?" Reid asked.

"No, I haven't," she answered. "Right now, I'm so confused. I don't know how to feel … maybe I'm in shock over all of this. One minute, I'm an only child, and the next, I have siblings. I'm having a hard time digesting all of this. It says here that Dr. Brookfield had four children, and one is a doctor here in this town. She's married to the chief of police. Have you heard of Dr. Brooke Kaufmann?"

"No, I haven't." He handed her the cup of coffee. "What are you going to do?"

"I don't know," Nicole answered, staring at the steam as it twisted and twirled and evaporated into the air. A faraway look settled in her eyes. She then said, "I've got three sisters and a brother … I know Mother would have said, 'Let it go, Nikki. You have me.' However, she's gone now. All these years, Mom let me believe that my father was dead. Then she told me that he was killed in Vietnam serving our country. I stopped asking questions after that because she always looked so pained when I asked her about my dad."

"Nikki, is it short for Nicole?" Reid asked.

"Yeah, my nickname growing up."

Chapter 29

Pico snored loudly on the couch. Myke sat slumped in a chair, his feet propped on the coffee table with a bowl of popcorn on his lap. The television had been turned up to drown out the steady rhythm of Pico's snoring. The five o'clock newscast caused Myke to sit up and listen.

"A house fire leveled the home of a prominent Manhattan physician and his wife, Dr. and Mrs. Kent Brookfield."

Myke reached over and shook Pico. "Wake up, Pico! You better listen to this!"

Startled by the roughness of Myke's hand, Pico jumped and asked, "What?" He swung his legs to the floor and rubbed his tired eyes.

"The Brookfield's' home burnt down last night with them in it, that's what!"

The newscaster had Pico's full attention. Pico's elbows rested on his knees with his hands cupping his chin as the newscaster recapped the story: "An early morning fire killed a prominent physician in Manhattan. Dr. Kent Brookfield and Mrs. Sharon Brookfield's bodies were found late this afternoon. Their deaths come as a shock to this small community of Manhattan. The immediate family members are in seclusion at this hour. We have spoken to Chief of Police Cliff Kaufmann, son-in-law of Dr. and Mrs. Brookfield. He said the origin of the fire will be investigated as an arson–homicide case."

"Oh, man, Pico. They were in the house and didn't make it out. My gut feeling told me to cry out and warn them. I thought that maybe that person I saw dart into the barn was Sharon's friend the ghost. But now that I think about it, it may have been a person and not that ghost darting into the barn. That person must have set the fire. It may have been murder."

"That could be. But why kill them?" Pico stared at Myke.

"I don't know, but I don't like it. Our timing couldn't have been worse. A murder was being committed last night, and we were there. Were they already dead before the fire engulfed the house?" Myke asked.

"I didn't hear anyone cry out for help. Did you, Myke?"

"No, I didn't."

Did you start that fire, Pico? Myke wondered. *That look on your face, I'll never forget it. Your eyes glowed with excitement when you saw the flames shooting from the rooftop.*

"Why are you looking at me like that?" Pico stammered. "I bet you're thinking that I started that fire, aren't you?" Pico looked at Myke with narrowed eyes.

"Well, yeah. I gotta admit that the thought did cross my mind. That look on your face in the car had me convinced that you had done it. After all, you were sent to prison on arson and theft charges."

"I wish I had never told you about those charges."

"That look of satisfaction, glee … the way you smiled. It really scared me. Besides, you went your way, and I went another before the fire started."

"Oh, amigo, I'm so disappointed in you. You thinking I started that fire … Man, I'm hurt. I didn't do it!"

"Well, what did you expect me to think when you were sent up to the big house for arson?"

"I told you that I was too drunk to remember what happened. When they found me, I was out cold in my car. I don't even remember driving to that house and parking in the driveway. And that gas can they found in my trunk … I was framed!"

"Yeah, you told me that story. But you would have suspected me if it was the other way around."

"Maybe I would have." Pico glared at Myke and shook his head in disgust. Here he had thought that they were friends. Then he added, "Maybe it was an electrical problem or something?"

"I hope it was. If it was murder, I wonder who had a grudge against Doc to do such an evil thing."

A long sigh escaped from Myke. He wanted to get even, not see them dead. Myke liked Mrs. Brookfield and would never have hurt her.

Chapter 30

The biting chill in the early morning air sent Brooke and her family scurrying into the little chapel off Amherst Avenue. The old sanctuary, a place of refuge for many, had been the home church for the Brookfield family for as long as they could remember. High above on the ceiling, fans were motionless, adding to the somber mood of the morning. The early-morning sun struck the colored glass and threw rainbow light across the red carpet. The beauty of the sanctuary that morning overwhelmed Brooke. Flowers overflowed the chapel and the appearance was like that of a flower shop. The altar and floor were lined thick with colorful mums, roses, carnations, and blooming potted flowering plants. *That would have pleased Mother,* Brooke thought.

Christmas three months earlier was the last time the Brookfield children were all together as a family in this church. That night, Christmas carols and bells rang out, proclaiming the birth of baby Jesus to Mary and Joseph. It brought back fond memories of Brooke's childhood and the Christmas pageant she and her siblings took part in: her mother fussing over her and her brother Jesse before the Christmas play, Daddy sitting in the first row with the old Polaroid movie camera ready to roll.

One year, she was asked to portray Mary, the mother of baby Jesus, and Jesse played the little shepherd boy. The children, dressed as angels, sang praises to welcome baby Jesus into this world. Then Pastor Ward read the story of the birth of baby Jesus.

The highlight after the play was the bag of candies, nuts, and fruits handed out as they were all ushered out the door and sent home to await St. Nick.

Once home, they would all gather in the kitchen for Mother's mincemeat pie and eggnog. Before they were allowed to eat, Daddy would call for a toast. He'd stand at the head of the table and gently strike the glass in his hand with his fork to get everyone's attention. He would then wish the family a prosperous new year in our Lord God. But this year, he had an additional request. "This time next year," he announced, "I'd like to see a grandbaby at this table for Christmas."

"Hear, hear!" Everyone chimed in. Eyes were directed at Cliff and Brooke. She was the only one married in the family.

Daddy looked at each of his daughters, and Morgan squirmed uncomfortably. "Don't look at me, Daddy! I'm not even married yet."

"Oh no, babe. I wasn't talking to you, sweetie." Daddy chuckled. "You've got your education to think about right now. Keep yourself pure for the man you marry. That's the best advice I can give to our children. Isn't that right, Sharon?"

"Right! With AIDS and other diseases hanging over our youth, abstinence is the only way," Mom answered.

That's Mother for you. But she was right, Brooke thought.

Doc turned and looked at Brooke sitting next to him.

"Brooke, you and Cliff have been married for six years, and you're a doctor. Cliff is the chief of the police department. When are you two going to start a family?

You're comfortable, financially set, and we're getting impatient. Do I have to explain to you how to bring this about?"

Daddy had really embarrassed Cliff that night. Cliff turned red as a ripe tomato, and the family roared with laughter.

Did Daddy know? Brooke had wondered. She had only found out that morning herself. Brooke had wanted to tell them that night, but Cliff thought it was too early. Cliff then suggested that they wait and surprise Daddy for his birthday in April. Now, they would never know or see their first grandchild.

Tears rolled down her cheeks. All was lost in the fire. Pictures, the collection of old Polaroid wheels that they enjoyed watching after the Christmas feast waiting for old St. Nick, and so much more lost.

fff

The Brookfield's' children made an early appearance at the church. A sign had been placed at the first three rows of the pew that said, "Reserved." Two closed caskets, side by side, stood against the altar cold and silent. The Brookfield family wanted to say their final goodbyes to their parents before the crowd showed up to pay their final respects.

Brooke held on to Cliff's arm as they made their way to the front of the sanctuary. Jesse, Brooke's brother and the only son of Dr. and Mrs. Brookfield, followed behind Cliff and Brooke. Close behind was Jenner Brookfield, a grade school teacher, with her fiancé, Eddie Parker. Eddie was a stockbroker out of Chicago. Their wedding date had been set for June. Now, with the death of their parents, they were contemplating canceling for a later date or a smaller wedding. The youngest, Morgan, a college freshman at Nebraska University, took a seat as if she were in a trance.

They sat staring at the caskets. Their parents' final resting places were coffins lined with white satin. Brooke looked up at the stained-glass image of Jesus the Shepherd. Jesus held a lamb in one hand and a staff in the other. Tears ran freely down her cheeks.

Why, Lord, did they have to die in such a way? They were good people, good parents, and most of all, they loved You, Lord! I am so angry at their senseless deaths. The muscles along Brooke's jaw tightened. *If you are such a loving God, why didn't you intervene, Lord? Why couldn't you have stopped this tragic death of our parents? Why did they have to die in such a gruesome way? Why, Lord, why, why, why?* Brooke's chin fell to her chest as a sob struggled to surface. In her lap, wet spots pooled on her black dress. *Oh, how I wish I had told Daddy that I am carrying his first grandchild. We could have made his last days so very happy.*

If I had only known how short their time on earth would have been ... A sob broke loose.

Cliff placed his arm around Brooke's shoulders, drawing her close to his side. She laid her head on his shoulder as she dabbed her eyes and blew her nose. Brooke stiffened and pulled away from Cliff's shoulder. "I should have told Daddy and Mom that I was pregnant," she said. *Why did I listen to you, Cliff?* she thought in anger, a force so great tearing through her very soul.

As if Cliff could read Brooke's thoughts, he spoke. "I'm sure that your dad and mom already know about their first grandchild. I bet they even know the sex." Flicking off a lint ball from her shoulder, he drew her head back onto his shoulder.

A steady flow of people filled the sanctuary as the angelic voice of Sadie Wells sang, "The Old Rugged Cross." Her voice filled the church as people continued to fill the sanctuary. It looked as though the whole community had turned up to bid farewell to the well-respected physician and his wife. Every seat was filled, and the vestibule was so crowded that people were lining the entryway.

Pastor Ward peeked into the room set aside for the family and softly said, "Are you ready?"

Cliff stood and took hold of Brooke's elbow, and they

followed the pastor out the door. Jesse, Jenner, Eddie, and Morgan followed close behind as Pastor Ward led them to the front of the sanctuary. As they walked to the front, people rose to their feet, and as they continued past, many dabbed their teary eyes. They stood as if they were at a wedding honoring the bride and the groom, but their faces were mournful and devoid of the joy of that moment.

Pastor Ward looked out into the sanctuary at all the faces and wondered what kind of closure his dearly departed friend would have wanted him to give. The question that Brooke had asked him days before came to mind. This question had been asked of him countless times by many people angry with God. They felt that God was an unjust God. He took the lives of their loved one's way before their time. This was the question, he thought, that needed to be addressed.

Doc and Sharon's closest friend and niece were both asked to speak. First to speak was Rick Bethel, owner of Rick's Café and a longtime friend of the family. He spoke fondly of Doc and the many sports they took part in while in high school together. But his fondest memory was the year the football team took the state championship. Doc made the touchdown that won the game by one point. The crowd had gone hysterical. Some jumped up and down, screaming and patting their companions on the back.

Others ran to the field and lifted the team members to their shoulders. No one since then had been able to break Doc's record on the yardage gained in that one year. Many colleges approached Doc with scholarship offers for football, but Doc had his sights set on playing football at a medical school, and he finally chose Kansas University. Doc went off that fall with a full football scholarship.

Rick went on to say how Doc chose to return to Manhattan to set up his practice, and he took care of Rick's family and many of those sitting there today. He mended many broken bones, gave out lots of prescription drugs to the sick, and counseled many ill and dying. Rick choked up with emotion and apologized. He cleared his throat, lowered his head, stepped away from the podium, and then returned to his seat.

Next, Doc and Sharon's niece came to the podium. Nervously, she brushed her blond hair to the side and cleared her throat. "Many of you know who I am. But for those of you who don't, my name is Ashley Booth. Uncle Kent and Aunt Sharon were very special people. They did not only love their family but also this community." As she went on, she touched on the highlights of her relationship with them and ended by saying, "They will be greatly missed by all who loved them dearly." Ashley looked over at her cousins who had lost their beloved parents. Her lips moved silently. "I love you!"

Ashley moved aside, and Pastor Ward stepped to the podium and began his eulogy. "Kent was better known by many of us as simply Doc. And yes, we are saddened by the tragic loss of Kent and Sharon Brookfield, but we should also be rejoicing! We all know where they went. They have gone to a better place, and one day, we will be united with them in His glorious kingdom. It was asked of me, why does God take good people in such a cruel way? This question has been asked of me many times and needs to be addressed. We live in a fallen world because of the sins of Adam and Eve.

"Doc and Sharon were good people, and, yes, they loved the Lord. Doc reached out to the sick and dying, and, yes, he prayed for many of you in this room. I asked myself, what would he want me to say about him and Sharon? Doc and I had talked on this subject in depth many times, and I believe that this is what he would want me to say to all of you.

"He would want me to tell you about God's saving grace. God did not promise that we would have no trials in life or that we'd have no troubles come our way. God does not take our family members or friends with violence. It's the evil and greed of this world that does that. No one knows when they turn a corner if death may be waiting to claim his or her life. Doc would have wanted me to ask you,

'Are you ready to meet your maker? Do you know where you will spend eternity?' Doc and Sharon have crossed over to a better place, and we should be rejoicing for them. Isaiah 57:1-2 (KJV) says, 'The righteous perishes, and no man takes it to heart; merciful men are taken away, none considering that the righteous is taken away from the evil to come. He shall enter into peace: they shall rest in their beds, each one walking in his uprightness.'"

Pastor Ward looked out at the many faces staring up at him and wondered how many heard what he had just said about God's saving grace.

fff

A somber mood hung heavy in the air, and Nicole and Reid left the sanctuary. Cirrus clouds like down feathers floated high above them.

"Are you all right, Nicole?" Reid asked.

Nicole looked over at Reid with sorrowful eyes. "I don't have the answers to my questions. I may never know what happened between my mother and Dr. Brookfield." Her shoulders slumped over; her eyes cast to the pavement. "I can't understand why my mother would never talk about him. Why would she tell me he had been killed in Vietnam? I guess I'll never know now, will I?"

"Well, sometimes it's best to let that unturned rock just lie. A bug that you're not ready to deal with just might crawl out and tell you things that you're not ready to hear."

"Yeah, I guess you're right on that point, and I like the way you put it. A bug under a rock! It might be a dirty and unwelcome bug. I've hit a dead end to my past."

"You know that pastor who delivered the eulogy? He may have the answers you're seeking. He talked as if he knew the doctor really well. Why don't you go and talk to him?"

"You might be right. I'll call him later today and make an appointment," she answered.

fff

An anxious feeling gnawed at Nicole's gut as she pulled into the parking lot of the church. The large white building that once housed a mobile home plant had been converted into a church. Drawing in a deep breath, she swung her feet out of the car and stared at the large-plated windows. Boston ferns graced the entryway where she entered the outer office. The pastor came out to greet her. "You must be the young lady who called yesterday. Nicole Martin, correct?" The pastor extended his hand, and Nicole took hold of it.

"Thank you for seeing me on such short notice, Pastor."

"Please come in and take a seat. Do you mind if I call you Nicole?"

"That's fine, Pastor."

"How can I help you? Your call about Dr. Brookfield did puzzle me."

Nicole stammered, "From your eulogy yesterday, I got the impression that you and Dr. Brookfield were friends."

"I'd like to think so, but God knew him best."

"Well, the reason I'm here is for me. I have unanswered questions about my father. I don't know if Dr. Brookfield ever discussed his past with you."

"His past?" The pastor's brow furrowed, and his chair squeaked as he leaned back. His elbows went to the armrest as he intertwined his fingers, allowing his pointer fingers to steeple under his chin. His eyes narrowed.

I believe I just might have hit the wrong button on this one, Nicole thought. She cleared her throat and fidgeted in her seat. She cast her eyes down and stared at her hands in her lap. "Let me start at the beginning so you'll understand where I'm coming from."

The pastor nodded. "That might help."

"I came to Manhattan six months ago in search of my identity. I didn't know where to begin my search other than my aunt telling me that Manhattan would be a good starting point. I became a student at the university and was working part-time for Ms. Shoemaker when Dr. Brookfield came to her office. I was unaware of who Dr. Brookfield was. I only knew that he had come to the office on business."

Pastor Ward listened to her story about how a note had fallen from Doc's pocket and set everything into motion. Thinking that Doc might return for his list, Nicole said she stuffed the notepaper into her jacket pocket and didn't give it another thought until she got home. That night, she pulled out the slip of paper, and things began to fall into place. She only found the mysterious letters that her mother had hidden away after her death. The handwriting on Dr. Brookfield's note had matched with the one on all the letters that were written to her mother.

Pastor Ward asked, "And who is your mother?"

"Loretta Martin," she answered.

The pastor's eyes seemed to grow in size as he inhaled deeply, just like Dr. Brookfield's eyes when she told him who her mother was.

Nicole then asked, "Did Dr. Brookfield ever discuss this with you, Pastor? I believe that Dr. Brookfield maybe have been my father."

Pastor Ward looked at Nicole with saddened eyes. He remembered the first time he had met her mother. Loretta walked into the sanctuary after the service had begun and quickly slid into the back pew. At the end of the service, he went over and introduced himself. She was a friendly and spirited person. She smiled with her eyes, and when she laughed, it was deep laughter that seemed to rise from her belly. She had just moved to Manhattan and was looking for work. She told him that she was a nurse, and he immediately introduced her to Dr. Brookfield, who was at the time looking for a temporary replacement, as his nurse would soon be going on maternity leave.

"Yes, I knew your mother."

Nicole's eyes lit up. "So, you did know her."

"Yes, I did. She came here to church. And did you say that your mother is deceased now?"

"She was killed last year in an auto accident. A hit-and-run," Nicole answered. "Please tell me what you do know, Pastor."

"You do have the right to know. I feel Doc would have wanted me to clear things up for him since he's unable to do it himself. It was a tragic mistake on both Doc's and your mother's part. They came to me for counseling, asking me for Godly advice and guidance. Your mother was early in her pregnancy with you. Sharon, Doc's wife, was also pregnant. It was a most difficult situation for both." He paused as he looked at Nicole. "Then one day after you were born, she packed up and left town. No one seems to know where she moved. I guess Doc did, but he never told anyone." Sad eyes looked out at Nicole.

Nicole sighed. "Thank you for telling me, Pastor. I can now find closure to my past." Gathering up her keys, Nicole stood.

"Can I offer you some advice, free of charge?"

"Sure," Nicole answered.

"Anger and hate are great destroyers of man. Forgiveness is a great release for man's soul. Don't allow anger to destroy the goodness in you. In your search for your identity, look to Christ. There are no illegitimate children, only illegitimate parents. Without God, life makes no sense. Nicole, you were in God's thoughts before you were even conceived. God has a purpose for your life. Seek His will in all that you do. He holds you in His hands with love."

Nicole cocked her head and gave the pastor a funny look. "I'm not sure I fully understand your meaning, Pastor."

"Read this." Pastor Ward handed her a book that encouraged people to live their purpose in life. "It will help give you a greater understanding of who you are in Christ. I pray that I've been able to clear up some of your long-unanswered questions. If you have any more questions, please feel free to call me anytime."

"Once again, thank you, Pastor."

Pastor Ward watched Nicole from his office window as she climbed into her car. His heart was saddened by the events of her life.

That young lady will never find out what brought her mother and Doc to my office. Her mother nearly made a tragic choice. Loretta wanted to abort the child she was carrying, and Doc was so against it. Doc was eventually able to talk her into going in and getting counsel from me. If she hadn't, that young woman wouldn't be here today. That secret will go with me to my grave, he thought. *I pray that she has found closure to her past. Help her find her identity in You, Lord. And most of all, help her to forgive the wrong that had brought all of this about. Amen.*

Chapter 31

Five days later, the local television news reported, "A Manhattan man has been taken into custody and arraigned in the arson-homicide of Dr. and Mrs. Brookfield. A fire five days ago leveled the home of the Brookfield's. Their bodies were found among the charred remnants of their home. Charles Walker's car has been identified as the vehicle seen leaving the scene of the fire. The car has been impounded by the police department, and the arrest was made."

A satisfied grin creased Myke's lips. *Now, you'll know what it feels like to be accused of a crime. I want you to feel the loneliness and know the fear of looking over your shoulder with all the violent criminals around you. Then, of course, there are your children. The kids in school will taunt and shun them because their daddy is a jailbird. It's payback time, Chucky.*

With Doc out of the picture, Myke knew Mattie would slowly crumble. She no longer had Doc telling her what to do and how to do it.

"How sweet it is!" he exclaimed. "I know she'll break. First, I'll work on the kids. Then she'll see how sincere I am and that I really have changed. The judge set up the conditions, and Mattie agreed to the supervised visitation, which means that she went along with the judge's decree. No problem! I'll be a very good boy. I'll show them a good time by taking them to the amusement park in Kansas City, and she'll see that I'm really trying. I'll move real slow and get in on the good side of her and—*wham!*—I'm back in my bed again." He grinned smugly. "One should forgive, shouldn't she?"

Two weeks later, at the warehouse, Myke felt a nudge from his fellow worker standing next to him. The supervisor was pointing in their direction, and four police officers and a plainclothes detective walked toward them. His partner standing next to him commented, "They're headed in our direction. Is it you or me that they're after?"

Myke was overcome with panic. In desperation, he looked around for the nearest exit. His instinct told him to run. He bolted toward the nearest door, leaping over the table and crashing into a stack of empty boxes. Stumbling, he fell to the ground on his knees. He frantically got back up on his feet, limped to the nearest door, and then slammed it open. The sun's rays struck him in the face, temporarily blinding him. His mind raced. *Run to the river!*

Turning to see how close they were behind him; he saw one of the officers sliding across the floor on the boxes he had knocked over. The other officers rushed past him. Myke slammed the door closed, picked up a two-by-four board that leaned against the wall, and slid it between the double door handles, barring the doors closed. Stretching his stride, he dug his sneakers deep into the gravel as he pushed off. He gritted his teeth, and his arms swung forward as he sprinted across the gravel toward the railroad track and beyond to the river.

Heaving and out of breath, he could hear the pounding on the metal doors behind him. Myke pushed his body, ignoring the burning pain in his lungs and legs. Then a voice rang out. "Stop, or I'll shoot!"

The muscles along Myke's jaw tightened as he clenched his teeth and hissed, "You're gonna have to shoot me! I'm not going back to prison."

A shot rang out behind Myke. "I won't hesitate to shoot you, Cooper!"

Myke's lungs felt like they were ready to burst. He slowed his stride to a stop. *This isn't worth getting killed for, man! I didn't kill the Doc and his wife.*

"Don't shoot. Please don't shoot!" He held his hands high over his head.

An officer, out of breath, placed his hands on Myke's shoulder. "Put your hands to the back of your neck, Coop, and spread eagle!" The officer breathed heavily down his neck.

Myke protested, "What am I being arrested for? I did nothing!"

"Then why did you run, Coop? Put your hands behind your neck and spread your legs," the detective ordered. "I'm not going to tell you again."

Once again, Myke's body was being violated. Hands traveled up his legs to his crotch and then up his body. "I have my rights!" Myke protested.

"We'll read you your rights, and you can put your complaints in with the judge."

"Read him his rights!" the detective ordered.

An officer stepped forward, "You have the *right* to remain silent. Anything you say can and will be used against you in a court of law. You have the *right* to an attorney. If you cannot afford an attorney, one will be provided for you. Do you understand your Miranda Rights?"

"Yeah, yeah, I understand. I've been through this before."

"Okay, Coop, you'll have your day in court." Myke's hands were pulled away from his neck and handcuffed behind his back.

"What did ya do, Myke?" a voice called out from the crowd that had gathered at the door that Myke had slammed out of and barred closed.

"All right. The show's over. Get back to work!" the supervisor ordered.

fff

Pico stood among the other workers, staring in disbelief. *I've got to get out of here, like today! Hide.*

He watched the door close behind the workers, and he hid himself behind the stack of pallets, watching Myke being escorted to the patrol car. Pico watched the patrol car drive down the street and told himself, *Run, make your break for the motel.* Pico took off in the opposite direction. Reaching the motel out of breath, he unlocked the door and shut it behind him, pulling back in surprise. The apartment was a mess. The cushioning from the couch was in disarray. The cabinet doors were thrown open. The sheets were stripped off the mattress and tipped off the frame of the bed and onto the floor. *The cops were here. I gotta take the next bus outa town.* Pico grabbed his duffel bag and shoved his clothes into the bag. *Wait. That shirt with all your cash.* Dumping out the duffel bag he had just packed, he found the western shirt with the snap pockets where he had stashed his extra cash. Removing the money, he counted it, five hundred dollars. *I wonder if the cops had found my cash, would they have taken it into evidence or pocketed it?* Pico smiled and put the cash into his wallet. Next, he went into the bathroom and grabbed his shaver, toothbrush, toothpaste, and deodorant.

He heard pounding at the door. Pico's heart raced. *The cops came back! Oh man, I'm dead.* He went to the peephole and saw Sher Shan. Sher Shan was standing in front of the door, his eyes shifting toward the street. He looked very nervous. Pico opened the door, and Sher Shan pushed past and closed the door behind him.

"What is going on?" Sher Shan asked. "The cops wanted to know what room Mr. Cooper was in and said that I needed to let them in to search for stolen items. Then they started to tearing up the place! I want you and Myke out of here. I don't need trouble. My wife is very upset about this."

"I'm leaving right now. Sorry about the mess the cops made. Tell your wife I am sorry."

Pico looked around for the last time at their motel room. *The cops really made a mess. The pigs!*

Chapter 32

Chief of Police Cliff Kaufmann and Dylan Blanton, a criminologist, drove to the scene of the fire. The charred remains of the house had collapsed into the basement. The red-brick fireplace, the only part of the house left standing, was covered with soot. The trees closest to the house were left in a skeletal state and were blackened.

Dylan, a broad and stocky man in his mid-forties, shuffled slowly to the barn where the safe had been secured. After setting his leather case down, he snapped it open and took out a pair of latex gloves.

"Not a pretty sight out there," Dylan said. "We've lost a good man in this community, not to mention, a fine woman."

"That we did …" Cliff looked over at the charred remains. "Well, let's get to work."

Dylan used a fine camel brush to dust the safe for possible fingerprints that would be sent to the criminal lab for identification. He stood and looked at the prints he had taken from the safe. "A good day's work, I'd say."

They could hear a car making its way down the slight incline of the gravel road leading to the house. With his work done, Dylan snapped his case closed and walked out the door of the barn to watch the car approach.

Cliff came up behind Dylan. "It's my wife with her brother and sisters."

In unison, Cliff and Brooke, both asked each other, "What are you doing here?"

Pained smiles etched their faces.

Cliff answered, "We're here to get prints off the safe. Police work." He smiled. "And you?"

"We came to see if we could find anything of Mom and Dad's. Is that okay? Have the police completed their investigation?"

"Yes, we've taken fingerprints off the safe and gathered up our evidence. Our work is done here. The fire department hasn't been out yet to determine what caused the fire. The police department and I suspect arson, but we really can't rule out lightning hitting the house, setting it on fire. The cinder hasn't cooled off yet, and you …" Cliff looked at Jesse and glanced over at his sisters. "You shouldn't go in there yet. Let it cool off first. Then after the fire department gives you the okay, you can go in. I don't know why you'd want to go in there, but you do what you feel is right."

Dylan cleared his throat. "I'm really sorry about your parents."

A sad smile curved Brooke's lips and then disappeared. "I am too, Dylan. When will you get the results of the fingerprints you've taken from the safe?" she asked.

"It may take a week, if not two, before we hear anything," Dylan answered.

"We need to head back to the station, Brooke. The sooner we get the prints processed, the sooner we'll get answers," Cliff added. "And I'll see you later today."

Brooke walked over to Morgan and placed her arm around her shoulder. Morgan stared silently at the rubble that once was their home. This was the first time she had been out to the house since the fire. Morgan had refused to accept the death of her parents, and now she stared at the aftermath. Tears began to well up in her eyes and roll off her lashes and down her cheeks at the realization that she would not be seeing their parents again. Her body shook uncontrollably. She heaved, gasping for air. Tears flowed freely. Her hands covered her mouth. She uttered, "No, no, this didn't happen. It couldn't have happened. Not to Mom and Dad! Not this way!" She slumped over with grief.

Brooke folded Morgan into her arms. Their sister, Jenner, and brother, Jesse, surrounded them and enveloped them in their protective arms. They all wept.

Chapter 33

A bolt of lightning snaked across the darkened sky as droplets of rain splattered across the windshield of the patrol car. At the city park, Myke watched the parents quickly gather up their young children and place them into vans and cars. After turning onto Juliette Street, they drove one block east to a two-story limestone building that housed the police station and prison.

"Remember this place, Coop?" the officer asked mockingly as he got out of the patrol car and opened the back door for Myke. The officer placed his hand on Myke's head and guided him out the door.

Detective Hamilton came around the car and took hold of his arm. "Welcome back, Coop! You just can't stay away from this luxurious hotel, can you?" He smiled as he led Myke into the building.

"Yeah, right. A five-star hotel with the best food in town." Myke smirked. As if he wanted to be there.

Phones were ringing, and Myke heard the crackling of a police radio coming across the switchboard. A middle-aged woman who was bent over her desk looked up. Her hair was pulled back and pinned with barrettes. She wore the light-blue uniform of a police officer. Hamilton walked toward her, leaned over the counter, and asked her to call the chief. "Tell him we've brought in Cooper."

Myke looked over at the detective in irritation and then asked, "You haven't answered my question yet. What are the charges?"

Hamilton looked at Myke and smiled, ignoring his question.

The woman behind the desk looked up at Hamilton. "The chief wants him in interrogation room 2."

"Let's go, Coop. Myke was shoved into a small room. The room was scantily furnished with a metal table and three chairs.

"Have a seat, Coop!" The guard pointed to a chair.

"These handcuffs are tight on my wrists! Can you take them off before I sit?" Myke asked the officer standing at the door.

Detective Ramos entered. "Let me have the key."

The guard handed Ramos the key, and he unlocked the cuffs. Myke sat in the chair he'd been told to sit in and rubbed his sore wrists.

"Not smart enough to stay away from this town, are you, Coop?" Ramos said, a smirk on his face.

Detective Ramos! Myke glared. *The most despised detective on the force. Smooth and cunning, he is.*

Four years ago, he had tricked Myke into believing that he was on his side. Very sympathetic, he was. He told Myke that Mattie deserved to be knocked around. It was a man's right. If he didn't stand his ground, he was nothing! He was smooth all right. He said the worst thing that could happen was a slap on the wrist with probation and counseling. Myke thought he was a cop he could trust. So, he opened up. Wrong move! All cops are dirty cops. Myke was gullible, naive, and stupid! That smile on Ramos's face, he'd never forget it. After he had spilled his guts, Ramos grinned and said, "I got you, punk!" Those were his exact words.

Well, Ramos hadn't changed one bit in four years. He was still that little, short, fat porker, only older. His once black hair was showing telltale signs of his aging. White streaks flecked through his hair, and it had begun to recede.

He thinks he's gonna play mind games with me again. Well, I'm wiser to his schemes, and I won't bite twice. I'm not young and stupid anymore!

The door opened, and a man walked in. The star on his collar identified him as the chief of police, and Myke immediately stiffened. The chief glared down at him. "I'm Cliff Kaufmann, the chief of police. Do you know why you're here?" Cliff asked, sitting on the edge of the metal desk.

"No, I don't." Myke eyed the chief with suspicion.

"Well, let me tell you why you're sitting in that chair. Two weeks ago, Dr. Brookfield's home was set on fire. Doc and his wife were unfortunately still in bed. They did not make it out. Footprints and tire tread impressions were collected, cast, and sent to the lab." Cliff tossed the pictures on the table of the charred remains of the home of Dr. Kent and Sharon Brookfield.

Myke looked at the pictures and cringed at the remains, pushing the pictures away. "Don't mean a thing to me," he said, trying his hardest to control his composure.

Cliff next pulled out a wrinkled, water-stained manila envelope in a sealed plastic bag. Cliff waved it in front of Myke's face. "The glue has your fingerprint nicely preserved on the flap."

Myke sat up straight. "Oh, no ... no way could you get my fingerprints off of that. I never saw it or touched it!"

"How could you not see it? Look at the picture." Cliff moved the pictures around and pointed one out. "See the tire marks. See the stone, see the envelope lying there? It's not more than a foot away from where the car had been parked." Cliff waited for an answer. "Cat got your tongue, Coop?"

"Well, now ... what's in here?" The chief opened the sealed bag and pulled out the petition. Some of the ink had smudged through the once-wet paper, which had been placed in a plastic bag. "See this?" Cliff laid the petition in front of Myke.

Myke stared down at it. "Yeah, so?"

"Read it, idiot. It's a petition with your name on it. It's not voting you as the most popular guy in town. It's a petition that Doc circulated around to keep you in prison, and when you found this on that rock, it made you real mad. So mad that you killed them. You threatened to kill Doc and Mattie in court. Remember that day?"

"I never saw that petition, and if I had, do you think I would have left it there? I would have destroyed it. I did not kill the Brookfield's." Myke stared at the chief with anger reflecting from his eyes.

"How do you explain the diamond earring of Mrs. Brookfield's found between the couch cushions in your motel room?"

Myke's mind raced. *That stupid ...* "Hey, man, I don't know anything about any diamond earring or that piece of paper. You can't pin this on me."

The chief of police walked around the metal desk and calmly set his hands down on the top of the desk, leaning forward and staring into Myke's face. "We know you and Pico Sanchez were released from prison the same day, and we also know he came to town with you. His prints were found on the silver candlestick dropped in the grass. Where is Sanchez?"

"I don't know," Myke answered.

"He has a rap sheet for arson and theft. Someone claimed to have seen you and him at the scene of the fire. Do you know anything about it?"

Rubbing his sore wrists, Myke answered, "No way anybody could have seen him or me. We were nowhere near the place!"

"Can you verify that?"

You may be walking into a trap. Be very careful how you answer his questions, Myke told himself. "No, I can't. Pico told me he was going to the movies. I didn't want to go. I was tired."

"Where were you the night of the fire?" the chief asked.

"Like I said, I was tired, and I stayed in the room watching a rental movie on television. I was alone."

"Okay, we'll let it go for now. Tell me, do you know where Sanchez is?"

Myke cupped his head in his hands and shook his head. "No, I don't. The last time I saw him, he was at the warehouse." *That son of a … he left me holding the bag. When I get my hands on the sucker, I'll kill him for this*, Myke thought in anger.

"Think about it, Coop. Sanchez's prints were found on a Coke can in a car belonging to Chuck Walker. We believe Sanchez stole the car the night of the murder and returned it early the next morning. Were you with Sanchez?"

"No, I was not with Pico. That stupid nut. I can't believe that he would steal my friend's car and kill Doc and the missus. And here I thought he was a friend. A friend doesn't do what he did." Myke slumped back in his chair.

"Where were you that Friday night, Coop?" the chief asked again.

"I told you, I was at home watching a movie I had rented."

"You won't mind if we check on this? What store did you rent it from?"

"The video store off Anderson."

Detective Ramos got up and left the room.

"Anyone see you there?" the chief asked.

"Yeah, there were people there."

A short time later, Ramos returned. "Coop did rent a movie early that afternoon," he told the chief. Turning to Myke, he said, "And, Coop, they say you didn't return it. You've got late fees."

"Coop, we're going to have to detain you until we find Sanchez," the chief said.

"Why, and what for?" Myke asked in an angry voice.

"Well, for starters, aiding and abetting. Secondly, you're a flight risk. And until we apprehend Sanchez, you'll be our guest here at the taxpayers' expense. Need more?"

"You can't put this on me!"

"Like I said, until you tell us where Sanchez is, you move to the top of our guest list. I'll repeat, we know

Sanchez was released the same day you were, and he's been a bad boy. Arrested for arson, robbery, and attempted murder. You're running with a bad boy, Coop."

"Attempted murder! He never told me about that charge!"

"Do you want to answer our questions as to where you and Sanchez were on the night of March 22?"

"Like I said, I was at home! Sanchez went to a movie." Myke became annoyed with the questioning. *How many times do I have to repeat myself to that idiot?*

Detective Ramos's fat fingers pulled a copy of the newspaper from the folder in his hand and showed it to Myke. "You know you could get life with no parole or the needle for this double murder."

"I murdered no one." Myke looked at Ramos with hatred in his eyes.

The chief slid off the table, his face in Myke's. "Four years ago, in the courtroom after being sentenced for nearly killing your wife and possession of a stolen gun, you threatened to kill your ex-wife and Dr. Brookfield. Where were you on the night of the fire?" the chief hissed.

"I told you, I was at the motel watching a rental movie."

"Was Pico Sanchez with you?" Ramos added.

"No. I told you, he went to the movie theater." Myke slouched low in his chair. He was tired of all the questions and knew it would serve no purpose for him to show his anger. It would get him nowhere, and it would only anger the detective.

"What movie?" Ramos asked, rubbing his knuckles.

"I don't remember," Myke answered.

"I can turn the other way; Coop. Ramos has a way with prisoners that leaves no bruises. Think about it." The chief smiled.

"All right! Pico has grandparents that he said we could go and visit. They would love to see him. He hasn't seen them in over fifteen years. That's all he said, and that's all I know."

"Where do his grandparents live?" The chief spoke in a low, controlled voice.

"I'm not his keeper!"

He watched the chief's face run from cream to red, and Cliff walked over to Myke and yanked him to his feet. His lips puckered, and his face showed his anger. The chief pulled him close. He stared into Myke's eyes, hissing profanity. "You no-good scum. You killed my wife's parents, and you're going down for it, you understand? Get that slime out of my sight, Ramos!"

"All right, all right!" Myke crumpled under the pressure.

The chief let go of Myke's shirt, smoothing the wrinkles out with his hands. "Good, I'm glad we've come to an understanding. Now, let's try this again. Where did Sanchez go?"

Myke cleared his throat. "He said he was going to skip over the border to Mexico City to see his grandparents. That's what he told me he was going to do."

Ramos looked angrily at Myke. "Can you explain this diamond earring found in your motel room?"

Ramos held up the one earring for him to see. Sweat beads formed on Myke's forehead and slowly rolled to the tip of his nose, teetering before falling and splattering on his hand. "I don't know how that earring got into our room. Maybe it fell out of Sanchez's pocket. I really don't know, honest."

"You better come clean, Coop. You want to take the rap for Sanchez and get sent up for a double murder? You'll get the needle, Coop."

"The death penalty! I'm not going down for this. I didn't do it!" Myke yelled. He was scared now. He ran his hands through his hair and thought, *what am I going to do*?

"Okay, I told Pico about the money that Doc kept at the house. He wanted me to go with him that night, and I told him I would not steal from them. He would have to go by himself. I wanted no part of it. Steal from them, that is. The missus, she treated me with kindness. She would bake cookies for me to take home to Mattie. Why would I do something like that?" Then Myke added, "I want an attorney! I have my rights."

Ramos walked to the door, opened it, and hollered out, "Hey, Pete, get this scum out of here and book him on disturbing the peace!"

"What?" Pete had a quizzical look on his face.

"Murder, Pete," Ramos said. "Lock 'im up for both murders."

fff

With the arrest of Myke Cooper, Chuck Walker was cleared of the murders and released from jail. Anger boiled in him, and Chuck had one thing on his mind: to confront Myke on the theft of his car and letting the blame fall at his doorstep.

Chuck received a brown envelope containing his belongings at the checkout station. Chuck thanked the clerk and then asked the officer behind the cage, "Can you tell me where Myke Cooper is being held?" He was holding his anger at bay.

The officer looked over a sheet of inmates. "He's in max," he answered.

Emptying the contents of the envelope on the counter, he dropped his change into his pocket and slipped his wallet into his back pocket. Picking up his car keys, Chuck asked, "My car, can I get my car back?"

"Parked out front."

"I need to talk to Cooper. Can I see him?"

"Let me call down to the jail." There was an exchange of words and a pause. The guard looked over at Chuck. "Was he brought in yesterday?"

Chuck looked puzzled. "That, I don't know. He could have been."

"Sign in on this log, empty your pockets again into this container, and put this visitor's badge on. Go through that door, and the officer at the other end of the hall will show you where to go."

Chuck nodded his thanks and removed his wallet, his keys, and change from his pocket again and went through the door into a well-lit hallway. At the end of the walkway, he was met by another guard. "Who are you here to see?"

"Myke Cooper," Chuck answered.

The guard opened the door and told Chuck to sit. Myke would be brought in shortly.

He sat in a small cubicle with a glass window that separated him from a cubicle the same size on the opposite side. A telephone hung on the wall in each cubicle. Chuck watched the door open slowly, and Myke ambled in with a guard behind him. Myke grabbed hold of the door frame when he saw Chuck sitting there. Myke turned to flee, and his face met the guard's chest.

"Sit down." The guard pointed to the chair. "You have a visitor, and you don't wanna be rude."

Chuck picked up the phone and motioned for Myke to do the same. Myke hesitated for a long moment. He stared at Chuck and then slowly reached for the receiver and placed it hesitantly against his ear. "Hey, Chuck, my old buddy. Let me explain. My so-called friend Pico, he stole your car. I had nothing to do with it. I'm really sorry, man!"

With clenched teeth, Chuck hissed, "You're lying. You were the only person who knew where I kept the spare key to the car. Do you have any idea what you put my wife and kids through, you bastard?" He stood up and struck the glass that separated him from Myke.

Myke jumped, knocking the chair over, and dropped the phone. The guards rushed forward and grabbed Myke's arm. "Your time is up."

Chuck's hand was then peeled off from the glass by another guard. "You don't want to do this. He may have deserved it, but you don't want to get yourself thrown back in prison for damaging property, do you?"

Chuck peeled the guard's fingers from his arm. Breathing heavily, he answered, "No, I guess not."

Chapter 34

Two days later, Myke was once again led into the interrogation room. The chief, Cliff Kaufmann, sat with one foot on the metal table. Detective Ramos sat next to him, and they were exchanging words as Myke was led in.

The chief looked up at Myke and directed him to sit, pointing at a chair. "How are you finding the accommodations here? I trust they are to your liking. Sorry, this isn't the Marriott." He grinned.

Myke felt that Cliff's remark didn't deserve an answer.

"Got enough to eat? How's the surprise meat?" Ramos asked.

This cop is a barrel of laughs! Myke thought. *Should I laugh or what?*

"What surprise meat?" Myke answered.

"Okay, all kidding aside, where did you say Sanchez went?" Ramos asked.

"I told you, he went to see his grandparents in Mexico City."

"We talked with Pico's soon-to-be ex-wife, and she said that he does not have any grandparents in Mexico City, as far as she knew."

"Then he lied to me. Honest, I only told you what he told me. Best I can tell you."

"You do know when we catch Sanchez, he's going to tell us what happened. Want to tell us your version before we get him?"

Myke was not going to tell them anything. He'd take his chances. He hadn't known Pico for long, but they had connected. Pico might not be smart, but he was loyal and a true friend. *We killed no one.* A smug look flashed across Myke's face, and he crossed his arms across his chest and stared off into nothing.

There was a knock at the door, and Ramos went over and cracked the door open. Words crossed between Ramos and the unseen person on the other side of the door. Ramos closed the door and buried his hands deep into his pants pockets. He looked at Myke. "Just thought you might be interested to know that Pico was caught trying to cross into Mexico. Do you have anything you want to tell us before he's extradited back to Kansas?"

Myke knew that would turn out to be a lie, an entrapment to get information from him, and he divulged nothing that could help the police.

fff

Back in the chief's office, a report lay on his desk from the crime lab. He picked up the papers and was reading the first line when the phone rang. He picked up the receiver and answered, "Yes, Beth?"

"Chief, the coroner is on line one."

"Thank you, Beth." He turned on line one. "This is Chief Kaufmann."

"Chief, I've completed the autopsies and blood work on the bodies of the Brookfield's. Their bodies are badly burned, and their death is inconclusive."

"So, nothing was found on or in the bodies to indicate foul play?"

"None that we can determine."

"Thanks for the update." Cliff went back to his reading. "A kerosene can tossed into the high grass had been found …" Cliff ran his hand across his chin, his thoughts drifting off, and the report he held dropped to his desk.

fff

Back at the laboratory, the chief reflected back. There were four fingerprints matched four people who had touched the safe: Dr. Brookfield, Sharon Brookfield, my wife Brooke, and me. The AFIS (Integrated Automated Fingerprint Identification System) database on fingerprints could not come up with a match for the fifth print. The print would have to be sent off to the Federal Bureau of Investigation in Washington, DC, for a level 3, and it could take up to eight weeks before the police could put a name to the fifth print, if at all.

Chapter 35

Shortly after Myke's arrest, an APB was sent out for the arrest of one Pico Sanchez. The focal point was narrowed down to the Mexican border. A picture and description of Pico was sent to the border guards in hopes of apprehending him trying to cross over. A week later, a phone call came in to the Riley County Police Department about the apprehension of Pico Sanchez, alias "Miguel Ramos," caught trying to enter Mexico.

Cliff Kaufmann grinned in satisfaction. *I've got both now.* Leaning over his desk, he pressed the intercom button. "Beth, get Ramos on the phone for me." The phone rang once, and Cliff snatched up the receiver. "Cliff here."

"Chief, this is Ramos."

"I've got a job for you if you want it. Sanchez will be landing at the airport in thirty minutes. He tried to cross the border using your name. If you're too busy, I'll get Detective Hamilton to bring him in."

"I just got off the phone with my brother, and he called to tell me the story. I'm on my way, and I'll even take Detective Hamilton with me. I can't pass up the chance of meeting this clown," Ramos said. "Besides, I've got a bona fide dispute against Sanchez for using my name to get over the border. My brother is the commandant of the guards, and the guards all know me. That stupid fool!"

fff

Detective Ramos was the first to greet Pico as he was led out of the aircraft in handcuffs. "So, you tried to use my name to get over the border, huh? That was a wrong move on your part. My brother is the commandant of the guards, and he made it a point to greet you trying to cross over the border." Ramos smiled broadly at Pico.

Pico glared at Ramos. His biggest regret was setting foot in this little town, followed by the day he set eyes on Myke Cooper. Disgust etched deeply across his face, and he spat on the asphalt.

fff

Grinning with satisfaction, the guard on duty strolled toward Myke's cell, swinging his baton. As he neared, he began to whistle "Jailhouse Rock," running the baton against the bars to make an irritating clunking sound that drew the attention of the other prisoners. Myke, with his hands tucked under his head, stared at the ceiling, listening to the bars rattle.

The guard stopped in front of Myke's cell. "Hey, Coop." He grinned in amusement. "Words out, Sanchez just landed here in Manhattan. Your partner in crime has been caught." The guard watched the expression on Myke's face change from annoyance to surprise.

So, they weren't lying when they said they caught him and were extraditing Pico back to Manhattan, Myke thought and muttered in disgust under his breath. "Why, that stupid fool ..." *All that talk about slipping over the border into Mexico and disappearing into the countryside. You dumb Mexican, we're both dead!* Myke's eyes narrowed in outrage.

Laughter bounced off the walls. "Hey, Coop! Your buddy got caught. You're screwed!" A fellow inmate snickered.

"Yeah, Coop, it's a shame to see a nice guy like you get sent up for a double murder. Did you know that the chief's wife, Dr. Kaufmann, was the daughter of Dr. and Mrs. Brookfield?" another voice taunted him.

"Screw you!" Myke hollered. As he paced the small cell, his thoughts raced wildly. *What the hell will Pico tell them now that he is in custody? Man, I could be in a lot of trouble for something I didn't do. The state of Kansas has the death penalty. Why did I come back to this stinking town anyway? Screw Mattie and the kids! I can't believe that I was so stupid to come back here for a woman who wants nothing to do with me.*

"You better get down on your knees and pray like you've never done before!" a cellmate called out, laughing.

"Prayer is not going to help him! He messed with the wrong people!" another cell mate yelled out and laughed.

"He sure did!" Laughter echoed down the line of cells.

"Shut up! All of you, just shut up! You wouldn't be here if you were on your knees, so don't preach to me," Myke said, and then he swore in anger.

Chapter 36

The detestable guard who enjoyed bringing Myke news appeared at his cell later that day. "Hey, Coop, you have a visitor."

Glancing up in annoyance, Myke asked, "Who is it?"

"She says she's your mother."

The magazine he was reading fell to his chest. *My mother! How did she find me?*

"Well, get up! Your mother is waiting," the guard snapped.

"Tell her I don't want to see her!" Myke snapped back sharply.

"She knew you'd say that. She told me to tell you that if you don't see her today, she'll keep coming back until you do."

"That's her choice. Tell that woman to go back to DC, where she belongs." *Why now, after all these years? She thinks she can just waltz back into my life like nothing ever happened?*

Myke was twelve years old when his father walked out on his mother. His life turned into a living hell. He watched his mother slip into depression and wallow in self-pity. She began drinking to ease her pain. She started with a couple of beers at night to help her relax so she could sleep. From beer, she graduated to vodka and gin and was drunk most of the day. Her drinking affected her work, and she was told to seek professional help for her problem. She refused to heed their warning and denied that she had a problem with drinking. One afternoon, Myke walked in from school and found her crying, a glass of vodka on the rocks in her hand. She had been told that morning to turn in her resignation or she'd be fired. The FBI had been her life. She sobbed. "They can't do this to me!"

The bitter memories buried deep brought back the sharp, pungent taste of the harsh words he had spoken as they flashed into his mind. "What did you expect, Mom? They tried to tell you that you have a drinking problem!

Look at you, and what you've got in your hand. It's not water; that's for sure!" Myke spat out in anger.

He remembered the anger in her eyes as she shot back at him, "How dare you use that tone on me! I'm your mother!" She jumped up in rage and came at him. Her hand came forward with great force, striking him across the face and sending his body crashing against the wall. Then verbal abuse spewed from her lips. "You're just like your father. No good and bad to the core!" she screamed in her drunken state. Her breath reeked of alcohol.

She had forced him to go to confession when she should have been in the confessional booth herself. The church became Myke's sanctuary. Father Jonathan took him under his wing and later asked him to be an altar boy. Mom said she was proud of him, words that he hadn't heard since his dad left them. She said it was a privilege and an honor to serve God and the church. But things didn't change. They were only shallow words spoken by a drunk.

Myke hated going home and began to spend long hours at the church. He did his homework there, and Father Jonathan helped him. Then things began to happen behind closed doors. Unable to talk to anyone, as his mother was always drunk and his dad simply wasn't there for him, Myke had no one to turn to. The person he looked up to and trusted was now abusing him.

The beatings increased as his mother's anger grew. She was never sober during the day anymore and seemed to delight in beating him for the silliest reasons: leaving the milk on the kitchen table or his shoes where she could stumble over them in her drunken stupor or because he looked at her the wrong way, sending a negative message. Myke remembered her throwing a knife at him in anger, cutting his arm badly enough that it required nine stitches.

Then two years went by, and she no longer bothered getting dressed in the morning and rarely bathed. The house had long gone by the wayside. Myke came come home from school only to find her passed out on the couch, her hair a tangled mess, and she reeked of booze. The support checks from Dad paid the rent, and the rest went to vodka and gin. He was left to fend for himself. When the money ran out, usually before the end of the month, she'd search his room for money, or she'd have him borrow money from his friends for beer. Myke hated borrowing money from his friends to support her addiction, especially when he had no means to repay them. It got to the point where they refused to loan him money.

His mother's behavior caused Myke a great deal of embarrassment. He had a hard time holding his head up in school. He was labeled "the kid of the town drunk." One day, his mother caught him with a can of beer and took a belt to him. She said she didn't want him to turn out like her. It was bad enough that he was his father's son!

Myke yelled back at her, "Do you know what the townspeople are calling you? The town drunk and whore! I'm ashamed that you're my mother!"

For that, she beat him black and blue and told him to get out and never come back. He ran from that house, never to return. Myke was fourteen years old and was on the streets of Washington DC.

Yeah, Myke thought, *I know what she's going to tell me*: "You deserve to be where you're at. You're bad to the core, just like your dad!" *I don't want to hear what she has to say. I don't need her.*

Chapter 37

Myke's refusal to see his mother found him on the way to the chief's office. His hands were handcuffed in front of him, and his legs were in the bothersome leg cuffs that rattled against the concrete floor with every step he took. The guard behind him gave him a shove to hurry him into the room.

"Come in, Coop." Cliff waved him in. "Sit down in that chair." He directed Myke with a point of his finger.

Myke couldn't understand why the chief had him brought to his office. Why not the interrogation room like all the other times? Why here? He did not notice the man sitting in the corner of the room when he entered.

"I want you to meet someone, Coop. This is Agent Ty Thomas from the FBI in Washington, DC."

Every fiber in Myke's body tensed. *FBI!* His thoughts raced. He knew enough to realize that when the FBI got involved, something big was going down. *What did Pico say when he was brought in?* A small-town death shouldn't have drawn the attention of the FBI. *What's going on here?* Myke, in deep thought, didn't hear the chief speak until he stood up and moved away from his desk.

"Agent Thomas is here and wants to talk to you in private," the chief said. "We will be right outside this door, so behave yourself, Coop."

Agent Thomas stood to his full height of six foot three inches. He wore a black knit top with the Polo logo on the left corner and tan slacks. It made Myke think of his father and the way he looked when he went off to the country club to golf.

Agent Thomas's hair was silver-white with flecks of black scattered throughout. His complexion was tan from being outdoors.

Myke stood up as Agent Thomas extended his hand. Myke's hands, still handcuffed, reached out awkwardly and took hold of his hand.

"Sorry about those handcuffs," the agent apologized. "Rules! Do you mind if I call you Myke?"

"No, sir."

fff

"Sit down, Myke. I have something to tell you." Agent Thomas paused and stared over at Myke. *A good-looking man*, Agent Thomas thought. *What a shame.*

Myke shifted uneasily in his chair. "What is it that you have to tell me?" The fear was present in Myke's eyes.

Agent Thomas seemed to become physically uncomfortable himself, and finally, he said, "I'm your mother's husband."

Myke reared back in surprise. "Excuse me?"

"I'm your mother's husband." His eyes rested on Myke's face. "You've refused to see your mother, and she's devastated. She came here to ask you for your forgiveness. She's ashamed of the way she treated you and what she did to drive you away. Your mother came here every day for almost a week. When she finally told me over the phone that you wouldn't speak to her, I flew down from DC. She's heartbroken." He paused and then leaned back in his chair. "I have gone over your case and believe that I can help you. But if you refuse your mother, we will be returning to Washington, and you're on your own. It's your choice. You decide. I hope you're a smart man. Swim this alone, and I guarantee you will go down. Sanchez has implicated you in the murder. He has turned state's evidence. Did they tell you?"

Myke hadn't heard, and a panicked expression flashed across his face. "Pico turned state's evidence! What did he say?"

"First, I need to ask you some questions. Where were you on the night of the fire?"

Myke decided then that it would be foolish to continue denying that he wasn't there. He had no idea what Pico might have told them, and he was simply tired of lying. Always be truthful, no matter what the cost. That was his mother's favorite saying. A verse he had learned long ago crept back to his memory: "The truth will set you free!" *Yeah, right*, Myke thought. *Where were you, God, when I needed you?*

Slouching back in his chair, Myke finally answered, "Yeah, I was there, and so was Pico. But we did not start the fire that burnt down Dr. Brookfield's home. We were there to break into the safe. I was told it held a lot of money. Pico said he could open it, but there was no safe in the furnace room. I've done a lot of bad things in my life but not murder."

"If you didn't set the fire, then who did?"

"It could have been an accident. I don't know. There was a storm earlier that night, it could have been lightning. But then again, I did see someone run into the barn. My feelings were that someone killed Doc and Mrs. Brookfield and set the house on fire. We just happened to be there. Our timing was all wrong. We're the victims here. I had this gut feeling that night, and how I wish I had listened to it!"

"There's got to be more to this. Why were you there that night?"

"I guess you could say to get even with Doc for firing me. And I needed the money. I was just out of prison, and I had no job. I gotta eat. Besides, I felt that Doc owed me back pay."

"Why didn't you talk to the doctor about this issue of your back pay?"

After a long pause, Myke answered, "I hated the guy for what he did to me. He helped put me behind bars, and he broke up my family. But I'm telling you, I didn't kill them or set the house on fire. I wasn't going to ask him for anything. We've been set up! We're victims too, not killers."

"Are you saying that you would have rather stolen from the doctor than confront him on your back pay?"

"I guess that's what I'm saying. But I didn't kill them."

"Can you prove that?"

"I can't prove anything. All I know is what I saw. Someone stood in the shadows watching us from the barn. At first, I thought it might be that ghost that Mrs. Brookfield talked about seeing around the barn. A woman dressed in a long green dress wearing a white bonnet and apron. Everyone knew that Mrs. Brookfield was a little off and paid no attention to her. And when I saw this dark figure standing at the barn, I thought it was that ghost that she always talked about. Pretty silly, huh? But there was something different about this ghost though. It wasn't wearing a dress."

"What do you mean by that?"

"That ghost wore pants."

Mr. Thomas cupped his hands and steepled his pointer fingers under his nose, "Okay … what about the car?"

"I only borrowed it. Before I was sent to prison, Chuck would let me borrow his car anytime he wasn't using it. I helped him rebuild that machine. His way of paying me back was letting me use the Cobra. I didn't think he'd mind. Besides, I had planned on getting it back to him before he knew it was gone."

"Why didn't you ask him if you could borrow the car? You're also facing charges of car theft on top of murder."

"It was late, and I didn't want to wake them. Like I said, I had planned on getting it back to him before morning. Anyway, didn't think he'd miss it. Besides, I filled up his tank with gas like I always did when I borrowed the car."

"You're in a lot of trouble, son."

"That's the understatement of the year, sir."

A solemn expression fell on Agent Thomas's face. He lowered his head, stared at his hands, and twisted his wedding band around his finger. He looked up at Myke, and his eyes softened. "Myke, will you talk to your mother?"

Will I talk to my mother! She ruined my life. Look at me! And you're asking me to talk to her, to be civil to her! Myke stared up at the ceiling; deep-seated anger began to stir within him. *What are you going to do, Myke?* he asked himself. *Kick a gift horse in the mouth? You wouldn't be that stupid, would you? What will it be? They want to help you. You really don't have a choice.* Clenching his teeth, Myke sucked in a deep breath and then answered, "Yeah, I'll talk to her."

"You've made a wise choice, son." Ty got up and shook Myke's hand. The handcuffs rattled with the movement.

"It's too bad that we had to meet under these circumstances. I'll get back with you as soon as I can."

Federal Agent Thomas left the room, and Ramos stepped in with a stupid smirk on his face. "So, your stepdaddy is FBI! Do you think he's going to get you off, Coop? I don't think so!"

Myke refused to acknowledge Ramos's sarcastic remark and sat staring out the window.

"Your mother is outside. You wanna see her?"

"Yeah, sure. Why not?" Myke answered.

Ramos stepped aside, and Myke's mother slipped past him into the room. Myke hadn't seen her in over ten years and didn't know what to say to her. She was still that tall, slender person, but she had dyed her hair blond. She wore blue slacks, a white blouse, and a red scarf around her neck.

Taken aback by her appearance, Myke stared at her for a long moment, and she returned the stare. The last time he'd seen her, she had been a mess. This woman standing in front of him was the woman he remembered from before his parents were divorced.

She slid into the chair next to him. She had aged; crow's-feet creased the corners of her eyes, and sadness was seeping from them.

"How did you find me?" Myke finally asked.

"The death of that doctor and his wife made national news. It was in the Washington newspaper and so was your name, implicating you in the murder."

"So, you think I did it, don't you?"

"If you tell me that you didn't do it, I will believe you."

"You believe me! Since when?"

"When times were better between us, you never lied to me, and I don't believe you would lie to me now."

"What happened to 'I told you you'd end up in jail. You're bad to the core, Myke'?"

"I should have never said those awful and hateful things to you. I have no excuse for the way I behaved." She lowered her head. "I'm truly sorry." Tears rolled down her cheek. "I was taking my anger and frustration out on you for the things your dad did to me. That was wrong."

"I didn't do it. Do you believe me?" Myke asked in a sarcastic tone.

Tears continued to roll down her cheeks, and with a stroke of her finger, she brushed them away. "Yes! I believe you." She looked directly into his eyes. "You could never lie to me with your eyes. Your eyes tell me that you're telling the truth." She looked at him sorrowfully, and in a weak voice, she asked again, "Can you ever find it in your heart to forgive me, Myke?"

He couldn't answer her. He needed time to heal, and like she said, she would know if he was lying.

She then told him of her attempt to find him years before. She had his picture put in every store window and tacked to every light post in hopes that someone would call her with his whereabouts. In her desperation, she said, she turned to God for help and gave up drinking.

"You were right, Myke. I was the town drunk. My problems drove you away." Again, she asked, "Can you find it in your heart to forgive me?" Her voice was pleading.

The diamond on her finger caught a ray of sunlight and flickered, drawing his attention to her hand. Myke quickly changed the subject. "When did you get married?"

She inhaled deeply, and a look of disappointment came over her face. Casting her eyes down at her hand, she answered, "Five years ago. Ty was a friend from the agency, and he knew I was looking for you and offered to help. You were constantly on the move. When we'd get word of where you were, you'd up and move. Then Ty saw this article in the paper and brought it to my attention. Ty's a good man, and I know you'll like him once you get to know him. He wants to help you, Myke, if you'll let him."

"Why?" Myke asked.

"Give him a chance, Myke. Ty has his connections. He is the director of the Federal Bureau of Investigation. Do you have a lawyer?"

Woo, the director of the Federal Bureau of Investigation ... He's top dog. "Yeah, a state-appointed one. I've talked to him once."

"Ty will do what he can to help you, Myke. I promise you."

Chapter 38

Brooke shook her head in anger. The senseless death of Packer King, a sixteen-year-old brought to the hospital in a comatose state, who later died on the operating table, forced open the door to a memory she so desperately fought to keep closed. Flashbacks to that dreadful night of her parents' deaths swooped down on her, engulfing her in rage. Her need to control her emotions, she rationalized, was to keep her sanity, but all the suppressed anger that lay dormant rushed to the surface. Her jaw muscles tightened. Her chest heaved in rage. *It's all so senseless!* She slouched over the scrub basin, resting her hands along the rim.

Dr. Bill Adams, with blood splattered on his surgical greens, walked into the small washroom, snapped off his latex gloves, and tossed them into the can marked "Hazardous Waste." Then he said in disgust, "What a waste of a young man's life!"

Tears poised on the bottom lids of Brooke's eyes welled into large beads, ready to pour down her cheeks. She leaned over the basin as the first drop rolled off her lashes and fell into the basin of suds. She chewed on her lower lip and was desperately trying to restrain the tears when a hiccup escaped.

"Are you all right, Brooke?" Dr. Adams asked as he removed his round wire-rimmed glasses to remove a spot of blood that had dried on the lens.

"No, I'm not all right!" A sob broke loose. "There was no need for all those senseless deaths. Why haven't the authorities torn up that old abandoned airstrip? This has been the second racing death on that tarmac! This could have been prevented." Tears gushed down her cheeks.

Droplets of tears fell into the soapy sink. "It's all so pointless. The death of my parents and now Packer ..." She choked back the sobs.

fff

Dr. Adams placed his hand on Brooke's shoulder, and she found herself in his arms in uncontrollable sobs. He understood her sorrow. Brooke's father, Dr. Brookfield, had been a close colleague. Dr. Adams had assisted Dr. Brookfield in the operating room many times. He himself was having a hard time comprehending how anyone could break into a family's home, rob them, and set their home on fire with the occupants still in bed.

No one is safe anymore, he thought.

"I'll tell Packer's parents. Get dressed and go on home, Brooke."

The hardest task any physician has to deal with is telling the parents that they were unable to save their child. Even if Packer had survived, he would have been in a vegetative state, requiring round-the-clock care. Dr. Adams loved what he did, but this was the gray area of his chosen profession. With the sad burden weighing heavily on his shoulders, he turned to his locker, stripped off the blood-splattered surgical greens, and slipped on his gray pants and white dress shirt. Hurriedly, he ran a comb through his brown hair. A worried thought leaped into his mind. Where was his son tonight? Was he with Packer and his other friends at the old airstrip?

Dr. Adams stood in the doorway of the waiting room,

sadness gripping his heart. He knew the King family well. Their sons had been friends since grade school. Barbara King's eyes were closed, her head on her husband's shoulder. Frank, Packer's father, stared up at Bill, searching his face, and gently shook Barbara awake. "Bill is here, Barb."

No words needed to be spoken. The expression on Dr. Adams's face spoke loudly. Barbara's face contorted in grief. "No, no, please, Bill ... No!"

fff

The clock on the nightstand illuminated the darkened bedroom. It was three o'clock in the morning when Brooke climbed into bed, wearily collapsing beside Cliff's sleeping body. Cliff rolled over and took Brooke into his arms.

"How is Packer doing?" Cliff asked.

"He didn't make it."

Cliff raised himself on his elbow and stared at Brooke. "He didn't make it? That's too bad." He lowered his head back onto the pillow. He sighed and said, "He was a promising young athlete with great potential. What a shame. I'll go talk to Phil Stokes sometime tomorrow about this. I'm sure that the city council members will be eager to pass a bill to have that old tarmac torn out immediately.

I don't think anyone will be opposed to that. No one in their right mind wants to see another of our young people in the morgue."

In a trembling voice, Brooke said, "The word's out that Zach Hopson may have caused both deaths out at the airstrip. He lures his classmates out to the tarmac with the promise that the winner gets a hundred dollars if they don't flinch first. He has even flashed the hundred-dollar bill around, baiting them into playing chicken. That has become a fatal game for two young men. Another death is more than I can handle at this point. I want those responsible for the death of my parents brought to justice! I want the death penalty to swing like a pendulum over their heads!" Her need for justice burned deep within her soul, and tears of anger streamed down her cheeks, soaking her pillow.

Cliff, for the first time, was at a loss for words. All he could do was hold her while she wept.

In a soft, gentle voice, he asked, "Why don't you take a leave of absence and go to San Jose to visit your aunt Martha? You've been talking about flying down to California to see her for some time now, Brooke."

"I can't do that! I can't miss the trial. I want to be in that courtroom when the verdict is read. Guilty! I want to hear the judge say 'murder in the first degree.' They are going to pay for the murder of my parents."

Chapter 39

The shackles on Sanchez's ankles jangled as he scuffled down the hall. The orange prison uniform was stamped with his cell number, 238, and his hands were handcuffed in front of him. The guard led Sanchez into a small interrogation room. The room looked much like the one in Kansas City—just as unfriendly and intimidating. Deep dread settled in his gut, causing him to feel nauseated. The guard pointed to a chair and told him to sit. Like an obedient child, he carefully wobbled over to the chair and sat.

The chief entered the room, with Detective Ramos following behind him. He felt the excitement of a hunting dog salivating before the kill.

Ramos grinned broadly. "Almost made it over the border. How did you get that fake ID using my name?"

Pico's heart quickened as his chest rose with every breath he took. He stared at a cobweb swaying in the steady stream of air coming from the air duct. He refused to make eye contact with Ramos. He felt great hate for this man standing a few feet away from him. *A Chicano turncoat!* Pico wanted to spit on the floor but thought that such an act would only make the Chicano strike out at him.

The chief sat back, quietly watching Sanchez. His fingers meshed together; his elbows rested on the armrest of the chair. When the chief finally spoke, Sanchez's eyes shifted from the web to the chief's face.

"Coop said that you robbed and killed the Brookfield's and then burned down their home to cover up the murder." Pausing, the chief waited for a response. Then he added, "Coop has turned state's evidence. You're going down for this."

Sanchez glared. *I know this game very well, and so does Myke. We're not stupid kids. You'll get nothing from me, and I'm sure Myke didn't turn state's evidence. I'll tell you nothing.*

"He also said that you have been convicted for arson and theft and that you spent time in the pen for it. Looking at your records here, he's not making that part up."

Pico sat stone-faced. *Who do they think they're kidding?*

"Did you kill them like Coop claimed?" Ramos asked, slamming the report down on the table.

"No!" Sanchez angrily answered. "I didn't set the fire or kill the Brookfield's!"

Ramos pointed to the report. "I have in front of me your records showing you were sent to the state prison in Leavenworth in 1987. You spent twelve years in prison and got out early on good behavior, and now this. You're a menace to society, Sanchez."

Yeah right, Myke turned state's evidence and the report sitting in front of you—fabricated, all fabricated. "I was framed!" Pico stated.

"That's what they all say." Ramos smiled.

"I don't remember breaking into that house or setting the place on fire."

"The reason you don't remember, Sanchez," Ramos cut in, "is because you were high on cocaine. Isn't that, right? It's all right here in this report."

A nervous twitch jerked Sanchez's head toward his

shoulder. "I don't remember anything. This guy loaded me up with cocaine, and the next morning, I'm in jail on arson charges and attempted murder. I gave all this information to the cops in Kansas City. I gave them the description of this guy Hank, and they did nothing with it. I'm a paid informant. Talk to Detective Fuller; he'll tell you. But they didn't believe me, and I went to prison! Like I said, I don't remember. I was set up to take the fall. I was the patsy."

"Then what you are saying is that you and Coop were in the wrong place at the wrong time and took the fall for the death of Doc and his wife? Is that what you are saying?" the chief asked.

"Yeah, that's what I am saying! We killed no one here in Manhattan. And I did not kill anyone in Kansas City. And I have never taken cocaine in my life. I don't remember anything other than waking up in jail, slapped with those charges."

"Enough of that case in Kansas City. We're talking about the murder here in Manhattan. How do you explain the fingerprints on the safe? You broke into the Brookfield's home, killed the Brookfield's, and then dragged the safe to the barn. To cover up the murder, you and Coop set the place on fire with them in bed, didn't you?" Ramos hollered at Sanchez.

What safe? There was no safe in the furnace room, and we wore gloves. Oh man, we're being framed! "No!" Pico spat out in anger. "I was on my way to Mexico two days before the fire. Cooper did it! I had nothing to do with it!"

"We checked the bus station records. You left two days after the fire, not two days before. Can you explain that?" Ramos asked.

"The bus station records are wrong! I'm not lying to you. I remember the broad asking me what date it was. She even laughed and said she couldn't remember eating lunch that day. As big as she was, how could she forget she didn't eat? She must have written down the date wrong."

The chief broke in. "Where did you get the money for the bus fare?"

"I had some money. It was enough to get me down to San Diego and over the border."

Then Ramos asked, "When you were caught trying to enter Tijuana, you had five hundred dollars on you. Where did you get that kind of money, and how did you get that fake ID to get over the border?"

"I worked for two weeks. When I got my paycheck, I quit."

"You quit your job ... From what personnel have on your records, you skipped out the day Coop was arrested at the warehouse. How do you explain that, my friend?"

I am not your friend! How am I going to get myself out of this mess? Sanchez thought. *I'm not going to take the rap for murder. I'm not going down easy.* His eyes darted from one face to another. *Oh, precious Jesus, help me out of this mess! I promise I'll turn my life around if only you'll help me, Lord. I promise!*

ƒ ƒ ƒ

The heat of the early afternoon caused Dottie Thomas's eyelids to flutter with sleep. Her husband had been gone longer than expected. It would have been smarter to wait inside the station where it was cooler than in this hot car. Shaking the sleep from her eyes, she saw the front door swing open from the rearview mirror. Ty walked toward the car, and she could see the agitation on his face. *It must not have gone well*, she thought. Ty slammed the door shut.

She then asked, "Is everything all right?"

Ty gripped the steering wheel and spoke through clenched teeth. "No, it's not! Your son is being railroaded for murder!"

"Railroaded? What do you mean railroaded?"

"It seems that the fifth fingerprint found on the safe was never sent off to Washington to be identified." He shook his head in disgust. "It's a good thing I went down to the forensic department to talk to Dr. Blanton after talking to your son."

"Is that why you took so long? What made you go down to see Dr. Blanton?" she asked in a voice tinged with deep concern.

"It's what Myke said. He said they never saw a safe in the furnace room. It looked to them like it had been moved. Myke's and Pico's prints could not have been found on that safe. I don't like it … I asked Dr. Blanton why the print had never been sent off. His lame excuse was that he went on vacation. He said he turned it over to his assistant, and, for some ungodly reason, it never was sent off. I don't buy it!" Ty held up the slide for Dottie to see. "I'm taking it to Washington myself to make sure it doesn't get buried under all their paperwork like it did here. They're moving quickly on his case, and it smells to high heaven. We've got to get that fingerprint identified before Myke must appear before a judge and jury. I'm sorry, Dottie. Here I am just rattling on, and I didn't ask you how your meeting went with your son."

"He's not ready to forgive me yet. I can understand his anger. It will take some time."

Mixed emotions churned through Dottie. She was pleased that Ty had taken an interest in her son's welfare and that he was making a great effort to try to clear her son of the murder charges. But worry also overwhelmed her. From what Ty had said, they were moving too quickly to set a trial date. Without Ty's help, Myke was facing the death penalty if they couldn't find enough evidence to prove him innocent of the charges against him. Desperate to put the shattered puzzle pieces of their lives back together, Dottie was willing to do anything to help her son.

Ty added, "My gut feeling tells me that your son is telling the truth. He didn't kill the doctor and his wife. Myke may have seen the killer out there that night. It's too bad that he didn't get a good look at that person."

Chapter 40

Leaning over the packing box, Nicole placed a neatly wrapped dish on top of another. The phone rang, and she straightened up, blowing a strand of hair out of her face in annoyance. *Who could that be?* Pausing, she contemplated whether to answer it. *It could be Reid*, she thought. It rang again, and she reached over and picked up the receiver.

Nicole answered, "Yes, I can come in tomorrow, Ms. Shoemaker. I'll see you at nine thirty tomorrow morning." She heard the click on the other end.

Huh, why couldn't Ms. Shoemaker tell me over the phone what she wanted? she wondered. *Why in her office tomorrow?* She didn't ponder the question for very long. Old newspapers were stacked on the dining room table. *Why do I put things off? I should have had this done already.*

Cuddles stood next to the table, crouching low. She watched the paper wobble at the edge of the table and slowly glided to the floor. She made a mad dash for it and slid across the wooden floor. Nicole laughed and rustled the paper. "Silly kitty."

Early for her appointment, Nicole made her way up to the second floor. The old wooden steps creaked on her way up. Her thoughts blocked out the sound. *Did I misfile a case that Ms. Shoemaker couldn't find or type up a document incorrectly? No, that can't be the problem. If that were the case, she would have asked me to come to the office yesterday. Well, you'll find out soon enough,* she told herself.

At the door, she stopped to look at the familiar bold black letters: Alexis Shoemaker, Esq. She placed her hand on the doorknob and pushed the door wide open. A young woman sat at Nicole's desk.

Well, she thought. *It didn't take Ms. Shoemaker very long to find a replacement.* Her heart sank, and she swallowed hard.

"Can I help you?" the young woman asked.

Nicole cleared her throat. "I'm Nicole Martin, here to see Ms. Shoemaker."

"Oh, yes! She's expecting you, and I am so happy to meet you! I'm Tracy. You're going to be a hard person to live up to. Ms. Shoemaker speaks very highly of you and your work for her."

"She does?" Nicole smiled in surprise. *And here I thought she was calling me for something she couldn't find.*

"Yeah, she does," Tracy said. "She told me that you were going home for the summer and would be back in the fall."

"Oh, so you're here only for the summer?"

"Yeah, I fill in where I can. I'm a Longhorn, also home for the summer. I'll tell Ms. Shoemaker that you're here."

"Thank you." Nicole exhaled in relief. *Then why does she have to see me?* Nicole wondered.

"You can go in." Tracy smiled.

Alexis sat at her desk writing on a notepad when she heard Nicole enter the room. She waved Nicole over to a chair. "Nicole, I'm so glad that you were able to make it in this morning on such short notice."

"It's okay. I'm just packing. My grandparents were called out of town unexpectedly yesterday and won't be back for a couple of weeks. So, I'm in no hurry to get back to an empty house."

Nicole sat in the chair that Alexis had pointed to. Small talk passed between them. Alexis then stiffened in her chair, and a mask of professionalism came over her. "The reason I called you in, Nicole, is to tell you that in an hour, there will be the reading of Dr. Brookfield's will."

"I don't understand. What does it have to do with me?" Nicole asked with a confused look on her face.

"Dr. Brookfield wanted to shield you from all of this, but I simply can't see how that can be done. Questions will be asked, and knowing Jesse, Dr. Brookfield's son, who is also an attorney, he's going to want proof."

"Proof? Proof of what?"

"That Dr. Brookfield was your father."

Nicole's hand went to her mouth, and she stared at Alexis, a look of bewilderment on her face.

"Nicole, are you all right?"

"Well …" Nicole paused. "I've had my suspicions after I saw him here at the office. And after Pastor Ward gave the eulogy at their funeral, Reid suggested that I go and talk to him. I made the appointment with Pastor Ward because I got the impression that he knew Dr. and Mrs. Brookfield and that they were good friends. Pastor Ward did confirm that Dr. Brookfield was indeed my father."

"I wondered if you had any suspicions. You looked very troubled that morning, and I'm glad that Pastor Ward was able to answer your questions. I've asked you to come because Doc has provided for you. You will share in the inheritance. I'm sorry, Nicole, to have to ask you to do this. Knowing Jesse, he will ask for your DNA. I feel that it would be in your best interest to get this done as soon as possible."

Nicole hardly heard a word. She sat numb, staring off with a blank look on her face. Her chest rose and fell in bewilderment.

"Nicole?"

Nicole's eyes shifted back to Alexis. "So, Alexis you think that Jesse will question my rights to the inheritance?" Nicole's voice cracked in anger. "I was not aware of any of this until now. I didn't ask for it. Well ... okay, let's get this over with. When do you want me to get this done?"

"I didn't think you'd fight this. I've made an appointment for you at one thirty this afternoon. Is that all right with you?"

"Yes, that will be just fine. I can finally put this question of who I am to rest." Nicole sank back into the chair, gathering her thoughts.

Sensing her discomfort, Alexis said, "It's just a technicality. Everything will be just fine. Jesse is the only obstacle I believe that you will have to deal with. I wanted to speak to you before Dr. Brookfield's children came in this morning. There is one other person besides family members mentioned in the will." Alexis's phone rang, and she picked up the phone. "Thank you, Tracy." Turning to Nicole, she said, "They're here."

fff

Brooke led the way up the creaky stairs, followed by her husband, Cliff. Behind Cliff, Jenner, Morgan, and Jesse trailed, holding up the rear. Their somber mood marred the day.

Mattie Cooper sat at her desk working on the business ledger. She looked up when she heard the procession on the stairs and noted the time. A sudden sharp pang of guilt flooded through her, and she dropped her head.

Oh, Myke, why did you do it? How can I face them? It was time for her to join the group in Alexis Shoemaker's office. She dreaded the thought of being in the same room with Dr. Brookfield's children because of what her ex-husband had done.

Cliff held the door open for Brooke, and she walked in. "We're here to see Ms. Shoemaker. We have a nine thirty appointment."

"Ms. Shoemaker is expecting you. Go right in," Tracy said.

Brooke walked over to the door, turned the knob, and pushed it open. As she entered, she drew back with a start.

A young woman sat in a chair across from Alexis.

Cliff walked into Brooke. "Come on. Go on in." He gave her a little push. When she wouldn't budge, he peered over her shoulder. "Oh!" He looked over at Alexis. "Are we early?"

"Oh, no. Please come in and have a seat."

Morgan stepped forward to see what was going on and asked, "Are we going to stand in the doorway or go in?" Walking around Brooke and Cliff, she found herself a seat.

Brooke could not take her eyes off Nicole. She felt as if she were looking into a mirror and seeing herself.

"Come, come," Alexis said. "Please come in and sit."

Cliff took hold of Brooke's hand and led her to a chair with Mattie following behind. Mattie squeezed around the closing door, entered the conference room, and shut the door behind her.

"Glad you joined us, Mattie." Alexis smiled at her. "Sit next to Nicole."

Mattie nodded and sat.

Nicole looked over at Mattie. *She must be the one Alexis started telling me about. I've seen her. Her office is a couple of doors down.* The others in the room didn't seem to pay much attention to the other woman who had just entered behind them.

Cliff spoke. "Who is this young lady, and why is she here?" He stared over at Nicole.

Alexis didn't know how to put it delicately and decided to be forthright with them. "This is your half-sister, Nicole."

Nicole looked at the faces that stared at her open-mouthed in disbelief. A voice rang out in anger, startling Nicole. "Why, this is absurd, Alexis!" Jesse snapped. "Why didn't you tell me, us …" He looked at his sisters. "That you were going to drop a bomb on all of us this morning? Or, for that matter, forewarn me about this young woman?"

"Now, Jesse, you as a lawyer should know that I am unable to divulge this kind of information before the reading of the will!" Alexis snapped. "As a lawyer, you don't get privileged information on this case, even when you're directly involved. Now, calm down, Jesse!"

Mattie, seeing the discomfort etched on Nicole's face, reached over and squeezed her hand gently. Nicole turned, looked at her, giving her a weak smile, and thanked her. She felt as if someone was staring at her, and she looked over at Cliff. He was glaring down at her. The look on his face sent a shiver down her spine.

In a tight and controlled voice, Cliff asked Alexis, "Why is she here? Did I hear you correctly say that she is their half-sister? And what other surprises do you have in your hat for us, Alexis? We know why Mattie is here, but why her?" He looked back at Nicole. His right eyebrow raised in objection. Brooke stared at Nicole with a curious look, and Morgan seemed to just sit there staring at Nicole.

What is going through their minds? Nicole wondered. *If only I could read their thoughts. Oh no, on second thought, I wouldn't want to read what they are thinking.*

fff

Tears welled up in Mattie's eyes. Doc had been good to her. He had become like a second father to her. In the will, he had left her the house on Sunset and twenty thousand dollars. Mattie was overwhelmed with gratitude.

Mattie reflected back to that day, which was a bit of a haze in her memory. All she remembered was a car coming at her as she fled for her life. Myke, in a drunken rage, threatened to kill her and the children. When she finally woke from the coma she had been in, she saw Dr. Brookfield leaning over her with a stethoscope at her chest. From that day on, Doc took Mattie and her children to his bosom. Doc went to court and made sure that Myke didn't get away with attempted murder. He took her and the children out of that depressing environment of poverty and moved her to a better neighborhood.

Nicole was to share equally in the family inheritance and it would not have happened if Alex hadn't told Doc that she was unable to add Nicole's name to the will without Sharon's signature. Doc in his crafty way of speaking to Sharon talked her into signing the will, willingly and unread.

Alexis set documents in front of Nicole and Mattie. "Sign here, and you can go."

Nicole and Mattie moved quickly. They just wanted to get out of that office and away from the family. They rushed out the door closing it behind them. Nicole and Mattie could hear loud voices coming from behind the closed door.

Oh my, Nicole thought, looking over at Mattie. "They are not too happy in there, are they?"

Mattie shook her head. Sadness reflected on her face. "I'm going to truly miss Doc, and so will my children. He was my friend and a grandpa to my children. It will never be the same without him."

Nicole smiled sadly. "I never got to know him. He was the dad I always longed for …"

"I'm truly sorry, Nicole. You would have really loved him. He was a good man." They embraced. "Welcome to the family, Nicole. You will always be welcome in my home." They departed, promising to keep in touch.

Darting down the stairs, Nicole stepped out into the sunlight. Relief fell over her, and she was glad to be away from those eyes filled with what she interpreted as contempt.

fff

Reid sat at the window of Rick's Café waiting for her. He stood when he saw her come out of the building and waved at her. Upon seeing him, Nicole rushed across the street and into the café.

With concern in his voice, Reid asked, "How'd it go, and why did Ms. Shoemaker want to talk to you?"

Plopping down in the chair next to him, she said, "Oh, it was awful, Reid. The way they looked at me, it made me feel like I had done something dreadfully wrong. They hate me, Reid!"

"What are you talking about?" he asked.

From the window of the café, Nicole saw Dr. Brooke Kaufmann step out onto the walkway, followed by her husband, Cliff, and her sisters, Morgan and Jenner. Morgan glanced across the street and saw Nicole sitting in the café, and she nodded in Nicole's direction. Heads turned to stare, and Nicole quickly looked away.

"They must hate me." Nicole sighed deeply. "Jesse insinuated that I am 'questionable,' their father's illegitimate daughter, their half-sister. Jesse and Cliff, they are upset because Dr. Brookfield put me in his will. I will get an equal portion. Alexis told me that she thought it would be in my best interest to have the DNA done to prove that I am Dr. Brookfield's biological daughter."

"Is that the reason Ms. Shoemaker called you into the office this morning?" A sympathetic frown was on his face. "Man, that must have been a shocker for you to find out that Dr. Brookfield added you into his will."

"Can you imagine the shock for them?" Nicole added.

"Yeah, a real big shock. When do you have to go in for the DNA test?" Reid asked.

"This afternoon at two thirty. Oh, they're coming this way, Reid. What are we going to do? Should we slip out the back door?"

"No, what back door? I think you should meet the challenge head-on. I'll leave if you want me to."

Panic flashed through Nicole's eyes. "No, please don't leave me alone with them!"

"They just walked through the door," Reid said.

"Oh, what am I going to do?" Nicole whispered.

"Nothing. They may be coming in for a cup of coffee like us. But on second thought, they're headed this way."

Brooke stopped in front of their table. "Can we talk?"

"Ah, yeah, sure. This is my boyfriend, Reid Starr." *I wonder where big brother Jesse is!* Nicole thought.

ƒƒƒ

Reid was startled by Nicole's remark. *Her boyfriend!* He had never heard her refer to him as her boyfriend before, and he liked it. He rolled it over in his head. Her boyfriend ... It took on a much more intimate sound, and he smiled to himself.

"Let's move over to a larger table in that corner, shall we?"

Reid and Nicole looked at each other.

"Sure," Nicole answered.

They stood and followed the others to a round table in the corner.

A waitress came by, and they all ordered coffee.

"Well," Brooke said, "this turned out to be quite an awakening for all of us to find out that we have a half-sister. Daddy had secrets that we were unaware of."

Nicole looked around at their faces. Morgan, who looked to be around her age, seemed more curious than upset. She even seemed to smile at her, which helped ease Nicole's discomfort. Brooke did most of the talking for the family. Cliff sat stone-faced and seemed to be sizing up the situation. Nicole immediately did not like him. Brooke, Jenner, and Morgan seemed nice enough though, and she felt more at ease with them.

And Ms. Shoemaker said that Jesse would want a DNA done. Can't he see the resemblance between his sister and Nicole? Reid glanced over at Nicole, then back at Brooke, and shook his head. He was trying not to be so obvious, but everyone noticed. *They must see the likeness between Brooke and Nicole*, Reid thought. Reid was annoyed. *I can't believe that he would put her through this.* He must be in denial, blind, or greedy.

Satisfied with their meeting, Brooke rose and pushed back her chair, and the others followed suit. "I'll get the check. The coffee is on me."

"Thank you!" Nicole said.

When they left, Nicole sighed in relief. "That wasn't so bad, but I'm glad it's over with."

"Boyfriend, huh?" Reid smiled.

"A slip of the tongue." She blushed.

"I like it, girlfriend … How about lunch? You're in no hurry, are you?"

"I've got that appointment this afternoon."

"I'll take you, if that's all right with you."

"I'd like that."

Chapter 41

Today, Myke was to appear before the judge. Deep dread gnawed in his gut. Nothing good ever happened in a courtroom from his experience.

The bailiff went over to a side door and knocked. The door opened, and Myke Cooper was led into the courtroom, escorted by the sheriff. Myke was wearing the county-issued orange jumpsuit. His eyes were cast to the floor in humiliation. The leg cuffs rattled against the wooden floor with every step he took. The handcuffs hung in front of him. Myke walked past the plaque of the Ten Commandments hanging on the wall, and he glanced up. His eyes came to rest on the sixth commandment: "Thou shalt not kill."

You know all things, Lord. So, you know that I killed no one. I am an innocent man!

The sheriff led Myke to the table where his new lawyer, Tim Bancroft, sat. Mr. Bancroft pointed to the handcuffs. "Remove them."

The guard took the keys hanging from his belt and removed them from Myke's wrists. He then slipped the cuffs over his belt and stepped back against the wall.

A hand came down on Myke's shoulder, and someone whispered in his ear, "Sorry, we're late." Dottie, Myke's mother, gently gave his shoulder a reassuring squeeze, and she and his stepfather, Ty, sat directly behind Myke.

The look on her face took him back to his childhood. That sweet smile he remembered from long ago had vanished after his parents' divorce. His heart ached with sorrow for all those lost years.

Myke was Dottie's only child, and she had spoiled him with love in the early years. He ran his fingers through his hair as fond memories rushed back. She'd tousle his hair as he walked out the door to the bus stop and put those little notes in his lunch box—notes of encouragement, a poem to brighten his day or simply to say, "I love you, Son, and I'll see you this evening."

Today in the courtroom, Myke had seen another look behind her smile. The expression in her eyes was one of pain and fear.

Myke's attorney had been watching him. With concern, he asked, "Are you all right, Cooper?"

"Yeah, I'm okay," Myke answered.

"All rise!" The bailiff's voice echoed through the chamber. All those present in the room rose to their feet as Judge Grant Collin entered the courtroom. Judge Collin, a tall man with thinning white hair, wore wire-rimmed glasses that sat low on his nose. The long black robe swished against his pant legs as he walked over to the bench. Before sitting, he ran his finger across the docket list. He looked over his glasses at the accused.

"The District of Riley County versus Myke Cooper," the bailiff announced.

Myke's lawyer, a slender man of average height in his mid-thirties with dark hair, stood and spoke. "Tim Bancroft for the defense, Your Honor."

The prosecuting attorney, short and plump in stature and with salt-and-pepper hair, pushed back his chair. The legs of the chair screeched against the wood floor like chalk against a blackboard. "Scott Dunne, prosecuting attorney, Your Honor."

"How does the defendant plead on the charges placed against him in the theft, arson, and murder of Dr. and Mrs. Brookfield?"

"We plead not guilty, Your Honor! And we request that Mr. Cooper be let out on bail, Your Honor."

Judge Collin looked over at the prosecuting attorney.

"Your Honor, the state requests that bail be denied on the grounds that Mr. Cooper is a flight risk."

Judge Collin lowered his glasses and looked over at Cooper. "I agree with you on that account. Bail denied. This court will set a trial date to commence on June 28." The gavel came down on the plate with a loud bang that resonated throughout the chamber.

Myke stood and turned to face his mother. She looked drained and tired. No words passed between them.

The sheriff came up behind Myke. "It's time to go. Let me have your wrists."

Myke obediently held out his hands, and the handcuffs were clamped tightly shut.

"Don't lose heart, Myke. Ty is doing everything he can to help you." Dottie smiled weakly.

"We'll get back to you real soon on our findings," Ty added with a more positive note. "Be patient! We're doing everything we can on this end to prove your innocence."

"Thank you for your help and for believing my story."

fff

Myke was led away, and Dottie watched her son disappear behind the closing door. Pangs of remorse coursed through her stomach. She placed her fingers on her lips as a soft sob escaped. Ty gathered his wife into his arms and held her tightly against his chest.

Mr. Bancroft stood for a moment, watching the scene. Clearing his throat, he extended his hand awkwardly. "I gather you're Cooper's parents. It's good to finally meet you, Mr. and Mrs. Thomas."

Ty took a firm grip on the extended hand. "Just call me Ty. This is my wife, Dottie. Thanks for taking on this case. You've come highly recommended as the best lawyer in this county."

Dottie unfolded from her husband's embrace and extended her hand in gratitude.

"Aren't you out of your jurisdiction?" Tim asked with a grin.

"A little bit." Ty smiled.

"Well, what did you find out in DC?" Tim asked.

"A lot!" Ty looked around him. "Is it safe to talk here?"

"Nope, reporters close by. Come with me. We can discuss this over lunch."

ƒƒƒ

Tim eased his car into the vacant spot in front of Harry's Fortress. The old red-brick building renovated years ago depicted a mix of the gothic architecture of the twelfth and sixteenth centuries. Buttresses were built against the outside walls with pointed arches. Inside, a large tapestry rug hung on the wall, depicting kings in battle. A vaulted ceiling and heavy columns graced the entry and hallway. Soft, low lights could be seen in the dining room.

They were early, and the restaurant was nearly empty of people. The host, wearing a black suit and black tie, stood at a small podium. "A table for three?" he asked.

"Yes," Tim answered.

"Booth or a table?"

"Is that booth available?" Tim pointed to the back of the restaurant.

"Yes, it is. Follow me." The waiter pulled three menus out and tucked them under his arm as he led the way.

Ty scanned the area before sitting down. A lone man sat in a booth in front of theirs. Dottie slid in, and Ty removed his jacket. After hanging it on the post of the booth, he sat next to Dottie while Tim slid into the seat in front of them.

fff

Reid, sitting in the next booth, caught sight of the shoulder revolver strapped to the man's chest. He didn't think much of it, only that they could be police.

fff

A moment of small talk passed between them, and Tim finally asked, "What did you find out in Washington?"

"I believe we've got a positive ID on that one fingerprint that was taken from the safe. I had to fly to Washington to make sure that this print didn't get lost again. It belongs to one Bud Kramer, also known as Dallas Wilcox. It seems that Wilcox got himself into trouble while in the army. He went to Leavenworth on attempted murder charges. Myke is innocent of the murders. I've got the evidence right there." Ty pointed at his jacket pocket.

Ty's attention was drawn to an attractive young woman standing in the archway. The light reflected off her auburn hair. The expression on her face told him that she had found the one she had been looking for.

Dottie followed his gaze. "What a beautiful young woman!" she said.

Quick with his words, Ty smiled and answered, "Yes, she is, but not as beautiful as you are!"

fff

Nicole stepped away from the light and into the dimly lit room, sauntering toward a table, her auburn hair bouncing with every step she took. She slid her slender body into the booth. "Have you been waiting long?" she asked Reid.

The waitress approached their table. "Are you ready to order?"

"No. My bill please," Reid said.

"Your bill … sir?" the waitress asked in a surprised tone.

"Yes, my bill, thank you!" Reid demanded.

"I'll get it right away." The waitress looked over at Nicole.

Nicole felt the stare of the waitress on her and refused to look up. *Why is he so angry?* She looked at her wristwatch. *I'm only a couple of minutes late.*

The waitress turned and left. Nicole then looked up at Reid. "I didn't think I was that late! Are you angry?"

On seeing the waitress coming toward them, Reid said to her, "We'll talk about it later."

The waitress placed the black folder in front of Reid. "Thank you and have a good day."

Reid slipped a few bills into the folder, letting it fall closed.

"Let's go!" Reid took Nicole by the elbow and led her through the archway.

Once outside, Nicole asked, tears brimming in her eyes, "What happened in there, and what is the matter with you?"

"Cops were sitting in the booth behind us."

"How do you know that?"

"They were talking about a fingerprint that had to be sent off. One said that they finally got the report back, and they think they know who killed Dr. and Mrs. Brookfield."

"But the newspaper reported that they've got the person that set the fire and killed the Brookfield's. What made you think they were cops?"

"I saw the gun one had strapped to his body. One may have been Mr. Cooper's lawyer and the other a detective or cop from what I could make out. I don't think they believe that Mr. Cooper set the fire or killed the Brookfield's."

"Who was the woman?"

"That, I don't know. All I heard her say when you walked in was that you were a beautiful woman."

Nicole blushed. "Hmm." She looked back at Harry's. "It would have been nice if you would have allowed me to make the choice as to whether to stay or not instead of rushing me out the door."

"I'm sorry, Nicole. I thought it would be too upsetting for you," Reid answered.

"Reid, I'm a big girl! Besides"—Nicole crossed her arms across her chest—"he meant nothing to me. He gave me his DNA, and that was all he did for me. I have no ties to him or my half-brother and sisters. They're just faces in a crowd like I am to them. Just a face."

"Well," he said, "I did what I thought was best for you. Finding your long-lost father, then poof, he's gone just like that. You've had a hard time dealing with their deaths. I'm sorry I spoiled your lunch. What can I say to make things right?"

"Jeez, Reid …" Her voice tightened with irritation.

"If you like, we can go back to Harry's." He looked down at her with pleading and apologetic eyes.

Her irritation began to slowly ebb when she looked into his pleading eyes. How could she stay angry with this man? Sighing, she finally yielded. "Let's just go get a sandwich down the street."

Reid smiled down at her and took her arm. "Wow! Remind me not to push the wrong button on you!"

Chapter 42

The high-pitched sound of the unoiled hinge on the cell door squeaked eerily as it clanked shut behind Myke. The sound sent a quiver through his flesh. He stared at the graffiti written on the white walls and shook his head. He looked around him, and his eyes fell on the familiar handwriting—his own.

He read, "The force of hate is greater than love! I'll see you in hell, Mattie."

The day he had written that, he had vowed he'd kill Mattie and Doc. His rage ran deep, and his chest heaved in remembrance as he stared at the message he wrote. It seemed like umpteen years ago. He did not want to reflect on that time in his life. The drunkenness, drugs, and abuse he inflicted on Mattie were all in the past, and he wanted to make things right again with her.

He read on, "Need a good listening ear and bail money? Call Grammy at 785-3652." *That's a new one*, he thought, and he smiled. "Hey, Grammy, I could sure use some money. Whaddya, you say, Grammy? Maybe I'll give you a call." He snickered.

The next message caught his attention. "The eyes of God are upon you. Repent of your sins or go to hell. Sin is sin."

Still another read, "Reverend makes national news; God hates all fags, but the Bible says that God loves everyone. God does not hate fags, only the sin they indulge in! Judge not lest ye be judged, Reverend!"

Yeah, Myke thought. *That reverend has turned up quite a stir. And just think of all those followers he has swayed into believing that lie. Pretty sad. A grisly testimony to the perversion of a man's soul in this century.*

Myke was debating as to whether he should add another testimony to the wall until the holding cell door squeaked open, and a prison guard stepped in. "Ready to go, Cooper?"

"Do I have a choice?" he answered smugly.

"In this place, you have no choice. You do as you're told!" the guard sarcastically answered.

Chapter 43

Nicole eased her car alongside the road and shifted into park. She desperately needed a moment to collect herself. Her world seemed to be crashing in around her. The weather fit her mood. The unseasonable, oppressive heat in the air promised a sultry afternoon. She felt as if she had climbed aboard a roller coaster plunging down a steep incline at a horrific speed and throwing her into a spiraling spin.

A ride that seems to never end. Let me off! Why did this have to happen to me? Sometimes I wish I had never gone in search of my identity! This has caused me more grief than

I'm ready to deal with in my life. That day Dr. Brookfield walked into the office, he carried himself in such a way that gave him an air of prominence. And his eyes ... his blue eyes glimmered with amusement as he walked toward me. I could not take my eyes off him. There was something about that man. In deep and troubling thought, she sighed as she remembered Doc walking up to her desk, introducing himself, and asking her name. Now, she recalled the glimmer in his eyes that went suddenly from delight to shock. He had taken a step back, groping for words, and then finally asked, "Is your mother's name Loretta Martin?"

When he asked where she was from, a pained and crooked smile creased his face. Sorrow filled his eyes. She would never forget that look in his eyes. It was forever engraved in her memory.

Shhh, Nicole! Get a grip, will ya! Slumping back in her seat, she watched the cars zoom past, headed for town. Her cell phone rang. She picked up the phone and answered, "This is Nicole."

"Nicole, this is Reid. Where are you?"

"I'm pulled over alongside Highway 24, heading out of town."

"What do you mean, alongside the road? Did your car break down? Did you have an accident?"

"No, I'm just feeling sorry for myself."

"What's going on?"

"I'm having a pity party. Wanna join me?" Her voice cracked with emotion.

"Why a pity party? Wanna talk about it?"

"I just feel as if my world has slipped off its axis, that's all." Nicole hiccupped and tried hard to suppress a sob.

"Explain yourself."

"I'm just confused right now. I can't think straight. Everything seems distorted in my life, and my emotions are in shambles. Why did my mother hide the truth from me, Reid?" Nicole placed her fingers across her mouth to keep her lips from trembling. "I've become so emotional it's beginning to scare me!"

"Don't be so hard on yourself, Nicole! You're not alone. All you've got to do is ask, and you know I'll come to you no matter where you are. You do know that, don't you?"

"Oh, Reid." Nicole cradled the phone on her shoulder. Her hand went to her forehead, and her fingers raked through her hair as she rested her head back against the headrest. "You cannot believe how much that really means to me for you to have said that. You are the first real friend that I have been able to really talk to since I moved here. Thank you for being a good listener and my friend." She sniffled and brushed away the steady stream of tears that flowed down her cheeks.

"I had hoped that I was more than just a friend, Nicole."

"I guess I didn't phrase that right. You're more than just a friend, Reid." Nicole looked up at the street sign and bolted upright, nearly losing the phone from her shoulder. She fumbled for words and finally asked, "Dr. Brookfield …"

"Yeah, what about him?"

"Do you remember his street address?"

"Why?"

"I'm just asking."

"The phone book is right here. Do you want me to look it up for you?"

"Could you please?"

There was a long pause as Reid flipped through the pages. He read her the street address. "What are you up to?" There was a pause. "Nicole, are you there?"

"Yes, I'm here."

"Are you okay?"

"Yeah, I'm okay now."

"Let's talk. Meet me at the Sweet Shop on Tuttle. It should not put you too far behind schedule. Besides, your grandparents aren't there, right?"

"No, they're not. But I don't like driving after sundown. I'll call you when I get home."

"All right. You drive carefully."

A coiling cloud of dust spiraled in the wake of an oncoming white truck. The truck came to a stop at the crossroad, and the driver cast a momentary look in Nicole's direction. He then glanced north and south for oncoming traffic and then back at Nicole. Smiling, he tipped his black cowboy hat and then accelerated, screeching the tires and leaving black tire marks burnt into the asphalt. The cowboy threw back his head and hollered, "Yahoo!" He sped off down the highway, headed for town.

"Show-off!" Nicole hissed. A blanket of dust settled on the hood of her car.

Chapter 44

The patrol car pulled alongside the unloading ramp of the county jail. Myke was led into the building and down to the lower level, where the other inmates were housed. A loud buzz ricocheted down the row of cells as the gate opened. The smell that permeated the air reminded him of the high school locker room. He twitched his nose at the smell of waste and body odor and said to himself, "So long, fresh air."

An inmate jeered as Myke walked past. "Hey, Coop! I heard that the judge that sent you up to the big house is an old buddy of Doc's. If he's the judge that gets your case again, you haven't got a prayer."

The guard removed his baton from his belt and struck the bars. "That's enough of that, Beckman!"

Beckman jumped back with profanity spewing from his mouth.

At Myke's cell door, the guard ordered Myke's cellmate to move back against the wall. Hammer did as he was told and moved to the far corner of the cell. The guard unlocked the door. Myke stepped into the cell, and the door closed behind him.

Hammer's skin was almond in color, and he was of mixed heritage. He was the tallest man Myke had ever seen at nearly seven feet tall. He walked over to the cell door and sucked air between his teeth. "One day, just give me a minute with that guard alone." Hammer's biceps rippled as he tightened his grip on the bars, watching the guard walk through the main gate. The buzz resounded loudly, and the guard disappeared around the corner with the gate slamming shut behind him.

Hammer turned and looked at Myke. A hideous snake was tattooed on Hammer's bicep. It curled up from his wrist as if it were slithering up his arm. Its tongue slithered out of its mouth at his shoulder. Its small red eyes seemed to focus on Myke, sending a shiver through him. Myke had done many crazy things in his life, but getting a tattoo was not one of them.

Hammer asked, "What's the verdict?"

Myke cursed. "They're holding me over for trial without bail. They're saying I'm a flight risk!" His nostrils flared as he snarled in anger. "Gonna have to stay in this smelly hole with you!"

"Hey, shut the hell up!" Hammer shot back, glaring at Myke. "I'm really a nice guy. Have I messed with you?"

"Yeah, right! You're a real good guy, all right. I can't imagine why you're in this smelly hole!"

Hammer flung the rolled-up magazine onto his cot and then flexed his tattooed biceps. The tongue of the snake seemed to quiver as if ready to strike.

In a low, hissing voice, Hammer said, "I'm going to ignore what you just said because you had a bad day, but …" Hammer walked over to Myke and stuck his long finger into his chest, backing him against the wall. "Do it again, and I'll hammer you, and you'll understand why they call me Hammer!" Hammer cursed and spit splattered into Myke's eye. "Do you understand me, Coop?"

Wiping his eye, Myke answered, "Yeah."

"Yeah, what!" Hammer glared at Myke.

"Yeah, I understand!" Myke adjusted his shirt and swallowed hard.

"I'm glad we have an understanding!" Breathing heavily, Hammer walked over to his cot, turned, and then looked over at Myke. Sniffing loudly, he bent over, picked up the magazine, and slapped it across the palm of his hand as he stared at Myke in anger.

Was that magazine he used to slap his hand a warning? The look in Hammer's eyes caused Myke to cower. He knew that he had stepped over the line. How was he going to wiggle his way on to Hammer's good side? He could be his link to safety. No one messed with Hammer or his friends.

Myke's thoughts reverted to his present situation. "How many times do I have to tell people around here that I didn't kill anyone!" He slammed his fist into the concrete wall.

Hammer looked up from his magazine. "What's your problem?"

"Oh. Ouch. Nothing…" Curse words followed. Myke shook his fist and drew his hand back to his chest, cradling it in pain. "I think I broke it," he bellowed.

"Knuckles and concrete don't mix. Didn't anyone ever tell you that? What you just did is a good way to find yourself in the infirmary," Hammer said. "Can you move your fingers?"

Myke tried to wiggle his fingers. "I don't know, but it's throbbing like hell."

"Let me look at it."

"Why, you a doctor or something?"

"Yeah, I am … or was."

"You're lying. You can't be a doctor!"

"No, I'm not lying. You're the only person I've told, so this is between you and me, correct?"

"Yeah, just between you and me. It wouldn't go any further. You've got my word on this. So, what happened to you to get yourself put in the slammer, Hammer? Hey, that rhymes. Slammer, Hammer." If looks could kill, Myke would be dead. "Okay, not funny."

"It's a long story. I worked at the hospital in the ER. But first, let me see your hand."

A doctor with a name like Hammer. That is maximum cruelty. What parent would give a kid a nickname like that? "How'd you come by that nickname, Hammer?" Myke asked. "Oh, ouch! You're hurting my hand."

"It looks like you may have fractured the fifth metacarpal bones here." Hammer pointed to the area. "You'll get a free pass to the emergency room for this."

Chapter 45

Just do it, Nicole! You're already here, she told herself. After turning the key in the ignition, she heard the engine start and shifted into drive. She turned onto the gravel road that the cowboy had just exited. The brome field stretched out for miles, and she felt very much at home. It reminded her of her granddad's farm in North Platte. A pinch of homesickness tugged at her heart. Out in the field, a lone tractor sat idle at the edge of the field. A hawk perched on the tractor's cab; its head tilted as it looked for prey.

As she traveled down the dirt road, her peripheral vision caught sight of a red mailbox partially hidden by an overgrowth of weeds. If it hadn't been for the color, she would have driven past it. Slamming on the brakes, dust flying past her window, she shifted into reverse and slowly eased the car alongside the red mailbox painted with nesting ladybugs. The stenciled address was painted in black. Bold numbers on the flap matched the address Reid had given to her. *This is it!* She stared in excitement.

Shifting back into drive, she pulled the car forward and looked down at the gravel driveway. The haunting black trees were void of the lush greenery of summer. At the end of the gravel driveway, the road had been blocked off with yellow tape, and a sign was placed to warn people: "NO TRESPASSING, CRIME SCENE."

Nicole let out a quivering breath, and her body shivered. Once again, a poignant feeling settled over her, pressing heavily on her chest. She sank low in her seat and focused on the road in front of her. Reprimanding herself, she said, "Get a grip and get over it, girl! Remember once that you didn't care if you ever saw him again, and you hated him for abandoning you and your mother!" *So why do I feel the way I do?* she asked herself. She had to admit that maybe it wasn't entirely his fault. Her mother first led her to believe that her father was killed in Vietnam. What was the reason behind all the lies?

She sighed wearily. Releasing the brake, she drove

down the dirt road. A tail of dust trailed in its wake. A pasture gate had been left open carelessly. *Maybe by that jerk who left tread marks on the asphalt as he whooped it up, waving his hat out the window.* Nicole shook her head and drove through the open gate. She must have driven a quarter of a mile in when she thought to herself, *you might have gone too far in. Will you be able to turn around?* Looking around her, she noticed the terrain was rocky, and she couldn't see how or where she could turn her car around. Slumping back in her seat, she glanced into the rearview mirror and watched the road disappear as she crested a hill.

She rolled the window down, allowing the wind to catch hold of her hair and toss it across her face. She brushed it away from her eyes and ran her hand over her head. *This is truly a beautiful countryside,* she thought. Her arm came to rest on the frame of the open window, and its warmth felt good on her skin.

The sound of the countryside captivated her, taking her mind off her problems. The crickets chirped in the tall grass, and the birds in a locust tree sang their song—a melody to lighten one's soul.

At the top of the hill, she brought the car to a stop. Below her was a panoramic view of the lake. Gulls circled low above a sandy beach dotted with geese.

The prairie grass rippled in the breeze. Cedar and elm trees dotted the rolling hills. Cattle meandered along a hill that went on for miles. The closeness to nature enveloped her, and the despondent feeling slowly melted away. *What a beautiful and tranquil spot*, she thought.

After turning the engine off, Nicole sat back and took in the beauty. A feeling of peace that she hadn't experienced in months settled over her. Time slowly slipped away from her, and when she looked at the digital clock in the car, it read 1:30 p.m. Time had passed too quickly. She started up the engine and threw the car into reverse. She felt the back-tire slip and drop. A sinking feeling grabbed hold of her belly. After shifting into drive, she pressed lightly on the gas, and the tires spun. As she rocked the car forward and backward, she realized she was getting nowhere. In frustration, she threw the car into reverse and stepped on the gas. The tires raced, kicking up the dirt. The earth would not let go of its tight grip.

"Aargh!" Nicole complained in irritation. Shoving the car door open, she walked to the back of the car. "I can't believe you did this, Nicole! Now, what are you going to do?" Folding her arms across her chest, she leaned back against the car in complete disgust. *I'll have to call Reid and have him come pull me out. He'll never let me live this down, especially since he warned me not to come alone.*

Reaching back into the car, Nicole pulled her cell phone from her purse and dialed Reid's number. *What am I going to say to him?* The ring of Reid's phone vibrated in her ear.

Reid picked up the phone on the third ring and answered. "What's up, girlfriend?"

"I need your help. My car is stuck in soft dirt. Can you come and pull me out?"

"Where are you?" he asked.

"Out in some field," Nicole said timidly. "Please, can you come and pull me out?"

"Okay, I'll come. But where exactly are you?"

"Well, I took a slight detour."

"Okay, tell me how to find you."

"I believe I'm still on the Brookfield's' property. I did take a little detour. Go past the red mailbox with the ladybugs on the right side of the road; then go about a fourth of a mile down the dirt road, and you'll see an open gate. Turn right, and follow the road. You'll see me. Thanks, Reid."

"I'll be there in twenty minutes. Stay put and stay out of trouble, you hear?"

"What kind of trouble can I get into?" Nicole asked.

"You wouldn't be in the predicament you're in if you had waited for me." With great emphasis, Reid added, "So stay put!"

"I need your help, Reid, not your lip service!" Clicking off her cell, she tossed the phone back into the car. She stuffed her hands into her back pockets, and her mouth tightened in a pout, mimicking Reid's words, she said, "Stay out of trouble! What kind of trouble can a person get into out here?"

She watched an eagle with extended wings hover low. It looked preoccupied watching the ground below. Suddenly, with great speed, it swooped down to earth as gracefully as a ballerina and then snatched up a small rabbit in its claws. With powerful, outstretched wings, the eagle gracefully pushed at the air, rising high above the earth and taking its prey across the lake. Nicole watched the eagle fade into a speck in the cerulean sky. She then began to weep for that little rabbit and its end. Batting away the tears, she sniffed. "Why did you have to die, Mother? I need you, and I miss you terribly."

It was just a rabbit, she told herself. *Pull yourself together*. Nicole looked around her. The valley opened up below her. A winding stream snaked through the land and emptied into a pond where horses had gathered to drink. Who would have thought that tragedy could have struck this ranch in such a violent way? Sighing, Nicole vowed not to allow the tragedy that took place here or the demise of that rabbit to destroy the tranquil peace that had settled over her.

From the pond, she followed the stream upward, and the sedate feeling was suddenly shattered. Below her, she saw the charred ground and the trees around it. Haphazardly blackened lumber protruded from what was once the basement. A limestone chimney blackened with soot stood tall and alone. The haunting, grotesque black tree limbs reached out into nothingness. A chill swept over Nicole, and goose bumps rippled up her arms and down her back.

Her eyes widened, and a soft cry rose from within. She turned and ran from the scene, returning to her car. Her heart raced, and her breath became shallow. She wrapped her arms around her waist to try to stop the trembling. She reprimanded herself. *You shouldn't have come!* The sight branded itself into her memory, reconstructing that horrible scene.

She kicked a pebble in anger and watched it roll to the ledge of a footpath—a path she had not noticed before. She pushed away from the car and went over to the edge of the path. Below her, the lip of the trail opened up to a once well-hidden clearing. A mound of dirt was stacked high with a shovel lying on top. *Someone has been very busy here*, she thought.

A shiny object flickered in the sunlight and caught her attention. She followed the trail down to where the object lay. A small, brown leather bag that must have been dropped was partially hidden by the tall weeds along the trail. Particles of gold dust and nuggets had seeped from the small opening onto the ground. Stooping down, she picked up the small leather pouch and looked inside. *Gold!* Looking around her, her gaze fell to the mound of dirt. A puzzled look appeared on her face, and she looked down at the dry leather bag that had stiffened with age. *What is gold doing in this part of the country? And what's going on here?* She stooped down and gathered up the gold that had spilled to the ground. A foreboding feeling came over her. Her heart thumped loudly against her chest. Her eyes darted from side to side, but she saw no one. Deep impressions made in the dirt led away from the mound of dirt to an overgrowth of trees. She followed the lines in the dirt, looking over her shoulder. She came to an overgrowth of hackberry trees around an opening in the earth. She thought it was an underground dugout. A door had been removed from its hinges, and it laid against the hillside.

As she neared, a heavy sadness seemed to fall over her like a dark cloud. She felt anxious and didn't know why. She felt as if someone were beckoning her to enter the earth. Glancing down at the bag of gold in her hand, the unsettling feeling slowly left her. She peered into the mouth of the dugout. A wheelbarrow was blocking the entryway. A flashlight and lantern had been placed in it. She picked up the flashlight and turned it on. She pulled away in fright as a sudden flashback of Dracula dressed in black with the flowing cape entered her thoughts. His face was whitened with painted-on makeup, and his fangs protruded from the sides of his lips. The fear she had felt as a child that was seared into her memory surfaced like pounding waves. Her legs felt like soft rubber that would not obey. A hand came down on her shoulder. Nicole jumped and screamed out in fright. Her cry bounced back into the recesses of the dugout.

"Nicole, it's me! Reid." Reid jerked his hand from her shoulder. Her heart pounded madly against her chest. She fell against the opening of the dugout, her hands to her pounding heart. She let out a whimper of relief. "Oh, Reid! You scared the heck out of me!"

"What are you doing in here? I told you to stay put! You had me worried when I couldn't find you!" he scolded.

"Look, Reid!" She pulled the bag of gold from her pocket and handed the small leather pouch to him. "It's gold!"

"Gold?" He emptied a small amount into his palm. "Where did you find this?"

"I found it at the foot of the pathway." She pointed in the direction past the mound of dirt.

"More than likely fool's gold." He brushed the gold back into the bag. "Besides, what would gold be doing in this part of the country anyway?"

"Exactly what I thought. Could this be the real thing?"

"I don't know. I'm not an expert. I couldn't tell you if it was the real thing or not." Reid took the flashlight from Nicole's hand and shined it into the inner chamber of the cave. "You've got my curiosity up. All right, since we're already here, let's go see what's inside."

Reid stooped low to avoid hitting his head on the doorframe. The passageway branched off in two directions. To the right were the living quarters for the family. The smell of mold and dampness greeted their nostrils. A fireplace was built into the outer wall of the hill. A large kettle hung from the metal arm. Nicole slipped her hand into Reid's back pocket and drew close to his side. A crude window had been chiseled out of the earth and boarded up. It allowed some light to filter in.

In a corner of the room, a table with a dusty, once-white tablecloth had been placed on the table. Tin plates and cups were arranged for a family of four. It looked as if they were getting ready to eat. Next to the table, a highchair stood with a plate and a cup on the tray. Food had been placed on the table, and the kettle hanging over the fireplace may have contained cooked food. Possibly a stew mix, Nicole thought. She guided Reid over to the kettle and removed the lid. There was a mass of something in it, but she couldn't tell what it might have been. It was dry and black. Reid didn't seem interested in what was in the kettle, and he slowly moved the light across the room. An antique bed with a starburst patchwork quilt looked as if someone was under the covers. A nightstand next to the bed had a kerosene lantern, a picture frame, and a Bible sitting on top opened.

Nicole went over and picked up the black-and-white photograph. A family with five children dressed in finery stood outside a Southern mansion. There were three girls in long ruffled dresses, and the two boys were dressed in jackets, white bow ties, and short knee pants. A Bible laying open on the stand and a book with the word *Journal* stamped on the cover was partially hidden under the Bible. Next to the bed was an elegantly carved baby cradle. Cobwebs laced it like a delicate curtain.

Nicole brushed the web away from the cradle and looked in. Shrieking back in fright, she grabbed hold of Reid's arm, buried her face in his shoulder, and cried out, "Ooh, it's a baby. How ghastly!"

A baby's body was covered with a quilt. The skull of the infant lay on a dusty pillow. Reid focused the light into the cradle. A spider startled by the bright light ran from the eye socket of the skull.

Nicole jumped and screamed, "How disgusting! I hate spiders! I simply hate them!" She shivered.

Reid stared down at the skeletal remains and back at Nicole. "Spider! What about the infant?" He stared at her oddly.

"I simply hate those long-legged things." She cringed. "They make my skin crawl."

"Talk about skin crawling, we had better leave this place, Nicole. Something bad happened here."

"Yeah, something sure did." Nicole looked around her, and her heart skipped a beat. "Do you hear that?"

"Hear what?"

"Someone's in here with us. I can hear someone crying, and it sounds like a woman weeping." Nicole tightened her grip on Reid's arm. "Listen … hear it?"

Reid stiffened. His eyes darted from side to side. "I don't hear a thing!" he answered, listening intently. "You're beginning to really spook me with your ghost. We had better get out of here. Like, right now!" Taking Nicole by the hand, he hissed. "Come on!" He tried to pull her toward the doorway.

"Wait!" Pulling her hand from his grip, she stepped around the cradle over to the nightstand and picked up the journal.

"What are you doing?"

"I can't leave this behind." The sobbing that Nicole had heard suddenly ceased. She felt a cold chill sweep past her, causing the hair on the nape of her neck to stand and goose bumps to bristle the hair on her arms. Something had crossed her path.

They made their way back up the hill with Nicole following close behind Reid, and she was glad to be out of that dark, musty-smelling, cold, damp dugout. On reaching the top of the hill, Reid stopped and crossed his arms over his chest, shook his head, and then paced.

Nicole watched him pace as he surveyed the situation, deep in thought. He finally concluded that the underground dugout was directly below Nicole's car, and the ground had simply given way under the weight. When he finally spoke, he said, "I hope the ground doesn't swallow your car up when I try to pull it out." He went over to his jeep, got in, and said a little prayer, "Oh, Lord God, help us with this task at hand."

Reid backed up his jeep and kept praying that he wouldn't find himself in the same predicament that Nicole had put herself into. Satisfied that he was still on safe ground, he took a deep breath of relief. "Thank you, Lord. Well, here goes!" Dragging the rope behind him, he went over to her little Mazda and tied a knot around the bumper. "Lord God, help us," Reid prayed.

"Are you ready, Nicole?" he asked.

"As ready as I'll ever be," she replied, sliding into the jeep next to him.

The jeep jerked hard, stretching the rope tight. The tires spun, kicking dirt into the air. The engine groaned with the weight of the Mazda. The ground seemed to move like waves receding back into the ocean, but the dirt was receding back into the hole. Nicole watched in horror as the ground began to fall in around her car. Seeing what was happening, Reid slammed his foot down hard on the accelerator, pulling the Mazda free from the sinkhole that had a tight grip on the tires.

"You did it. You did it!" Nicole screamed in elation. "You're my hero!"

He noticed the dimple in her left cheek and the twinkle in her eyes as she grinned up at him. How could he not love her? "We did have a scare there for a moment, didn't we?" Reid looked over at her. "Wanna go and get a Coke now?"

"Why not? I'm in no hurry. My grandparents were called out of town unexpectedly." Getting out of the jeep, she then added, "I'll follow you into town."

Chapter 46

The sweet smell of freshly-baked bread and pastry greeted Nicole's and Reid's nostrils as the door to the cafe swung open. Her stomach growled at the pleasing aroma. Reid ordered two chocolate éclairs and two large Pepsis. After getting their order, they went to the farthest corner to sit, away from those who might unintentionally overhear their conversation. Taking a bite of the éclair, Nicole then licked the chocolate off her fingers and opened the journal.

"I wondered why you just had to have that book. It's only a diary, and only women write in them."

Nicole looked up at Reid. "Well, yes. It is a woman's journal." Nicole pointed to the word stamped on the cover. "This journal may hold a wealth of information on who these people were and what happened."

"Okay, read it to me then. You've got my interest up," Reid said as chocolate smeared on his cheek.

Leaning forward, she wiped the chocolate from his face. "Messy, messy!" she said, licking the chocolate from her fingertips.

Reid blushed with embarrassment. "That's what my mother would say."

Nicole's eyes fell to the page, and she began to read.

Wheeling, Virginia

February 1, 1858

Property of Marianne Kent

Today is the happiest day of my life. Nathaniel has asked me to marry him.

Nathaniel is the overseer of Papa's slaves and his right-hand man. Papa has always talked very highly of Nathaniel and said Nathaniel was like a son to him. Nathaniel said he would ask Papa for my hand in marriage after the harvest of the tobacco. Papa was always in a good mood after the sale. It will be very difficult for me not to say anything to Papa and Mama.

February 2, 1858

Papa is furious, and he's yelling at Mama. I stopped to listen outside the library door. I heard him say, "I told Marianne that Major Maddox would be here this afternoon, and she disappears. Major Maddox has a promising career in the Union Army. John was a West Point graduate and would be a tremendous asset to this family. What is wrong with your daughter? One day, John will run for president of the United States. Think of the prestige she would have as the first lady of this nation!"

Papa wants me to marry Major Maddox and compromise my happiness with Nathaniel for prestige! Prestige … for whom?

Mama saw me standing at the slightly open door that she had left ajar and beckoned me to join them.

I walked in an announced, "I won't marry John, Papa. John makes me shudder. Deep craters scar his face, and he's fifteen years older than I am. I don't love him."

With that remark, I have been banished to my room until, as Papa put it, "I come to my senses."

February 3, 1858

Early this afternoon, I saw Major Maddox ride off in great haste. He took the whip in his hand and struck the horse's rump. Papa, with his hands to his back, paced the long stoop with an angry frown on his face. I had snuck out of my room this afternoon and didn't want to speak to the major. When Papa saw me coming up the path, he hollered angrily, "Where have you been? Mammy has been frantically looking for you. You disobeyed me and ran off after you had been banished to your room."

It seems that Major Maddox had come for an answer to his proposal of marriage two days before, and he came today wanting an answer. John left and was very upset with me for not being at the house when he came calling. In anger, Papa demanded to know what my answer would be to John.

Fear ran rampant. How could I tell him that I had accepted another man's proposal of marriage? Cowering, I finally answered, "I love another gentleman."

Papa fell backward in surprise and then demanded that I tell him who the scoundrel was. I told him it was Nathaniel. Papa went mad and said he would shoot him! Papa then stormed into the house. I have never been so scared in all my life. Papa returned with a rifle and stomped the butt of the Winchester on the stoop in front of me, shouting, "What does love have to do with this? Your mother was only fifteen when she married. That is a year younger than you. You'll learn to love him as your mother did me!"

February 4, 1858

I've been banished to my room for three more days. My nanny since birth, Mammy Addiah, has been bringing all of my meals to me. I am not allowed to sup with the rest of the family until I come around to seeing Papa's view on this issue of my marriage to Major Maddox.

February 5, 1858

I have just got to get word to Nathaniel. Wonder if Mammy Addiah has said anything to Nathaniel or if she would take a message to him from me. I'll ask her when she comes to bring up my supper tonight.

February 6, 1858

Mammy is angry with me and refuses to get involved. She refuses to listen to anything I have to say. What am I going to do?

February 7, 1858

Mammy Addiah is very upset this morning. It seems that Ben, her son, has known about Nathaniel and me for some time. Mammy's angry because Ben never told her. Ben is like a brother to me, and he would never betray me, even to Mammy.

February 8, 1858

Papa has summoned me to the library. Mammy's stern look pierced down at me as she brushed my long hair. I begged her to tell me what to do, and she refused to get between me and Papa.

On shaky legs, I made my way down the stairs and stood motionless in the doorway.

Papa beckoned me to enter and sit. He then told me that the wedding date had been set for October 12. Major Maddox had agreed on that date.

I looked over at Mama with pleading eyes. Mama refused to look at me. She knew how I felt, and yet she would not stand up for me. Why am I not so surprised by this? She would never go against Papa's wishes.

February 9, 1858

Mammy Addiah is against Nathaniel and my plans to marry. She says that I must obey my papa. I threatened to run away with Nathaniel. Mammy shook her head sadly, her lip turned down, and she said to me, "Love makes people do foolish things. You in love, chile, and I s'pose nothing going to stop the heart that in love." Mammy Addiah took me into her arms and held me as I sobbed. "You're the only one who's ever understood me. Mammy, please give me your blessing, or we'll run off." I begged her. Mammy couldn't bear the thought of me doing such a thing. Her warm, loving black hands cupped my face. "You surely do love that Nathaniel, don't ya, chile?" she said. "You know us black folks are gonna be negger's in a woodpile for this, chile. Your papa is gonna be mighty mad over your defiance!"

Reid looked up at Nicole and exclaimed, "She's going to pass up a fortune and maybe one day being the first lady of our nation, for love. I don't understand her." Reid shook his head and smiled.

"Oh, Reid." An impatient, irritated frown flashed on Nicole's face. She set the journal down, a cloud of sadness blanketing over her. "Like Mammy said, one does crazy things when in love. I feel so badly for Marianne." Nicole's thoughts drifted back to her mother and Dr. Brookfield.

Mother would surely understand what Marianne had gone through.

"Where are you, Nicole? Come back."

Looking across the table at Reid, she smiled. *And to think he didn't want me to pick up this journal.* She smiled back at him.

February 10, 1858

Mama came into my room this morning and said Papa was planning the biggest wedding this side of the Mason-Dixon Line. She seemed pleased at the wedding preparations. She said that Papa talked with Major Maddox and told him that I had accepted his proposal in marriage and that he had their blessing.

I wept bitter tears. How could Papa tell Major Maddox that I would marry him? Mama knows that I love Nathaniel. Tears flowed down my cheeks, and I flung myself across my bed sobbing in grief. Mama was beside herself and at a loss on how she could comfort me.

February 11, 1858

I've got to get word to Nathaniel, but how am I going to get out of this room? I'm so miserable I could scream.

Mammy Addiah brought up my lunch. "Mammy," I begged, "please, Mammy, leave the door unlocked. I've got to talk to Nathaniel."

"Yer papa, he's never done whip none of his slaves, an' I ain't gonna be de first one. You don't know what you axing me to do, Missy." She pouted. "I ain't gonna do it!"

Setting the tray down, Mammy looked at me with disgusted eyes. "Uh-uh," she said and then she locked the door behind her.

Five minutes later, I heard the key in the lock, and Mammy walked in. "De colonel, he axing fer ya an' wants ter see ya in de library, Missy. Hurry up an' tidy yerself." Mammy went over to the dresser and picked up a hairbrush. "Sit, chile!"

Papa sat behind his mahogany desk, bent over his ledger. He removed his round-rimmed glasses when I entered the room and set them down on the desk. Staring up at me, he proceeded to tell me how very disappointed he was in me. "A bright future is before you!"

What bright future? I asked myself. Papa said it was for my own good and for the good of our family.

"Well?" Papa hollered at me.

My fingers were crossed behind my back. I prayed that the Lord would forgive me of my terrible lie that I was just about to tell. I told Papa that I would marry Major Maddox. Papa beamed broadly, and I was given the freedom to move about the house.

February 12, 1858

I found Nathaniel in the shed this morning and told him that Papa had arranged for my marriage to Major Maddox this fall. Nathaniel's outburst of anger frightened me. I have never seen him so angry. He threatened to kill Maddox rather than have me in his bed. I told Nathaniel we could run away and get married, and he said he needed to think things through.

Tonight, I could hear pebbles striking my bedroom window, and when I looked out, to my surprise, it was Nathaniel. He waved at me to come out. He had spoken to Mama, and she told him that she would take care of everything.

February 13, 1858

Mama found me by the swimming hole this morning. My heart was heavy with sorrow. She sat next to me on the fallen tree trunk and folded her hands in her lap. She then asked me, "Are you really going to marry Major Maddox?" I had to admit to Mama that I had lied to Papa, and God was going to punish me for it. I simply couldn't marry the major. "I don't love him, Mama."

Mama looked at me with saddened eyes and wanted to know what I was going to do. I told Mama that Nathaniel and me, we were going to run off and get married. She said she would not allow me to marry without her being by my side. Then she said she'd take care of everything.

I'm so afraid for Mama. What is she up to? And what if Papa finds out?

February 14, 1858

Abraham, the elder of the nigger camp, married us tonight, and this is the happiest day of my life. Twirling in front of the mirror, I giggled like a young girl. I ran my hand down the soft green satin and felt so beautiful.

Mammy fussed with my hair, adjusting the black curls hanging loosely down my back. She smiled proudly as she put the finishing touch to the bow and pulled away. She looked at me with approval and then said, "It's time, honey chile."

Mama busted through the door, out of breath. Papa, with his demands, kept her busy. She held out a string of black pearls and showed me the engraving on the clasp: MK, 2/14/1858. Papa gave the pearls to Mama on her wedding day, and now she was giving them to me. She held them up so proudly and asked me to turn around so she could place the pearls around my neck.

My heart raced with joy as I picked up my skirt and rushed out the door. Nathaniel was so handsome; he took my breath away. He was wearing mustard-colored breeches, a white shirt with a black bow tie, and a jacket of a darker shade of mustard. His eyes were as blue as the sky, and the color of his hair was that of yellow tobacco leaves ripening under the hot sun.

Abraham held the broom that Ben had carved and asked, "Are you sure you wanna do this?"

We looked into each other's eyes and smiled. "Yes," we answered, and then we nodded our heads.

Abraham held his arm upright with the broom in his

hand. He walked around us blessing our marriage and praying that the unity would bring us healthy children. He then laid the broom on the ground and said, "In the eyes of our Lord, jump over the broom of matrimony."

We met with Ben after the wedding, to discuss the route we would be taking to the gold fields in California. Ben will be the only one to know of our travel plans.

Black pearls, Nicole thought. *My grandmother was given a strand of pearls when she married. That's very odd. The initials on the clasp were also MK, but I don't remember seeing the date. Like Marianne, Grammy's pearls were also handed down to her. Grammy said they would be mine one day when I married.* "Oh, Reid, I feel like I've seen those pearls."

"Where have you seen them?" Reid asked.

"My grandmother has a strand of pearls with the initials MK engraved on the clasp. Isn't that odd?" She stared off with a blank look on her face. "But I don't remember seeing a date."

"Hey, maybe you and Marianne are connected. You know, related."

Nicole gave Reid one of those looks. "Yeah, right." She rolled her eyes.

"Okay, not funny."

February 16, 1858

This has been the happiest day of my life—waking with Nathaniel at my side. We will be leaving Wheeling at first sunrise and will be taking the Wheeling Suspension Bridge into Ohio, heading for Zanesville, Ohio. Then we'll head on down to Logan, where Nathaniel said his brother resided. From there, we'll go to Columbus, Dayton, Hamilton, and then into Indiana. We'll go to Bloomington and then down to Flat Rock, Illinois. From Illinois, we'll go to St. Louis, where we plan on hooking up with the wagon train for California. The long journey is still ahead of us.

February 17, 1858

Nathaniel said he thought that we may have only made twelve miles from Wheeling today. It was getting late, and we had to find a place to spend the night before darkness set in. Traveling across the country in a wagon has not been very comfortable. It's almost as bad as being in a saddle all day. But married life is blissful, and it makes up for the discomfort of the trail. Nathaniel is teaching me how to cook over an open campfire.

February 20, 1858

Today is the day that Nathaniel has dreaded. We woke up to snow falling to the earth. We prayed that the Lord would make the snowfall light, or we would have to find a place to hole up in until the snow let up. If we can make it to Logan, we will hopefully stay with Nathaniel's brother.

February 21, 1858

Our prayers have been answered, and the snow was light. We got about two inches of snowfall.

March 4, 1858

This is going to be a long journey to the gold fields. I am not sure if I am up to traveling so very far away from home. Nathaniel is in good humor, and that has helped me accept the discomfort of the long ride. At times, I prefer to walk beside the wagon to get the stiffness out of my legs, and I'll take the reins from Nathaniel to give him a break.

I fall into bed at night after the preparations of supper and then the cleanup. I'm too tired to log in our events of the day most evenings.

March 16, 1858

We finally made it into Logan and came upon a beautiful cascading waterfall in Hocking Hills. It is a sight to behold. Water rolled off the high cliff into a pool of clear, aqua-blue water. Looking down from where we stood, we could see small and large fish at the bottom of the pool. Icicles hung from the edges of the cliff. Nathaniel was so excited at having fresh fish for supper. He said he would hunt for venison tomorrow.

Nathaniel went off to scout for a good place to set up camp and found a deep cave that would protect us from the storm coming our way. He built a fire to cook the fish he had caught. With our bellies full, we settled in front of the fire, and I read from God's Word. The winds picked up and howled outside of the cave. We snuggled close under the quilt, falling asleep to the sound of the trees being tossed about by the wind.

March 17, 1858

Nathaniel's hand came gently down on my shoulder, waking me. He said the wildlife was plentiful. He saw a buck at the cave's mouth this morning. He had made breakfast and handed me a plate of bacon and eggs and the last of the bread. The smell of bacon turned my stomach, and I'm unable to eat.

By midmorning, I was feeling a lot better when Nathaniel walked into camp with a buck draped over the back of his horse. Reaching up, he pulled the young buck off the horse's back, and it fell to my feet—its mouth open and its tongue hung out to the dirt.

"What are you going to do with it?" I asked Nathaniel.

"Skin it, my dear." Nathaniel whipped out his hunting knife and sliced down its stomach. Some of its contents slid out onto the ground.

I gagged, and my hand went to my lips. "Oh, Nathaniel, I'm going to be sick." I hurried off to the nearest tree and lost my breakfast.

"She must be pregnant." Nicole smiled.

"Pregnant! So soon after they're married?"

"It does happen, you know!"

The bell jingled over the door, and a man with a wide-brimmed hat walked in.

"That's the jerk I saw leaving the dirt road onto Highway 24 this morning."

"I know him. Hey, Dallas!" Reid called out.

"Hey, Reid, what are you doing on this side of town?" Dallas walked over to their table, extending his hand in greeting.

He saw the journal in Nicole's hand. "Mighty old-looking book you've got there," he said.

Closing the journal, Nicole slipped it off the table onto her lap. "It is," she answered.

Dallas turned back to Reid. "So, what have you been up to, Reid? Taking the summer off from basketball?"

"No, some of us met this morning for a two-hour practice."

Dallas looked over and winked. *Does he recognize me from the highway?* Nicole wondered.

"Why don't you join us?" Reid offered.

"I'd like that. I'll go get my coffee." Dallas turned and left.

Annoyed, Nicole asked, "Did you have to ask him to join us?"

"Why? I didn't think you'd object." He looked at her quizzically. "Is something wrong?"

"I can't put my finger on it, but there's something about him that makes my skin crawl. Maybe it's those slanted, shifty brown eyes. How do you know him anyway?" she asked.

"I met him in Aggieville at one of the bars."

"You drink?" She stared at Reid.

"No, I don't drink. I'm usually the designated driver. I don't want to see my friends or someone else killed by their drunken driving."

Dallas returned and pulled out a chair. "Who's your pretty friend?" he asked, winking at Nicole.

"This is Nicole."

Dallas extended his calloused hand, which had dirt caked under the fingernails. She took it and shook his hand. She then dropped hers under the table and wiped her hand on her jeans as she smiled up at him.

"So, you're Reid's girlfriend, huh?" Dallas asked.

Nicole ignored his comment. The men talked for a while, and Dallas stayed longer than Nicole wanted him to. She was anxious to get back to the journal. When he finally said he had to get back to work, she was relieved and glad to see him stand. The men shook hands, and Dallas looked down at her. "I'll let you get back to your reading, little lady."

Nicole watched Dallas get into his pickup. Gunning his engine, he waved as he drove off.

"It's getting late," Reid said. "I know you don't like to drive after dark. Why don't you stay at my place? My roommate is gone for the summer, and you can use his room. I'm sure he won't mind," Reid said. "Promise, I'll behave myself."

"Okay, if you promise. I know that Cuddles will want out of her cage. She's been cooped up for too long."

fff

Once settled in, Nicole curled up on the sofa with Cuddles curling up in her lap. Reid came from the kitchen and handed her a glass of iced tea.

Opening the journal, she let it fall onto the last page she had read.

She continued to read.

March 18, 1858

This morning while loading up the wagon, to my delight, Ben came walking into camp. I was so happy to see him that I didn't notice the crooked and painful smile that flashed across his face as he walked toward us. His shoulders slumped forward, which was so unlike him. Fatigue and pain were engraved deep in his dark brow. In my excitement, I ran to him and threw my arms around his chest. Ben winced in pain and drew his shoulder back. "What's the matter, Ben?" I asked. Walking around him to get a look at his back, I found blood had seeped through his thin coat.

Nathaniel followed behind me and saw Ben's back.

"Dear Jesus! Who did this to you?" he demanded.

"The new Massa Handcock," Ben said through gritted teeth. "He whipped me fer running away, Massa Nathaniel."

"I'll kill that man for what he did to you," Nathaniel said in rage. "Come to the fire and sit." Nathaniel peeled the dry bloody shirt from Ben's back. Ben groaned in pain. "How did you find us, Ben?"

"I knew where you were headed. You told me, and I didn't have much trouble following the wagon tracks until it began to snow. I just kept heading west." Then Ben told us that Papa, Mama, and Mammy had sent him after us. They were fearful for our safety. Ben didn't get very far when Massa Dudley Hancock caught him. Nathaniel asked Ben who Hancock was, and he was told that Hancock had replaced Nathaniel when Papa found out that we had jumped the broom and run off. Papa, Ben said, was very upset by Missy's disobedience. "Your mama, she begged and pleaded with your papa and asked de colonel to let me go and look after ya. Your papa, he finally come around to seeing her point. I did not run off, Massa Nathaniel."

"I believe you, Ben," Nathaniel said.

Ben winced in pain. "If Mammy hadn't heard the ruckus coming from the shed, Dudley would have killed me with that there whip," Ben said. "Nobod' mess with Mammy's chile or the wrath of Mammy is gonna be on them. Except fer de colonel, Missy." Ben furrowed his brow in pain and tried to smile. "Colonel Thaddeus an' yer mama, Mammy knows them the big bosses. She cottons to nobod' else!"

In anger, Nathaniel clenched his teeth. "Did Colonel Thaddeus order this done to you to set an example for the other slaves?"

"Nooo, sir!" Ben shook his head. "Colonel Thaddeus, he sent me to you. He'd never order one of his darkies to be whipped. Not Colonel Thaddeus, he's a good man." Ben then laughed. "Colonel Thaddeus was so mad when he come into the barn and saw what Dudley had done to me. He took the whip from Mammy's hands and turned the whip on Dudley. The colonel then tells Dudley to get off his plantation."

Ben reached into his back pocket and pulled out a crumpled piece of paper. "This here is fer you, Missy, from the colonel." Ben handed her the letter.

The smell of Papa's pipe tobacco greeted my nostrils, and she inhaled deeply. I loved the tobacco smell when Papa lit up his pipe. Homesickness gripped me. Oh, Papa.

I miss you so. Marianne ran her finger over the letter T that was melted and pressed into the black wax.

She hesitated for a moment, and then she slipped her finger under the lip of the envelope, breaking the wax seal.

Nicole turned the page, eager to read what the letter said, and a discolored paper fell from between the pages and teetered on her lap. She made a hasty grab for the letter before it could slip off her lap onto the dirt and into the fire. Nicole carefully unfolded the letter and looked up at Reid. "It's a letter from my papa." She began to read it out loud.

February 28, 1858

Dear Marianne,

I was very angry at your disobedience and your defiant nature in the way you ran off to marry Nathaniel. To my great displeasure, your mother finally told me that Abraham married you and Nathaniel. To protect Mammy Addiah, your mother kept her out of sight and claimed she was ill. Abraham worked in the fields until nightfall. It is not an easy task for me to admit that I was wrong. I love you too much to disown my beloved daughter. I believed that your love for Nathaniel was a silly young girl's infatuation that would soon pass. I see now that I should have taken you seriously. You're married now, and your mother is worried sick about you. Come home! Your mama told me that you and Nathaniel were headed for the gold fields of California. If you decide to continue on your journey, I'll understand. I am sending Ben to you. I have enclosed papers for Ben's freedom. The stipulation is that as long as you are in the gold fields, he is to stay by your side and protect you and Nathaniel. Ben's a good man. I trust him with my life and now yours.

Major Maddox has proposed marriage to your sister Gracie. The wedding will take place next spring when she turns sixteen. Please come home.

Sincerely,

Your Papa

Nicole cleared her throat. "My father has forgiven me and wants us to return home. I pray that Gracie is happy with the decision she made to marry the major."

"Yeah, she's forgiven only because her father pawned Gracie off to the major. He'll keep the future president in the family. Makes you wonder if the colonel wasn't buying prestige for his family's name by marrying Gracie off to the major and the future president," Reid added.

"Yeah, I see your point. I wondered what Major Maddox would have gotten out of that marriage to Marianne. Did he love Marianne, or was he so flippant? Maybe he was after the colonel's name to get himself into the White House. He couldn't get Marianne, so he went after her sister Gracie. I'm glad that Marianne followed her heart. She's better off."

April 14, 1858

Two months have passed swiftly. I can hardly believe that Nathaniel and I have been married for this long. Our travel progress has been very slow. We are making eight to twelve miles a day on a good day. The ground is still frozen, but when the rain comes—and that could be any day now—it will be difficult to travel in the mud and slush. Nathaniel is pushing the horses hard, and I feel so badly for them. At night, Ben and I see to it that Patches and Sugar Foot get a good rub down and an extra ration of oat and barley. Ben asked me tonight if I was with child.

I wondered why I was sick every morning, and it never crossed my mind that I could be pregnant. Then Ben asked if Massa Nathaniel knew. I wasn't sure if Nathaniel suspected, and I told Ben that I'd tell him sometime tonight. At the news of my pregnancy, Nathaniel was so very excited that he was going to be a papa. He began making plans for when we get to Whitewater Canal in Indiana. He was going to let the horses graze for a couple of days and let me rest. He and Ben went out hunting to restock our supply of meat and will later head to town to restock our supplies of staples and feed for the horses.

"Marianne told Nathaniel that she's pregnant!" Nicole said in excitement.

"Oh, that's good," Reid replied.

Men ... Nicole thought. "Well, all I can say is that I am so grateful for cars. I know that I couldn't handle traveling by wagon. It's hard enough to drive from one state to another in an automobile," Nicole said, skipping some of the pages.

August 21, 1858

We finally made it to St. Louis, Missouri, and we were told that it was not advisable to head for the gold fields this time of the year. The winters would be harsh in Colorado if one made it through. They told us of the Donner party traveling through the Sierra Nevada Mountains in October 1846. An early and terrible winter was on its way, and the Donner party was caught in the pass, and many died in the freezing conditions.

We checked around and found that some of the travelers are going on to Topeka, Kansas. St. Louis is crawling with people staying over for the winter. We will spend the winter in Kansas and head out for California in early spring.

August 27, 1858

Ben found a fallen oak tree outside of Topeka. He and Nathaniel went out to cut the needed wood. Ben said he was going to carve the cradle in gold for our baby. "Nothing but the best for Missy and Nathaniel's baby!" Ben beamed with pride.

Nicole wrinkled her brow. "The cradle was carved in gold?" Reid grinned at her expression. "I doubt that. The cradle would have been taken a long time ago. Besides, we would have noticed it if it had been carved in gold."

"Yeah, you're right about that."

The wooden floor creaked, and Nicole heard the sound of heels softly clicking on the bare floor. The room turned cold, and the hair on Nicole's arms stood. Cuddles felt it too. The fur on her back bristled, and she hissed, jumped off Nicole's lap, ran to the bedroom, and crawled under the bed.

"What's with her?" Reid asked.

"Listen. Didn't you hear someone walking across the floor?"

"No, I didn't hear anything."

Reid looked around him and tilted his head, listening intently.

"Didn't you feel that sudden drop in temperature in here?"

"Yeah, I felt the chill. I wondered where that cold draft could be coming from." He rubbed his arms.

"Listen. Do you hear that?"

"Hear what?"

"I can hear a woman sobbing. Can you hear her?"

The shape of a woman's body began to take form. She was wearing a long pale-green satin dress. Her eyes pleaded, and her hands were outstretched. "Help me please!" she beseeched. "My baby, my husband." She seemed to be beckoning them to follow her as she passed through the wall.

"What was that?" Reid stammered.

"I believe we may have just encountered a spiritual being."

Reid's face was devoid of color.

"Never in my life did I expect to see what I just did."

"You saw her! I'm so glad you saw her too. I'm not seeing things. And you did see her pass right through the wall and disappear, didn't you? That dress." Nicole picked up the journal and flipped back the pages. "Here it is!" She read out loud, "'Running my hands down the soft green satin. My black curls hanging loosely down my back.' Reid, we've got to go back to the dugout."

"What for?" Reid asked.

"I've got to get another look at that cradle."

"It's not a very good idea to go back there. If caught, we'd be accused of trespassing. It is private property, you know."

"I am aware of that! But I am family! So how could I be trespassing?"

"You can't prove that right now. You haven't gotten the DNA results yet, Nicole. They'd laugh at you, not to mention arrest you."

"Well, let them laugh!" Irritation tainted her voice. "If you don't want to go with me, I'll go by myself!" she blurted out in anger, glaring up at him.

Reid stared back at her in disbelief.

Turning her back, she went over to the counter and picked up her car keys and purse. Pausing, Nicole looked back at him. Reid sat there staring out the window. Heavy-hearted, she turned and went to the door. Her hand went to the doorknob, and she paused, sighing. *What have I done?*

"Wait! I can't let you go alone." Reid stood and walked over to her. He took the car keys from her hand. "You do realize that it could be dangerous for us to be out there, don't you? That gold bag that you found yesterday may have been what they were digging for. Men have been known to kill for gold. We may be putting our lives in danger."

"Yes, I know that. But you saw Marianne, didn't you?"

"Yes, I did. I never believed that I'd see a spiritual being. Never in my wildest dreams did I think I'd ever see one."

"Well, then, you did hear her grieving for her baby and husband, didn't you?"

"Yes, I did. All right, let's go."

"Wait." Nicole went to the coffee table and picked up the journal. "I can't leave this behind."

On the way to the dugout, Nicole let the pages slip through her fingers once again and read on:

August 28, 1858

Nathaniel and Ben found a quaint little house on the edge of town yesterday. I am so excited. This little house has two bedrooms, and Ben won't have to sleep in the barn with the horses this winter. What is even more exciting is that Nathaniel and Ben found a job in a furniture store where they will make tables, chairs, bed frames, and dressers. With Ben's talent in carving, Ben will be able to use the equipment to work on the cradle with Nathaniel's help. They will begin work on Monday.

I am so glad that we came to an agreement on moving on to Topeka. With the baby coming in November, I am thankful that I will have someone here to deliver our first child. We will head out as soon as they give us the word in spring that it is safe to travel west with the wagon train.

September 4, 1858

I found a doctor who will deliver our baby when the time comes. I really like Dr. Ruttman. He is a caring person.

September 14, 1858

Went to see Dr. Ruttman today, and he said I was doing well, and the expected date of delivery had not changed. I am getting so very big, and our baby is so very active. I've gotten a letter off to Mama telling her of her first grandchild's birth date, which will be a week or so before Thanksgiving.

September 20, 1858

It has been a real hard pregnancy for me. I am so tired most of the time that I have a hard time getting around. My belly is so large that I can't see my feet. Ben or Nathaniel, they have to help me put on my shoes every morning. They think it is so very funny, and I still have another two months to go.

September 25, 1858

Nathaniel and Ben came in late tonight, towing the cradle behind them. They finally put the last finishing touch on the cradle tonight, with the exception of the spindle, at the furniture store. The spindle caps are not in place and will be completed when we get to California.

Nathaniel and Ben are so very proud of their work, and it is beautiful. Three people who have seen the cradle have placed an order in for one similar to ours. The boss was so very pleased with the three orders that he is giving them a bonus for every cradle ordered.

November 20, 1858

Annie came into the world in the wee hours of the morning. I am so very glad that Dr. Ruttman was not out of town on a house call. Annie is a beautiful baby, and Nathaniel and Ben are pleased that she is a healthy baby. Nathaniel had hoped for a son but is just as happy with a daughter. "A son next time," Nathaniel had said.

Chapter 47

By midafternoon, Nicole and Reid were driving past the mailbox painted with the red ladybugs. The pasture gate that had been left open that morning was now closed. A sign was hung on the gate, and it read, "No Trespassing!"

"Now, what are we going to do? Did you see that sign?"

"Yes, I did. I'm family, remember? Pull in there." Nicole pointed toward a dirt road partially hidden by weeds and trees.

"Okay, now what?"

"Let's go," she said with a determined look on her face. "I'm not going to let a 'No Trespassing' sign scare me off."

"It will be our heads, if caught." He looked at Nicole for a long moment. The stern stare she returned told him she was not going to budge. Sighing, he turned the engine off. He reached over and opened the glove compartment. "We may need this," he said and held up the flashlight.

The walk to the dugout turned out to be a pleasant one. A gentle breeze rippled the tall prairie grass. The swaying of the grass brought back fond memories of a family trip to the ocean. One day, she thought, she would return to the ocean. She looked out at the prairie grass, and she could almost feel the ocean wave break around her legs and see her feet vanishing beneath the swirling sand, the receding tide drawing the golden sand back into the ocean.

The wind ceased, and the prairie grass went still.

They passed grazing cows that got spooked, causing them to bolt in all directions. The horses ignored their presence and just swished their tails in contentment as they continued to graze on the green grass. A young painted filly stood close by, and Nicole stopped to admire her. Reaching down, she pulled out a handful of grass and clicked her tongue. She went over to the filly and gently brushed the grass across her nose. The filly yanked the grass from her hand and chewed it greedily. When Nicole reached up to rub her nose, she bolted back in fright and galloped away.

"What are you doing? I thought we were in a hurry," Reid asked.

"Oh, come on!" Taking hold of his arm, she turned him in the direction of the dugout. "My granddaddy raised horses, so I've been around them all my life. For my tenth birthday, Granddaddy bought me a filly just like that one. I miss my grandparents and the ranch. For a moment, I felt like I was at home."

They walked in silence until she felt Reid's hand brush against hers. He looked over at her and smiled, taking her hand in his. Her heart flip-flopped in her chest, and she felt a tingle surge through her body.

On reaching their destination, they heard voices coming from the dugout.

"Wait here," Reid whispered. He made his way up to the ledge and looked over. His head suddenly came down, and he eased his way back to Nicole's side.

"What's going on down there?" she asked.

"There's a white pickup at the bottom of the gorge, and someone is coming out of the dugout."

Muffled voices drifted up.

"What do we do now?" Nicole asked.

Reid whispered, "Stay put and be quiet. That's what we're going to do." His finger went to his lips.

"Where do you want me to stack the bags of gold? Do you want me to put them in the back of the truck?" a voice called out.

Reid tilted his head. *I know that voice.*

"No!" came the reply. "Put them in the back of the cab and be careful. Those bags are very old and fragile."

The truck door squeaked open, and they heard a thump.

"It's a real shame …"

"What is?"

"Wasn't there any other way we could have dealt with this problem? Did they have to be killed? Couldn't you have reasoned with Doc?"

"There was no reasoning with Doc. He's a stubborn old man bent on doing things his way. Do I have to remind you that all this gold would have been buried under tons of dirt or found by someone on the worksite? As it turned out, we had to dig half of the hill out to unearth the gold since you carelessly fell against that pillar."

"That was an accident, not intentional. I stumbled over

the shovel and fell against the support pillar. Besides, the dugout had already begun to cave in, and I was nearly buried alive. My question was about Doc and his wife. Did they have to be killed? They were good people, and I hated to see them go the way they did."

The confession startled Nicole. "They murdered the Brookfield's! That voice sounds very familiar. In the coffee shop this morning, is it that guy? What's his name... Dallas, that's it!"

"Yup. Do you know what this means?" Reid whispered in her ear. "We're in a lot of trouble if we're caught here. They killed two people! They won't hesitate in killing two more. Stay right here, and don't move." Reid crawled back up the embankment, drew himself up, and peered over the side.

Dallas reached into his back pocket and pulled out a red handkerchief. He removed his hat and wiped the sweat from his forehead. As he did, he turned and looked in the direction where Reid was hiding at the top of the hill. His hand went to his forehead, and he squinted.

Reid flattened himself and pushed his way back down to Nicole's side.

"It's going to be a hot night, boss." Dallas stuffed the hankie back into his pocket.

Nicole rolled onto her back and watched a flock of geese fly low over the lake. They gracefully glided toward the water's surface. The beauty and grace of the fowl seemed to dissipate with her despair. The tranquil peace had lost its beauty.

With the last bag of gold loaded, Dallas hooted with glee. "We're unbelievably rich!" He laughed.

The word *rich* struck a raw nerve, and Nicole blurted out, "Rich? They murdered two people for that gold. They killed him!" Nicole choked back a sob. "I needed him." She sniffed. *I've missed all the things a daddy does for his daughter—hold me when I'm hurting, kiss my tears away when I'm sad, run behind my bike, and cheer me on like my friend's daddy did. He'll never walk me down the aisle when I marry*—she looked over at Reid—*or hold our firstborn.*

Tears rolled down her cheek, and she shook with silent anger. "How could they do such an awful thing! An innocent man is in jail for a murder he did not commit." Nicole could hardly contain the rage she felt inside of her. "They murdered my father!"

Reid's hand clamped hard over her mouth. "Shhh!" He pushed her head to the ground.

"Did you hear something, boss?"

"Yeah, I sure did. Get up there, and check it out."

Dallas snatched up the shotgun and headed up the hill.

Chapter 48

The guard inserted the key into the cell door. "Stand back, Hammer," the guard ordered.

Hammer did as he was told and moved to the far corner of the cell. The cell door was pushed open, Myke walked past the guard, and the guard said, "Behave yourself, Coop. I don't want to have to take you back to the infirmary. It costs the taxpayers big bucks every time you do something stupid."

"Yeah, yeah!" Myke answered.

The cell door closed behind him. His hand had been placed in a cast up to his elbow.

"So, what did the doctor say?" Hammer asked.

"I told the doctor you were my cellmate and about your diagnosis too. He asked me how you were doing, and I told him you were having a party in prison, loving every minute of your visit here."

Hammer smiled. "What's his name?"

"His name?" Myke ran his hand across the white cast, as if in deep thought. "Oh yeah, Hamilton. That's it, Dr. Hamilton. He's pretty old, white hair and all. You know the guy?"

"Yeah, I know him. He's a real nice guy. He hadn't been in the ER for very long. He was telling me that retirement wasn't all that great. He was going crazy looking at four walls, and his wife couldn't stand his hanging around the house. They were driving each other nuts. So, he decided to go back to work a couple of nights, and he ended up here. So, tell me, what did Dr. Hamilton say?"

"The x-ray confirmed your diagnosis. I fractured the metacarpals, and he slapped this on my arm. Wanna sign it?" Myke asked.

Chapter 49

"He's coming. Move!" Reid scooted past Nicole down the embankment toward a pile of granite rock. Fear coursed through Nicole's body as she followed close behind Reid. Her heart was pounding, and she was breathing heavily. She made it down the embankment, reaching Reid's side, and collapsed against the cool granite slab.

Dallas's straw hat could be seen as he crested the hill with a rifle slung over his shoulder. His masculine figure was clad in dirty blue jeans and a short-sleeved brown plaid shirt. He lifted the hat that sat low on his forehead and scanned the area. Nicole pulled at Reid's sleeve and pointed. "Look."

Dallas slid down the hill toward them. Reid grabbed hold of her arm, dragging her toward the ravine that she was pointing to. They scrambled in and hid between the rocks.

"See anything?" the voice called out from the other side of the hill.

"Nah, not a thing. It must have been some animal." His voice trailed off behind him.

Nicole looked down at her shoes—they were covered with cattle dung. She had stepped into a patty. Cringing, she looked around her. The area they had entered was littered with droppings.

"That was a close one. I'm sure glad you saw this ravine." Reid looked down at her shoe. "You stepped into something very messy."

"Do tell! You pulled me into it," she said.

He made an awful face. "I did? Sorry about that. But it was you who pointed out this ravine. Here, let me help you clean off your shoe."

A short while later, they heard Dallas say, "Whaddya say we go get a beer after we unload?"

"Can't. I told the wife I'd take her out to dinner. If I, were you, I'd stay out of the bars tonight."

"I'll drink if I want to. I'm not on your time clock," Dallas answered.

Dead silence followed that remark.

"Sorry, boss, I didn't mean it that way! I'll stay out of Pete's."

Doors slammed, and Reid and Nicole heard the diesel engine turn over.

"They're leaving," Reid whispered.

"Well, it's about time! Did you see the face of that man with Dallas?" Nicole asked.

"Wish I had. We've got to report what we just heard."

"Not before I see that cradle. I feel a connection to Marianne. I really feel that she has been trying to tell Sharon something for a long time. Maybe I can be that person who can help her."

"Well, that really puzzles me. They must have been God-fearing people. It looked like they read the Bible with it open on the nightstand. I would have thought that Nathaniel's and the baby's spirits would have definitely gone to be with God. Why is Marianne's spirit roaming the earth?" Reid asked.

"That is a very good question. Why is she still here? Could it be because from what we've read, she wasn't right in the head? That is a puzzle, and we'll only find out the answer when we get to heaven."

fff

The western sky glowed with an orange hue. The sun sat on the edge of the world and suddenly slipped off, disappearing from sight, and the earth turned to darkness.

"Well, that settles that. It's too late now. We'll have to come back in the morning," Reid said.

"We've got the flashlight. Just a peek, please," Nicole begged.

"What about your fear of dark places?" he asked.

"I'm not alone. You're with me. Besides, I have faith that He will give me the courage I need."

How could he say no to her when she looked at him with those pleading eyes? Reid hoped that he wouldn't regret giving in to her.

"All right, you win. Stay close to my side."

They made their way down to the dugout and entered the cavity. As they drew near the sleep area, the air became very cold. Marianne's form suddenly materialized, and she radiated light and pointed under the bed. The bright light that Marianne radiated startled Reed. "That light is almost blinding. Marianne is here, isn't she? If she is, I can't see her this time. What is she trying to tell us?"

"Yes, she's here. What is it, Marianne?" Nicole asked. "Over there." Nicole pointed, walking over to the bed, where Marianne was beckoning her to go. "Under the bed, you want me to look under the bed? What's under the bed, Marianne?"

Reid went over to the bed, lifting the skirt, and aimed the light so that Nicole could see.

"There's another journal under the bed," Nicole said. "That's what she's trying to tell us, and I don't think I can reach it. It's too far pushed under. Besides that spider might be under there."

"I'll get it." Reid got on his hands and knees to retrieve the journal, and he handed it to Nicole. "We had better go. We can come back later to get a better look at the cradle when we have more light in here and more time."

The reflecting light faded, and the room cast flickering shadows as Marianne's spirit vanished. She seemed to be satisfied at their finding the other journal.

Reid put his arm around Nicole's shoulders and guided her out of the dugout. A half-moon gave off enough light to guide their way back to the car. The flashlight was beginning to dim, and they would soon be in darkness.

"You know, sometimes people can really fool you. I really thought I had Dallas figured out. I wonder if he would have used that shotgun if he had found us," Reid said.

"What gun?"

"Didn't you see that shotgun?"

"No! I saw no gun. You had your hand on my head, pressing my face into the dirt. How could I have seen anything?"

"I did?" Specks of dirt dotted Nicole's forehead. Reaching over, he gently brushed it off. "I'm sorry. I didn't realize I was being so forceful with you. I was only trying to keep you quiet."

The flashlight beam slowly grew faint until it went out. The shrill of a coyote's howl pierced the night air, causing Nicole to grab hold of Reid's arm.

Reid held up the flashlight. "We're on our own. Don't let go of my arm."

"That's one thing you don't have to worry about," Nicole said. They were walking in silence when they heard another cry of a coyote.

A grin creased Reid's lip. "Do you remember our first meeting?" he asked.

"How could I forget that day?" She laughed. "I really didn't intend to hit you in the head with that snowball. I was aiming for your backpack. I didn't think I could throw it that far. It really scared me when it hit you in the back of the head. Then you turned and looked directly at me. Oh boy, you were mad."

Reid chuckled. "You should have seen the expression on your face when I picked up the snow and began to pack it."

"Gosh!" She laughed. "I was in a frantic hurry to get my car keys out of my backpack when that snowball hit me in the face."

"If you hadn't tossed that snowball, we might not have ever met. You do know that, don't you?" Reid stated.

"That I do. It was the best day of my life." She bent down to pick up a stick and dragged it in the dirt behind her. He reached over and took the stick from her hand, tossed it into the grass, and took her hand in his.

Chapter 50

Cliff clenched his teeth. The remark that Dallas had just made enraged him. *So, he thinks he's going to be rich? And that the gold will be shared equally? Well, that's the most asinine thought he's ever had. Finding the gold on Doc's land doesn't make him an equal partner.* Cliff snorted in annoyance. *He's just a ranch hand doing odd jobs around the place, not a family member who gets equal rights to anything. Who does he think he is? He forgets who he is dealing with. I am not his buddy.* Cliff cursed under his breath. *He's an absolute idiot and a liability, as far as I am concerned.*

Dallas heard Cliff curse and glanced over.

"Is something the matter, boss?"

Ignoring the question, Cliff turned the truck onto Sharingbrook Circle, a cul-de-sac lined with upper-class homes. With his mouth agape, Dallas stared. He hadn't been on this side of town in years. The last time he drove this way, it was open pastureland.

Dallas whistled. "Your house?" He looked up at the two-story white house. The patting sound of the automatic water sprinkling system caught Dallas's attention. He had never seen anything like it. "You don't have to stand there with a water hose!" Dallas exclaimed.

"No, the underground system does all the work for you."

"Man." Dallas looked around him. The grass was as plush as carpet, and purple French hydrangea lined the white picket fence, dividing the properties. "One day soon, I'll have a house just like this one." Dallas stared in utter awe.

Cliff smirked. *So, he thinks.*

The touch of a button on a little black box on Cliff's visor sent the garage door upward. It disappeared above the doorway. They drove into the garage, and the door slowly descended behind them.

ƒƒƒ

"This garage is bigger than my mobile home," Dallas said. And he thought, *I wonder what the inside of the house looks like.*

Cliff ignored his remark and went over to the back wall. He pressed in a code that unlocked a concealed door that slid open, revealing shelves up against the wall.

"Wow!" Dallas walked over. "That's pretty fancy!"

"I had it put in to store the gold. Not bad for a real quick job, and they did an excellent job on short notice." He stood back and glowed with pride. "Okay, let's get to work. We've gotta hurry before my wife gets home."

Dallas opened the back door of the truck and smiled at the wealth lying on the seat and floor of the cab. He looked around and saw the chief disappear into the house. This was his moment. Dallas removed the chewing tobacco from his shirt pocket and put the bag of gold in its place, and then he slipped the tobacco into the pocket of his jeans instead. Dallas inhaled with excitement. *Yes, sir,* he told himself, *one day, you're going to find me living uptown like the big boys!*

ƒƒƒ

Cliff returned with two bottles of water and handed one to Dallas. "What are you doing standing around? Didn't I tell you to unload the gold?"

"Yes, sir, that you did." He pointed to the floor of the cab. "See the bags of gold on the floor, it's done and on the shelf. I'm not standing around and doing nothing! Thanks for the water," Dallas added.

They worked at a steady pace until Dallas asked, "By the way, Chief, when do I get paid?" He had slipped another bag of gold into his jean jacket pocket while the chief's back was turned.

Cliff stood upright and flexed his muscles. "You'll get paid in due time. I've been in contact with a friend from South Africa. His family oversees a gold mine in that part of the world. Haven't confirmed anything yet, but I will soon."

"Do I know your friend from Africa?"

"No, he's no one you would know." *Besides*, Cliff thought, *you'd be the last person I'd confide in. I'm no fool!*

fff

African ... what is he up to? Is there anyone in town from South Africa that I might know? Dallas wondered. *Huh, parents that mine for gold in South Africa. Who could that be? That's someone I need to befriend.*

Cliff took Dallas home and firmly said, "Stay out of the bars tonight, you understand? If you gotta have a drink,

drink at home. I can't have you running around Manhattan telling everyone you're rich." He barked, "There's too much at stake here."

Dallas glared at him. *He can't tell me what to do! If I want to drink, I'll drink, and he's not going to dictate to me. He's probably mad because I forgot to pick up the dynamite this morning. Well, I can't understand what the big deal is all about. Like he never forgets.*

Chapter 51

As the first glow of dawn became visible through the bedroom window, Nicole slipped out of her borrowed bed. She went to the window and watched the sun climb over the horizon. *Well, Marianne, let's put the mystery of the golden cradle to rest today.* She went into the kitchen and put on the coffee. Mentally, she ran through her next move. *I need to shower and dress before Reid wakes.* Quietly, she slipped into the bathroom and turned on the water, humming softly as she undressed.

With her hair combed and dried, she hurriedly dressed and went to Reid's bedroom door and knocked. "Reid, are you awake?"

"Yes, I'm awake. I'll be out in a minute," he answered.

Pouring herself a cup of coffee, Nicole went over to the coffee table and picked up the journal they had found under the bed. *What hidden secrets will this journal reveal?*

"Good morning." Reid's voice was cheerful. "How did you sleep?"

"Not well."

"How come?"

"I couldn't get Marianne out of my thoughts. I wondered if they ever made it back to Virginia."

"That's something we may never know. Have you read the second journal yet?"

"I haven't started yet. I was waiting for you."

Balancing his coffee, Reid sat next to her. "Okay, you can read now."

August 26, 1860

We have been in Colorado for nearly three years. Nathaniel says it's time for us to return to Virginia. I have received letters from Mama that it was rumored a civil war was ready to break out. Mama's last letter states that she is worried about us and wants us to return home. Papa is in failing health, and Lieutenant General Maddox has been summoned to Washington DC, and my sister Gracie is beside herself with worry. Nathaniel is needed back at the plantation.

August 27, 1860

I'm pregnant again and haven't got the heart to tell Nathaniel. I'll be showing soon and entering my fifth month. The wagons are nearly loaded with our personal effects and supplies for the trip back to Virginia. We will leave at first light tomorrow. Annie will be two in November, and she's such a big help already at her young age. Big Ben simply adores her, and she follows him everywhere.

August 28, 1860

Nathaniel and Ben, they are driving the horses hard. They want to make it to St. Louis, Missouri, before the first snowfall. I'm beginning to wonder if it would have been better for us to weather the winter in Colorado until spring.

Reid looked in from the kitchen and asked, "Are you hungry?"

"I'm starved. What have you got to eat?"

"How does bagel and cream cheese sound?"

"I'll help." Setting the journal on the coffee table, she got up, went into the kitchen, refilled her cup with coffee, and waited on the bagels.

"They're leaving too late in the season. They may not make it to Missouri," Reid said.

"You think so?" Nicole asked.

The bagels popped from the toaster, Nicole helped spread the cream cheese thickly on top, and they went back into the living room to eat. Taking a bite, Nicole bent over, picking up the journal, and looked at the next entry.

August 30, 1860

Ben rode into camp and said he thought three men may have been following us. He said that he had seen them three days ago and that they were camped about three miles behind us. We are going to have to be very careful. Ben wants to split up to throw them off. Nathaniel doesn't think it's a good idea. "We need to stay together," Nathaniel told him.

September 2, 1860

The three men that we thought were following us have finally left the area. Tonight, will be the first night that we will be able to get a decent night's sleep. Nathaniel and Ben had been taking turns standing watch.

September 6, 1860

I am simply too exhausted to write in this journal. The trip is tiring, and Annie is very unhappy at being cooped up in this wagon. Nathaniel and Big Ben help as much as they can.

September 8, 1860

Nathaniel said we may be in Kansas. He thought that we had entered the Flint Hills and gone too far north. It is extremely cold and windy. The strong wind cuts right through our thin coats. The wind carries the dirt high into the air, darkening the sky, making it look like night. All that dirt in the air has made it difficult to breathe. We wear hankies tied around our noses and mouths to keep us from breathing the dirt into our lungs. Annie cries bitterly and complains that she is so very cold, and I fear for her. Ben rode in from scouting the area and said he found a cave that we could hole up in until the weather clears.

September 10, 1860

This cave has turned out to be a real blessing. It is a vein that runs deep, a cavity that is large enough for us to set up housekeeping. Nathaniel and Ben work feverishly to install the cooking stove. A hole in the side of the earth had to be made to put the chimney through. Once that is completed, I'll be able to cook, and it will provide some heat to take out the chill in this dugout.

Annie has settled down and is playing quietly, to our relief.

September 16, 1860

It's been a while since I last wrote. The weather here in Kansas is so unpredictable that Nathaniel and Ben thought it would be best to stay put. The trip would be too hard on Annie. Wildlife is plentiful, and the men thought it would be a good time to stock up on meat. They have plans on scouting out the area for a nearby town to get the needed supplies if we have to spend the winter here. Nathaniel thought Fort Riley would be the closest. We had stopped there on our way to Council Grove with the wagon train.

September 23, 1860

It feels like we're going to have an early winter. Kansas is so very cold. We had plans on staying put until the weather warmed up some. But it continues to stay cold, and the wind is so unceasing. The first snow fell this afternoon, and I took Annie out to play. She loved the snow. Now that we are staying until spring, Nathaniel and Ben have fashioned a door to keep the wind and snow out of the dugout.

November 1, 1860

Thanksgiving is coming upon us, and my thoughts are heavy with my family. I wrote a letter to Mama in hope that Nathaniel and Big Ben would find a town to mail this letter. I am so very worried about Papa since Mama's last letter told me of his failing health.

November 15, 1860

I am so grateful that Papa sent Ben to us. I don't know what we would have done without him. The men are headed out this morning for Fort Riley for the second time for more supplies and a birthday present for Annie. Annie's birthday is in ten days.

It is also a great way for them to get news concerning the Civil War and also to let them know of our location and how we are getting along. Ben did mention to one of the officers that he had felt that three men might have been following us before we entered the Flint Hills.

November 19, 1860

Nathaniel and Ben made it in from Council Grove. Fort Riley did not have the needs for a child. They had been gone for nearly ten days, and I was so worried. Annie kept asking for her papa and Ben. I was in tears when they pulled up in the buckboard. I ran out and scolded them in anger. They apologized profusely and said they were glad they made it in when they did. The weather was not looking good, and they wondered when the snow would begin to fall.

When I finally settled down, they asked me to stay in the dugout with Annie. They had her birthday presents and didn't want her to see them. But my suspicion is they don't want me to see what they have bought me.

November 20, 1860

Today is Annie's birthday, and she is so excited. She is two today. I baked Annie a cake yesterday, and we frosted it together this morning. She jumped up and down with glee. Ben gave her a baby doll, and Nathaniel bought her two needed dresses, a bonnet, and a heavy winter coat. She is growing so fast. Nathaniel also picked up the needed things for a newborn and bought me many bulks of colored yarn and a new winter coat.

Nathaniel and Ben had bought themselves heavy winter coats and parade around the room, showing off their needed heavy winter jackets. Their coats from Colorado would not have held up for another hard winter. Nathaniel said if it wasn't for the gold, we could not have afforded what they bought. This was a happy day for all.

November 28, 1860

Yesterday, Nathaniel and Ben came home with a turkey. Ben held the turkey by its legs and proclaimed, "A Thanksgiving feast. It is a day to thank our Lord for supplying all of our needs, for keeping us safe and our bellies full. I am so thankful that I have my family around me." Ben smiled at us. "This cave has provided warmth and safety, and it has become our home for the winter."

December 3, 1860

Annie has had a cold with a fever for days, but she is doing much better today.

It must have snowed two feet last night. I am glad that Ben found a safe place for the horses. Another cavern was later found not very far from us to shelter the horses from the hard wind and cold. The horses seem very content to stay in this small valley. There is plenty dry prairie grass for them to graze on, and the lake is close by for water.

December 20, 1860

Ben will place a rocking horse under the tree on Christmas Eve for Annie. He stepped back in pride, looking at his masterpiece. Hiding it from Annie has been a challenge. She is so curious that Ben is afraid she'll find it before Santa gets here. Christmas is in five days. Ben went down to the creek and cut down a cedar tree. Smiling broadly, he dragged it in. What little Christmas decorations we have made have been placed on the tree. Annie is so excited, although I don't think she fully understands.

December 25, 1860

What an exciting morning! We didn't have much to give to one another, but we had each other. Annie loved the rocking horse that Ben carved for her. I knitted two scarves—one for Nathaniel and the other for Ben. Nathaniel shot a turkey two days ago, and I put it on to cook last night. The welcoming smell this morning put a dance to my step. Ben presented me with four sweet potatoes. I was so thrilled and told them so. This has been the best Christmas celebration ever.

January 1, 1861

Little Ben came into this world early this morning. Nathaniel is a proud papa of a son, and Big Ben is thrilled that we named our son after him. Annie won't leave my side. She loves her little brother and wants to hold him all the time.

I am so tired from the long labor. How I wish Mama was here.

"Oh, Reid, she had a New Year's Day baby. A little boy. Marianne must have given more information on the cradle, don't you think? I'm going to skip some of the pages and come back to this later," Nicole said.

March 27, 1861

Nathaniel rushed into the dugout with fear on his face. "Where's Ben?" he asked in a most fearful voice.

I told Nathaniel that Ben went hunting to restock our supplies for our journey home, and then I asked him, "Why?"

Three men had set up camp by the lake. Nathaniel said that he went down to see what they were up to when one said they saw a darkie in the area. They were looking for a runaway slave seen in these here parts.

Nathaniel told them that Kansas was a free state, and they had no call to be running a slave down in this country. It seems that there was a large bounty for the one they were looking for. They didn't care if he was free or not. Ben was a nigger, and they had come to get him. Then Nathaniel said they told him that they had followed a lone wagon last fall, but due to the weather turning cold so early last year, they turned back. They didn't think the travelers would get very far and would have to hole up somewhere around the area where they had left them for the winter.

March 28, 1861

Ben can be gone for days at a time when he's hunting. He did not come in last night, and Nathaniel spent a sleepless night waiting on his return. Nathaniel said those three men were bounty hunters. Bounty on a runaway slave can fetch up to $1,500 depending on the size of the slave. One like Ben would fetch an easy $1,500. Those men, Nathaniel said, don't care if he's got papers saying he's free. Papers can be destroyed, and Ben would never be able to prove he's a free man, and he would be sold back into slavery.

March 29, 1861

Little Ben, a demanding infant, began to cry, and Nathaniel went over to the cradle and picked him up. He handed him to me, saying, "Keep him quiet and Annie inside." He was going to go look for Ben. Nathaniel went over to the fireplace, removed his rifle from its stand, and stuffed the shells into his jacket pocket. He kissed us as he went out the door. It would be the last time I'd feel his kiss and see him alive.

Time seemed to move slowly as I waited for Nathaniel and Ben's return. Anxiety began to seep in as I sat there nervously staring at the door. Then I heard Nathaniel's voice. "Hey, what are you doing on my land?"

"This here your property?" I heard a man ask.

Nathaniel answered, "It sure is, and I'd be most appreciative if you fellows would kindly move on."

Ben must have come out of hiding and joined Nathaniel. The men had come too close to the dugout, and Ben had been watching them from a distance.

"That there, he's your nigger slave?" I heard a man ask.

"Ben here is a free man," Nathaniel replied.

There was a cross of words, and the man said that papers meant nothing to them and that they'd take Ben, even if they had to use force to take him.

Little Ben pulled away from my breast upon hearing the strangers' voices. He looked up at me. Seeing my fear, he puckered his lower lip, and I knew what he was about to do. I pressed his mouth to my breast to quiet him and rocked him back and forth as he struggled to free himself from my tight grip. Then I heard the guns fire. Terrified, I paced the dirt floor, waiting for Nathaniel to enter and tell me everything was all right, and that the three men had left.

Annie asked, "What's that noise, Mama?"

I felt Little Ben's body go limp in my arms. Looking down at him, I saw that his face had turned blue, and his eyes had rolled back. I began to scream for Little Ben to breathe, shaking him and pounding his back.

More shots rang out, but I was oblivious to the sounds. I kept hollering for Nathaniel to come and help me. Our baby had stopped breathing.

The door burst open, nearly knocking me over, and Ben stood in the doorway. Grief clouded his face. "Ben, Little Ben has stopped breathing. Please, Ben, help me!"

Big Ben took Little Ben from my arms and pounded on his back. "Breathe, Little Ben, breathe! Please breathe." He turned Little Ben over and tried to breathe life back into his little body by breathing into his mouth. "Come on, little fella, breathe fer your Uncle Ben," Ben pleaded.

Little Ben was not responsive. I ran my finger through his hair; his scalp was warm to the touch, and yet there was no life. Anxiously, I looked around for Nathaniel. "Where's Nathaniel, Ben?"

Ben didn't answer. He walked over to the cradle and placed Little Ben in his bed. Leaning on the cradle, his head lowered, he answered, "Massa Nathaniel … the bounty hunter, they kill him." Ben's body shook in grief.

I then noticed the powder and bloodstain on Ben's jacket. Ben had also been shot. He then told me that he and Nathaniel had killed two of the bounty hunters and that he wounded the third, who had gotten away. One of the bounty hunters had killed Nathaniel.

Ben went out and brought Nathaniel in and placed him in bed next to Little Ben's cradle. Nathaniel had been shot in the head, above his right eye.

Ben then said we needed to leave Kansas right away and that I was to gather up what we needed. The food supplies and clothing, he said, were the necessities. We needed to travel light, and the furniture would have to stay. He was going to get the horses and wagon and bring them around front. Ben also promised to come back for Nathaniel and Little Ben once he had us safely back in Virginia.

Nicole hiccupped and wiped the tears that streamed down her cheeks. She sighed. "That is why the remains were in the dugout, and Marianne has not been able to rest. Her baby and husband died tragic deaths. This is so sad." Tears welled up again in Nicole's eyes.

"There was nothing mentioned about the gold or the cradle, and did you notice if Annie's rocking horse was there?" Reid asked.

"Did we finish the first journal?"

"I don't think so. You skipped some pages, remember? We'll go back to it. This second journal has been really interesting and yet, a very sad ending for Marianne's family and Ben."

Chapter 52

Cliff Kaufmann rose early and went to the Farmers' Co-op on old Highway 24 between Manhattan and Wamego—a trip that had put him into a bad frame of mind. The co-op was just down the road from the mobile home park where Dallas lived. *And how could he forget …*

Pulling into the parking stall in front of the store, Cliff got out of his pickup and slammed the door shut when he heard a voice call his name. Turning, he saw the manager, Fred Wells, headed his way.

"What brings you out to this side of town?" Fred extended his hand in greeting.

"Well, whaddya know, Fred?"

"Not much," Fred answered. "How can I help you, my friend?"

"I'm here to pick up the dynamite I ordered a week ago."

"I had it ready for Dallas to pick up. What happened? Did he forget?" Fred asked, pushing the door open as Cliff walked past him. "This was a special order, and I knew you were waiting on it. I even called him yesterday morning and left a message on his answering machine, telling him it was ready for him, and that it's been here for a week."

Cliff shook his head in disgust. "Yeah, he sure did forget." Irritation tainted his voice. "He's not very dependable. His time at the farm may be short."

"That's too bad. He's a real nice guy. But lately he's been acting kinda funny, like he's on drugs or something. I don't think I'd trust him with dynamite the way he's been behaving. What are you going to do with the dynamite?" Fred asked.

"Doc had talked about clearing out the north pasture so he could plant hay. He wanted the dynamite for tree stumps. I told him a couple of months ago I'd do it for him. I feel pretty bad about not doing it when he asked me to do it." Reaching for his back pocket, Cliff pulled out his wallet. "How much do I owe you?"

"I can put it on your bill, Cliff."

"No, I'll pay for this in cash."

Chapter 53

Nicole went to the bedroom and picked up the first journal that she had laid on the dresser. Flipping through the pages, she came to the page they had last read. Placing her finger between the pages, she went back into the living room and sat next to Reid. "Ready?" she said.

"Ready, read on," he answered.

April 25, 1858

Nathaniel and Ben found a good place to set up camp along Cherry Creek. The first day out, Ben came into camp hollering that he had found gold. Getting supper ready went to the wayside. As the sun set, I realized that we hadn't had a bite to eat since breakfast.

May 1, 1858

Ben has finally added the spindles to the cradle. "Here it is, finally done as I promis' ya." Ben smiled with pride, and I wept with joy over the beauty of it.

The heads carved in gold depict Ben's grandfather, the chief of his tribe, and other chiefs who went on to be with their ancestors. It is beautiful to look at. Ben said that the chiefs were the protector of our baby and that they would watch over him.

"Let's go back to the dugout. I have got to get a better look at that cradle," Reid said in eager anticipation.

I couldn't believe what was coming out of Reid's mouth. *He wants to go back to the dugout.*

"Did you see the heads? I don't remember seeing heads. Did you see them?" he asked.

"No. If I had, the cradle would have been here sitting in front of us. The heads were covered from what I could see in that semi-dark cave."

fff

A weary feeling crept over Reid as they walked down the slope to the dugout. Instead of the one dirt mound they had seen the day before, they were staring at two mounds of dirt. *A lot of digging has taken place in a short time*, Reid thought, and he wondered if Nicole had noticed. At the entrance of the dugout, Reid turned on the flashlight. "Are you ready for this?" he asked.

"Yes, as ready as I'll ever be."

"Take hold of my arm." He extended his elbow, and she did not hesitate to hook her arm through his.

fff

They stepped into the dark recesses of the dugout, and a sudden rush of fear caused Nicole to shudder uncontrollably. *Why the fear now? I thought I had it under control*, she thought.

"Are you okay?" Reid asked.

"Uh-huh," she answered. She wasn't going to let him know how terrified she had become. She could feel her muscles cramp with tension. It took great effort for her to place one foot in front of the other. *You're being silly*, she told herself. She forced her legs to move with only the light from the flashlight as their guide. *Why this sudden uneasy feeling?*

Reid stopped in front of the cradle. "Here it is, untouched by man for over a hundred years." He stepped in closer to get a better look. Nicole held back, looking over at the bed. She remembered reading the entry in the journal that told of Nathaniel's body being brought in and placed on the bed by Little Ben's cradle. "Is Nathaniel under that quilt?" she asked.

"I don't know. Want me to check?"

"Could you, please?"

The star-pattern quilt of flower patches and stripes had been placed neatly over Nathaniel's body. Dust covered the quilt, and when Reid took hold of the corner, she could see particles flaking off in the light. The skull had been shattered above its right eye. It was just the way Marianne had described it.

"He's there, all right," Reid said. He draped the quilt back over Nathaniel's skull.

"Those poor people … Ben never made it back for them," she said sadly. "He must have been caught by the bounty hunters."

"Come over here, Nicole." She followed Reid to the cradle.

The cradle looked exactly like the drawings and the description Marianne had given in her journal. The base depicted a tree trunk. The upper half was delicately carved with branches and leaves. Birds perched on the limbs and looked into the cradle as if singing. Nicole had never seen anything like it. Baby socks had been placed on the tops of all four posts, and Nicole removed one.

"Look, Reid!" A golden head of an African warrior sparkled as the beam of light fell on the head. "It's absolutely beautiful!" Nicole gasped in excitement.

Awestruck by the beauty, Reid whispered, "It truly is a work of art." He shined the light on each warrior's head as Nicole removed the socks. "Ben did an absolutely beautiful job at carving the heads in gold, at that." He then directed the light onto the baby's skeleton. A spider, startled by the bright light, ran back into the eye socket.

"Argh!" She quivered. "There's that spider again!"

Chapter 54

Standing under the showerhead, Dallas allowed the spray to wash the day's grime from his body. The hot water soothed his aching muscles. After turning the water off, he shook the droplets from his hair and ran his hands across his face. The conversation he'd had with Cliff, the chief, seeped back to remind him, and he swore. *He doesn't own me. I only said that I wouldn't go to Pete's. I'm celebrating my good fortune tonight whether he likes it or not. I'm not on his time clock, and I'll do as I darn, please.* Hurriedly, Dallas got dressed, slipping on his new boots. He ran the palm of his hand over his black Nocona dress boots, pleased with his new purchase. He walked over to the mirror. *You good-looking son of a gun!* He grinned back at his reflection, running his hand across his damp black hair. Pleased with himself, he pointed his finger at his reflection, flipped his thumb, and winked. He felt that his life had taken a drastic turn since finding the dugout and all that gold. A Discover card had come in the mail days before, allowing him to splurge on himself.

Buy now, pay later, he thought. *When the gold is cashed in for American dollars, I'll be on easy street living the good life. Life is sweet!* Dallas turned and walked out the door.

Friday night in Manhattan, Aggieville, was where he wanted to be. Teenage boys not old enough to drink cruised down Moro Street, honking their horns and whistling at the pretty girls. *So juvenile*, he thought. *Was I ever like that?* He chuckled to himself. *Yeah, you were.* He laughed. But then, he wasn't there for the teenage girls.

A young couple walked out of the Polar Ice Cream Bar with ice cream cones. He sighed. *Life seems to have slipped by me, and I'm not getting any younger*, he thought. *I have no one hanging on my arm, looking up into my eyes with love.* A sad feeling crept in, and then he sat up straight. *But it won't be for long!*

It was going to be rough finding a parking stall at this hour of the evening. When people parked, they stayed. A taillight flashed on, and Dallas hit the brakes. *Tonight, is my lucky night!* A spot opened up in front of the Shot Gun Tavern, a favorite tavern of ropers and wannabe cowboys. He pulled in to the stall, got out, and locked the car door. Once inside the tavern, he looked around for a familiar face and saw no one. *It must be too early. Maybe they are all down at Pete's. I'll go check later.* A potbelly stove stood in the middle of the room, radiating heat, and bar tables circled cozily around it. Off in a corner, people gathered around a rider with his black hair slicked back. He straddled an electronic bucking horse with one hand, holding tightly to the saddle horn. The rider's legs flared out, his arm held high to keep his balance, and he yelled "Yee-haw!" with bystanders shouting encouragement.

Orders of beer, Coke, hamburgers, and fries were delivered to the patrons. Dallas ordered his usual: a Coors Light, cheeseburger, and fries. A young redhead wearing a low-cut top walked in. He watched her glide across the room, headed in his direction. They made eye contact, and she smiled at him. Clearing his throat with excitement, he returned the smile. *All right*, he thought.

She walked past Dallas. The excitement in his eyes faded, and the smile disappeared. She sauntered over to a young man sitting a couple of seats down from Dallas. She laid her arm across his shoulder, looked down at him, and asked, "Have you been waiting long?"

"Nah, just got here," he answered.

A look of disappointment flashed across Dallas's face, and he hissed, "Slut!" His order was set in front of him. Loading the fries with ketchup, he greedily scarfed down the burger and fries, washing it down with the cold beer.

Unbeknownst to him, an undercover cop slid into the empty seat next to him. She was on the lookout for minors with fake IDs. He looked over at her and liked what he saw. She was an attractive brunette with captivating green eyes and delicate features. She wore a low-cut purple top with the Wildcat logo and tight blue jeans. She looked to be around nineteen to twenty years of age.

Dallas switched from the light beer to bourbon and water. Sipping his drink, he glanced her way. She seemed preoccupied, as if she was looking for someone. After four beers and a second bourbon and water, Dallas was beginning to feel a little tipsy and bold. "Hi! My name's Dallas. What's yours?"

She looked over at Dallas, stared at him for a moment, and then answered, "Mac."

"Funny name for a lady," he slurred.

"Ms. Mackey to you!" she stated and moved a seat over from him.

"You're a bit of a snot, aren't you, little lady?"

She ignored his remark and turned to the woman sitting in the seat next to her.

"Well, let me tell you …" He hiccupped and held his third bourbon up to his lips. He slurped it down. Setting the glass down, he continued, "You'll be sorry you snubbed me, Miss High-and-Mighty." He leaned over and whispered, "I'm a rich man! I found gold on the doc's property. That I did."

She looked back at him and stared. "Are you for real?"

"That's the truth!" he added. Lifting his glass, he toasted her with a wink. "Here's to you, little miss. And, yes, I'm for real."

"Show me the gold."

"You want to come to my place?" A drunken, crooked, sheepish grin smeared across his face. He belched again. "I think I've had too much to drink." Suddenly, he put his hand to his mouth. A queasy look flashed on his face.

"Are you all right?" she asked him.

"Ohhh!" he groaned. "I've gotta go to the john!"

Soon after, Dallas returned to his seat. "I feel a lot better. Do you still want to go to my place?" He winked.

"Sure." Officer Renee Mackey helped him off the stool and held him up as he weaved unsteadily to her car.

"Hold on for just a second while I catch my breath," Dallas said. "The pavement won't stop moving." Clammy perspiration began to form on his forehead, and Dallas leaned over, puking on the ground.

Mac unlocked the car door. "Feeling better?" she asked with a faint grin on her lips.

"Never better," he answered.

"Okay, Dallas, in you go. If you feel like you're gonna get sick again, let me know so that I can pull over to the side of the road. No need for you to mess up my car." She held the door open for him. "By the way, what's your address?" she asked.

"Let me get into the car first; then I'll give you, my address."

Dallas got in, and she shut the door behind him.

At the back of the car, she removed her radio from a clip on her belt. "Dispatcher, this is 77 Riley. I have a drunk and disorderly, and I'm bringing him in. Over."

"Seventy-seven Riley, do you need backup?"

Officer Mackey walked over to the driver's window and leaned over, looking in to check on Dallas. Dallas's head was slumped over to one side, and his eyes were closed. He was snoring loudly. "Negative! He's out cold now. Bringing him in, over and out."

After clipping her cell phone back onto her belt, she opened the door and slid into the car. The smell of Dallas filled the small space. His snoring was steady and explosive.

Nah, I don't need backup. He's a drunken pussycat. She smiled. Officer Mac inserted the key, started the engine, and eased the car out of the parking stall into the traffic lane. Looking over at Dallas, she thought, *Boy, he's in for a rude awakening when he wakes tomorrow morning and finds himself behind bars.*

ƒƒƒ

"Oh, my head," Dallas groaned, licking his lips. An uneasy feeling crept over him. *Where am I?* His hands flew from his forehead. His eyes went wide, and he thought, *I must be dreaming!* He laid his arm back across his eyes. *Okay, let's try this again.* Removing his arm, he found himself staring at the cold steel bars. *This can't be.* Dallas jumped to his feet too quickly. Stumbling, he groaned, "My head!" He slumped over and sat back onto the cot, his hand to his forehead. He slowly got up again, walked over to the bars, and yelled, "Guard, guard!"

A guard peered around the corner and answered, "Whaddya want?"

"Why am I in here?"

"Disorderly conduct, resisting arrest, and inciting a brawl. Need more?"

"You've gotta be kidding!" he screamed. "I don't remember any of it."

"No, I'm not kidding. You've got one phone call. Wanna call your lawyer?"

"No, get me the chief. I wanna talk to the chief of police, and now!"

The guard laughed. "You want to talk to the chief! Yeah, right. He's got better things to do than mess with the likes of you!"

"He's a good friend of mine, I'm telling you."

"Yeah, sure, he's a good friend … He's a good friend of mine too." The guard smirked.

Dallas was getting nowhere. *Think, Dallas, think!* he told himself. *Oh, man! What did I do last night? The boss … oh, will he ever be mad when he finds out that I'm in jail if he doesn't know already. How am I going to talk my way out of this one? He'll kill me. What do I do now?* Dallas fell back onto his cot and ran his fingers through his greased-down hair, allowing his head to fall into his cupped hands.

"Guard, I need my cell phone to make a call. Can I have my phone?" Dallas asked.

"Like I said, if you need to make a phone call, the phone is hanging on the wall."

"No, I need my own cell phone."

"No can do," the guard shot back.

Chapter 55

Early the next morning, Officer Mackey went to the station to fill out her report on the arrest of one Bud Kramer, alias Dallas Wilcox. Since the case involved the chief's in-laws, Officer Mackey wanted to personally hand him the report. She felt that she might have stumbled onto something very important. Dallas's claims of finding bags of gold on Dr. Brookfield's land might prove Dallas had a hand in the murders. The suspects behind bars, Myke Cooper and Pico Sanchez, might be innocent after all. Cooper had denied any wrongdoing in the deaths, and Mac was inclined to believe him. Thief, yes. Sanchez, however, had a record of arson and theft. Sanchez was a more likely candidate to be an accomplice to the crime.

Officer Mackey held up the report. *This could be my big break! If I can clear this Cooper guy of murder ...* Mac's eyes brightened with anticipation. *This could place me in a position for that detective promotion I've wanted. No more deadbeat, juvenile drinking arrests and charging tavern owners for serving alcohol to minors. I hate that scene!*

fff

At eight thirty that morning, Chief Kaufmann walked past Officer Mackey. Officer Dan Phillips nudged her. "Hey, Mac, the chief's in." He pointed with his eyes.

Looking up, Officer Mackey called out, "Chief!"

The chief turned and looked at her. "Yes, Officer?"

"I have a report here on an arrest I made last night that you will find highly interesting, sir."

"Come to my office, Officer." Her name seemed to escape him, and he looked at her nametag.

"It's Mackey, sir."

"Ah, yes, Officer Mackey."

The chief held the door open, and Officer Mackey stepped past him. After closing the door, the chief went to his desk and picked up his mail. After flipping through it, he then tossed it back on his desk. "What have you got for me, Officer Mackey?"

"I arrested a man last night who claimed to have found gold on your father-in-law's property. I thought you'd want to be the first to see this." She handed the report to the chief.

The chief took the report from her, looking at her oddly. Rustling the sheets of paper, he brought it up to eye level and read. Stiffening, he inhaled and held his breath for a long moment. *Why, that stupid fool! I told him to stay out of Aggieville last night.* The chief swore under his breath. *I should have killed him and been done with it!*

The look on the chief's face puzzled Officer Mackey. She thought he'd be glad at the arrest. Instead, he looked highly irritated by it. "Is everything all right, sir?" she asked.

Highly agitated by Dallas's stupidity, the chief looked up at Officer Mackey. "Everything is just fine. Good work, Officer Mackey."

"Will you be getting a search warrant for his residence, sir?"

With a wave of his hand, he said, "I'll call Judge Sanders right now, and I'll have Detective Paulino pick up the search warrant. But first, I want to question this guy concerning the gold."

"Sir, if you don't mind, I'd like to be in on the search."

"I'll tell Detective Paulino about your request."

"Thank you, sir! I really appreciate it." She turned and left the chief's office.

Officer Mackey gave Officer Phillips a thumbs-up. "The chief said he'll tell Paulino I want in on the search!"

Officer Phillips smiled and patted her arm. "Glad you're coming along on this one. You deserve it."

ƒ ƒ ƒ

The chief dropped heavily into his chair, staring at the report lying on his desk. His heart pounding, his mouth dry, he picked up his coffee and stared into the cup in anger. He couldn't believe that Dallas would defy his orders after he told him to stay out of Aggieville. And to top it off, he'd gotten himself stinking drunk and blabbed his mouth to an undercover officer about the gold. That complete idiot got himself arrested on trumped-up charges and thrown into jail. *I knew I couldn't trust him.* Cliff got up and paced. *Dallas stole from me! I need to make it over to his place and get the bags of gold before the detective gets there. Then I need to talk to Dallas.*

Cliff raced out the door, and as he passed his assistant, he said, "Nancy, when I get back, have Wilcox brought to the interrogation room. And get a hold of Paulino and tell him to get a search warrant to search Dallas's place ASAP!" *It will give me enough time to get the gold before the search warrant is issued.* His thoughts raced wildly.

"Yes, sir," Nancy answered as the chief slammed out the doors.

fff

Wow, I've never seen the chief so angry before. I'd hate to be in Dallas's shoes. Nancy shook her head.

Hurriedly the chief drove to the mobile home park where Dallas resided. The door was unlocked, and he walked into Dallas's mobile home and looked around; it was a real pigsty. Lying on the coffee table were the two bags of gold that Dallas had stuffed into his pocket. *That thief!* He removed the bag of marbles from his pocket and switched them out. *That will make Officer Mac look very foolish. Poor girl, she had hoped that this would get her off that juvenile beat. Well, I'll see that she gets that promotion down the road. She did do a real good job—too good as a matter of fact.*

fff

Dallas was taken into the interrogation room as soon as the chief made it back to the office. A cold chill tingled down Dallas's spine as he walked down to the interrogation room. His thoughts ran wild, and fear suddenly coursed through his body. *Where's the chief when you need him? If he doesn't show up soon …*

Dallas was pushed into the interrogation room, and Lt. Bailey pulled on the gray steel chair. "Sit!" he ordered.

Dallas sat and looked around him. His eyes fell on the one-way mirror. *Could the boss be standing behind that mirror watching and listening?* Dallas squirmed uncomfortably in his seat. Then he asked, "Why am I here, and why was I locked up?"

"For starters, you're in a heap of trouble, Dallas. One, you assaulted an officer. You were drunk and disorderly—"

"What? I did what? You've got to be kidding me. Assaulting an officer?"

"Why would I kid you about something this serious?"

A worried look formed on Dallas's face. His eyes darted toward the closed door. He thought he heard someone on the other side of the door. *Maybe it's the boss.*

Lt. Bailey continued, "Do you remember talking to a brunette last night by the name of Mac?"

"Yeah, I kinda remember a lady by that name. Why?"

"Well, Officer Mackey—"

"Officer Mackey!" Dallas's mouth fell open.

"Yes, Officer Mackey is an undercover cop. Didn't you know that?" Lt. Bailey grinned.

Oh, man ... What did I say last night to that cop? Oh, man, the boss is gonna lay a brick when he hears that I'm in the slammer ... if he hasn't already heard, that is.

Lt. Bailey said something to Dallas that Dallas didn't hear, so he asked the lieutenant to repeat himself.

"I said the chief will want to talk to you since it involves his deceased in-laws. He should be in shortly. Do you want something to drink?" Lt. Bailey asked.

"Yeah, a cup of coffee for this hangover," Dallas answered nervously. *What am I going to say in my defense about what happened last night?* The room was cool, yet sweat beads formed on his forehead.

The door swung open, and in stepped the chief. "Go take a coffee break, Mitch. Chocolate doughnuts in the break room."

"Sure thing, Chief."

Dallas stiffened in his chair. He followed the pacing movement of the chief. Afraid to speak, Dallas said nothing. When the chief spoke, he jumped.

"In this place, you're to call me 'chief,' not 'boss'! Do you understand?" Cliff spoke in a gruff voice, resting his hands on the edge of the table. His breathing came deep and raspy. Dallas had never seen the chief so angry. He leaned in toward Dallas and hissed into his ear, "How could you be so stupid! And what were you thinking? Well?" Cliff stared down at Dallas. "I want you to speak in a low voice to me so no one can hear us, do you understand?"

"Yes, Chief," Dallas whispered. "I don't understand. What do you mean, Chief?"

The chief grabbed hold of Dallas's collar and twisted it tightly around his neck, yanking him up on his feet. In a low voice, the chief hissed, "Didn't I tell you to stay out of Aggieville last night?"

"Ahh, that you did, Chief, but I can explain," he whispered.

"It had better be good!"

"I just went out for one drink to celebrate our good fortune. Just one drink." Dallas held up a finger. "That was all I had."

"Just one! I heard that you got yourself stinking drunk last night. Why do you think you're here in the slammer? I heard that you tried to pick up a cop last night."

"Chief, I really didn't know she was an undercover cop. It's her fault that I got drunk, and I don't remember telling her about the gold. Honest, Chief."

"Keep your voice down!" The chief released Dallas's collar and shoved him back into his seat in disgust.

"You said plenty last night. In fact, you had too much to drink for your own good."

"Chief, I didn't tell her a thing. It's all lies."

"Are you telling me that she lied about all of this?" The chief pulled out two bags of gold from his pocket. "You stole from me, you thief!"

Dallas's eyes widened with fear. His lip twitched, and he began to fidget in his chair, hopelessly lost for words. His mind searched for an excuse, but nothing came.

"A search warrant will be issued to search your place as soon as I leave here. Once again, I have to clean up your mess! You tell Detective Paulino that you know nothing about the gold and that you have no idea of what Officer Mackey is talking about. You're going to have to discredit Officer Mackey's claims, and you'll be out of here in twenty-four hours. So, don't screw up on me. Do you understand?"

"Yeah, I understand," Dallas answered. "I'll deny everything that lying bitch said." Squirming in his seat, Dallas thought, *Should I tell the boss what I found at the ranch? Maybe by telling him, it will take his mind off the gold.* "One more thing, Chief, I went out to the dugout to get the shovels that you said I forgot to load in the pickup yesterday, and I found footprints by the pile of granite rocks. It looks to me like someone may have been hiding there. It was not an animal, but a man and possibly a woman or a child. For them to hide like that, I wonder what they heard."

The chief stopped and pivoted around. "Are you sure about this?"

"Couldn't be any surer, Chief."

Turning, the chief rushed out the door, brushing past Officer Mackey. "Chief, I've got orders to take the prisoner back to his cell," she said.

"Do it!" Cliff answered as he rushed past her.

fff

Wow, he's in a great hurry, Officer Mackey thought, watching him rush down the hall to his office. *Is this going to be one of those days?* she thought.

Dallas sat calmly in his chair, feeling secure that the chief would take care of everything and he'd be out by morning. *One more night in the slammer can't be that bad. The food is free, after all.*

Officer Mackey walked in. "Remember me?" she asked.

"You're not that undercover cop, Mac, are you?"

"The same. Stand up and put your hands behind your back."

"I thought Detective Paulino was going to question me?"

"Do I have to repeat myself?" she asked.

Dallas stood and turned around, placing his hands behind his back. The handcuffs clicked into place.

"Detective Paulino has been called out, and he's on assignment. He'll get to you later on today." Officer Mackey took him by the arm and escorted him down a long hallway to a waiting elevator. The elevator descended into the basement where the jailer awaited his arrival.

"You would have made a lousy bed partner!" Dallas shouted as the elevator door closed. Dallas grinned to himself, feeling smug about his crude remark.

The jailer narrowed his eyes. "That was uncalled for." The guard yanked the handcuffs on Dallas's wrist to hurry him back to his cell.

Dallas cringed in pain. "Yeah, well, it served her right," he said.

"You wouldn't be in trouble if you had more respect for authority. Remarks like that get you nowhere."

fff

"Did Paulino get that search warrant I asked for?" Cliff asked.

"Yes, Chief," Nancy answered. "Detective Paulino just entered the building, and he's headed to your office, sir."

With the search warrant in their possession, Detective Paulino, Officer Dan Phillips, and Officer Renee Mackey drove to the mobile home park where Dallas Wilcox resided. Detective Paulino tried the door, and it was unlocked. The curtains were drawn, and the room was semi-dark. It would take a few minutes for their eyes to adjust to the dimness of the room.

Officer Mackey reached over and turned on the light.

"We can see much better with the lights on," she said.

Detective Paulino heard a car drive up and looked out the door to see Agent Ty Thomas. *What would the FBI be doing here?* Paulino waited at the door then hollered out, "How can I help you Agent Thomas?"

"I heard about the search warrant and thought you could use some help." Agent Ty Thomas answered.

Detective Paulino's brow wrinkled. "I hadn't heard of any FBI being assigned to this case."

"I'm here as an observer. Hopefully I can be of some help." Agent Thomas answered Detective Paulino.

"Okay. You're an observer. Just stay out of the way. Let's do what we came out here to do, men!" Detective Paulino snapped.

Officer Mackey walked past Paulino and headed for the kitchen. He sniffed the air. "Man, this place smells!"

Dallas's place was a pigpen. Empty pizza boxes were tossed by the back door among the newspapers. Coors cans overflowed the trash and littered the floor. Dishes were stacked high on and in the sink, and roaches scurried for a place to hide. They didn't have much of a problem finding one.

Agent Thomas waded through the clothing that trailed down the hallway to the one bedroom in the back of the mobile home. The top of the dresser was piled high with clothes and more papers. He pulled open the top drawer and moved the clothing to one side. Agent Thomas noticed a bulge under the lining and pulled it back. It was a brown manila folder, nine-and-a-half-by-five inches in dimensions, with the name "Sharon Brookfield" written on the front. Agent Thomas whistled and walked to the open doorway. "Look what I have here!"

"Aren't you an observer here?" Detective Paulino asked.

A sheepish grin creased Agent Thomas's face. "You could use a hand, couldn't you?"

"Off the record, of course. What is it, heroin?"

"No, something a lot more important than heroin," he answered.

"What could be more important than finding drugs?"

"Savings bonds made out to Sharon Brookfield. Wasn't the safe broken into and money and savings bonds stolen?" Agent Thomas asked.

"Well, well, well, Dallas." Detective Paulino walked over to Agent Thomas. "Let me see those bonds!" He grinned. "We got him on stolen property. Let's see what's in these bags I just found."

He shook the contents into his open palm, and marbles rolled out. Red, yellow, white, and blue cat's-eye marbles. A couple fell—*Plunk! Plunk!*—and rolled across the vinyl floor before being stopped by a shirt lying on the floor.

"What is this?" Detective Paulino said in surprise, shaking out the second bag. "Marbles! Where's the gold." Detective Paulino looked over at Officer Mackey with a disgusted look on his face. "Gold, huh?"

She raised her hands. "He said he and his partner found bags of gold on the property, sir." She walked over to where Detective Paulino stood, shaking her head. "I don't know what to say."

Agent Thomas, Myke Cooper's step-father, went over to the coffee table where detective Paulino found the leather bags and went down on his left knee. Leaning over his right leg, he ran his finger across the carpet and came up with specks of gold. "Hey, come see what I just found!" He held his finger up for them to see. "What do you think? Looks like gold flecks, don't you think?"

"Let's hope it is gold. Have this analyzed at the lab," Detective Paulino added.

Mac took out a sample container out of her pocket and handed the plastic bag to the agent, he carefully brushed the gold dust into it.

"Thank you, Agent Thomas." A sigh of relief she exhaled.

Detective Paulino looked around the room. Something was just not right here. His instincts told him something was amiss. *A drunk doesn't lie, not about something like this. Well now, let's see here. Two bags of marbles, gold dust on the floor, savings bonds with the name Sharon Brookfield on it. It doesn't add up.* "What do you make of this?" he asked Officer Phillips. Detective Paulino tossed the bag of marbles back onto the coffee table.

"Someone may have gotten here before we did and cleaned up the place," Officer Phillips answered. He looked around. "They missed the trash and the clothing trailing through this place. Could this have been a plant to frame Dallas?"

Chapter 56

In despair, Nicole asked, "What are we going to do with the baby and Nathaniel?" She felt the heavy burden of Marianne's anguish. "I feel deep down that Marianne wants us to put them to rest, but how are we going to do that?" she said in a mournful voice. Her sadness hung in the air like an early-morning mist, sending a shiver down her back.

"I really don't know what we're going to do," Reid answered. "We'll put the baby in bed with Nathaniel. We're taking the cradle, and I feel that placing Little Ben in bed with his daddy is the right thing to do."

"Yeah, I feel that's what we need to do for Marianne." Nicole's thoughts went back to the journal and the gold. *What did she mean when she wrote that Ben was going to carve the cradle in gold? There has got to be a hidden secret somewhere.*

"Ready to do what we came here for?" Reid asked.

"Yes." Nicole hooked her arm through Reid's. Muscle spasms once again rippled through her arm. Her fear of dark places caused her muscles to tense.

Reid patted her hand. "I'm here with you. You'll be all right."

"I know I will be." Her lips curved into a tight smile.

The shuffling of their sneakers echoed off the wall as they proceeded through the mouth of the dugout. They entered the living chamber, and the uneasiness she had felt subsided. She unlocked her arm from Reid's and walked up to the cradle. She let out a quivering breath. Sadness engulfed her as she stared down at the skeletal remains of Little Ben. *A tragic death for such a little one. No wonder Marianne is unable to rest.*

The starburst quilt that little Ben was wrapped in was covered with dust. Seeing Nicole at ease, Reid walked over to the bed where Nathaniel lay and pulled back the covers. The dust caught by the light drifted and danced in the air.

Nicole cringed at the sight of Nathaniel's splintered skull where the bullet had entered.

"Let's do what we came here to do." Bending over the cradle, Reid took hold of one end of the starburst quilt. "Ready?" He looked at Nicole. "Lift Little Ben gently."

"Wait! Make sure that the spider is not in his eye socket."

Marianne stood off in a corner watching the scene unfold with happiness. She had reached out too many people for over a century and finally found someone receptive to her and willing to help.

Nicole pulled back in fright. Her eyes went large with fear. The brown spider had taken up residence in Little Ben's eye socket. The light had drawn it out. Its small body with its long brown legs scurried across the skull and ran across the quilt. It paused and calculated its next move. Nicole backed away. "Get rid of it, Reid!"

With a flick of his finger, he sent the spider flying across the room. It ran up the wall and disappeared between the cracks of the boarded-up window. Sighing with relief, Nicole took hold of the ends and cautiously lifted the quilt. The skull moved, and she froze. "His head, it moved!"

"It's okay, Nicole. It won't come away from his body." Reid crossed his fingers as he spoke.

"Are you sure? I don't want the skull rolling off onto the dirt floor." Her voice trembled.

"Here, let me hold him."

Reid stared at her in disbelief. "You want to what?"

"Put him into my arms."

"Are you sure?"

"Yes, I feel that this is what Marianne wants me to do."

ƒƒƒ

Reid wavered with uncertainty. *What is she thinking? She wants me to put the baby's bones into her arms! She has become so involved with Marianne and her plight*, Reid thought.

"Well, are you going to do it?" she asked.

"Okay. If that's what you really want me to do." He slid his hands under the quilt, gently scooped Little Ben up into his arms, and handed him to her. Nicole cradled Little Ben in her arms. This had been the moment that Marianne had been waiting for. She just wanted to touch and hold her baby one more time.

Marianne stepped behind Nicole. "Don't be afraid, Nicole. Allow me to hold my baby through you."

Nicole could feel Marianne's joy and her overwhelming love for her infant son. Nicole's heart quickened with excitement. She was seeing through Marianne's eyes, and Little Ben was a living baby in her arms.

"I see Little Ben, Reid. He's smiling up at me. Oh, he's a pretty baby. He has the bluest eyes, heart-shaped lips, and hardly any hair on his head. Oh, I wish you could see him, Reid." Little Ben's little fingers reached up and touched her cheek as he cooed. "He touched my cheek, Reid!" She rubbed the baby's skull gently as one would a live child.

Reid couldn't believe what she was doing. His mouth dropped to his chest, and his eyes were large in surprise.

Chapter 57

The prison doors clanged open, and the prisoners filed out of their cells like redneck bikers ready to paint the town red. One shouted, "You're ten minutes late! That means we stay out ten minutes later." In unison, they all cheered in agreement, falling into line.

"You think so?" Officer Banta said. He strolled down the line of prisoners, his hands to his back with the baton held in place.

Myke felt someone staring at him. He looked down the line and stopped at Dallas. Myke gave Dallas a sidelong glance that clearly gave the other man an uneasy feeling.

Dallas dropped his gaze and stared down at the floor. Rumor had it that Dallas was arrested for having stocks and bond certificates belonging to Mrs. Brookfield in his possession. They were supposedly found in his mobile home during a drug raid.

Dallas has done a lot of bad things in his life, but drugs were not one of them, Myke said to himself. *I can see him stealing those bonds from her. Murderer.* Myke could hardly wait to confront Dallas in the courtyard.

"What are you glaring at, Coop?" Banta asked Myke. "There's not going to be any trouble, right?"

"No, no trouble," he answered.

"Good."

Banta, a short, stocky African American prison guard, ruled his cellblock through intimidation. He bullied the convicts into submission with threats of using his baton to crack heads, and on a number of occasions, he had to reinforce his threat with action. Banta stopped in front of Dallas and stuck his baton into his chest. His wide lips tightened in a grin. Using his baton, he pushed Dallas back into his cell. "Not you!" he said.

A stunned expression radiated from Dallas's face, and he stammered, "Why? What did I do?"

Banta ignored Dallas's question and barked orders out to the other guards. "Take them out, Smithie!"

Smithies, a redheaded guard with freckles splattering across his face, waved his baton toward the door. "Okay, you guys, you know the rules. Let's go, and be quick about it." In single file, the prisoners marched out into the open courtyard. Dallas watched as the door closed behind them.

Banta walked into the cell next to Dallas and flipped the mattress over. With a knife, he slit the edge open. Forks and butter knives fell to the floor. "You dumb fool," Banta said. "Did you think you could get away with this?" Banta's steely black eyes glared down at the silverware and then over at Dallas.

"Wait a minute. I didn't steal all of that. I haven't been here long enough to hide them, let alone steal them. I thought security was tight in this place. Who told you about that stuff in the mattress anyway? I've been set up!" Dallas hissed through clenched teeth.

"You don't know?" Banta answered. "There's a snitch around every corner you turn in here. As one of my teachers used to tell us in school, 'I have eyes behind the back of my head.' Now, put your hands on your head and back up against the cell door," he demanded.

"That mattress isn't mine. That stain was not on my bed. It looks like blood. That mattress belongs to Steve. I had no idea that Steve was smuggling silverware out of the kitchen. He does the cooking around here. He must have switched the mattress, and that is the honest truth."

A malicious grin crinkled Banta's lip. "You wouldn't know the truth if it smacked you in the face. Back up against the cell bars with your hands on your head."

"Why? I don't know anything about this," Dallas said, with fear in his eyes.

"I'm not going to tell you again. I wasn't born yesterday. I have been a jailer for twenty years, and I have heard and seen it all. Do as I say, Dallas."

Fear rippled through Dallas's body. That look on Banta's face was evil. That stare conveyed a message that he would do bodily harm to him if he didn't do as he was told. Dallas put his hands on his head and leaned back against the bars.

Banta went out the cell door and stood behind Dallas with the bars between them. He slipped his right arm around Dallas's neck and slammed Dallas's head against the bars. Dallas reached for Banta's arm, struggling against the tight grip he had on his throat. He tightened his jaw muscles, and the veins in his neck protruded as he gasped for air. The room slowly spun around and began to turn black, and Dallas's body fell limp. Banta tied the rope to the upper bars and hoisted Dallas's body off the ground. A stool was placed on its side next to his feet. Banta went about ransacking Dallas's cell and tossed a knife under his bed. Pleased, he turned and locked the cell door behind him.

Chapter 58

Dust trailed behind the dirty white pickup with the words, "WASH ME!" written across the tailgate. On seeing the writing, Cliff was irritated. But he had more pressing things to attend to than washing his dirty pickup. He slowed the truck down until it came to a stop in front of the closed pasture gate to Doc's land. A sign was wired to the steel gate with the warning "No Trespassing!"

He unlatched the gate and swung it open. His peripheral vision caught sight of a flickering light. He stared past the open field toward a cluster of trees and watched intently for movement. Cumulus clouds crossed the path of the sun, and the flickering stopped. *It's probably the sun reflecting off a car mirror*, Cliff thought. *Kids!*

Doc had once mentioned that he thought kids were cutting across his land to get to the sandy beach below. *I will ticket them if I ever catch them trespassing on my land. That will stop their shenanigans.*

Cliff closed the gate and got back into the truck, slamming the door shut, and drove down the dirt road. He was so peeved about the high price he had paid Banta to see to the demise of Dallas that he didn't notice the gulls flying overhead. Nor did he notice the rabbit that darted out from the tall prairie grass in front of the pickup. He had no time to enjoy the beauty of God's creation or to dawdle in religious hoopla.

A grin slowly creased Cliff's lips, and he thought, *Well, Banta, a little adjustment to the brake line on that old Chevy will take care of my problem.*

He drove the half a mile in and pulled up to the rock quarry above the dugout. He got out of the truck and looked at the ground. His hands went to his hips. Shaking his head in disgust, he growled, "Dallas, you idiot! Animal, huh! The two-legged kind. You thought you could wiggle yourself out of this by telling me that you had found the tracks after the fact. That is just one more reason I can't have the likes of you around."

Cliff heard voices below him. "What are these kids doing in this area anyway? The dugout is nowhere close to the lake," he hissed through clenched teeth. "I'll scare them so bad that they'll never trespass on my land again."

Cliff bent low, scrambling up the hill on his hands and knees. At the top, he lay flat and peered over the side. A woman with auburn hair stepped into the clearing, her hair pulled back in a ponytail. If it were not for her petite size, he would have thought it was his wife, Brooke. The woman gently set down an elegantly carved cradle and rubbed her shoulder. She then collapsed onto the mound of dirt. Her arm went to her forehead, shielding her eyes. A tall young man with light hair joined her at her side.

"I don't think I can carry this cradle back to the jeep," she said. "It feels as if it's been filled with lead."

Cliff's hand went to his shoulder holster, and he unfastened the strap. *Why, it's Reid Starr, the basketball player from the university.* What in heaven's name is he doing here? He watched the young athlete walk around the cradle and then turn, facing the sun, looking in the direction where Cliff hid.

Reid's hand went over his eyes. "Boy, that sun is beating down on us."

Cliff dropped his head to the ground and was in deep thought. What was his next move going to be?

"It must be around three o'clock," Reid said to Nicole. "Let me rest for a minute, and then I'll go get the jeep and bring it here."

"I'll go with you. The cradle is not going anywhere."

Cliff stiffened and arched an eyebrow. The only person who knew about this place was Dallas. Had he been talking? And if so, how many people did he tell while inebriated? A villainous haze hovered over Cliff. It slowly descended, engulfing him. Betrayal and rage sheered through his gut. *Never trust anyone!* Glaring down at the two young people, he got up and dusted off his slacks. With icy composure, he made his way down the hill.

Reid saw a tall figure coming toward them. He took hold of Nicole's arm. "Turn very slowly. There's a man behind you."

"Yeah, right! This is not the time to be funny, Reid."

But his facial expression told her he wasn't being funny. She slowly pivoted around. Startled, she stepped back, grabbing hold of Reid's arm. It was not the farmer in blue jeans and with a straw hat on his head she had seen earlier. He was a well-dressed man with a gun holster fastened around his shoulder. His attire was definitely not one of a farmer or rancher. There was something very familiar about him, but at that moment, her mind did not register his face, only the gun and the predicament that they were in.

"Oh, boy," she said. "We're in a lot of trouble. He's doesn't look too happy."

"Trouble!" Cliff drew in his breath. "That's an understatement. You're trespassing on private property." His eyes narrowed. "I've seen you before. Why, you're the young woman that Doc claimed to be his bastard daughter. What's your name? Nicole, is it? You were in the lawyer's office at the reading of the will, weren't you?"

Nicole's lips puckered, and her eyes grew large as she wrestled with rage. "Bastard daughter! How dare you?"

Planting herself firmly, she stuck her hands down her coverall pockets in defiance. "Yes, I was there in Ms. Shoemaker's office, and I am his daughter."

"That, my dear, is very questionable," Cliff answered. "How dare you imply—"

Reid tugged at her sleeve. "The gun, Nicole, he's got a gun," he whispered through the corner of his lips.

She yanked her arm away from Reid's grip, glaring at Cliff. Anger spilled from her eyes.

"I dare!" Cliff grinned mockingly. "I have every right to question your legitimacy, young lady."

Being called a bastard child enraged Nicole, and that smirk on Cliff's face took her over the edge. In anger, she lashed out. "Why, you—"

"Don't, Nicole," Reid pleaded.

Nicole looked over at Reid and bit her lip. She wanted to curse at this man, but she would not allow the words that she wanted to say to draw her into sin. "How dare you imply that I would lie? I have letters from Dr. Brookfield that he sent to my mother," she said angrily.

Reid looked over at Nicole with pleading eyes. "Nicole, please," he said softly.

Cliff tossed his head back and laughed. "Letters! Well, your DNA has been sent off to the lab. We will soon find out your identity." He looked over at the cradle, and his jaw hardened.

"Stay put and don't do anything stupid!" he snarled as he walked over to the elegantly carved cradle. *Why didn't I notice the cradle before?* He ran his hand up the length of the heavily carved post and was totally mesmerized by its beauty. His hand stopped at the cap, and he removed the infant sock covering it. Cliff fell back in shock, his mouth agape. "It's gold?"

The ghostly figure of Marianne swooped over the cradle, circling around Cliff. Nicole saw the dramatic entry of Marianne and felt the cold chill tingle down her spine. She squeezed Reid's hand.

"Yes, I felt her presence," he whispered.

Cliff's eyes glowed with greed, and he said, "Theft, to be added to the charges of trespassing." A rush of exhilaration swept through him, and he removed the other three socks from the caps.

Marianne stood at his side, watching him run his finger along the golden face. "This is more than beautiful! It's worth …" Cliff's eyelids seemed to flutter as he caressed the golden face. He ran his finger across the eye, and it suddenly snapped open, staring back at him. Alarmed, Cliff drew back. He watched the nostrils flare and its wide lip's part to show its displeasure at being disturbed.

"Did … did you see that?" Cliff asked.

"See what?" Reid stammered.

"You didn't see the eyes open?" Cliff could feel the hairs on the nape of his neck stiffen.

Reid drew up his shoulders. "No. We saw nothing."

Cliff's nostrils flared in fear. *This is crazy. I must be hallucinating. This is not possible.* He continued to stare at the golden head. The eyes opened, and the facial features changed. Cliff reeled back and yelled, "No, no! Get away from me!"

The warrior's face had changed, and Cliff was staring at Doc, his now-deceased father-in-law.

Doc's mouth moved. "Murderer!" His eyes closed.

Cliff stammered. "Murderer? Who's doing this?" Cliff looked over at Reid and Nicole. "Didn't you see that and hear what it said?"

"See what? We heard nothing," Nicole answered. "What is wrong with him?"

Reid caught sight of a sudden movement on the hill. Officer Dan Phillips stood up from the crouched position he was in. He placed a finger across his lips.

"Get away from me, Sharon! You're dead!" Cliff stumbled and fell, dropping the gun. He scrambled backward on his hands, kicking away with his heels, and reached for his gun. He fired. One could hear the sound of the bullet as it impacted the cradle, splintering the wood. Cliff hollered, "Leave me alone, Dallas!"

"He's gone mad!" Nicole whispered in sudden fear.

Reid took hold of Nicole's arm and slowly moved toward Officer Phillips. Cliff pivoted quickly around and yelled, "Stop, or I'll shoot you!"

"Chief, you don't want to shoot anyone. Put the gun down," Officer Phillips instructed.

Cliff turned in the direction of the voice. "What are you doing here, Dan?"

"Trespassers were seen crossing Doc's land, and the rancher was concerned about your dynamiting here. He didn't want the kid's hurt. Let me take them in, Chief."

"I can't let you do that, Dan." Cliff raised his gun and fired. The bullet struck Dan in the chest, and he stumbled back, falling to the ground. Nicole covered her ears and screamed hysterically. Reid grabbed hold of her, pulled her down, and placed his body over hers to shield her. They could hear a click made by the gun. The gun had misfired. A sudden, cold chill quickly swept past them.

Nicole's sobs ceased, and she peered through Reid's arm. She saw the frozen fear on Cliff's face as a mist appeared in front of him. The shape of a man slowly appeared. The ghost had placed the infant into Marianne's arms.

"Nathaniel," Nicole whispered.

Marianne caressed the baby in her arm in a protective embrace. She moved toward the dugout that was once a safe haven for her family.

Cliff's hands shook with uncontrollable fear. He reached for the dynamite in his back pocket and for the lighter. With shaking hands, he repeatedly flicked the lighter, trying to light the wick on the dynamite. The lighter finally flickered on, and Cliff lit the dynamite and tossed it toward Nathaniel's ghostly figure. It passed through him and headed toward the dugout entrance, where Marianne and the baby stood. The loud boom shook the ground. A cloud of dust and large dirt clods rained down, striking Nicole, Reid, and Officer Phillips. A pickaxe stuck out of the ground near the mound of dirt. The force of the blast knocked Cliff backward and off his feet.

Nicole screamed out and buried her face against Reid's chest, blocking out the sight of the chief falling onto the pickaxe.

Officer Phillips ran down the hill toward them, his hand to his chest where the bullet had struck him, and he asked, "Are you kids okay?"

"Yes, we're okay. What about you?" Reid moved off Nicole, staring at the hole in his shirt.

Dan patted his chest. "If I didn't have my bulletproof vest on ... well, I wouldn't be standing here."

Officer Philips looked over at the chief and sighed remorsefully. "Ah, Chief."

The pickaxe protruded through Cliff's chest. His eyes stared at them in horror and pain. He raised his hand. "Help me," he pleaded. Then a sudden void entered his eyes, and his body went limp.

Chapter 59

A stern warning from the district attorney's office kept Nicole in Manhattan. Rumor at the Riley County Jail had it that Dallas did not commit suicide but in fact was murdered by one of their own officers.

The gold that Dallas had bragged about finding to Officer Mac was missing. With Dallas's death, they had no way of knowing if he had fabricated that story.

Murder and missing gold had the community humming with greed. People were caught on the Lazy B Ranch with metal detectors in hopes of finding the lost gold.

An investigation was ordered to determine what had happened on the Lazy B and the cause of the chief's death.

Detective Ramos, Detective Paulino, Officer Phillips, Nicole Martin, and Reid Starr sat in a conference room behind closed doors. An uncomfortable air lingered in the room.

Ramos spoke. "We all know what happened at the Lazy B. Now, we could drag the chief's name through the mud and hurt many people, especially Dr. Kaufmann, who is also pregnant, I've been told. I don't believe she could handle the news of what happened at the Lazy B and that her parents may have been murdered possibly by her husband, the chief. She's had a very difficult time dealing with the death of her parents and now her husband."

"What are you suggesting?" Officer Phillips asked.

Ramos looked over at Nicole and Reid.

"Silence," he said.

"Silence? What do you mean by silence?" Nicole asked.

Ramos lowered his head and tapped his fat fingers on the tabletop. "The chief is dead. Whatever he has done will never be known. Dallas, his accomplice, is also dead, and we are looking into Officer Banta. He is our primary suspect in Dallas's murder."

"Murder!" Reid sat up in his chair. "Not suicide?"

"No. We don't believe it was suicide."

"What does Banta have to say about all of this?" Officer Phillips asked.

"Banta's body has been found by a fisherman. His car went off a cliff at the lake, and he was found pinned behind the steering wheel of his car. All involved are dead."

Nicole asked, "What about Myke and Pico?"

Ramos then added, "Myke's stepfather, Ty Thomas, an FBI agent out of DC, cleared Myke and Pico of the murder charges and for setting the fire to the Brookfield's' home. Myke and Pico will be charged with breaking and entering and felony theft." The end … or is it?

www.ingramcontent.com/pod-product-compliance
Ingram Content Group UK Ltd.
Pitfield, Milton Keynes, MK11 3LW, UK
UKHW041409180426
11947UKWH00007B/24